Silicone 5.0

Jorge Majfud

HUMANUS PUBLISHING H.

Silicone 5.0
© Jorge Majfud 2025
ISBN: 978-1-956760-39-2
© Illegal Humanus Publishing H.
© Humanus │ 2025
First Spanish Edition: Baile del Sol, Spain, 2018
humanus.info
E-Mail: editor@humanus.info

They killed you over there on the other side, who knows when, and now you think you're chasing something, but in reality, you're running from your own corpse. You're a fugitive who thinks he's the detective.

On the Other Side

Until His Body Said Enough

WHEN THE HEART ATTACK STRUCK on Saturday, March 17, Facundo Walsh Ocampo was in his apartment at 1420 Atlantic Avenue in Daytona Beach, close to ten at night, trying to open the front door so someone would see him lying in the hallway and call 911. To make matters worse, someone was loudly playing Selena singing "Bidi Bidi Bom Bom," so he knew no one would hear him fall on the hallway floor, shiny as a petrified pool. Not even Silvanna, of course, who at that moment was in the kitchen, in a box, in a fetal position, motionless and with her eyes open, as if they were her eyes, but unable to hear.

Everything had happened as he imagined it at twenty-two, when he was still a lonely student walking through the port of Buenos Aires, entertained by watching or daydreaming about the flags of distant countries, fluttering in a strange southern sky. He remembered a summer afternoon on a beach on the other side, in Uruguay, when he had written in the margin of Joseph Schumpeter's book "History of Economic Analysis": today a master's at Oxford, tomorrow another at Berkeley; today one million, tomorrow two, and if not, a heart attack and to hell with all this accumulation. It wasn't a profound thought, he reflected, almost forty years later. Just a truth—simple, insignificant, rather disappointing, as truths often are when you've solved almost all the problems that kept you occupied for so long, when you've burned through all your great expectations in life and don't know how to be happy because you were trained your whole life for something else.

He had moved the day before, and perhaps the physical exertion, the emotional exhaustion of the divorce, the discovery or suspicion that his identity had been stolen in Mexico, had all contributed to pushing his health to the limit. He had been sitting for a long time in silence, accompanied only by a glass of whisky without ice, staring into the dark depths of the ocean, imagining explanations for his colleagues at the company, explanations about something that shouldn't matter to them. He had spent even more time trying to explain to himself why everything he had considered important in life, in his life as a productive man, had suddenly stopped mattering. For almost thirty years he had tracked the Dow Jones and the Nasdaq in the Wall Street Journal, day after day, suffering like an Italian soccer fan cheering for Boca Juniors, hoping the blessed stocks wouldn't stop rising while the Merval and Ibovespa collapsed, out of pure and petty revenge against four or five despicable individuals he knew in Buenos Aires and São Paulo—and suddenly all he wanted was for the Dow Jones, the Nikkei, and all the rest to crash, along with all his own investments and his national fantasies of living in the world's leading economic power, where people really know how to get things done, where the winners are.

Thirty years…, he had said to himself, as if pronouncing the magic words that would reveal the answers to so much confusion. The answers never came. The darkness of the sea remained before his eyes; he could no longer even make out the faint line separating the sky from the water. That night he had downed his second whisky just as he began to feel a strange pain in his left hand. He had taken off his watch. He had tried to ignore the discomfort, but the very fear of falling into an abyss had made him feel even worse. He rubbed his unresponsive hand, like when you wake up at night with a dead arm and struggle to understand that the blood hadn't been circulating properly.

3

It wasn't unusual for the net to break at its weakest thread, he thought a day later, in the hospital. His father had also ended his days with heart problems. The Walsh family had weak hearts. Tata José, as his nieces called him when they had barely learned to babble a few words, had died a year after his first heart attack. Facundo calculated: his father was 77. Eighteen years older than him, though at 59 the gap feels much smaller than one imagines. Maybe medicine had advanced a lot since then, but his father had lived a less stressful life. His mother…Now that he thought about it, he wasn't sure what his mother had died of. He'd heard something about respiratory failure, something about pneumonia, but he'd never asked why his mother had been walking on the beach in the middle of winter, in the rain, that day. Had she argued with his father? What story lay behind that dramatic moment he, her son, hadn't questioned until now, when death came to visit him and there were no living witnesses left, aside from scattered fragments of a reality slowly sinking into the depths of the past? Back then, the news of his mother's death had left him so dazed he hadn't even cried, and any explanation would've seemed natural and sufficient, like a child accepting that storks from Paris bring babies, that mice leave money under the pillow every time you lose a tooth, or any of the other filthy lies we're accustomed to and refuse to let go of at any cost until reality, all by itself, through disappointment or sheer involuntary maturation, resigns us to the truth, to a new truth, or to the loss of the only ones we had left standing.

He barely remembered his mother coming back home, almost forced by her husband, angry, drying her head with a towel (that defenseless head, that pained face he loved so much), tucking her under a blue quilt in her bed, bringing her a hot tea to bed, and a few days later the ambulance taking her to the hospital, from where she came out on a stretcher covered by a white sheet, headed to the funeral home. Did his mother suffer from depression? Did her brother's disappearance a few months earlier have something to do with that night on the beach? Had she discovered her husband had a fling with a young actress from experimental theater? (Where did this persistent idea, surely false, come from?)

In 1977, Tata José had tried, without success, to return to acting, his youthful calling, thwarted by material needs, as he called them with exaggerated irony. It didn't work out, and probably it all ended with arguments about the French girl. But that same year his uncle Roberto had disappeared (when exactly? how?), so Facundo couldn't clarify the real reasons why his mother had gotten lost one winter evening and night on Martínez beach walk, walking or sitting on a cold stone, in the drizzle. Had she gone to the river as we all go to the water searching for our own soul? Had she tried to kill herself, as they say Alfonsina did? He would never know. In any case, she did it as we all do in less definitive ways, abandoning ourselves to irresponsible habits, like drinking too much or walking in winter rain. From the hospital he only remembered a room where people drank coffee and watched a black-and-white TV. Argentina was playing Hungary. He never forgot the score (5 to 1) and the people's celebrations. He remembered names like Leopoldo Jacinto Luque as if they were Maradona. The slow, painfully slow penalty by Osvaldo Ardiles, saved by the Hungarian goalkeeper, and a mustached man yelling ¡Pajero de mierda! Diego Maradona stepping onto the field while a very pretty young girl asks who he is and a fat man throws his hands up to the sky, as if pretending to be offended by the question. Facundo's nerves at the start of the match had turned into a certain euphoria shared by the men in the room. After the game ended, suddenly, like someone waking at night and remembering a bad earlier experience, he remembered his mother was dying on the fourth floor. She died that same night, maybe before Argentina scored the fourth goal and Facundo stood up to celebrate, arms almost raised.

Returning to his body, he shook his head as if swatting a fly. He looked at the monitor with his heartbeats drawn in green. He was alone in the dark room at Memorial Medical Center. With difficulty, he stretched his hand and reached for his phone. He searched for that Argentina vs. Hungary match on YouTube. He found some fragments. He didn't recognize any of the images, but he confirmed that it had all happened on February 27, 1977. For some reason, he had always confused that date with February 29, which was actually his mother's birthday. But that year there was no February 29. And there was no birthday.

Back at Daytona apartment

UPON RETURNING TO THE LONELINESS of the apartment, he didn't bother investigating the identity theft. He didn't take Silvanna out of her box. He knew that if he did, he'd have to cut her into pieces and distribute her one night across different trash bins in the city.

He couldn't avoid the depression. Dr. Menéndez had warned him that sadness was an expected effect during the recovery period. Those things never change and are controlled with a pill. After all, he thought as he popped the first one into his mouth, we're still just intelligent machines.

Facundo didn't stop taking the nitroglycerin or the other yellow or pink pills, but what the doctor had so poetically called sadness felt to him like nothing less than depression. If we're predictable machines, his sadness wasn't solely due to the weakened muscles of his injured heart. The near absence of Elena had kept him awake for several days. No one can make you feel as guilty as a woman can, whether you've dropped the two atomic bombs on Hiroshima and Nagasaki or eaten the last piece of chocolate.

At least in practice, Elena was no longer his wife, she surely didn't love him anymore (surely not; for sure), but anyone would've visited a friend more than once and for more than ten minutes. His friends hadn't rushed over either desperately, he told himself, with irony. The last day, he had seen Henrry Rodríguez, Jeff Al Ferro, and Roxane, Robertson's secretary. For each of them, perhaps with the exception of Roxane, it had been more of a formality. The smiles, the optimistic jokes, were the same ones Facundo knew from his days as a top-tier salesman. The one who stayed the longest was Ernesto, the unbearable Ernesto, but that was probably because his brother-in-law had a flexible schedule at the College and enjoyed chatting for free more than he did teaching his classes.

Alexa, the young girl Elena had adopted like a pet, undocumented and without other commitments, hadn't come to see him. Why should that surprise him? Long before, Facundo had suspected that someone had told the girl never to stay in the house when Elena wasn't there, as if every man were a potential deviant. If it was her mother, he could understand it. If it was Elena... Alexa didn't dislike her, but it was clear the girl was terrified of him, and Facundo had never made an effort to clear things up. It had never mattered to him, though perhaps he'd been too oblivious because, given his profession, he knew that not a few young girls like her, having barely failed in their attempts to touch the glory of modeling, would latch onto anything that could be interpreted as abuse by a good lawyer. There was no shortage of material and old creeps, either.

Elena felt the absence of a daughter much more than he did (at least he'd never had time to think about it, until now) and Alexa had practically fallen from the sky at a delicate moment. She was a girl in her early youth, brought from Venezuela by her mother at the age of seven. Elena had met her at a casting for a Publix ad campaign, a chain of high-quality food products where they choose blonde, Barbie-like girls to bag groceries and offer to accompany customers to their cars. But Alexa hadn't been chosen for the ad due to her poor English. To speak broken English or English with a Spanish accent, they had a model with a more Latina look, like a Mexican from Oaxaca. A few months later, Elena ran into her again at the Nuestra Belleza Latina contest on Univisión, where she didn't make the cut due to the mysterious criteria only the judges or organizers seem to understand. By then, she was fourteen, and Elena took her on as a protégé. At seventeen, the girl was at a stage of exploring her womanly charms. Maybe Elena was grooming her to be a model and, for obvious reasons, didn't want to accept any help from Facundo. Alexa was a young woman whose looks perfectly fit the beauty industry's standards (tall, thin, light eyes, full lips, sensual body, expressionless face), but she was undocumented, so Facundo didn't see any possibility for Elena to exploit that raw diamond.

He sank back into the armchair and the now tasteless, forbidden whiskey. He returned to remembering that February 27, 1977, which had visited him in the hospital. Then he drifted to November 25, 2005, another moment of family agony. The dates belonged to entirely different worlds. He imagined his own: April 22, 2019. He drank the last drop of whiskey and gave himself a few more years: August 16, 2021. His uncle Ernesto, José's brother, had also died of a heart attack, though he had survived almost three years after a series of surgeries, bypasses, and several stays in the ICU of the Hospital Ramos Mejía. So, aside from his shitty life, so full of successes, the problem came from an invisible sperm of his father.

Then he moved a little closer to himself. When he started feeling unwell, the night of March 17, he heard as if Elena herself were there telling him that Men are very handsome until a woman leaves them and then they cry and agonize just as a woman is used to crying for years, without her man understanding her, because men stop understanding their wives a few years into marriage. Or at least they don't feel the same empathy as before, when they were in love, when they would enchant their wives just by being moved by their problems, trying to listen to them, as a real man knows how to listen.

That night, nine days after his heart attack, after regaining some strength and allowing himself the excess of two whiskeys, he opened one of the cardboard boxes cluttering a corner of the apartment, searched for Schumpeter's economics book, and finally found page 271, where that marginal note was still written, scribbled one summer, probably the summer of '86, one of those summers so full of youth that it feels like the poets' eternity.

He remembered the exact moment when he wrote those words. In truth, they had been the expression of a strong moment of skepticism, though not of sadness. He remembered a sailboat with the Australian flag, with an exaggerated clarity, considering he didn't remember much else from that afternoon. Not the day, not the year, not how he had ended up there. It was probably a beach near Uncle Alberto's house by the Rambla de los Argentinos, in Piriápolis.

The lapses in his memory, Dr. Menéndez had said, were the consequence of having had his heart stopped for too long. The lack of oxygen had inevitably caused some brain damage, most likely reversible, since the brain, they now knew, is a very plastic organ and regenerates itself. Of course, memory is a mystery. While skills like moving, thinking, speaking, or remembering can be recovered through new connections, even new neurons, it would be impossible to recover any information from the neurons that had died. A stroke erases entire years, whole chunks of life, like a tsunami wiping out an ancient coastal city. But it was also possible that forgetting was just a consequence of a disconnection. Otherwise, it wouldn't make sense how people normally recover memories after many decades, especially when they're dying. When Elena visited him in the hospital, she seemed in a hurry. Perhaps that had been the first time Facundo remembered the Argentina vs. Hungary match in 1977, after forty years of not visiting that important corner of his existence.

The truth was that the first sign of concern had come before the heart attack. One afternoon he had returned to the house in Ponte Vedra earlier than usual and couldn't remember the alarm code, those four simple numbers he pressed every day to go to work and again when he returned. 0211. Elena had entered it the day the ADT technician had programmed the alarm. Why did you choose those numbers? Facundo had asked her one night when they got home. I don't know, she had said, I just came up with four random numbers, by chance. But Facundo knew that codes and PINs were rarely chosen at random. Especially not when a damn technician, always in a hurry, urges you to pick one. They always refer to something that exists in the present or persists in the past. It wasn't the date they met, nor their first time together, nor their wedding day. It could have been some other date from her intimacy not shared with him, one of those things he knew he would never find out and, perhaps, didn't even have the right to know. February 11, in Spanish, or November 2, in English. Impossible to guess what that little number hid, which he had to memorize and which one afternoon he suddenly forgot. That's why the alarm started going off first, and then the phone. An ADT agent asked if there was a problem, to which Facundo, still stunned by the forgetfulness and the unbearable noise of the alarm, hesitatingly said that there was no problem. The woman asked for the PIN, and Facundo couldn't answer. 0221, he said. Then he corrected himself, trying to type with his index finger on an imaginary keyboard in the air: No, sorry: 0122... The woman hung up, and five minutes later the patrol car arrived, starting to ask uncomfortable questions. Can you tell me your name? Can you show me your ID? After looking at his driver's license, the officer seemed to have fewer doubts than he did. He

14

told Facundo to have a good rest and left. Things really work in this country, Facundo thought to himself. They really do... As long as you have the money to pay for them.

The doctor downplayed it. It wasn't Alzheimer's or anything like that, just stress. After the heart attack, the same thing. It seemed to Facundo that the doctor didn't remember the previous incident with the house alarm and the police, even though he had everything stored in his digital memory that grew every minute from his tablet with every irrelevant detail his patient shared. Facundo didn't want to remind him about the alarm. He was tired or, like everyone else, preferred to simplify things, deny reality, or avoid the well-known "via crusis" through different medical labs—more out of the doctor's legal precaution than out of genuine need. So he said nothing. He just wanted to hear that he was fine and get out of there as soon as possible.

He shouldn't be surprised, the doctor told him, if he didn't remember the most basic things that anyone should remember to live a normal life, such as his home address, his phone number, and so many other things. Dr. Menéndez had treated some cases of people around Facundo's age who had developed Capgras syndrome, in which the individual becomes convinced that their loved ones have been replaced by imposters. It's as terrible as Alzheimer's, if not worse, Dr. Menéndez had said, shaking his head, as if hinting that he hadn't cured any of them.

However, after a week of rest and solitude, Facundo Walsh Ocampo seemed to have recovered. He seemed to be the same person he was before the heart attack. Then, he imposed three weeks of rest on himself, without consulting or considering the responsibilities he still had at the company.

He only focused on resolving the identity theft issue and getting rid of Silvanna as soon as possible.

Identity theft

THE FIRST TIME HE SAW THE NAME Patio del Virrey was on Sunday, January 14th, almost two months before the heart attack. He remembered it because the following Monday was Martin Luther King Day. A purchase of 144 dollars, likely a purchase and withdrawal, had been made with one of his alternate cards a week earlier, on January 6th. He couldn't recall why he hadn't paid attention to it. Maybe because Tijuana and the supermarket felt familiar to him, because the amount was trivial, or because at the time he was up to his neck with Jeff's new project (elevating the modeling industry by granting university scholarships to the candidates), or for some other reason that now eluded him.

He went through his credit card statements again. For a moment, he became furious. Not because of the amount stolen but simply because of the idea of the theft. If there was anything in this world that made his blood pressure rise, it was the thought that someone had taken advantage of him. He couldn't stand the slightest notion or suspicion of having been deceived or manipulated, even though Ernesto always told him that such things were nonsense, because we're all systematically deceived and manipulated by greater forces. We only call it deception when someone from below proves to us that we're fools, not when we fulfill our role as wage slaves, which we do with resignation, if not with pride.

Facundo wiped his face with his hand to banish the image of Ernesto at the Starbucks in Princeton. He couldn't stand it when he got all intellectual like that, speaking in a complicated way. That time, he was about to ask him why he didn't just move to Cuba, but he'd already asked him that years ago and he'd already answered, so he opted for the American way: let him talk, words are forgotten. At least the ones we don't like. He tolerated him because, aside from being his brother-in-law, the black sheep of the family and Elena's shame, Facundo knew, or thought, that Ernesto was a natural-born loser, and his only consolation was feeling proud of his condition as a loser, an impossible mix (as he himself said) of Socrates, Jesus Christ, and Che Guevara, three criminals executed by the justice of the powerful of their time.

"The first was executed by a democracy (with slaves) that was an empire" Ernesto had said, with that preference for finding patterns," the second by an empire that was proud to be one, and the third by another democracy with slaves that has spent its entire life trying not to be called an empire.

He tried to remember. He had been in Tijuana the previous year, but the fact that someone made a purchase in January of that year was concerning. Had he lost the card there? It couldn't be just that, because it wasn't a credit card but a debit card, meaning the thief must have had his PIN to use it. But what was the PIN? He couldn't recall. The worst-case scenario was that it was the same number he used for most of his cards. On the other hand, it was also a mystery that the amount was so modest and that in the following two months, the thief hadn't made any other withdrawals until March 16th.

He finished the rest of the whiskey and told himself, No, I'm not that stupid. I wouldn't use the same PIN for the alternate card. So what was it? Impossible to remember. He tried, but realized it was out of reach. By the second whiskey, he could never recall secondary names. Let alone alternate codes. Maybe in the morning, with a clearer head. Anyway, he used one of those cards when traveling in complicated countries because they had a very low monthly spending limit, just survival, about a thousand or two dollars, if he remembered correctly, nothing to regret in case of theft.

But on March 26th, he detected a new purchase of $75.06 debited by the same supermarket, Patio del Virrey. He searched online. The business didn't even have an official website. After an hour, he found a phone number. Mini mercado Patio del Rey. He called, explained the problem to three different people before they left him on hold for an absurd amount of time. He hung up, called back several times. Finally, a young woman informed him that they had looked into his case and found no irregularities. He hung up, cursed the Mexicans, corrupt from Moctezuma to Peña Nieto, and threw the phone onto a pile of mail waiting on the table.

He looked at the untouched cup of coffee, probably cold by now. The doctor had forbidden him from drinking coffee or any alcohol, without even knowing that for some time now, Facundo had been mixing the two, to relax and to stay awake. The truth is, he thought, doctors can't forbid anything. They're too harmless to forbid anything. At best, they're like priests in their glory days, when everyone revered them, but both they and their parishioners did something else.

The table was full of letters, many of which, he knew, he would never open. Most were advertisements trying to pass as personalized letters, some handwritten or appearing to be handwritten. The effort of technology to create something imperfect was admirable. He couldn't get angry because he knew what that subtle aggression was, that desperate strategy to seduce thousands of strangers, and had always felt a sort of solidarity or empathy. "Among oxen, there are no goring," his uncle Alberto used to say. "Let everyone scratch with the nails they have," his father-in-law would say—or rather, his ex-father-in-law, though he didn't know it yet. But for a moment he thought, and only for a moment, of the effort of all those who worked in advertising agencies, like refined violinists playing for a deaf man, and he even thought of the number of trees, paper mills, printers, trucks, energy that had been invested in that absurd waste that had, ultimately, collided with an indifferent wall called FACUNDO. Just a year earlier, he had argued in a café that thanks to all of that, people still did business, and the poor still had jobs in the most unsuspected corners of the world. Thanks to all that waste in rich countries, thousands of the poor had something to put in their mouths. A good argument. Nothing but hypocrisy, like every salesman's argument, advertisement, propaganda.

What had happened since then? Ernesto said it didn't matter what facts occurred around a believer. The believer would never change their religion, ideology, or soccer team because of any objective fact, any indisputable result. It didn't matter if a ship was sinking with its crew. We are all captains of our own ship and sink with it, never admitting that we steered it straight onto the sharp rocks in the middle of the night. Unless some change happens before, and changes, the real changes in an individual, always come from within. A mystery harder to solve than the nature of the Holy Trinity or the sex of angels, but one that, normally, people don't want to face, as if the resolution of the riddle held no salvation.

"I find less conflict between God and a radical humanist" Ernesto had said, "than between God and the religious. Have you seen those ridiculous videos of sermons by self-proclaimed pastors chosen by God, exorcising people who writhe hysterically on the floor? Well, they never, ever appear in the news of major media outlets, but these are the ones who will define elections and the fate of societies in many parts of the world in the years to come. Are you sure you've never seen them? Really? I find it hard to believe. Well, it must be that you're too busy with important business, and I don't have a normal job. One day, when you have nothing to do, like me, you can watch them on YouTube. There's always some pastor denouncing Jazz or some twelve-tone music as an instrument of the Devil. Some even prove it with tangled pentagraphic theories. Others see it in the allegorical design of the dollar bill. Illuminati and all those theories for the intellectually challenged. They insist that the Devil is in a symbol here, in another there. In the name of a beer or in the shape of a condom. In some insignificant symbol, as if it were the primary means the Devil uses to control the world."

"The Devil is in the fine print…"

"That. It's always said that the Devil is in the details… Oh, no, no. The Devil, if he actually exists, of course, if he's not just some poor devil, is in the big things. The Devil is in the hatred of a proper religious person because their neighbor or the journalist from Channel X is gay or activist Z is poor. The Devil is in a nation supporting an invasion that leads to the slaughter of a million innocents in the name of freedom, of democracy, and then no one cares, because they're busy demonizing the poor who come here to work illegally. They talk big about the Law, yet they're the first to violate the most basic laws. And they do it all with pride and fanaticism (what they call moderation) in the name of God, because if there's anything popular and repetitive to the point of nausea in this shitty world, for the last few thousand years, it's hating and humiliating, hating and killing, all in the name of God."

"Brother-in-law," Facundo had said, somewhat ironically, "You should seek professional help. You're losing perspective on things…"

"Of course, we critics are always the radicals, the ones out of touch with reality and all that. In the world of big business, it's not like that. It's the world where realism, moderation, sanity, pragmatism reign… If you kill someone with a shot to the head, that's a horrific crime. If you kill thousands of people slowly over the course of a few years, that's good business. Did you hear the latest about Bayer? And about Monsanto? They really know how to do it. No one's ever going to recommend they seek professional help. Or jail time."

That time, he said goodbye to Ernesto with a smile. Perhaps, silently, to himself (or to his most superficial self?) he called him, as he had so many times before, as only one can from the heights of Success and which is so characteristic of that culture: poor loser.

Now, further removed in time and geography, there was something unsettling him. He didn't want to say it was something that distressed him, because he detested the dramatics of Elena and her brother Ernesto. He still thought the same way, but something had changed. Either the ship had crashed into the rocks, or he had managed to change course for reasons he wasn't entirely clear about. Something, which he couldn't quite pinpoint, had run its course. No mystery, really, considering the moment he was going through. He looked at the letters with promises of great deals and solutions to nonexistent problems and felt they were like the seeds in a certain biblical parable, the ones that fell on stone and withered away. Or something like that. Facundo the skeptic (he thought, in Ernesto's voice), the man who once had faith in all those very same things.

What to do with that mountain of letters and envelopes, aside from shredding them carefully so as not to throw his personal data in the trash, where they might end up in the hands of some identity thief? Should he also sue every company that robbed him of several minutes of his life every day by making him open and read advertisements that seemed to include some relevant notification about his home, his credit, or his latest tax return? Even in the most irrelevant advertisements, his personal data was included: full name, address, date of birth ("Happy Birthday, Mr. Walsh!"), and an unsuspected series about his own interests and hobbies. The last time he had been looking at cruises online, he started receiving brochures with offers for Caribbean cruises. He didn't know how or who collected this data, but it worked very well. Apparently... No, not apparently: undoubtedly, they knew his weaknesses (perhaps better than Elena) and, obviously, they knew where he lived and where he usually traveled. Sometimes they exaggerated a bit, like when he had been reading an article from the University of North Carolina about the effects of alcohol on health, and two days later he received a 30 percent discount offer for a detox treatment, an invitation from Alcoholics Anonymous along with a voucher for a 450cc sample of cognac with the purchase of two bottles of Ballantine's. The other offers for shoes, massages, and fruit-scented condoms might have been due to Elena's past internet searches. Every day, he had to empty his mailbox of these endless advertisements for dentists, pizzas delivered to his door, and "scratch the coupon to see if you've won an invitation to check out Toyota Dealer's new cars!"

Through those mysterious algorithmic connections (mysterious only for those who aren't Google engineers, of course), he had tried to search for something about advertising, data theft, and identity theft, and probably due to a combination with his previous searches about his health problem, he ended up on a paragraph from Ernesto's friend, another one of those despicable individuals, a professor who lives in Jacksonville: "One of my characters has suffered a heart attack, so I've been searching online for symptoms and hospitals where he lives. Now I'm receiving all sorts of advertisements for health insurance and treatments. I hope this doesn't raise my health insurance premium and that none of the other characters decide to commit a crime (something very likely in a novel) because things are going to get complicated for me."

"I hope you die first," Facundo said, slamming the laptop shut so hard it made a noise as if it had broken somewhere.

With infinite weariness, he picked up the phone again to file a complaint with the bank. All he could confirm was that, after filling out the corresponding online form, he would have to wait a few weeks until his case was processed and a resolution was issued, which would be sent via traditional mail directly to his home. Generally, he preferred to lose the money than waste even an hour entangled in these typical disputes with credit card companies and insurance companies. They always win through exhaustion, counting on the fact that you have a job that's either interesting enough or suffocating enough to not dedicate so much time to complaints and fights that always end with sarcasm or, directly, with an insult from the frustrated customer and an equally insulting *"Thank-you-for-choosing-us-it's-been-a-pleasure-doing-business-with-you"* from the cyborg employee of the relentless bureaucratic machinery of large private corporations.

He searched for the email generated by H&R Block when he filed his last tax return in February and paid extra, as he did every year, for a Peace of Mind. That service, pompously named... how else could you phrase that Frankenstein of Peace of Mind...? Tranquility? Psychological Insurance? Sleep Easy? Existential Relief...? Fear Business? What the hell? Anyway, he found in an email the so-called Peace of Mind which informed him that before activating his IDENTITY THEFT PROTECTION, he had to open an account and go through a bullshit process that he thought he had already done years ago, but which, in any case, for it to work properly, had to be updated every year and, even then, it didn't guarantee that someone, in the end, wouldn't steal his identity; an item he had acknowledged by clicking on ACCEPT TERMS at the bottom of a 12,234-word contract with tiny text that, obviously, he hadn't finished reading, not even the first or the last paragraph.

Fifteen years ago, when he was still young and didn't have as much money, he had broken down from stress trying to prove to the health insurance company Aetna that he was in perfect health, and if he had requested a change of insurer, it was only because he had to move states, from New York to Florida, and the new company didn't work with the previous insurer, its competitor Blue Cross and Blue Shield. He recalled that night almost indifferently. Insurance companies are called that, just like that, they're called that, INSURERS, insurance, because they always make sure they won't lose money, and to do that, they have to confirm that the future client doesn't need them!" he had shouted that night, while Ernesto's daughters, still little girls, played on the floor and Elena told him not to set a bad example for the nieces, that the girls would absorb all his stress and bad mood and that, as a result, they wouldn't grow up to be happy adults. But he, only he, or the person he was twenty years ago, was right, he thought. Like any bank, those damned insurers only lend money to someone who can prove they don't need it. In the end, they're businesses, and business is business, a sacred and unquestionable activity, if there ever was one. Only the damned states can afford not to think about profits... In the end, his case was accepted three weeks later, after an entire package of Tylenol, several nights of cursing and being unable to sleep, and five thousand dollars for a private doctor to prove that he had never been operated on for a testicle but for a harmless ganglion in his hand, which, for all intents and purposes, was just as useless, and which reappeared like magic a month after the careful and very professional surgery by Dr. Kaplan and which he himself resolved a month later in his office, like in the Middle Ages, by bursting it, not with a Bible but with two copies of Rich Dad Poor Dad by Kiyosaki together. That's how he resolved, definitively, the problem of the ganglion, which was not recorded in any medical file. But who could think of such stupidity as bursting a ganglion in the hand, a biblical cyst, like in the times of Almanzor and Alfonso the Wise, with a single blow from a book, without the intervention of a professional and without a medical record? It was his fault. He had first had surgery and then burst a ganglion, not a testicle. By the time the new insurance company finally confirmed it was a ganglion, not a testicle, and accepted his application so they could start billing monthly, he already had two swollen testicles and the beginning of a cardiac arrhythmia from which he never recovered, he said during a casual dinner in Miami, after the last female colleague had left. At least that's what he thought for a long time without daring to go to the doctor to rule out the possibility of arrhythmia, so as not to leave a record of any possible or real illness that could complicate things later. He knew they would take him through different clinics and all kinds of tests (the more the better, because the damned insurers paid for it) until, at the end of the process, they would recommend he take a vacation, in the best case, or prescribe him a drug (also mostly paid for by the insurers) which, as usual, he wouldn't take so as not to have to return to the same doctor due to the side effects. The last time, during an annual checkup, he hadn't answered with a firm No to the question of whether he sometimes felt sad, and after the nurse left the room, the famous doctor appeared with a prescription for something called Happytilaunesterone that would solve the problem. Or almost. The only drawback was the side effects he read after buying the little bottle at the pharmacy: possible episodes of bipolarity and suicidal tendencies.

Jeff's marvelous idea of the six million

ONE OF THE ENVELOPES WAS ADDRESSED to him. The sender, Jey Hay, Jeff Al Ferro's pseudonym, allowed him to guess the contents. Jeff congratulated him on the last meeting in Kuala Lumpur where the pre-agreement on the AR21 androids had been signed. He should congratulate him on the achievement and, above all, for not giving up at the first rejection, something like scoring a goal in stoppage time, he seemed to hear Jeff's voice, always resorting to soccer metaphors.

More than persuading him, Jeff had pressured him to sell the idea to Bolton Co. In fact, as always, he already had the strategy planned long before Facundo accepted. Jeff's principle of action, he had once admitted during an end-of-year meeting, came from his early algebra studies at Stony Brook University. Like the geniuses of Apple and Facebook, he too had discovered his goldmine, one ordinary day in a classroom. Like those geniuses, he too had dropped out of school to dedicate himself fully to what really mattered. That's why he never even graduated with a BS, but had been a thousand times more successful than the nerds in the class who now had master's degrees in science and taught in high school for forty thousand dollars a year. He had never been skilled at math, but from that brief enlightening experience he had learned something that would serve him for life. Like in an equation with an unknown, he said, one must frame the situation as if the result were already known. $x2+3x=0$. Before starting, we know the result is zero. All that's left is to solve for x, in this case with two results, meaning something, an obstacle between the start of a great business and the final result, which we already know, or foresee. The difference is that it's not an inevitable reality, like the weather, but one we are going to create. If the equation is worth it, all that's left is to solve for the unknown. It becomes reality. If not, it should be abandoned before any effort.

It vanishes. It never existed or will exist. That's our world, and its creators are us, the businessmen, the busy men.

That afternoon at the Starbucks in a Barnes & Noble (in Manhattan or Philadelphia, he couldn't remember) Jeff had shown him an article from a Silicon Valley publication on Artificial Intelligence and machine translation. A skeptical professor argued that these marvels of digital technology were fallible because they couldn't grasp the broader context of a culture. According to this Dr. Majfud, there were ideas and feelings that only humans could understand and sometimes not even we, humans, understand other humans, this corrupter of innocent minds had said.

Jeff had paused to look at him for a second, like a hunter eyeing his prey through the scope of his rifle. That last sentence, he said, had inspired him: and sometimes not even humans can understand other humans, he repeated. For reasons the author of that little phrase could never have imagined, there lay the key to a business that could not only make it rain money for the company but was going to change the history of humanity.

Facundo laughed. After another silence, he took a sip of coffee and asked.

"What do you mean, specifically?"

Jeff fidgeted in his chair. He was about to say something but instead answered with another question:

"What if one day an algorithm is developed that can decipher human emotions better than humans themselves? Yes, I see. It seems ridiculous. Maybe that day is still far off, but the important thing is to sell the idea so others can develop it. That's how everything works. Isn't that exactly what Kennedy did with his vision of reaching the Moon? That's something you and I know better than anyone: if you don't aim for the Moon, you won't even jump the fence with the neighbor."

"Psychoanalytic machines?" asked Facundo.

"Why not? Or at least robots that give us a clue about our own feelings. Come on, let's think seriously. When your stomach or back hurts, where do you go? To the doctor. And who's responsible for the solution? The doctor, who studied for it and who we pay for it. But when you go to the psychologist, things get a lot more complicated. Who's responsible for curing you of a trauma, no matter how small, one of those we all have in our collection and which, thanks to them, make you a creative and productive man? You, of course, not the psychologist. Not the professional, but the patient. The only sure thing is that they'll charge you, and in fact, they ask for your credit card before you even enter the office. Just in case, after forty minutes of chatting, the patient doesn't have the three hundred dollars. And I'm talking about a cheap psychologist, one of those who doesn't inspire much confidence, not so much because of the nonsense they say but because of how little they charge. A year ago, I had to give in to one of those exhausting domestic arguments (which ended at two in the morning with the classic 'Yes, dear, we'll go get professional help' because I was exhausted and had a partners' meeting at 8:00 a.m.) and ended up going to couples therapy at Silvanna's whim. Result? After three months of therapy and $10,800 (plus taxes), we weren't cured, and it was my fault. It was my fault before and, in the end, I was still stuck with that tumor hanging from my balls. You see, women aren't bad or at fault for anything, are they?"

Facundo let out a laugh that caught the attention of an old man with the face of a sad Benny Hill, sitting two tables away.

"Partly, it's like that," Jeff continued. "Surely the fault was and is mine. I'm too cynical to believe in fairy tales, and that's one of my limitations, I have to admit, not just as a person but as a professional. Some time ago, on one of those long and boring flights that

35

feel like death, I read an article about Neanderthals. I was struck by the idea that our ancestors exterminated them because the big-nosed little men were too realistic and pragmatic. Once they disappeared, the little men of the forest, the foreigners, became the gnomes in fairy tales. Isn't that a wicked irony? We, on the other hand, believed in all kinds of myths, and that's why we survived. Why was I so impressed by this theory? I asked myself many times until I came to a crucial conclusion: as I read it, I felt, as a businessman, identified with that realism and pragmatism of the Neanderthals, and it was hard to accept that they had disappeared for those very reasons that have always been the banners of our profession, of our essence. But there was a detail, a mistake, I realized much later. We're not like the extinct Neanderthals but like the survivors, the victorious Cro-Magnons. Why? Because businessmen aren't pragmatic or realistic but the opposite. We dream, and that's how we create the world…"

"I thought there was something about it that reminded me of my brother-in-law," said Facundo.

"The crazy one from college?" asked Jeff.

"Forget it."

"Well," Jeff continued, "in the end, the only thing I understood from all those attacks and reproaches from Silvanna, with the heroic professional support of the therapist, is that a woman doesn't want you to solve her problems but to listen to her. But not just any way. No. I listened to her, but, every now and then, my face betrayed some distraction or, worse, some exhaustion. It's not easy to have the endurance of a woman at two in the morning talking about things you don't understand. When listening to her, I had to put on an understanding face. Do you understand what I'm saying?"

"I think not," complained Facundo, tired. "Don't forget I'm coming from Berlin, and for me, it's two in the morning."

"I'll sum it up for you," said Jeff, unable to control his new tic: a strong wink with his right eye followed by a kind of smile that lasted fractions of a second. "Women are different from men, but the solutions can be very similar. If I were a well-programmed doll, we would've never had any problems. That's according to her and according to our therapist. I'm still trying to understand what it was that I didn't understand about putting on an understanding face. Something that any doll or robot capable of listening and learning could've resolved much better and much earlier than I did. Of course, the robot wouldn't have to get up at 5:45 a.m. to be ready and in a good mood for the shareholders' meeting at 8:00. It wouldn't even have to sleep two hours. That's what it means to be a real man. Or whatever you call this thing you see here."

Jeff breathed tiredly, took a breath, winked again, and continued, this time without the three-centisecond smile, probably drowned in an older gesture, a kind of kiss to nowhere, one of those expressions normal people make when thinking about a past mistake:

"In other words, both women and men need substitutes that are neither women nor men but abstractions of each, improved versions, with their virtues and without their defects, like vitamins that are neither apples that cause diarrhea, nor carrots that cause constipation, but just that, vitamins that our body needs."

"In short," interrupted Facundo, "the therapist didn't work for you…"

"We weren't cured, at least. I say at least because I don't know if it provided Silvanna with some gain, like some kind of existential legitimization or a new imaginary romance with the little doctor, because he sure was good at listening. After all, that's what his profession consists of. Knowing how to listen. We didn't solve 'The Problem', but I paid a fortune, much more than for the heart surgery. You tell your whole private life to a guy with the face of a good sage, like a Catholic priest without a cassock or a crucifix but surrounded by little African and Buddhist statues, and in the end, the fault lies with the husband, who is usually the one resisting believing in the healer due to macho biases."

At this point, Jeff waved his hand as if swatting a flying insect in front of his face and said:

"Let's leave that now. What I'm getting at is that with therapist dolls (notice I said therapist, not therapeutic, so as not to objectify them), people will not only have faster and more reliable solutions, but it'll be enough to press a little button to completely erase the memory. So that stuff about telling your private life to a jerk in a cassock or with a doctor's title won't be a problem anymore. And if it doesn't get erased, it won't matter, because the little robot won't care much about it either, nor will she denounce you on CNN for having kissed her thirty years ago. In fact, I doubt any version of those will last that long."

"I don't know," insisted Facundo, looking at his watch and trying to bring the conversation to an end. "Maybe the professor has a point about that, about how not even people understand each other…"

"That's the point!" said Jeff, like someone who realizes they've spent an hour trying to explain something to a child with no result. "That's the problem, but not the solution. We don't even understand ourselves. How many have any idea of their own traumas? Worse yet, how many have an idea of what someone in front of us is thinking or feeling, like you and I are now? Especially if the person in front of us is a woman, or someone who doesn't share our culture. Or are you going to tell me you know your wife's fantasies?"

"Let's not get into that," said Facundo, annoyed. "You know I don't like mixing the personal…"

"Well, think then of any other example. My wife Silvanna, if you want. Don't tell me you've never looked at her breasts because I won't believe you. No one can avoid looking at Silvanna's breasts because they're firm, perched above a wasp waist, and that's inevitable. I'd say it's the exact opposite of a Mayan Indian. Did you see those fleshy lips? Silvanna is a real Barbie, and I'm not stupid enough as to think that other men, even colleagues like you, have never looked at her breasts or lips or who knows what else. Yes, I know, she has a BA from Princeton, but that's not visible, and few pay attention to it. Not just because of our profession, which has many connections in the fashion and beauty industry, but by common sense, anyone knows that a thousand times more important than a Harvard PhD is an ass graced by nature and well cared for by man. But our society is so hypocritical that it condemns what it desires. Let me put it more clearly: it condemns what it desires. Does it bother me that people look at Silvanna's ass? That even my colleagues imagine those perfect lips kissing them? That she secretly reciprocates all that lascivious fantasy? Of course it does. But what can a reasonable man do? Follow her everywhere with a camera and threaten every man who looks at her? Or do we not also look at other variations of the same beauty? Your wife is pretty too (I say this respectfully, objectively), but don't tell me you'd dislike it if one day Silvanna showed up at your office and planted a kiss on your mouth. I'd be furious, but not you, let's be honest. If you say no, you're a damn hypocrite son of a bitch. It's the same for them, Silvanna, the secretary, the new intern from Minnesota, your wife…"

"I told you to drop it," said Facundo. "Private is private. We all know that every now and then we go to the bathroom to pee and we do it with our private parts, but that doesn't mean we're going to start doing it in the hallways just because it's something natural. That's what bathrooms are for."

"I don't know," said Jeff. "Wait for some movement to arise in favor of PEEING IN THE STREET

WITHOUT THE CHAINS OF THE PATRIARCHY or something like that… God let me live long enough to enjoy it."

Facundo looked him in the eyes but didn't find his gaze. It was lost in a kind of euphoria about giving birth to a great idea called Half a Million. Suddenly, he remembered the almost whispered words of Jeff's secretary, Tina, who said her boss was addicted to caffeine and that after his fourth Starbucks at four in the afternoon, the effect on him was the same as Mr. Robertson's after his fourth Corona Premier at nine.

"No problem," concluded Jeff, interpreting Facundo's silence and gaze as a response. "You don't need to answer any of my questions. Everyone knows you're a decent guy. In other words, a repressed individual. A properly repressed one. Something quite unusual for an Argentine. Maybe you Americanized yourself too much, bought into all the crap we preach here like a manual for the Good American, the upright puritan who doesn't catcall a beautiful woman at a construction site but then, after two hours of watching porn online, rapes the neighbor's daughter and even the cat, then strangles both; the proper English gentleman who goes to church on Sundays and on Mondays waves a Confederate flag, not because he hates Black people and Mexicans—which he does—

but because it's part of the tradition, of his pure essence, different from those ugly rapists on the other side of the border, and he thanks God for living in a country chosen by Him, amidst thousands and millions of sexual deviants and serial killers, and you ended up more Catholic than the Pope. I'm not going to ask you if you've imagined touching Silvanna's tits. You'd never tell me, and I don't care, and I wouldn't want to hear it. One isn't responsible for their disgusting desires and has the right to freedom of imagination, protected by the First Amendment, which happens to be the only freedom that hasn't been fully regulated yet. Either way, I know it, I know at least you've looked at Silvanna's tits, and because I understand human nature, no one in the company has ever beaten me. As the cliché goes, the essential is invisible to the eye. A great truth, but for the wrong reasons. Do you remember when that deal with NORDSTROM WAS DEAD? NORDSTROM DOESN'T JUST BELIEVE IN DIVERSITY, IT VIEWS IT AS GOOD BUSINESS. Neither Robert nor Nath could revive it. A couple of incompetent fools with good reputations, with appearances that resist any feminine opposition, in other words, two decorative elements for the company, and nothing more. When that ship was sinking, who did they call? Who? Do you remember? Of course you do. They called The

Shark Jeff. Everyone thinks I don't know they call me "the shark," but it doesn't bother me. On the contrary. They called The Shark Jeff, and Jeff devoured them all."

"Until Ivanka Trump showed up and left you like a mere minnow."

"That's another story. After all, no one is invincible, especially when the president's daughter gets in your way. But in our league, at our level, why do they always call The Shark Jeff when the game gets tough? Why? Because Jeff is bad? No, quite the opposite. Because Jeff is good, very good. At least at what he does. I know what I'm doing and I do it well. Why? For one simple, very simple reason. Because I don't lie to myself. I'm not a hypocrite who murders half the population and then kneels in church convinced that God will forgive him and open the gates of Heaven for him. I can lie to a lot of people, but never to myself. What bothers me the most is hypocrisy. Like romantic idealism, which leads to nothing but lie after lie. How do I know if Silvanna isn't turned on by some colleague I don't even know? Imagine, after ten years of marriage, the poor woman must be so bored with the same routine, the predictable kisses, the familiar caresses, the same hamburger and fries, the same McDonald's, no matter how much I try to spice up the menu, the natural lack of intense emotions like me, that guy who, when he walks, is always the same from behind and from the front. Who knows. I'm not saying Silvanna doesn't love me, as her husband, but for her to have erotic dreams about me, there's probably a distance here to Mars."

"Stop it" complained Facundo. "I'm not interested. In fact, it bothers me when you use me as your psychoanalyst."

"See?" remarked Jeff. "Even friends aren't good for confessions anymore. Once I told half my story to Jaime and he called me a machista. Did you notice how machistas are today's communists? You can't say anything serious without getting hit with the social censorship of political correctness. A robot, on the other hand, if it could learn from living with one of us, would've already detected a problem in your resistance to hearing the truth. Do you understand the central idea I'm trying to explain?"

"I have a right to my own traumas" replied Facundo, visibly annoyed. "Besides, I have to go."

"Yes, I know. That thing about the right to trauma isn't up for debate. We're not here to pity each other but to do business. But if we don't understand how the world works, we can't even sell a jug of water in the desert."

"OK" said Facundo. "I'll take note, and we'll talk about your project later. Honestly, I'm exhausted and I can't make sense of what you're proposing right now. But I'll take care of it. It's almost eight here. Two in the morning in Berlin. My biological clock is still there."

"I almost forgot you're a human being…"

"Still am…"

"A robot that had intimacy with its owner, someone capable of learning and processing thousands of emotions per second, would already have an effective response. The best response. In the not-too-distant future, they'll be more reliable than we are."

"A horror."

"A horror for human narcissism, which five hundred years after Copernicus still believes it's the center of the universe. Look at the bright side: the military industry, as always, is already way ahead with killer robots. What are drones that kill from a distance, if not that? No one talks about the families that have disappeared under the night bombings of these metallic little birds in the Middle East. Disappeared in every possible sense. We don't know if they were bad people or not-so-bad kids who happened to be passing by, playing war with a stick. Sticks are more dangerous than the AK15s they sell at Walmart, did you know that? Soon there'll be insect drones capable of picking out the bad kid and eliminating him in any corner of the world. Or bacteria drones, more likely."

"There will always be the problem of defining who the bad kid is."

"No, no, not at all. For military logic (which, nowadays, is the same as democracy's logic) the bad guys are always the others, and don't overthink it. The definition of what's good or what's bad doesn't matter in the slightest. The only thing that matters is who has power and who doesn't. The former have always been and will always be the good ones. It's the best and only objective way to solve the dilemma. Everything else is just talk."

"I know you, comb-seller" laughed Facundo. "Now, what's the bright side of your product?"

"The bright side is that, in my project (my masterpiece before I retire, God willing) we're not going to invest in developing new ideas of extermination but the opposite. We're not going to invest in war but in love."

"I'm melting... My brother-in-law says the protest by Google engineers against artificial intelligence applied to war drones is because they all came from American universities, anti-war and anti-patriotic strongholds in the middle of a war-mongering and chauvinistic country."

"I believe it. Universities don't just teach algorithms. But it won't always be that way."

"In the end, they got Google not to renew the contract with the Department of Defense. When I found out, I didn't know if that was a good thing, just when I thought it might be a good thing."

"To hell with all of it. The Marxists are draining my brain. Let them entertain themselves with old books and their miserable salaries. Leave that silliness aside and let's focus on reality. Or rather, the reality that's coming. Doesn't investing in love strike you as a respectable argument? We could reach an understanding with the slackers of the sixties, those hairy anti-Vietnam types who walked around naked and smoked pot while others died in distant countries fighting to protect their freedoms. Now that communists are no longer a threat, what better than making love to an android that, for the first time in history, will be therapeutic in every sense? Sex, psychoanalysis, and hygiene, all for the first time in human history."

"Yes, probably" admitted Facundo, somewhat uncomfortable to find that the insufferable Jeff was about to convince him once again. "Not bad. You almost had me. It's the best thing you've said since you started your coffee. It might be the best thing we've done in twenty years. Though we won't be around to see it."

"No, maybe we won't see it. But we'll have been the first to imagine it and the first to promote it. The profits won't be insignificant either, as you can imagine."

"You said the same thing about the model scholarship project," said Facundo.

"Wasn't that your idea?" asked Jeff.

"I don't think so. I don't have good ideas, and if I do I've got to credit them to you, since you're the boss."

"In the end, we could only give out six or seven scholarships" said Jeff, feigning defeat. "But at least we made seven young girls happy who believed they had earned them through their intellectual potential."

"I think it was more. Almost twenty, at a cost of sixty thousand dollars a year each, up to four years. Almost five million, which at twenty percent leaves us less than a million for the division."

"For the entire division, as usual… I don't want to downplay the achievement, but, as you know, it's pocket change. We didn't make history with that. Do you know what these last two projects have in common? The models have to pretend to be robots to be appealing, and the robots will have to pretend to be human to be successful. We've talked about that many times. Haven't we? Do you remember you always told me the irony of our products was that the more frigid the models appeared, the more attractive they seemed? I don't know if it's me, but when you were more cynical, you had better ideas. A bit more aggressive, I'd say. Or am I wrong?"

"I'm getting old."

"You told me the best girls always walk as if they were disgusted by what they were doing or as if they were bad in bed. Well, it doesn't matter if you regret your macho past now, what matters or what comforts is that twenty of the scholarship recipients are now enjoying themselves on one of the campuses of the wonderful universities this country has (with no less merit than the basketball players sitting next to them in the classroom) and that at least one, or two, might become lawyers, fluid engineers, or forensic doctors."

"Some will make it..." said Facundo. "That's what I told myself in every interview, so I wouldn't feel bad. There are so many idiot men who get ahead just because they think they have two heads and the one downstairs thinks too."

"Tell me about it, I voted for Trump. I wanted to see how far one of our own could go, and maybe I went overboard. Either way, the scholarship project was a good one, and in passing, we did someone some good. But, as I was saying, that was a very minor project, to get us through the inexplicable low activity of last year. This other one is a megaproject that won't just bring us a tsunami of dollars but will also make us participants in the great Revolution of the century, with a capital R."

"It worries me" said Facundo. "You sound like the president."

"I'm worried about you. You've been acting a bit strange for some time now."

Facundo stood up. It was eight-fifteen. He was exhausted. Jeff, confident he had planted his idea in one of his closest and most effective collaborators, patted him on the back and told him to get some sleep early. In the morning, Jeff was going to do the same work with Richard, at that same Starbucks, and Facundo didn't know it. For Jeff, Richard was a less skilled player, a benchwarmer, but he had to secure his enthusiastic participation, in case Facundo backed out of taking the lead in Malaysia.

After three weeks of studying Jeff's latest project, Facundo agreed to participate. Jeff was unpleasant in many ways, but very good at what he did. He could convince anyone that the earth is flat and, in passing, gather fervent followers capable of going door to door announcing the good news of a project to expand their area.

Two weeks later, Facundo had met with the board of Bolton Co. in Los Angeles. It wasn't a good start. The board wasn't convinced by the proposal, and Facundo, with his experience in hand, flew to Kuala Lumpur a month later, where it turned out to be easier than expected. The Asians, accustomed to nothingness, to the eternal margin, and surprised by the unstoppable streak of multi-million-dollar deals, joined any quixotic venture, any proposal. Facundo thought that if he had to sell Martian water, the first place he should go was that part of the world.

Finally, he had managed to sell Jeff's idea in Malaysia, and that Manila envelope undoubtedly confirmed the success of his efforts.

He set it aside but didn't open it.

That's how Facundo had sold Jeff's idea in Seoul

ANOTHER ENVELOPE ADDRESSED to him. The sender was from XiNotch Co., a substitute for Xin Co., one of Mr. Xi's companies, who probably wasn't actually named Xi but, for all practical purposes, it was the same because few knew that Mr. Xi was the largest shareholder of the company producing the RealPerson dolls, and few, like him, Facundo, had had the opportunity to meet him in person.

"This letter is for you, Silvanna," he said, as if she could hear him.

He opened the rough-textured envelope, carefully misaligned as if it had been sent by Khufu from ancient Egypt. In a perfect world, imperfection and even poverty are signs of distinction and, of course, cost much more. The first word he instinctively searched for and read was the most important: congratulations... Below it, the signature of Mr. C. Lopes, the Filipino who signed all the company's letters and who (Facundo suspected) didn't even own a bicycle. A man around forty, with stiff, still unanimously black hair, though with some wrinkles betraying him around his eyes, whose job was to take responsibility for anything said in the name of the company that, for some reason in some country, turned out to be inappropriate, illegal, or simply a miscalculation. An employee with one of those exorbitant salaries that are hinted at by his Rolex, his always new blue-beige jacket worth a thousand dollars (much uglier than the fifty-dollar brown corduroy Saddlebred suit Ernesto had worn for as long as he could remember), his culinary tastes, his three-day escapades to England or Spain to watch Barcelona play against Liverpool, and by other more private whims when he wasn't in the service of the Company. A kind of modern mercenary (if not a prostitute) who indulged in various luxuries but didn't even have the right to call himself by the name his parents gave him at birth. An invented character, surrounded by a fake world with the sole purpose of keeping the company within the strict and secret bounds of legality. Someone bulletproof against any lawsuit, any hint of dignity. He was just as useful for taking responsibility for Mr. Xi's misguided opinion on a new law in Qatar or the United States as he was for taking credit for a night of sex with a scorned Brazilian woman who had somehow, no one ever knows how, found the email of Mr. Xi's wife.

Facundo read the rest of the letter. He was a few days away from achieving the biggest contract of his career. Or, at least, a pre-contract that would grant him exclusive use of the EM (Emotion Processor) of the RealPerson dolls. A year ago, two at most, he would have leapt with euphoria. For much less he had celebrated, though in absolute silence, like Maradona celebrating one of his goals, jumping and punching the air with a fist. Now, the big news reached him like a newspaper that, even before picking it up off the floor, we already know has nothing important to report.

The name, RealPerson, had been decided after a lengthy two-hour dispute in Seoul, around a large shiny wooden table, in a room without the typical floor-to-ceiling windows of executive buildings in Korea or Kuala Lumpur, as if it were a secret meeting of a Cold War military command. Someone had observed that the name might come off as a bit pretentious, but Sir David, the expert in marketing psychology, dismissed this possibility, assuring that perceptions could be shaped by advertising and the prestige of the product itself; that one shouldn't forget that the consumer, above all, was an animal, human, but an animal nonetheless, with a body and a deep psychology very similar to any other primate, that what differentiated us from our evolutionary cousins was, precisely, the most superficial, like makeup on women, and that the only thing that couldn't be changed, only exploited, were the four or five basic instincts, such as sex, hunger, power, and revenge, in that strict order. Success, according to Sir

David, is expressed through these basic and common elements of the consumer animal.

Both RealWoman and RealGirl (the more fake something is, the more Real they add in front) were dismissed due to the potential lawsuits from feminist groups, rather than the inconvenience that the company also produced male dolls.

"Feminazis" the representative from the Houston board had clarified. "Those women who stopped being women... They complain about being objectified, about having their breasts touched, but they're the first ones to go topless in public. They call that a protest against the patriarchy."

"It's possible to see it the other way around" said the one from Chicago: "men get offended by those breast-baring protests but applaud when there's a butt contest."

"I don't know, it's not the same."

"No, of course it's not the same. One group is dangerous. The others, the ones in the contest, are under control. It's not the same as the eleven Pussy Riots from Russia versus the thirty million obedient and very conservative pussys, all those proper churchgoing coochies and charity event attendees who when they menstruate say it's lipstick and who voted for the pussy-grabbing president of our country, blessed by God."

"For the Lord's sake, let's drop that."

"What's the difference between the porn star, Stormy Daniels, and Mrs. Melania Trump? One is retired and doesn't speak English well."

Someone complained with a timid sigh and requested that politics not be discussed, and certainly not the Russians, who had also committed blasphemy, but another beside them, as always happens in these kinds of meetings, reinforced the apparent outburst before any opposing stance could gain ground.

"*Feminazis*," insisted the one from Houston.

"Thanks to whom," said the representative from Singapore, a Brazilian with an intrusive nose that he could have easily fixed years ago "our products exist and thanks to whom the RealPerson will bring about the Revolution of the century."

"That's right" confirmed another. "If there were no demand, we wouldn't even bother to think of a solution."

"If only women were more feminine... But no, now they're all feminists. I don't know the statistics, but I'd venture to say almost all of them are lesbians..."

"You wouldn't say that at your daughter's school parents' meeting."

"I'm no genius, but neither am I that."

"Yesterday I was at a fashion show. The clothes bore me, it's not for me if it's not on my stock list. But what's inside…"

"Well, that at least can truly be called a woman…"

"Of course, they're better than the bitter feminazis, but even in that case, one should ask, what is Real about those beautiful (I repeat, beautiful, absolutely beautiful) girls who strut down fashion runways like blind robots about to trip."

"At least our products can smile."

"Exactly!"

"Then, millions of other young girls copy them and, as if that weren't enough, they call themselves 'authentic,' 'unique,' 'my greatest merit is being myself.'"

"That's precisely why" explained the expert in consumer psychology. "Because people believe what they need to believe, meaning the opposite of what it really is, exactly like when someone buys a bottle of water because they're thirsty. If they wanted another type of pleasure, maybe they'd buy a Coca-Cola or a beer. That's the only reason someone buys a bottle of water, because they're thirsty."

"How true!"

"Nothing is more real than our RealPerson."

"If it's up to me, they already have my vote."

For Facundo, the only clear thing was the idea of Real, because in a world where everything is fake, or almost everything, selling the idea of Real is the greatest obsession and, therefore, the best business. Like Sir David's bottle of water. Real food, Realpolitik, Real facts… Uncle Alberto had already suspected our world several decades in advance: The ads for small cars always emphasize the virtues of their spacious interiors, he had said once, back in the summer of 1976, Facundo remembered, walking along the beach at Piriápolis, who knows why and who knows why Facundo had never forgotten such modest ideas as that one, which now seemed to reach their true dimension.

The secret weapon of XiNotch Co. to outperform the Californian RealDoll was going to be its ability to respond to the emotional, rather than physical, needs of its owner (one of the sacred laws of this new product was that you could only speak about consumers in the singular).

In fact, this had been the central argument of Facundo's strategy in defense of the Emo (emotional) component, that afternoon in Singapore:

Today (he had argued), when it was his turn to present after the discussion and consequent vote on the product's name "people trust robots and all kinds of software to care for or reveal physical illnesses. That psycho-cultural stage is already mature and will not be an obstacle to overcome. With software and by simply looking at their phone's camera, consumers can know their blood pressure, their heart rate, and how many calories they need to burn to avoid reaching the critical index that separates diabetics from the rest of humanity. Aren't you all listening to me, right now, in Mandarin, Malay, English, and Korean, while I'm speaking in Spanish? Maybe not in the Mandarin of Confucius or the great Xi Jinping, but you understand me, don't you? Today, a car can take us to any point in a city while we rest, while we nap or read the news on the roof or on the same road. Even the car can suggest where to go on the weekend, what movie to watch, what book to read, which political party to vote for according to our own needs, and if it's the best day of the month to have sex or not. Above all, if we were women, this would be crucial data. An intelligent device can smell the level of testosterone or estrogen. Of course, nothing is easier to measure than the amount of these elements in the human body. At least no more difficult than measuring our car's oil level. In fact, I would say that the latter, the measurement of estrogen and a woman's sexual desire, is more difficult to measure without any software (unanimous laughter from the board). Last week, in San Diego, with a Starbucks coffee in hand, while pretending to be interested in one of the competitor's products, a RealDoll told me, "Don't look at me just as a woman you want to sleep with. I can also listen to your problems. Wouldn't you use your car just to listen to the radio, right? (Facundo had made a theatrical pause while looking at each member of the board) Do you realize? (he continued) Even Proto-Artificial-Intelligence is capable of teaching us things that we, with our anachronistic pride of believing ourselves the center of creation and the Universe, never understood before. This revelation was just a coincidence because I later learned that our competition in California doesn't pay much attention to the emotional or intellectual aspect of their dolls. Their strategy is to provide high-quality sex, hyperreal sex, augmented reality sex, but sex in the end, and little more. (Facundo paused, like an exhausted preacher leaning on his pulpit for a moment, before continuing with more calm.) But it's not just artificial intelligence that has much to teach us. Everything we think we know today is false. Or imprecise. New studies reveal, for example, that the ones who consume the most pornography where violence is exerted against women are, precisely, women. It seems that women and respectable husbands are offended by humiliation or caveman behavior, but they can't stop desiring what offends them. These are not just statistics, which are often unreliable. No, gentlemen. This is the reality of the entire universe gathered by Big Data analysis. That's what it's about. That's the future of immense, incalculable profits. Those who don't understand where we're headed will go bankrupt. Why should XiNotch's dolls be limited to satisfying their owners, like the competitor's dolls, when they can also provide reliable therapy? This is our point of greatest interest and critical importance. If a robot can operate on our heart, it can also tell us what's happening, what's going on with our lives. And not just that, they can also provide therapy beyond being sexual companions. This is the niche of the future. The future, I'm talking about the future. No, no. It's not enough to create the best silicone buttocks (the kind one couldn't distinguish between a flesh-and-blood woman and a silicone woman), it's not enough to create the best lips that kiss better than our wives and, even better, better than those young girls who want to be actresses, confuse us with Hollywood agents, and stamp a kiss on our mouths without us asking, and we don't follow through with the game just out of fear of being sued for harassment, abuse of authority, or something like that. No, I'm not referring to anything as superficial as that, although (let's not lie) as necessary as breathing. It's about understanding us (they understanding us and not always the other way around, as if women were the only beings with needs to be understood). It's about creating women capable of sleeping with us without complaining that it hurts and, after consummating what must be consummated, capable of listening to us and giving us the solution to our problems. Because someone who buys a twenty-thousand-dollar doll is someone who has a problem. That is, someone like any of us, which makes for a potential consumer base of at least one billion individuals. If they don't have any problem, if they're a priest of a yet-to-be-born sect, if they're a being from another world or pretend to be one, they likely still need something more than sex, because otherwise they would resort to more economical options. After all, any prostitute in Hamburg or Buenos Aires would do the same for three hundred or five hundred dollars, depending on the country. In fact, we shouldn't keep talking about "dolls," because this is an outdated concept. Very outdated. XiNotch's women will no longer be passive beings but intelligent ones, and if we continue investing in this technology, they will also become sensitive beings, much sooner than we think. With the added advantage of being at the service of their client, their owner. The client will be able to choose the characteristics of each woman (submissive, unyielding, rebellious, enslaved, proud, understanding, abused...), even of each man, and in this case no one will be able to sue anyone or organize a march in defense of a XiNotch, which would be ridiculous, for obvious reasons. Those who understand this will be understanding the world that awaits us just around the corner. Those who can't see it will be left out of the business, that is, out of the world.

The nine representatives of XiNotch applauded him as they had never done before. After convincing the board, he began to convince himself, as if it were a reflex. The truth had come out of his mouth, created by the inevitable circumstances of business, but almost immediately they had convinced the messenger himself.

That time he was brilliant. Not because he believed what he was saying but, precisely, because he didn't believe any of it. But his client did believe him, and that's what mattered. That was the only thing that mattered. And that's why he now received confirmation of the deal to be signed on June 25 of this year, in Honolulu, perhaps to close the deal halfway there or because Mr. Lopes or Mr. Xi himself was thinking of taking a vacation.

How Silvanna Achieved Immortality

HE TOOK TWO SIPS OF COLD coffee, as a way of interrupting those thoughts, and reopened his bank account.

"I should revive you, Silvanna," Facundo said, without taking his eyes off the screen. "Besides sleeping with me and understanding my problems like no one else in this world, you should be able to make coffee. Did you hear me? Can you still listen to what I say, without me having to poke you to activate you?"

He mimicked an unfamiliar voice: "Chauvinist, chauvinist! Facundo, you're a disgusting chauvinist! Because of you, I couldn't develop as a woman!"

He stopped.

"No, no," he said, now in a more serious tone. "Let's see. That's something Elena would have said, not Silvanna. Silvanna knew how to play in a man's world, and that's why she could win."

He verified that the mysterious purchases had been made on dates when he hadn't been in Tijuana. Back then, he had traveled to Mexico City for three days, for the Lecor case, the BMW one, but he hadn't returned to that city. That was certain. So, he had no doubts. His credit card had been stolen, or at least the number along with the verification code. He searched his wallets, the carry-on bags he usually takes when traveling, in every pocket of his jackets and coats, and didn't find it.

He thought the simplest, most reasonable thing was to cancel the card, request a credit report to confirm that his identity hadn't been stolen, and forget about those small sums.

But he did neither. His hunter's instinct told him to wait, that there was something more. A businessman never reveals everything he knows, even if he doesn't know why. That's the golden rule that inevitably leads to unexpected benefits, no matter the nature of the problem. There's a reason glass is fragile. Because it's transparent, he thought.

He got up and went to the bathroom, as a mechanical and easy, though never entirely effective, way of interrupting a thought.

It all started back in 1996, with a Tamagotchi, he thought. Those little keychains the Japanese tried to keep alive by feeding and caring for them as if they were living beings. The business left fortunes in the hands of a few alive and spread like a virus through the rest of humanity, like a Prozombic plague. Then came the robot dogs that children confined to their homes could pet, with the advantage that they didn't poop or need feeding when the family was away. Those things reacted as if they felt affection, some kind of fondness or, at least, pleasure. Of course, back then, it was still a primitive reaction, not very sophisticated: a little bark, a somewhat repetitive tail wag, not too different from ancient dogs. What could be expected from that generation that spent every day confined to their homes for more time than prisoners in jails, while their parents locked themselves in their offices for twelve hours, often out of honor, doing nothing? When they don't die from overwork. They even have a word for that, karoshi. Uncle Alberto would have translated karoshi as "dumbass." And on this side? What could be expected from a generation of kids obsessed with McDonald's Happy Meals (businessmen have always been misunderstood poets), except for obese adults, heart-attacked before their time? Or maybe everything had started much earlier, and our job, as Jeff said, was to understand human nature and nudge it in the direction it was already heading, as they advised doing in Argentina with crazies.

As he unzipped his pants, he made a gesture of deep exhaustion. He thought that, for some mysterious reason, some other kind of inoculation, perhaps ideological, a part of himself had adopted Ernesto's little speeches. The same must have been done with their students, he thought, even though Ernesto defended himself against this accusation by saying that if it were true that teachers indoctrinated youth, it was far worse the indoctrination churches did with those same individuals as soon as they were weaned and still learning to walk, not for a measly four years but for almost their entire lives.

He stood firmly in front of the throne, ready to return half a liter of perfectly filtered coffee to nature. He looked at his penis and tried to relax so the stream of urine could come out. Whenever he was obsessed with some idea, he couldn't pee without grounding himself and thinking about something resolved, something past and concluded, like a Hollywood movie. But until he snapped out of his thoughts, he couldn't release. He often spent long minutes in that position, his penis held by his fingers like a statue that doesn't know why it's there. He thought again about death, about the easy decomposition of this member without bones, a decomposition as quick and easy as that of a woman's perfect breasts, like the most perfect idea, the most persistent memory, the tallest tower. This idea of futility relaxed him for a moment, and he was able to fulfill that tiny objective: peeing.

As he watched the transparent stream of urine splashing into the toilet bowl, with its corresponding noise, a deliberately loud noise that he no longer needed to suppress as he had done for the last thirty years, he thought that, in reality, Tamagotchi hadn't been the first signs of the Second Nature. When we learned to cultivate the land (he thought), we discovered the plow, which did it better. Humanity began to eat better and grow, while we could no longer stop cultivating the land and producing more and more. When we learned to spin and calculate, we discovered the spinning wheel and the calculator, which did it better. When robots could do almost any job, and we had free time to think, we discovered Artificial Intelligence, which could think and feel faster and more efficiently. Then, we no longer needed to work, think, feel, or do anything.

"Maybe I should take Silvanna out of her box," he said, "and sleep with her."

Immediately he thought that would be impossible. It would be definitively disgusting, knowing he had to get rid of her as soon as possible.

He lay back on the bed and thought about her once more. Almost 24 hours before flying to Kuala Lumpur, he had run into Silvanna at Café Don Sancho, where he usually had lunch on days he went to the office. Silvanna had greeted him the moment he stepped through the old doorway, so he had no choice but to sit at her table. Any other option would have been understood as a slight.

Silvanna seemed very cheerful that afternoon. However, as he had always suspected, she was a full-time actress. Perhaps like all of us, though not all of us are so good at it.

At first, Facundo felt uncomfortable. It would have been just another encounter between two somewhat familiar people if Jeff hadn't bombarded him with that barrage of psychoanalytic deductions in their last conversation at the Starbucks in the Barnes & Noble, less than a month ago.

Reluctantly, Facundo tried not to look at Silvanna's breasts, as her husband had claimed all men who crossed her path did. The white blouse she wore was made of such a fine fabric that it was impossible not to notice her erect nipples. Perhaps they weren't actually erect (as he had vaguely thought, maybe associating it with some improbable arousal), but rather, that's how they naturally were all day, slightly firm. In any case, she must have known, and as Jeff had said, there's nothing more erotic in a woman than her bad intentions. That's why he wouldn't trade a single meaningful glance for a hundred pairs of breasts.

After a roundabout exchange of casual comments, the kind people make when they don't know what to say, Silvanna had congratulated him on his achievement, on the "Olympic medal" from Kuala Lumpur.

"Did Jeff tell you?" Facundo asked.

"Obviously."

"Not so obvious," Facundo stammered. "Out of sheer modesty, I haven't even mentioned it to my wife."

"What?" she exclaimed, surprised.

"You know, the whole thing about selling silicone dolls..."

"Come on! Those dolls aren't just dolls, and they're not just silicone. And Elena doesn't know about your latest big deal? It's a marvel. If I were you, I'd have already published it in the Wall Street Journal, Business Insider, and Bloomberg News."

"Well… I see it as being professional, like a lawyer who has to defend a criminal in court…"

"Or like an actor who has to do a porn scene…"

Facundo didn't respond. He looked toward the café where the employee was calling a customer named Sean or John. He could never clearly distinguish between the two names' pronunciations.

"Are you ashamed of having succeeded in selling Jeff's idea?" Silvanna asked.

"Now that you mention it… maybe, yes."

"Don't be foolish," she insisted.

Facundo felt like a child. Like a child, he couldn't look at one of her nipples without embarrassment. Her calling him foolish wasn't an insult but rather a sign of excess familiarity, he thought hours later. For hours, he couldn't stop thinking about that strange and revealing encounter, the combination of symbols, like her red lips marked on the plastic coffee cup, the futile attempt to guess one of the two English names in the employee's call, the word *foolish* coming from Silvanna's white teeth, and the outline of her left nipple defiantly challenging the thin fabric that pretended to cover it.

For the first time in three years of seeing her sporadically at work or in the building's elevator, Facundo had confirmed everything Jeff had said about her. It was true—Silvanna had breasts that were impossible to overlook. Not that they were excessively large. It wasn't about that kind of vulgarity, but rather a form of perfection that was hard to explain, the way one can't explain a certain gaze. Her breasts seemed to reveal a kind of artistic youth that persisted in her beyond the few years it usually lasts in other women. He thought about it and decided that this idea, or whatever it was called, would never cross the boundaries of his lips. He wasn't going to jeopardize thirty years of professional effort over a few careless words. It was also true about her waist. It was carefully narrow. Even when seated, it didn't reveal the slightest hint of fat or that natural softness we start to feel ashamed of after turning thirty or thirty-five. Yes, culture, education, macho values, patriarchy, blah, blah, blah... All of that was true, he thought. But one is what one is, with their testosterone and their lack of refinement. For better or worse, a Barbie to him and his generation would always be a Barbie.

Silvanna must have been around thirty, with many hours of gym time each week. She had always seemed like an arrogant woman to him, perhaps because she knew she was beautiful—perfectly, standardly beautiful, a mix of Claudia Schiffer and Nicole Kidman in their twenties. Or, simply, because she was Jeff's wife.

He also couldn't avoid looking at her full lips, something she didn't try to hide but rather accentuated with lip gloss (sold by brands like Etnia Cosmetics, as if civilized women, by necessity, should be dry), a gloss that left the impression of her having just run her tongue over them a second before.

In contrast, Facundo thought, compared to her husband, Silvanna had blue eyes, but her gaze wasn't particularly deep or unsettling. He didn't know how to put it, but there was something about her look that never went beyond, that didn't grab attention like her nipples outlined beneath the white Lycra.

Perhaps because of this or some other detail, the infamous rumor had spread that she was frigid. Or maybe Jeff himself had confessed it to someone who couldn't keep the secret. He would never know that, and (he thought then, mistaken) it also didn't say anything to him nor did it matter in the slightest.

She noticed that Facundo had looked at her, even if it was only for a fraction of a second, and said:

"So, are you leaving tomorrow?"

"Yes… tomorrow," said Facundo, returning to his body. "Tomorrow, 7:45 AM, Miami-London-Kuala Lumpur… You're well informed."

"Of course," she said. "That has been one of the most talked-about cases in the company and its surroundings. Congratulations again. If you have a long layover at Heathrow, I recommend eating at the Bridge Bar and Eating House. They have original Guinness."

"Well, thanks. I'll keep it in mind. Guinness is too heavy for my taste, but I'll balance it with a Heineken."

"Can I give you another piece of advice?"

"Of course, go ahead."

"If there's one thing you shouldn't have, it's any shame for success. You should tell Elena. Or do you have secrets with her? Sorry, I take that back. It's not my business, right?"

Facundo didn't know what to say. It was too obvious.

"A professional job," she insisted, "is just that. A professional job. You have to acknowledge it, not be ashamed of it. I'm sure you would never have sold the

AR21 idea the way you did with even a drop of doubt or shyness."

"Of course not. But when I work, I'm an actor. Haven't you noticed that actors always say they're really shy? It makes you wonder why they chose that career, but it actually makes sense…"

"And when you have lunch with a friend, you're shy," said Silvanna. "But you know what? You're always working."

"Always?"

"Yes, always. Or almost always. Much more than anyone would be willing to admit to themselves. Look, I'll be honest with you…"

Silvanna made a thoughtful pause, almost forced, folded her napkin into a triangle, and said:

"Jeff mentioned to me that they're going to need an image, and they're going to have trouble finding one that doesn't resemble any individual on this planet, to avoid any lawsuits. The poor guy can't sleep thinking about it."

"True, that's going to be a real headache," confirmed Facundo, signaling the waitress. "Even if we invent a face and a body, there'll always be someone in the world who resembles it, who identifies with it, and who sues us for it. They'll claim we found them on some social network, those things where nowadays everyone's an expert. We won't fix it with an aspirin, and it's very likely the Big Idea will end right there…"

"Well, no, you're wrong," she said. "It's not that hard. No need to dramatize. For me, it would be an honor for them to use my image."

Facundo looked at her. He must have furrowed his brow or opened his eyes in a special way because she laughed heartily. It wasn't a pose. She seemed to enjoy it.

"Didn't you know I was in modeling before marrying Jeff?"

"I think he mentioned something. But…"

"But nothing. Just as the Mona Lisa was immortalized by Leonardo da Vinci, I want my last work, my best work, to be modeling for the AR21. In fact, I want them to use my voice, my way of being, whatever. Everything. I'll sign any contract, relinquishing any rights. I don't even expect much economically. If there's something, better, because I'll need it in the coming years, but the amount will never be a problem, it's negotiable."

"This isn't like that porn actress's confidentiality agreement for the president, is it?"

"Don't worry. It won't be a confidentiality agreement or anything silent. I won't even be able to blackmail anyone. That's the world that's coming, kid. Androids won't complain about being abused, and people even less."

The waitress who had shouted Sean or John interrupted them, asking if she could clear the plates. She asked if they wanted anything else. Facundo said no. He asked her to bring the bill for the cheesecake and the lemon pie.

Silvanna leaned her elbows on the table and rested her chin on her intertwined fingers. While Facundo dismissed the waitress, she kept looking at him with a slight smile, an intimidating smile. Then she took out her card, and he told her no, not to worry, that he would pay. When the young woman walked away with her credit card, Facundo mumbled something unintelligible. She smiled again, as if at that moment she were watching her son William playing on the beach.

"Her name is Lexie," said Silvanna. "Poor, young, and pretty. Look at her if you want, but she's a lesbian. A bit shy around people, but a fire in bed. She left Idaho because they found her out,. *I-the-whore*, she says."

Facundo said nothing. He tried to avoid Silvanna's gaze. Finally, he said:

"It's insane."

She kept smiling as she looked into his eyes.

"What part is insane?"

"Did you tell Jeff?" he asked.

"No."

Facundo laughed heartily. At the next table, an elderly man looked at him curiously, as if he were the same man who had watched him at the Barnes & Noble Starbucks three weeks earlier. As if he were, he thought, the very same one.

"I'm glad it amuses you," she said.

"Forget it," said Facundo, "It's not because Jeff is a colleague. In fact, although I respect him, I can't say he's my best friend. Not even close."

"I know…"

"Anyway, what you're proposing is something I wouldn't do to my worst enemy."

"Oh, please!" she said, now getting serious, "Men wouldn't dare sleep with their best friend's wife, but they'll sleep with anyone else. I mean, by simple logic, their codes of honor don't allow them to betray their friends, but they're fine betraying their own wives."

"I hadn't thought of it that way. Either way, it's not my case."

"Neither is mine," she said, "If I speak from any experience, it's that I know men better than anyone could imagine, though, at least until now, I never let them put their hands on me without permission. But, from constant exposure, I can read their looks and double-meaning words. Right from the start, I realized you had no intention of trying to conquer me, which is something I find very attractive in a man, I can't deny it. When a man looks at me and doesn't even think about trying to kiss me or take me to a hotel, that's something I value immensely. Sometimes, women just want to be admired. Maybe because we learned that since we were little, but now it's too late to turn feminist or to enjoy soccer, like you men. Or perhaps an alpha male like Jeff doesn't enjoy the hunt and being admired for his business predator achievements, which, in the end, is the same thing?"

Silvanna paused, as if she were talking too much or wasting time. She glanced at her watch and said.

"Anyway, listen, I know you have to go. I'm not proposing that you sleep with me, nor am I interested. It's just my job. The job I've always wanted to do, modeling, and that the admirable Jeff, with that magical subtlety of being able to convince even the devil, prevented me from doing since we first met at a fashion show, since we got married, and even more since we had William."

She stopped abruptly and immediately suppressed a kind of sob, with a hard, stone-like expression.

"In a few years, I'll grow old," she continued, furrowing her brow and looking Facundo in the eye. "Men won't turn to look at me anymore. You think I don't know that? There was always something in me that kept me from having the success everyone predicted for me when I was eighteen or nineteen, when I started walking on the most important runways in the world. Didn't you know? I'm sure no one does, no one remembers. I used to save newspaper clippings as if they were something important. Now no one remembers the photos. They've even disappeared from the internet. They've been erased, because everything saved there vanishes in just a few years. Those grand dreams are worth less today than this cup, look…"

Silvanna throws the empty cup into a slot reserved for coffee cups and misses. Facundo stands up, picks it up from the floor, and places it in the right spot. Then he returns to the table without saying a word.

"Maybe it wasn't Jeff," she continued, "Maybe it wasn't Jeff who murdered all those wonderful dreams, as I've always thought, but that's something I'll never be able to know. Don't make that face. I know you're acting, like the proper man you've learned to be since you came to this blessed country. Am I wrong? Never mind, you're not going to tell me anyway, and if you do, I won't believe you. But you're Argentine, not a Yankee, don't forget that. Though, of course, whatever nationality you are, you'll still be a man."

"We all have murdered dreams," said Facundo. "It's part of the human condition. We grow old and can no longer dream like we did when we were twenty. So we look for other emotions to replace them. Some find alcohol, others women…"

"Now you sound very wise. As if everything were equal and the same happened to anyone just because they're aging. It's not like that. I'm sure that for a man, wrinkling and not attracting attention isn't as dramatic. You never think about that. You grow old and richer and think you can sleep with a young girl who convinces you that, deep down, even if it doesn't seem like it, you're wonderful walking down the street (with that attractive belly over your belt and that marvelous little curve in your back) and even convinces you that you're amazing in bed despite the gray hair on your chest and your balls." For us it's different…

Silvanna paused and cupped her breasts.

"Look at these," she said. "Don't be shy. Look at them. Or haven't you been staring at them just a moment ago, before the waitress arrived? Hers (did I tell you her name is Lexie even though the tag on her chest says Emma?), hers are small, almost masculine. They haven't been kissed enough yet to blossom. Yeah, I know you've been looking. Relax, I'm not saying it to scold you. I'm not even going to judge you for being so nice. In a few years, I'll get depressed when men stop looking at them. I'm telling you because it's something women always think about. If a man looks at us, we purse our lips as if it bothered us, like, 'What-a-disgusting-pig,' but one day comes when we curse them and call them queer in our heads because they walk past without even glancing at the merchandise on the shelf, as if we had an expired date. In five or ten years, these dears, which have accompanied me everywhere, will become flabby. They won't be straight-point-and-curve anymore, but round-round, without a point and with a bigger cup, like for drunks. And here," she pointed to her eyes "some wrinkles will appear. And here" (hips) "I won't even tell you. And so on everything else."

"Life compensates us with other things…" said Facundo.

"Oh, boy!" she complained.

She folded the napkin again, this time into a smaller, fatter triangle:

"Yeah, yeah, I know. What matters is inner beauty, and all that nonsense. Well, it's not that it's necessarily nonsense, but right now I'm interested in that beauty that has always made Silvanna Silvanna, and not Jeff, not Facundo, not Einstein, not Mother Teresa. And I don't want that Silvanna to die."

"As for me," said Facundo, "the only thing I can't imagine is Jeff, knowing that thousands of Silvannas are being raped every night all over the world…"

"Oh, no, Facundo," she said, tired. "You're just as chauvinistic as Jeff. I'm not his property. I'm an individual, a human being, even if I'm a woman. I have my own expectations for life. Anyway, I thought you… I don't know… at least…"

"And you, wouldn't it bother you?"

"That thousands of strangers sleep with my image? No, no. Definitely not. On the contrary. Do you think I don't know that many men have probably jerked off after meeting me? How many have made love to their wives thinking they were doing it with me? In the end, we, they do the same thing. Even in that, we're human beings, like you. But what can I do about all that? Complain? No, quite the opposite."

There was a long silence, which Silvanna herself broke. She looked into his eyes again (Facundo couldn't explain how Silvanna wasn't Jeff, being more dominant than him):

"So, what do you say?" she said.

Facundo thought that Jeff and Silvanna had something in common, something that had led them, deceived, like most, into marriage. Both were promiscuous, if not in fact, at least in how they verbalized their little vices and their incurable obsessions. Narcissism, for example, explained both of their obsessions with hunting, conquest, and sex. But she was more dominant than him, and he had ended up being the victor.

"Aren't you going to say anything?" she insisted.

"You are crazy," said Facundo.

"I'm not asking about that. Will you do it or not?"

"No, of course not. I can't."

She smiled and said:

"You know what? Yes, you will."

She immediately stood up to leave and said:

"Do you think I'm doing it out of narcissism…?"

It was then that Silvanna revealed things he never would have wanted to hear. Not because he didn't suspect them in some way, but because he didn't want to hear them. Then she told him:

"I'll send you the material when you're traveling. The CEO of Rommes and the one from RealPerson in Kuala Lumpur need the prototype, and you know what? They've already found it. Both have fallen in love with Lady K."

"Who is Lady K...?" asked Facundo "Oops!"

"I'll send you the material for the prototype when you're traveling," said Silvanna, smiling again.

"If I were you, I wouldn't be so optimistic," said Facundo. "Don't count on me."

"You'll see," she said. "It's just a matter of time."

Seemed stupid, acted stupid, but wasn't.

FINALLY, ON MAY 21ST, Facundo had agreed and signed in Kuala Lumpur that the AR21s would be created in Silvanna's image and likeness. He had decided it out of spite, but he didn't regret it. During the thirteen-hour flight from London to Kuala Lumpur, he had thought, over and over, about the last words he had heard Silvanna say.

"Do you think I'm doing it out of narcissism? Well, twenty years ago I might have done it out of narcissism. All models suffer from this syndrome. Either we dedicate ourselves to the profession because we're narcissists or we become narcissists from staring at ourselves in the mirror and competing for others' attention. But it's not just for that reason. It's for another, less innocent reason. Revenge? Maybe. Call it whatever you want…"

For a moment, Facundo had intuited the explanation behind that gaze, beautiful but distant, insensitive, filled with rage.

"Revenge against who?" he had asked.

"You don't need to play dumb," she had replied.

"Fine. I can guess."

"You guessed right. I'm going to get my revenge on him before I divorce him."

"I had no idea you were going to separate."

"There's no other way."

"Was he unfaithful?"

Silvanna laughed.

"You don't know, do you?" she said, looking him in the eye.

"No. I have no reason to. I know Jeff is a bit… unique…"

"Unique…"

"He sometimes says foolish things, but that's a far cry from knowing about his private life."

"You've never seen anything?"

"No. Like I said, aside from enduring his sexist jokes, I've never seen anything, if that's what you're looking to confirm."

"I've never seen anything," she repeated, tired. "Well, neither have I. That's the problem."

Silvanna had taken out her card to pay for the cheesecake. Before or after him, he couldn't remember. It didn't matter, except for his growing obsession with recalling every detail with precision. This happened to him when he was alone in airports, in hotels in the middle of nowhere. He remembered telling her not to worry that he would pay, so she slung her golden purse over her shoulder and, before standing up, said:

"I didn't see anything either. Until I knew. And you won't see anything either. Until you know."

She stood up and left.

A few hours later, almost dozing off over his phone at two in the afternoon, from one of the tables at Klia Airport in Kuala Lumpur, he sent her an email. He was intrigued by your last words, he wrote. He thought that by then she'd be asleep, that she'd respond hours later. But no. She replied almost immediately, with the material she had promised for the board meeting. Facundo imagined her in bed, next to

Jeff, asleep or knocked out by four whiskies. She reminded him that the RealPerson board members already had the same material, and that she was sending it to him so he wouldn't seem surprised during the meeting. It wouldn't be advisable. Not a word to clarify the mystery she had left hanging in the air during their last meeting at Starbucks.

Facundo asked her again but received no response.

Fifty minutes later, at the Regis Hotel in Kuala Lumpur, at 5 pm, after a strong coffee and feeling somewhat more awake, he insisted again. He threatened her. He told her to forget the proposal of using her image for the androids.

He received no reply. It was five in the morning in Orlando.

At eleven at night, he fell asleep with the tablet beside him, no news whatsoever. Nine hours later, just as he went down for breakfast, he had a reply from Silvanna: with her last words, she had meant that Jeff had deceived both of them, her and him, Facundo (Jeff had just left for the office). That for more details, he should ask Elena.

At first, Facundo thought, or wanted to think, that Silvanna was acting out of spite and wanted to involve him to support her plans. But he couldn't help but think and search his memory for any detail that could align with her theory. Half an hour later, he received another email with the date and the hotel where Jeff had stayed in New York, in June 2016: Park Hyatt Hotel, room 411. Didn't he remember any trip Elena took around that date? Silvanna wrote.

Silvanna's words had hit him like a punch to the gut. She had written, at the end, I actually liked you the last time we met. Really liked you :) But things are what they are. <3

Facundo searched through his email and found the address of another hotel that same week in 2016, the Ritz-Carlton, two blocks from the Hyatt. Elena had gone to visit Mariela, who was passing through the United States. He, Facundo, hadn't been able to accompany her due to work, so he stayed in Orlando while she took a well-deserved week in Manhattan.

Facundo canceled the meeting with the RealPerson board until the next day, citing discomfort from the long trip. That always worked because, besides, it was almost always true. He searched for Mariela's phone number and, after several attempts, managed to reach her in Buenos Aires. Indeed, Mariela had been in New York a few years earlier, but she hadn't ended up seeing Elena, "because of those things where you always plan something when you're traveling and in the end nothing goes as planned," she had said. Mariela didn't remember why Elena hadn't been able to go to New York. Finally, after some hesitation, she remembered, or thought she remembered. A deliberate ambiguity in her words revealed that, suddenly, Mariela had understood that Facundo wanted to know something about Elena. In his haste, Facundo hadn't been able to sell that unexpected call with a believable story. Mariela, who wasn't particularly sharp, had suspected something just a few minutes later. As an old friend, she couldn't say anything that might compromise Elena. If necessary, she would lie, like all complicit friends, those true friends who only lie honestly. "Actually, I wasn't there in 2016," she said, "but in 2015," with a fake, scatterbrained voice, speaking the way the upper class talks in Villa Devoto, as if they had a lisp or were studying French. 'I was going to return in 2016, but I'm not sure if I did, I mean, I don't know if I returned that year or the next. Oh, Facundo, you caught me driving and this… you know how Buenos Aires is at this hour…'

How Silvanna would finally cleanse humanity

THE FIRST PROTOTYPE OF THE K GIRLS, as he secretly called them, was ready seven months later. Seven-month babies born out of market urgency. If you don't sell during Thanksgiving or Christmas, you won't sell at any other time of the year, they said in Atlanta. Not only were they an unparalleled copy of Silvanna's face, but the new company, RealPerson, founded less than two years earlier, had in its possession a technology that could only have been stolen from a series of universities around the world. It was absolutely impossible for them to have achieved that progress in such a short time. In fact, it was likely they had stolen some ideas from him too. He remembered, for example, that during the product presentation, one of the board members had noted the potential resistance from a significant portion of consumers to having sex with a computer.

"I always said," he joked, "that the only thing we haven't done with our computers is have sex... and there's a reason it's the last thing."

"Even if the silicone perfectly imitates the color and texture of female skin," added another, "there will always be the idea that inside they're full of wires."

Facundo knew that those initial unfavorable opinions didn't necessarily mean rejection. Unlike political fanatics (that is, the people, the consumers), businesspeople were always willing to change their minds about any topic if that change meant greater profits. What businesspeople sought with those initial signs of disagreement was to be fully convinced by the person presenting.

At that time, Facundo had replied that perhaps that was a problem that had survived due to a lack of imagination, not so much because of technical limitations, since one always imagines an android filled with wires, chips, and all sorts of plastics and copper wires because of movies and the latest prototypes from the competition.

"Probably," he said, "no one has thought yet of replacing all that with flexible conductors like silicone, like flesh itself. It could be pork flesh or artificial meat, created in labs, not necessarily human flesh. Aren't there millions of people who've received a pig's aorta after a heart attack? Aren't there labs already growing human ears in a little bottle or on the side of a patient's abdomen who's lost an ear? In the future, in fact, androids will store information in artificial DNA, not in chips. Chips will be a symbol of the past. Alongside silicone and artificial DNA wiring, veins and arteries of red ink will run, to foster empathy with the owner and even to satisfy, therapeutically, the base instincts of a potential killer. Soon, any of you will have as much trouble identifying a human from an android as we do today not knowing if our children are really ours until we do a DNA test."

That last comment had triggered a full burst of laughter from the board, with the exception of the only woman present. Facundo knew that without a certain dose of humor, it was impossible to win over the buyer's trust. He had secretly stolen this tip from Ernesto, who had once said that a mandatory little joke was always necessary in the speeches of presidents of big countries when proposing the invasion of a small one. Or perhaps he hadn't stolen it, but since then he had been doing it more consciously.

"How can all of this be done?" someone asked from the far end of the table. The question from the white-bearded shareholder resonated in his earpiece with a Madrid accent from a female voice: "How could all of this be done?"

Facundo smiled, but managed to return to the game, like in the last century, more precisely on a December evening in 1971, when he had leaned over the glass marbles to make the final winning move after his mother shouted at him from a window to come eat, that it was already too dark. That little corner of Artigas Street didn't have many lights. None, in fact. The winner would take the prettiest marble, a blue, red, and yellow one that was worth more than the million dollars he was about to pocket if he responded correctly.

"Well, that's not our problem," Facundo said, with conviction or feigning conviction. "Like Bill Gates, like Zuckerberg, we don't need to invent anything new to take advantage of centuries of human progress, to make a few billion dollars in a few years and, incidentally, take all the credit for a revolution that changed the world for the better."

A single chuckle confirmed that, at least, someone had gotten the sarcastic side of the idea. Back then, automatic translators still struggled with irony and other human subtleties, which is why Facundo had grown accustomed to using more of a robotic, simplified, but effective language. It was likely (he had reflected during his last flight to San Diego) that when androids with artificial intelligence learn more from humans, by then humans will have already been modified by androids in the same way that translators and voice synthesizers had changed their own accents and had simplified human language.

"Someone might question whether a world inhabited by androids is a positive revolution," Facundo, the salesman, continued, "but, without a doubt, it will be, like every triumphant revolution. Of course, there will always be the dissatisfied, but in this case, they'll have the great benefit of returning their wife, or their husband, or exchanging them for a more expensive model, which, no matter how expensive, will never be as costly as a divorce."

More laughter from the board. This time the translation must have been more effective. Facundo knew he had them in his pocket and finished with a more serious tone, like a bullfighter who drives the final sword into the noble beast's cross.

As he finished his presentation, he quickly shuffled through images of potential models, faces he had plagiarized at the last minute from different websites. One of them must have been a mistake. No, it was. The face of Argentine congresswoman Lalita Carrió appeared with some exotic glasses. He liked Carrió politically, but it seemed he had been reading some related news and, out of exhaustion and whisky, had accidentally copied her photo for his presentation. With a hint of frustration, he said:

"Sorry, this image must be a mistake. They call her 'alpargata rosada'..."

He pressed the remote and moved on to a very pretty young woman, but someone on the board didn't understand the automatic translation, which must have been (Facundo thought) something like "This woman is known as a pink sandal." But Facundo didn't have time to invent a lie and, automatically, the right answer came out:

"They call her 'alpargata rosada' because no gaucho would ever wear her."

The Korean who asked the question pressed the translator to his ear and remained thoughtful. Facundo was glad he didn't understand the translation and that artificial intelligence wasn't so cultured yet. Probably the Korean heard: "They call her a pink slipper because no cowboy needs her." Urban classes wear slippers; surely they were completely inappropriate for a rural worker. It sounded more like a political statement, which, in a presentation about artificial wives, made little sense.

There was a white, impenetrable silence in the room.

"You just have to have the right nose for future business," he said, "and let our employees, with their proud PhDs, materialize our vision. You see, there's another new area, currently unexplored."

There was unanimous applause from the nine attendees, he remembered later, with displeasure, sitting on his toilet at home. Then he went to the kitchen and poured himself a disgusting gulp of artichoke. Cinarin, thistle. He couldn't remember what the hell it was called in Spanish. He did remember the extract and the brand Uncle Alberto used in Uruguay. Chofitol. That was something you could never forget.

He went back to his desk and, as he was about to set the glass of whiskey down on the table, next to the mouse, it fell to the floor. The remaining whiskey spilled, but the glass didn't break. In the United States, there's no drama like that because most middle-class homes have carpeted floors. Some are more expensive than others, but they're all the same. In La Plata, when Facundo as a kid and fell off a chair, he'd hit his head on the cold tiles of his parents' house. Somehow, in some mysterious way, he had survived all that without any obvious signs of mental retardation and had managed to be successful in his field, despite the tile-floor injuries, despite the lead pipes that carried water to the house, and despite the Colgate toothpaste tubes, which were also made of lead. As a kid, they used to have fun melting lead to make little parts for imaginary machines. When glasses fell, they shattered.

This one didn't. The glass stared back at him from the comfort of the carpet, almost empty now, with a tiny piece of ice melting on the endless synthetic fibers.

He looked back at the screen. The final result, though predictable, was no less impressive. The Silvanna from Kuala Lumpur laughed like Silvanna (the real one, the fake one), but she looked better, more human, as if she were genuinely happy to see you there and was thinking about something forbidden or something only she knew. Her breasts, her waist, and who knows what other details (provided by the interested party herself through photos, videos, and who knows, maybe even holographic sessions during her emergency trip to Los Angeles for a fashion show) were faithful to the model. The only challenge left for RealPerson was to make them walk, but for now, they could sit, hold an intelligent conversation, lie down, and engage in various types of sexual relations.

The most astonishing thing, Facundo thought in the solitude of his apartment after his second whiskey, was that the perfect copy of Silvanna couldn't walk but had already incorporated every possible advancement in artificial intelligence. That is, while he was numbing himself with a second whiskey to get a couple of hours of sleep, stressed over his divorce from Elena and the more recent suspicion that his identity had been stolen in Mexico, Silvanna, the copy of Silvanna, was learning from the world of humans at an unimaginable speed. In a couple of years, she'd complete elementary school, high school, university, and an unsuspected wealth of human experience. Of course, she hadn't started from scratch, like a baby, because the experts at RealPerson would have filled her with information and experience from hundreds of other programs that understood human beings better than any human. Artificial intelligence, at Johnson & Johnson and other companies in the United States, was already being used to read the resumes of hundreds of thousands of job applicants. Even more, AI could predict with great precision when an employee would quit their job, when they'd ask for a raise, how many times they'd get drunk each month, and even how their sex life could affect their productivity. A whole capital of knowledge that would one day become obsolete when companies managed to replace those complicated beings with Silvannas, who, besides doing their job effectively, could sit on their bosses' laps without the ethical and legal complications that combination of activities entails today between humans. Then, there'll be Jeffs everywhere, and probably Facundos too, improved versions, of course. Will there be Ernestos? Yes, maybe some, to add diversity to the offerings, just like we sell deliberately imperfect products today, Peruvian crafts made in Chinese factories, toys to assemble, mystery novels, and the like. The Jeffs wouldn't make sexist jokes, the Facundos wouldn't drink whiskey, the Ernestos wouldn't speak seriously, and the Silvannas wouldn't sue anyone for abuse. No worker would need to sleep or ask for leave for any sleep disorder. In a later stage, Silvannas would sleep with other Jeffs and other Facundos. There'd be screams of pleasure, insults, punches thrown in electronic restaurants. None of it original. But what does it matter?

As he sipped his third whiskey, he had one last, even more unsettling thought: before that stage where humans would become strange, scarce, irrelevant beings, the psychologists of the future would be mathematicians, and they wouldn't be human. Something worse, he thought: if AIs, if androids, can predict human behavior using statistics and algorithms, like the resume readers, that means we humans are more mechanical than we think. That is to say, if we are still human, it is because we cannot clearly predict the behavior of others, nor our own. We repeat the same mistakes, the same wars, the same orgasms. We cannot see the future with any clarity, not because it's impossible, as AIs are proving, but for the less heroic reason that we have serious intellectual and emotional limitations. Not knowing if, or when, we'll divorce our eternal love makes us more human. Not knowing the date of our death makes us more human. We don't want to stop being human because we are terrified of the deepest truths and don't want to know the details.

Facundo took a deep breath and exhaled slowly and forcefully, as if he were smoking. Silvanna, Jeff, Elena, he thought. What was the obsession with conquest and sex if not an excessive attempt to forget? Like alcohol, like money, like any other addiction. Perhaps, in the not-too-distant future, that will become another product that generates new profits: achieving forgetfulness, achieving ignorance, reaching a certain degree of chaos in a perfect world or, at least, an inhuman one, organized by benevolent machines. Hadn't we already seen glimpses of this? When we discovered machines a couple of centuries ago, we didn't become more human—we became more machinelike. Now that we've discovered Artificial Intelligence and will soon grow accustomed to Artificial Humans, we won't become more human but, more likely, more inhuman, more Artificial Humans. Probably inferior. Less intelligent, less sensitive, less kind. Less. Nothing. As it should be.

The boss of bosses, welcomes Silvanna

NOW HE SAW HER CLEARLY. Silvanna smiled on the screen as she looked at the camera, like a shy, inexperienced schoolgirl. He could see every detail of her face, her gaze, visibly enhanced, sweeter, humanized... She looked more exciting, more alive, perhaps because he was seeing her from his own alcohol-sunken solitude. Or maybe the psychologists (better said, the engineers) at RealPerson had detected in the real Silvanna that slight flaw of a cold, robotic gaze and had corrected it by combining ten or perhaps one hundred gazes previously defined as attractive by some software. For some obscure reason (he thought), the correction had taken a few years off Silvanna's appearance. The attractive component included the selling of youth, like the very young Hatsune Miku, the nonexistent singer from Japan. Because youth makes even the ugliest woman beautiful, and a consumer, like a prehistoric gatherer,

103

appreciates the freshest fruit most. Even more so, the hunter values tender meat.

He, like very few, like the three or four chosen ones in the world, could verify everything being sold in the promotional video in reality, in the actual product that, at that very moment, rested just a few meters away, inside the FedEx box. He had only seen her hair, her nose, and her knees, and had closed the box again. He pictured Elena and Jeff visiting him in that modest apartment, a visit obliged by the recovering heart attack victim. Maybe neither of them would bother, like a boxer refraining from delivering a final blow to a fallen opponent, and some stranger would take care of showcasing the exotic marvel of 21st-century technology when he sold the apartment.

The AR21 had just made history, and very few on the planet were aware of it. They would never know. For some time, consumers would settle for these substitutes, grow accustomed to them, until someone thought of the trend of offering real humans again. A new big, huge, magnificent business, but not for now. That would add excitement to rapes, to crimes, like the excitement of the rich, like that of the king of Spain when he goes to Africa to kill an old elephant that still impresses, more for its size than its danger.

Even so, Facundo knew he would be the last one to touch one of the Silvannas, if he ever even got to touch the product. Why this conviction? Now that he was getting divorced, he was free to do whatever he wanted, apart from abusing whiskey, with an android or a real woman, or more or less real. His incapacity was similar, but more severe, to not being able to urinate in airport urinals. In fact, he even struggled to do so if he couldn't find an isolated cubicle, like one in the Kalahari Desert. He hated this mania of having to look for a cubicle in a corner, without the sight of someone else's shoe under the partition while urinating or defecating as if they were at home, making all sorts of noises or talking on the phone as if that operation went unnoticed by their sphincters. Not him, he couldn't. His damned modesty prevented it, as if he could be recognized by the sound of his stream. In short, those little secret stupidities that make us who we are.

He had been offered a trial session in Hong Kong, a Silvanna in his hotel room under absolute privacy and discretion, following the rigorous protocol the company used with its biggest clients, but he had declined, citing lack of time. One of the worst excuses a human being can give for not having sex or for not doing their job, but bad answers always serve as a wall that protects the inalienable right to have a private life, even if one doesn't even have a life.

Without leaving evidence, he slipped the name Jeff Al Ferro to the secretary of RealPerson (he wrote it on a small piece of paper that he then crumpled and flushed down a toilet), but with the address of Leonard Gasper, Jeff's regional boss, for a free promotional shipment of the product. Anything could be passed off as a mistake. A few months later, he was informed that they had sent three copies to the United States, the first three girls who would conquer America, like Columbus's three tiny caravels. One, to his new address in Daytona, even though he never signed the request. Another to Jeff in Orlando. The third, to Mr. Gasper, the boss of bosses in Las Vegas. The Malaysians and Chinese from the Hong Kong subsidiary knew that the biggest market was in China, but they needed to recover their investment as soon as possible by selling the first prototypes at exorbitant prices in Europe and the United States before foreseeable competition forced them to lower the price, and for that, nothing better than starting with the main promoter, Facundo, and the owner of almost everything else, Mr. Gasper.

At this moment (the ocean had turned into a black rectangle, almost as black as the sky, probably cloudy), Facundo tried to bring that impossible day to a close, one his nerves couldn't digest. He was going to turn off the computers, but first he went to the bathroom. As he brushed his teeth and observed his haggard reflection in the mirror, with dark circles and visible gray hairs beginning to conquer his jet-black mane, he imagined the fat Gasper receiving the package, a reinforced cardboard box with a Silvanna folded in half. What would The Godfather see first? he wondered. Silvanna's buttocks facing upwards or, better yet, Silvanna's face between her thighs, as if she were a contortionist?

The fat Gasper knew her from the seminars and the first supervisor meetings, because Jeff always brought her, for decoration or because she was jealous and didn't let him travel without her. That changed at some point. Perhaps her boredom or his need to flirt with other women in hotel bars made things easier.

Without a doubt, the Atlanta dinner of 2015 or 2016 was decisive. In many ways. One of those moments when the future of some people is decided, and no one notices the importance of the details until it's too late or when it's all long past and almost no one remembers the real reasons.

Facundo was there, at the same white tablecloth table with black napkins, a bouquet of tropical flowers in the center and a bald Turk with twisted mustaches serving the wine with a ceremony more fitting for the court of King Louis XIV than for 21st-century businessmen. Almost at the end of the dinner, when the exhaustion from a day of work and the drowsiness from a giant lobster, sacrificed just minutes earlier (more out of snobbery than for the special flavor of a recently deceased being) began to be digested with difficulty, when the women were on dessert and the men on their third glass of high-end Rioja, vintage 1996 (shamefully lacking the best of all, the 1995), Silvanna laughed at a photograph of the governor of New Jersey, Chris Christie. A dramatic and crucial moment for the destiny of two or three existences seated at that very table.

For a woman, one glass is more than enough, and if, on top of that, you add the irresistible sugar of dessert (a toxic combination if there ever was one), the results can be disastrous. For the same reason, Facundo barely drank alcohol at those dinners, just enough to be polite and so they wouldn't mistake him for a Muslim because of his not-entirely-white skin. Although he was very resistant to its effects, he knew it only took one colleague or supervisor to consider that dinner a mere extension of work. Not by chance, the company paid for it. Just like when you send an email, every word belongs to the company and, like all great companies, his was a small absolutist state that no one had elected and was not controlled by its inhabitants, forever terrified of the imminent and always distressing exile of being fired. The company potentially owns everything, Facundo had once thought, except burps and farts, since they currently hold no market value.

"Breathe, honey," Jeff had said, smiling, as he took the phone from her.

When Jeff saw the photograph of the New Jersey governor, he burst out laughing and passed the phone to the person next to him. After five or six variations of the same laughter, the phone inevitably ended up in Mr. Gasper's hands, and he was the only one who didn't laugh. Everyone knew he was a Republican, one of the most conservative, likely a member and donor of the Tea Party, the Rifle Association, and the Assemblies of God, but Facundo always suspected something else. Something deeper. The photo of the governor was from that baseball game at Yankee Stadium where Christie had symbolically participated at the beginning. Symbolic in every sense. He had worn a tight white pair of pants that revealed not only the politician's exaggerated belly but also practically non-existent male genitalia, as if Homer Simpson had been created in his image and likeness. The governor seemed proud of his image, but not all of his followers were.

"Do you know why Christie participated in that spectacle?" someone said. "Because he's going to run as a presidential candidate for the Republican Party."

"Oh, boy," Silvanna said. "A politician with no sense of personal image will never become president."

"He became governor," Gasper had said.

"That was before he flaunted his belly at Yankee Stadium," Silvanna said, looking at the representative from California as she took her phone back. "But look, isn't he just like Homer Simpson? Asexual, like all comics made for children."

Jeff laughed at the comparison. He gestured to the waiter and pointed at his glass. In passing, he glanced at Luisa Scott, the manager of the Massachusetts team.

"I insist that the success of any product," Silvanna said, "even a politician, is based on image. Am I saying something new? Why does something so obvious need to be explained? It's not just us, men and women in the world of business. Even Jesus had to be made blonder and blue-eyed so he could sell.

"Well, let's not go down that road," Jeff said.

The last glass of wine had left him pleasantly relaxed, but his sense of caution and his nose for danger kept him always on alert. Something that (he had once said) you can't count on in a woman or a repressed man. To make matters worse, Jeff suspected that some unwanted friendship had lingered from a course on International Business he had taken at FIU, surely not from the specific business classes but from one of those humanistic filler courses that always sneak into American university programs. For months, he tried to track down the idiot who still must have been in touch with her, but without success. One day, he walked into a Pakistani café and read: When you get home, hit your wife. You won't know why, but she will. The owner had said it was a joke, a satire on machismo, that he would never do such a thing, though he knew some ultraconservative neighbor in Islamabad who would do it every day, that in Pakistan they had had a female prime minister, twice, Benazir Bhutto, while in free-democratic— equal—America they were still waiting for a woman president. His annoyance, Jeff later thought, stemmed from the fact that, more or less, that was what he himself did when he got home, in a bad mood from his failed attempts to discover who the

111

Silicone 5.0

bookworm was who had managed the miracle of turning a runway model into an intellectual practically overnight.

"But even when He's depicted agonizing on the cross, it's done with style" Silvanna continued. "No belly, no double chin, nothing that could ruin a fashion show, whether male or female. Heretical, you said? The heretics are the ones who created those images. So much so that if someone comes along with a different representation, like those made by scientists, the Jesus with darker skin, rather ugly in the face, people get angry or come out with that line about how the race and appearance of the Savior don't matter. If they don't matter, then why are so many upset about a darker-skinned, rather ugly Jesus? Why always blonde, like the angels in heaven? Same with a politician, gentlemen, but in a more subtle and sophisticated way. Did you see the sculptures of Trump that some satirical artist put on street corners in various cities, with a tiny penis, all because of that debate with the senator from Florida, Marquito?"

The one from Massachusetts let out a chuckle she suppressed too late. She looked at Jeff, who was staring at her, and lowered her head.

Jeff placed a hand on Silvanna's thigh and insisted she drop it. That it was getting boring. But

112

Silvanna seemed even more annoyed, though she could still hide it. Typical effect of wine when one's not used to it, Jeff thought: after the relaxation comes the euphoria and, finally, the uncontrollable rage, often cathartic. This last part was what was starting to worry him.

"We're getting late," Jeff said.

"Those artists who created the naked Trumps, with bellies and no penises, think they're so clever," Silvanna said. "The left thinks they're smart because they dominate culture, but that's exactly why they don't dominate politics. Does anyone remember when they said John Kerry had demolished George Bush in the last debate? How naïve! George W, with that drunk face that didn't even understand they were throwing two towers at him, came out triumphant for obvious reasons. There's no people more anti-intellectual than America-ns. Haven't you noticed? The same will happen with the sculptures of Trump and his little penis. I bet millions of men will feel identified and vote for the billionaire. Any sociologist knows that ideas are just a facade, they matter little to nothing. Someone said politics is merely a game of emotions, and they're right. Except emotions need flesh to latch onto, simple things like a phrase and an image. If this man, the obese governor of New Jersey, doesn't even have a decent image consultant, he'll never be president."

"Such a great truth," said the one from Alabama. "Besides, in this country, we need someone who knows how to manage an image. Someone from the industry."

Silvanna laughed again and added, turning her phone around for everyone to see:

"This man should go on a diet, urgently. But not just for politics. In fact, being president doesn't matter at all. As everyone knows, obesity affects men's sex life and, by the way, with those weapons the governor boasts about, we're not going to win any wars."

"And a country without wars…" insisted the one from Massachusetts. "Have you noticed we're always saving someone, some ungrateful person?"

Facundo had noticed, from the beginning, that both Mr. Gasper and Jeff were competing for the attention of the manager from Massachusetts, whose name he had completely forgotten. The woman was as beautiful as Silvanna, but for a predator, it's not about having the most beautiful woman but about never losing in the conquest, in the hunt, in the war. That's called testosterone, and any successful businessman is always equipped with a considerable amount of this hormone, like any good athlete or wrestling champion. Conquering, hunting is always more important than keeping the prey. The prey might enjoy observing this competition between the two males, especially because she knew neither would give her the satisfaction, other than warming up the game by looking at one and then the other. Jeff was with his wife, which made him a safer and more tempting competitor for the prey. Not by chance (Facundo had remembered, being somewhat of an expert on the subject, central to any marketing strategy) studies suggest that when a woman is attracted to a man, especially if she gets him to look at her, she always looks at his partner. The prettier the partner, the higher the self-esteem of the player.

The one from Massachusetts seemed to lean towards the Homer Simpson, towards Mr. Gasper, but this could just be a crude strategy. Because Jeff was with his wife or because she knew who the real boss was. Because there's nothing better than wounding a male's self-esteem.

With a sharp tone (his only mistake that night, like a goalkeeper who leads his team to the World Cup final and, due to a delayed reaction, lets in the decisive goal), Jeff emphasized Silvanna's words alluding to the candidate's lack of weapons, the governor of New Jersey who resembled Mr. Gasper in his pronounced belly but, unlike the governor, no one could estimate the size of his penis based on how he dressed.

At a meeting prior to the one in Atlanta (in Tampa, if he remembered correctly) Mr. Gasper had mocked himself, saying his wife had asked him to go on a diet because he was starting to look more and more like Homer Simpson. Literally. He, on the other hand, had proposed wearing a wig and growing a mustache. He'd said it as if the idea proved that, despite being fat and bald, he was smarter than the rest. But at that meeting in Atlanta, two years later, no one knew yet that Mr. Gasper was in the process of divorcing. Later, the rumor circulated (among the men in the Orlando offices) that his wife had cheated on him, probably just once, with one of his employees, a skinny, dark-skinned guy but with very large feet. And everyone knows what they say about men with big feet. The wives of millionaires (someone said in the corner by the office coffee machine) if they don't dedicate themselves to something serious, even if it's spinning on a distaff, sooner or later end up getting bored of luxury and falling back into the pleasures of poverty.

"Anyway, Trump is going to win," said Alonso, the florid representative from California. "Did you watch the last debate in Detroit? Even CNN titled it 'Donald Trump defends size of his penis.'"

Not by accident, but inadvertently, little Alonso had just thrown gasoline on a fire that was beyond his understanding.

"I think I'm not understanding this conversation," said Mr. Gasper. "It must be because I haven't watched the news in many years, much less political debates. They're pitiful. What is all this they're talking about?"

"Well," said Alonso, "it seems it all started with Mr. Trump calling Senator Marco Rubio 'Little Marco,' Markie, alluding to his short stature, both physical and personal, and the other candidate responded at an event, I don't know where, I guess in Florida, something like... let's see, in Spanish it would be... Short but I get the job done. I don't know the English..."

Jeff laughed heartily, and the one from Massachusetts, who must have known Spanish, being a good representative of the Boston elite, whispered the translation into Mr. Gasper's ear.

"Maybe not with those exact words," Alonso clarified, "but Little Marco responded that everyone knows what men with small hands are like and called for attention to Trump's hands. He didn't realize that

117

only Trump can play dirty, that it's not for just anyone. So, in Detroit, Mr. Trump showed his hands and confirmed, as always, that he had no problems with size. No problem, I assure you. Everyone knew what he was referring to."

"Everyone?"

"Everyone, even the journalist, what's her name? Yes, Megyn Kelly, who pretended not to notice. So virginal, the poor thing, who was later threatened with death because Trump suggested she looked a bit aggressive because she was menstruating. Of course, all with extreme subtlety. Remember that phrase, 'You could see the blood coming out of her eyes,' and on the other hand…"

"Enough," Silvanna complained. "Let's not be vulgar."

"Vulgar?" Alonso protested. "Who? Don't you remember that recording where Mr. Trump said you have to grab women by the pussy? Surely millions of decent women, the kind who wear Amish-style dresses, buttoned up to the neck, very conservative, churchgoers every Sunday, are going to vote for him. Didn't you see the hysterical rallies in his support? I'd bet my hands on the fire that they're going to vote for him. That's what it's all about, isn't it? Fuck me, fuck me hard, and tell me I'm a virgin."

"Alright, alright," said Jeff, "be that as it may, Mr. Trump objectively represents half of this great nation. When he says he could stand on Fifth Avenue and shoot people and still not lose votes, it must be for some very, very profound reason. That's why he can also sleep with all the Russian prostitutes he wants and never lose the support of the evangelicals who are in favor of the traditional family."

"There must be some kind of morbid attraction in sleeping with the enemy, right?" said Jeff.

Silvanna laughed. Mr. Gasper didn't. You never know what words, even the most innocent, can find dramatic resonance in someone hiding unsuspected stories and veiled personal prejudices. Jeff left the one from Massachusetts and focused on his boss. That night he suddenly realized the boss couldn't stand him, found him arrogant, and the mere idea that Jeff had risen in popularity in a way that even Mr. Gasper, in the best years of Ronald Reagan, had never achieved, made him sick. Anyone could find Jeff arrogant, but it was eating Mr. Gasper alive, and Jeff didn't understand it until that night, too late.

A few years later (thought Facundo, shortly after trying to reconstruct that decisive night, like an archaeologist carefully unearthing different shards of pottery and trying to piece together what they were once a part of), Mr. Gasper, almost on the verge of retirement, was about to meet the Silvanna that was the product of Jeff's great idea and Facundo's historic efforts in Kuala Lumpur.

Until that day, more than two years after that dinner in Atlanta, until December 22, 2021, Jeff didn't know the final outcome. He had only seen a collection of potential faces, almost all Asiatic, Japanese for their paleness, for their geisha-like look, but later he didn't bother to have them send him a photo of the AR21. He had only been interested in the business and the prospect of future profits from the three percent of final sales. Surely, they would soon send it to Jeff, and Facundo wouldn't be there to see his reaction, to hear his curses and shouts of fury.

What a pity, thought Facundo.

Exhausted, he glanced at the glass still on the floor. He didn't pick it up. He barely had the strength to grab the mouse and play the video he had just received from Kuala Lumpur.

"Jangan jadi bodoh," said Silvanna.

Facundo laughed. They had managed to replicate Silvanna's expression in a way that was impossible to surpass.

"Jangan jadi bodoh," Silvanna repeated.

Facundo reached for his translator and, placing it in his ear, heard Silvanna's voice with a slightly different accent, a hint of Argentinian, saying:

"Don't be stupid."

Finally, remember something. A night in Tijuana

THE NEWS ABOUT XINOTCH hadn't made him happy. He had waited months for that confirmation with exaggerated anxiety, and now, when it arrived, it left him with a mix of indifference and dissatisfaction. Again, he tried to accept the special circumstances he was going through: the divorce, Jeff's impending rage, his struggles to sleep at night and stay awake during the day, his memory loss caused by stress, the heart attack, or both, which at times became evident, like when he couldn't remember the alias from his penultimate business venture, the password to his most used secret email, or one of his better-known fake Twitter identities, which he considered more authentic than his real account, since under the name Alfredo Smith he had vented all his true thoughts about feminism, the dictatorship of diversity, wealth redistribution… Although his true thoughts, his true self, were only true for some time, only during that stage of his life that lasted from when he turned forty-five, fourteen years ago, until a few months before his divorce.

Then he paused for a moment by the window. The ocean and the sky were a single dark blur, indistinguishable. At that moment, thousands, millions of marine predators would be killing their prey. Thousands of miles away, dozens of people would be dying under bombs, all while outside the Universe seemed calm, in a dark calmness, very much like non-existence. Then he thought that for many years he had fought to achieve some economic stability, a family without shocks, with a daughter without high school problems that never came, with a wife without worries or depression who also never came without worries and without depression. Nothing out of this world, not even his obsession with making ten million before turning sixty. At some point, some of that happened, especially the nearly ten million just before turning sixty. Nothing by chance.

He had missed the ten million by a hair, he told himself, more with irony than regret, as if he were no longer himself and could now laugh at the other Facundo who had been and, at some impossible-to-pinpoint moment, had ceased to be.

Immediately he had an even darker thought. Or clearer. When he set the goal of reaching ten million, it must have been around 2001. He wasn't sure, but roughly it must have been that year. Then he returned to his computer, went to the statistics site of the U.S. Department of Labor, and confirmed the obvious. Those ten million weren't even ten million.

According to the Bureau of Labor Statistics consumer price index, the dollar experienced an average inflation rate of 2.10% per year. Prices in 2001 are 29.72% lower than prices in 2018. In other words, 10,000,000 dollars in 2018 is equivalent in purchasing power to 7,028,084.56 in 2001, a difference of 2,971,915.44 over 17 years.

In seventeen years, his dream had depreciated by 29.72 percent. His nearly ten million today would have been just $7,028,084.56 in 2001.

He smiled as if he were pleased to see himself defeated, fallen into the mud after desperately trying to climb a hill too high for his abilities. A confirmation that exonerated him from keeping the madness alive. For a man, for a business tiger, this detail couldn't have gone unnoticed for nearly twenty years. What happens is that each person sees what they want to see and understands what they want to understand. Now, when the Facundo of the ten million had died of a heart attack in a hallway of a mediocre middle-class apartment in Daytona, he could think better, he could see the Universe from another point of view. Then, objective data appeared that even a schoolchild would have understood much earlier.

But, after some years, he realized that instability and uncertainties are not only inevitable but preferable to complete security. Perhaps that's why so many successful people in the news end up miserably because of problems with other men's wives. After all, it must be a stroke of luck for a father not to know when his daughter would appear with her first—her first panic attacks, like some ancestor she never knew, with her first failures, like everyone else. Now, suddenly, he understood that it was a blessing not to know where his bones would end up nor when he would die.

He returned to his computer and checked his bank account once more. Since last September, there had been six withdrawals in the Tijuana area, four of sixty-two and two of a hundred each. The only expense, for $32.16, had been charged by a restaurant called Cola de Pez. It was the first on the list. Facundo remembered this place perfectly. Well, not perfectly, but he was sure he had dined there, with live music, with people smoking nearby. He remembered feeling

annoyed or reacting with some irritation to the rude-
ness of those at the next table, but he recalled it with
a certain nostalgia. He remembered the many beers
he had drunk, the prawns and shrimp with lemon
wedges. He recalled the modesty of the place, the bare
and dying lights hanging from the ceiling—not out
of snobbery (as they often do on this side when they
play at being poor and the customer has to pay more
for it), but out of genuine necessity. He remembered
the people passing by on the street, talking as if they
were in their own homes, the owner going out of her
way to offer him the best of the house.

He tried to find more information about Cola de
Pez. Before he could open a new page, he saw CNN's
Breaking News, a red banner warning of a school
shooting in Florida. He read the headlines. At least a
dozen dead. He closed the page. The event had happened far from there. He glanced at his work email
(no news from Martin in Chicago), his personal email
(Elena persisted in her silence), and then opened the
Google search bar and typed

"cola de pez restaurante méxico."

How had he ended up there? he wondered, finding no answer. He never ventured into dangerous
places. It was impossible that any of his clients had
recommended it. He had chosen a small table next to

a large window without glass. Shortly after, a very thin man had sat down in the chair across from him without asking. He took a piece of bread while saying, "if I may, maestro." He was blind, or nearly so, but he wore no glasses or carried a cane. Facundo said nothing, and the man seemed to understand.

"Don't worry, maestro, I'm leaving now," he had said.

But he didn't leave until an hour later. Facundo barely remembered what he had said, only that during that hour he didn't stop talking, nor did he stop leaving long silences that felt as if he were still speaking without speaking, silences that heralded new revelations, entirely lacking in interest. At least for Facundo.

Facundo bought him a beer, and the blind man explained that, in reality, the restaurant was called One Way, but everyone knew it as Cola de Pez because of the owner. Thirty years ago, she had been a very beautiful woman, but no one had ever managed to sleep with her.

"María!" the blind man almost shouted.

After a few minutes, the owner approached and told him not to bother her customers.

"Am I bothering you, sir?" the blind man asked.

Facundo felt a deep smell of curry or some oriental spice that María carried on her apron. He remembered that the traditional Mexican al pastor taco, which overwhelms newcomers to the country with its aromas and mysteries, had been imported and adapted by Lebanese immigrants two or three generations ago. The same smell he had felt in Morocco and Jordan, but the language had put up a heavy barrier when he wanted to know about the ingredients, about how and who prepared them in that place. That night in Amman, he had seen two young American women, two very pretty blondes in shorts, challenging the conventions of that Arab restaurant, full of men. If they had hoped to live an anecdote, something typical of backward or stagnant societies from the time of Hammurabi, to tell in developed societies, they had no luck. No one had said a word to them. Facundo had been unable to understand either them or the others. Only that smell, ancient, poor—that is, truly rich, millennia-old.

"It's fine," Facundo had said, in a tone that meant both yes and no at the same time.

"María," the blind man insisted, "tell the Argentine friend why Cola de Pez is called that."

"Go to hell, José," she said.

"Why don't you ever want to say why your restaurant is called that?"

"Because I felt like calling it that," she said, picking up one of the empty plates. "And stop bothering. Would the gentleman like to try the crab omelet? It's a house specialty."

"Okay, let's try it," said Facundo.

"You're still the prettiest in Baja California," the blind man insisted. "I don't know if it's the same beyond because I've never traveled that far in my damn life."

"Go home, José. Don't bother my customers," the owner said and left.

"Tell me, you who come from afar," the blind man said, "don't you think she's a beautiful woman? A woman with that voice can't be ugly. Don't you think? I always had a good eye for women, and women didn't dislike it when I looked at them. Until I got older and poverty became more obvious. You can see it in the teeth, in the sun wrinkles, in the hunger, in the clothes. The rich don't have construction accidents either. They don't go blind from work or get a pittance as compensation."

Facundo said nothing, but the blind man insisted:

"Please, tell me. Please."

The blind man's words sounded like a prayer that woke Facundo from a slight drunkenness, more the result of the place's joy than the first beers.

"Don't you plan to tell me? Yes, I know, gringos don't say those things about women. Once in a while, they kill one, rape another, but always with style. Truly gentlemen."

"Why do you call me a gringo? I'm not a gringo."

"But you live in the United States."

"How do you know?"

"I don't know how I know. I just know that I know, and it's useless for you to lie to me. After thirty years of living in Tijuana, you can just smell who comes from the other side, and whether they come from above to mock everything that doesn't work here, or if they're crawling, or if they were kicked in the ass and fell headfirst into their parents' land. Don't worry, I'm not going to kidnap you to ask for a million-dollar ransom. I just wanted you to tell me if you think María is beautiful."

"She's a beautiful woman," Facundo conceded.

"Beautiful, beautiful," the blind man insisted. "It sounds like you're selling a scarf."

**The Washington Post: URGENT: FLORIDA.
TWENTY YOUNG PEOPLE KILLED BY ONE OF THEIR CLASSMATES**

The president claims it's not the time to politicize the tragedy by discussing gun control and proliferation in the country and calls for prayer. Several photos show the killer posing with an AR15 and a flag in the background. The Post clarifies that the photos were taken from the killer's Facebook page shortly before it was deleted.

Facundo laughed and confirmed:

"You're right. She's not just beautiful but rather very beautiful."

"Now you sound more authentic," the blind man said. "I can tell you really think María is beautiful. Do you see wrinkles around her eyes?"

Facundo laughed and poured him more beer.

"Tell me, seriously. Don't take it lightly."

"I don't know," said Facundo. "I don't know, I haven't noticed that. I'm not the one in love with her."

The blind man fell silent for a long time and finally said:

"Not just the blind can see what others don't see."

Then, faking cheerfulness, he drank from his glass and said:

"Anyway, do you know why this place is called Cola de Pez? They say she was a mermaid."

"Who?"

CNN, Fox News, CBS, USA Today. They were all on the same thing. The world ends from time to time, and then no one remembers.

But the present didn't give up so easily

ELENA STILL HADN'T GIVEN ANY SIGN. Surely she had been upset by his last email. Someone had tagged him on Facebook. Someone named Emma Claris. He was going to dismiss it, but he ended up opening his account to see a photo from the latest symposium in Chicago on New Administrative Persuasion Strategies. He had forgotten that selfie and couldn't remember this Emma, who appeared as one of his Facebook friends. She looked nice. She had a broad smile, an African trace in the face of a blonde woman, the kind he and magazine photographers liked. Either way, he didn't remember her. Maybe she was interested in the younger guy who appeared next to him. Or maybe she wasn't interested in any of those who appeared there but just wanted to show off that she had been at the same table, at the same symposium as Dr.

Mohammed El Salamin, an eminence in the circle of the International Business University of Dubai, as he found out that same night.

The phone rang. It wasn't Elena. An unknown number. Probably telemarketing. Him, Facundo, a victim of telemarketing. Typical. The lion harassed by hyenas. They had him fed up. He probably needed to change his number again. He didn't answer. If it's important, he thought, let them leave a message. He needed to learn to say no. If you were a woman, someone had told him (who?), you'd be a whore. Why? he had complained. Because you don't know how to say no, they had said. He didn't remember. Well, yes, now he remembered. It was Karl, a colleague he barely knew because he, Facundo, had joined the Company a month before the said Karl committed suicide one early morning in the office, the same one occupied by the new one, Joana. Joana didn't commit suicide. She got pregnant, was abandoned, and had to leave the job. Maybe because of these quirks of fate, her position was filled by Joan, a guy incapable of getting pregnant, very sharp and ambitious as a rat, a trait that brought the company a thousand times more profit than the willingness and servility of Joana and ten thousand times more than all of Einstein's intelligence.

The present, in the form of his tired body, kept him sunk in an armchair, but something kept dragging him, again and again, to that night in Tijuana, while new details emerged from his memory, like an ancient wooden galleon suddenly surfacing, revealing more details than explanations, when the sea retreats dangerously beyond normal for a low tide, just before a tsunami. Like when one tries to focus on reading and other thoughts leave you reading like a blind man, these memories prevented him from attending to the most urgent matters.

"The owner," the blind man insisted, "her. María. They said she was a mermaid. Who knows where they got the idea that mermaids are beautiful… Must have been fantasies of sailors without women, tired of eating fish. Imagine a beautiful woman with fish fins instead of long, soft legs. Well, of course, there's no nickname without an explanation. Before the reform, many travelers passed through here. They were enchanted by her, but there was no way. There was no way. It wasn't because of her tight dress but because of her integrity, because of that very thing that lasts in her to this day, though much less tempted by sailors and the slippery dollars of the tourists who used to come here back then, always just passing through, because Cola de Pez wasn't and never was in a tourist area. You're not a tourist. You're a businessman. Someone more interesting than the tourists, but just as stupid."

"Thank you."

Microsoft Outlook. Central Authentication Service. Log in. Eleven new. Two urgent. In a group email sent to all colleagues, Ramiro insists on giving his opinion on the danger of North Korean missiles when he hasn't been able to close a miserable contract in Singapore. Nothing really important. Nor in his GMail, apart from the endless travel offers from Orbitz and Expedia. He would mark them as spam if it weren't that... (New email, Google alert as it happens: the Patriots' eagles defeat The Eagles 27 to 24. Orbitz: Wow! These hotel deals under $99 are summer's best steal!) If it weren't that there was always the possibility of using one of those services at some point. He looked at his two phones, as if they were drunk and resting next to his coffee cup. He woke them up with his right index finger. No MSN, SMS, ICUP. Elena knew how to play with her silences. The two mobiles looked like big insects, a mutation reflecting Global Warming, with their luminous bellies facing upward, like those fireflies he used to catch as a child on his grandfather's farm in Argentina, but a hundred or two hundred times bigger. A hundred or two hundred times less important, less alive. Luminous corpses. The big difference was the smell. Before, things had scents. They weren't as strong as the ones now. They were just real scents, scents that mattered. In the smell of his grandmother's fritters, there was a whole world, there were his parents, the beach of the summer of 1986, the sound of the eucalyptus trees embraced by the wind like the waves of the sea, the skeptical story of his grandfather who believed in nothing about a woman announcing the end of the world in the store where they sold their watermelons. Why do people live in fear and desire to live for all eternity? asked the grandfather, with a smile that brought him infinite peace. Why so much fear? Why aren't they content with the years they have to live and nothing more? That's it. Enough. Where's the drama? The grandfather was grateful to be alive and didn't want to live forever, like the blonde woman at the store. But the woman had become furious when she found out the grandfather didn't care about dying and returning to nature. In fact, the grandfather wanted to be cremated and have his ashes given to a tree, to help it grow. The woman, visibly upset, had threatened him with hell. If he didn't believe in eternal life, he should burn in hell, eternally. So, what kind of loving God was she talking about? asked grandfather Ursino. The grandfather wasn't afraid of God. Not because he felt stronger, nor because he was an atheist, but because he didn't understand the logic of things. Why would the Creator of the Universe go to church? But why does the God of Love need to be Feared? Why, if humanity had emerged from Love, had God decided to create sinful beings only to condemn them to the flames of eternal fire? he questioned. Either God was Sadistic or nothing else was anything but the product of fear from His small, stupid creatures. Why must one suffer from the fear of others, distilled into an endless repertoire of threats? What have we done wrong to all those people who spend their time praying but are always so angry? They speak of Love, and they look at us with hatred. They can't burn us in the squares anymore, as they used to, but if it were legal, they'd gladly do it. They talk about the joy of having discovered the Lord, and they dump all their rage on us. Why don't they settle for the eternal life they've earned on their own and leave the rest of us in peace…? Why do people go to pray in churches if, when they pray, no one knows what they're asking God for? They could do it at home, in a park, on the train. But no. They have to do it in churches, the exact opposite of what Jesus recommended, that bit about discretion in a corner. But why in churches, those lavish temples of pride in the name of humility, if Jesus always had a problem with temples? Because Jesus said, 'You are Peter, and on this rock I will build my church,' they repeat with feigned calm. They don't mention that a page later, the same Jesus, when things got heated, corrects Himself and says, 'Peter, get behind me, you are a hindrance to me.' Oh no, but all true believers must go to pray in churches. They kneel, close their eyes, and no one knows what they're asking the Creator of the Universe. Because churches are not places where God goes to listen but where earthly power is exerted...

His grandmother listened and didn't respond. She believed in that God, though she didn't know exactly which God or whether the woman from the watermelon store was right or simply delirious, as if in an asylum.

Yes, all of that was in the smell of his grandmother's fritters. In contrast, the smell of the perfect donuts parading on the rollers of the Krispy Kreme where he had been on Saturday, was just that, the smell of donuts, perfect fritters, sugary and greasy, fried with recycled oil and never touched by a disgusting human being. Of course, yes, in thirty or forty years, that child who on Saturday watched, mesmerized, the parade of donuts on the mechanical rollers from the other side of the glass, will remember all of it with the same nostalgia, with the same sense of wonder. That is, if by then people still have time for so much unproductive distraction, as apparently he himself did when he was supposed to be planning the approach strategy for his next trip to Shanghai.

He took another sip of coffee, disgustingly cold. He looked at his two luminous bugs. He thought again, as if there were no urgency. A new pencil, an eraser, the smell of grass when Facundo knelt in the dark to pick up one of those little bugs of light he had caught with a swipe of his hand. After rescuing it from the depths of the grass, he would stand up and shout at his brother with a triumphant gesture. In dictionary Spanish, they called them fireflies, but the kids called them *bichitos de luz*. At that moment, he would trade his two phones for just one of those, he thought. But no, the luminous phones drew him in. He was the insect circling the light, and that was as absurd as everything else.

"No," the blind man insisted, "don't take it personally. I'm speaking in general terms. The two types of featherless bipeds, tourists and businessmen, are equally stupid. Arrogant by action or omission. Unhappy as a rule. More or less corpses convinced of their superiority. Haven't you seen how the skulls laugh? Well, that's what tourists and businessmen are like. They're always laughing, but they're dead…"

True, that pitifully poor blind man spoke as if he had read the Greek philosophers. Did it catch your attention? Diogenes was not a professor at Harvard.

"Maybe you're right," Facundo had said, almost defensively. "I imagine you were a businessman too."

"Maybe, yes. There's no greater capitalist than a street vendor. Except that when capitalists like us fail, they don't call us capitalists. They call us parasites, communists, or something like that. But let's leave it at that, friend. I don't want to torture you with poor people's struggles, with the struggles of a resentful poor man, as my cousin says. I have a cousin on the other side, you see. I should be thanking you for the beer, actually. So, cheers!"

THE FLORIDA SENATOR PROPOSES ALLOWING TEACHERS AND STUDENTS TO CARRY WEAPONS IN SCHOOLS FOR PERSONAL PROTECTION.

Another senator from Georgia or Mississippi goes even further, claiming that preschoolers should be armed, because they could never defend themselves against a terrorist with just a pencil sharpener. He later clarified that…

Fed up with all that immaculate filth, he closed all the news windows and returned (or tried to return) to the central problem. He couldn't recall the other expenses on dates when, obviously, he hadn't been in Mexico. He had returned in January for the Camerino case but didn't remember having been to the Patio del Virrey supermarket. Normally, he had breakfast at hotels and ate at restaurants recommended by clients.

He finished the whisky left in his glass, as if it were an obligation. Better to do harm than to waste, he remembered his uncle Alberto once saying, complaining about the excessive amounts of food people force themselves to eat during the holidays.

To one side, he saw the paper where he had been collecting numbers and letters over the past few months. They were all crossed out with a thin but deep line, as if slashed. They had been the futile attempts to guess the password to Elena's email. At least the email he knew of and, supposedly, the one she used most often. He had tried, in vain, every possible date and name. He could have hired Dominus Dominicus, the hacker from Singapore, one of the best in the world, who had provided invaluable service to the company a few years back, but he didn't want to expose her to the possibility of others reading her emails.

Suddenly, he felt the impulse to write a number along with the name of a friend from Buenos Aires, but it hung in the air. It had been a fleeting moment, like an epiphany, but the number had vanished, evaporated with the alcohol. Alejandra was the only one who knew when Elena had her first relationship in Buenos Aires. Because it's a woman's thing (he thought) to remember the date they lost their virginity. Surely the boyfriend didn't remember, just as Elena didn't recall the date they first had intimacy at her parents' house in Philadelphia.

He fell asleep on the couch. Strangely, he didn't wake up until six hours later, with a slight discomfort, as if he had just fallen off a cliff. For a moment, he felt like he had been running away from something, but he couldn't recall any dream. Not even the simplest image. Maybe just an idea, or the sensation of having gotten up to open the balcony's sliding door and discovering that the balcony had no railings. Had he walked over the abyss, and that's where the feeling of vertigo came from? He had lost that habit of remembering dreams, so much so that he could describe dreams from his youth, from his childhood, but not his recent ones, not a single one from the last few years, as if growing old was the same as losing the ability to dream, just as the elderly close to death can't smile, just as a child can't smile in their first months of life.

He sat up to check the time on his bedside clock. A piece of paper folded in two blocked the 7:35 from view. He moved the paper to better see the time and noticed something written on it. He must have written it himself at some point during the night, as he used to do when he was a student in Buenos Aires and wrote, like many young people, sentimental lines they pompously considered poems.

He read:

consciousness
that state incapable
of conceiving
something so simple
as nonexistence

Right at the worst moment

THE DISCOVERY THAT HIS IDENTITY had been stolen had come at the worst moment of his life. It always happens that way. Sometimes days, weeks, or months go by without a big client, without a trip, without a new idea, without a new demand from the Board, without an interesting investment that would yield juicy profits, apart from the adrenaline rush, and then one day everything piles up, like when you don't check your email over the weekend and on Monday you're overwhelmed by so many urgent matters.

Either it was a coincidence or everything was connected by causes he couldn't quite understand. That tangle of minor urgencies was exacerbated by the divorce, his sleep troubles, his difficulty staying awake, and the identity theft in that godforsaken country.

In reality, he wasn't entirely sure if his identity had truly been stolen or if it was just a case of a card being skillfully used by a thief who, judging by the amounts, wasn't even a major criminal. But the old fear was always there, no matter how many Peace of Mind services he contracted with H&R Block and other companies, and it would descend upon him at the slightest suspicion. That's what happens to someone when they have nine million dollars in the bank and high hopes in various stocks, he thought, as if trying to console himself. Many would love to have these problems, he murmured, as if someone else were speaking to him.

In any case, it had come at the worst possible time, just when he had decided to take a three-week leave. Dr. Kaufmann had assured him that his recent difficulty sleeping and his even greater difficulty staying awake and focused during business meetings or while driving was a result of the heart attack. When he mentioned that he had experienced some of that long before, Dr. Kaufmann told him it was likely due to a liver weakness, poor eating habits, or even some undetected virus that traditional tests hadn't picked up after countless useless back-and-forth visits to his office and the best clinics in Florida. Like any doctor, he prescribed no more than one glass of wine a day and, if possible, to eliminate the 7:30 PM whiskey. He also mentioned that thing about stress. Even the old ladies from his childhood, his grandmother Hortensia's friends, used to say it: You need to relax, girl. Those dizzy spells are from nerves. Which is pretty much the same as saying: give the problem less importance, and the problem will become less important. Until his grandmother died of a stroke, most likely due to her habit of eating everything fried in pork fat on a wood stove that filled that enormous country kitchen with smoke from morning till night. It could have been the grease, the cakes, or the smoke, even though humanity was supposed to have

144

developed a tolerance to wood smoke after hundreds of thousands of years breathing it, dating back to the cave days.

Yes, sure, Doctor, blame it on stress too. You're definitely never wrong about that, though you don't need years of university to figure it out. Nowadays, everyone lives under stress, and especially him, after Elena proposed the divorce and a month later he found out she was likely going to keep the houses in Boca Raton and Ponte Vedra, and he'd be left with the summer apartment in Daytona. The lawyers would scrutinize every corner and every movement in his bank accounts, and Elena would discover that the family fortune, just in stocks and savings accounts, wasn't around seven million, as she thought, but had already surpassed nine. Another great argument for her claimant lawyers. Not to mention the mess of explaining those purchases in Tijuana on dates when he was supposedly in the country. If there was one thing Elena wouldn't believe, it was the identity theft story. It wasn't in her interest either. Over the years, he had learned that she convinced herself of the reality of her own imagination. Every time he didn't answer the phone immediately during his trips to Asia or Latin America, she imagined him in bed with some woman. Once, he thought that Elena's imagination had something to do with her own habits, or at least her own desires. Maybe she wasn't sleeping with strangers in every city across the country, but she might have had some experiences he'd never know about.

Surely, she would keep the majority of the shared assets, which, naturally, would be enjoyed by some freeloader. The freeloader, a better lover than him, younger, less stressed, and less occupied, would enjoy her money, enjoy all the life he himself hadn't had in the last twenty or thirty years.

That's how the world works, and he, Facundo, who always prided himself on being a practical, effective man who understood reality for his own benefit, would end up crushed by the machinery, like any ignorant failure he'd ever crossed paths with. Like blind José.

She would find a partner much sooner than him. That much was, at least, certain. If he even... He had burned all the promises of eternal love and living together, even beyond death, and he wasn't willing to repeat those teenage poet verses again. The dark swallows will return, to hang their nests on your balcony. She wasn't the type of woman to be without someone by her side who would remind her every day that she was a great woman. The thick honeysuckle will return, climbing over the walls of your garden. According to self-help manuals, that's what women need—someone to repeat to them every day that they are wonderful, valuable, unique. You're worth it. You're one of a kind. There's no one like you. What a woman needs is a man who values her. That job is easy for a stranger, for a new acquaintance who can lift a woman's self-esteem (or her indignation, depending on the adventurer's appearance) with just one glance (*The burning words of love will return, resounding in your ears*), but it's an almost impossible task for a husband, even more so for someone who spends their life solving problems. Problems solved, at best, merit nothing more than a cold, very cold "thank you very much." Who sincerely appreciates the value of the trees every day for the air we breathe?

The thick honeysuckle will return
climbing over the walls of your garden,
and once more in the afternoon, even more beautiful,
their flowers will open.

The perpetual encouragement, the incessant feeding of self-esteem, was a superstition created by the publishing market, he thought. Or maybe it was simply true, and he had failed at this. Which was strange for a businessman accustomed to selling obelisks and stars in the sky, like any romantic poet. He, on the other hand, didn't need anyone to tell him he was a great man because he had believed it for a long time. Thanks to good business deals, of course, because Elena had made it her mission to humiliate him in bed with her indifference, which he didn't even translate into the infidelity she accused him of.

He rubbed his face with both hands and thought that he was only thinking all of this out of resentment. There's nothing better than accusing yourself to ease the feeling of injustice in your own flesh. Strange that Grandma didn't say that before. What was different was the lawyers, Elena, and her freeloader feasting on the fruit of so many years of his systematic, meticulous, and obsessive effort. That was anything but subjective, but if he couldn't stop thinking, he'd surely end up like Grandma Hortensia, with a stroke, or like Grandpa Ramón, with a heart attack, long before either of them.

Dr. Kaufman's nurse had asked those annoying questions she always asks at the beginning, almost without thinking. One of them read: Have you felt sad for more than a day in the past week? Facundo told her maybe, and the nurse, without looking at him, insisted, with some irritation: Yes or No? There's no room in the system for any philosophical explanation. To which Facundo said, Well, yes, I haven't felt terribly happy in the last two days. The woman left the office, and half an hour later Dr. Kaufman came in with a prescription. An antidepressant. When Facundo arrived at the CVS pharmacy, they were waiting for him with the bottle ready. That was efficiency. He returned to the apartment and, before taking it, read the side effects: possible suicidal thoughts and paranoid episodes. Three hundred and fifty dollars down the drain, but it was worth such expensive trash. Dr. Kaufman was a good guy and an even better professional, Facundo thought. But he's in the business, and for someone like Facundo himself, who's been in the business for some time…

He couldn't find the words to finish the sentence. The idea, the intuition, hung in the air and vanished like the day before in his memory. It was that exhaustion that washed over him again. If he went to bed too early, he'd be awake within half an hour and unable to sleep the rest of the night.

It was also true that if he hadn't taken that leave, away from the office and the arguments with Elena, he probably never would have discovered those mysterious purchases in Tijuana, let alone the missing backup credit card. Every six months, sometimes every four, the bank would send him a new credit card to replace one that was working perfectly fine, all as a precautionary security measure. So, for that security, he had to update the databases of countless services every so often, many of which he didn't even remember, like the subscription to the landscaping company that showed up every two months to spray the lawns of the houses in Boca Ratón and Ponte Vedra with something that was supposed to kill insects. The fear of insects, like all fears, is another big business. Termites can ruin an entire house and years of savings. They had also discovered a flea capable of transmitting a parasite that ate your brain in a matter of hours, worse than a zombie. Viruses and antiviruses. Things that can always be real. There was always a monthly fee to pay; an insurance, the prevention of some catastrophe like a hurricane or a murderous neighbor, and so on, a long list of ten or fifteen services that overcharged him fifty or a hundred dollars every time the automatic payment failed because the bank (as a routine security measure) had replaced the card and he didn't respond within twenty-four hours. None of that was known or worried Elena. He solved the problems. All of them, except for boosting her self-esteem as she deserved.

He thought of Grandma Hortensia. Who knows if her stroke wasn't due to cholesterol but because that fate was already written in her DNA? How did his mother die? No idea. But it was possible, he thought, that his condition had something to do with that ticking time bomb which is an illness or a weakness decided at the precise moment his parents finished having sex, one summer afternoon in the little beach house. His existence, that is, the existence of the Universe, defined by a lottery where in a single orgasm billions of possible combinations play out and only one, by pure chance, ends up being Me, that sort of false but inevitable god from which one sees, feels, and believes to understand the entire Universe. He remembered reading in The Economist something about the DNA of divorced people. His parents hadn't divorced because she died young, at only 42 years old.

He went to the study and took the magazine from under the whiskey glass. He hadn't finished it yesterday. Around eleven at night, it had started to disgust him, and at that hour in the morning, it smelled disgusting, almost as disgusting as an extinguished cigarette. The distant calm of nine at night was as inexplicable and unfounded as the apathy, almost depression, at seven in the morning, ten minutes before coffee. Throughout the same day, he thought, one goes through all the emotional stages, translated into ideas throughout the history of philosophy. Thus, depending on the chemistry of the liver, the thyroid, or testosterone, one goes, like a little paper boat in a flooded street after the rain, from Spencer's positivism to Sartre's nausea, passing naturally through stoicism, idealism, cynicism, and all the other ideas of the Greeks which he, also for an inexplicable reason, imagined as witty, fun, and carefree people, perhaps because, as always, real problems only exist in the present.

He poured the whiskey into the kitchen sink and looked for the article on divorces. On one page, it detailed the growing colony of wealthy Americans emigrating to Mexico, like those in the Ajijic colony by Lake Chapala, seeking tranquility and less crime. Further on, a section with perfume advertising some extremely luxurious shirts and a tie for just a hundred dollars. Something similar to the Rolexes worth thousands of dollars which he, despite all his experience, still couldn't distinguish from a ten-dollar Chinese watch. The millionaire Elon Musk, of SpaceX, managed to launch the biggest rocket in the world and send a pretty car, quite fake, like the dummy driving it, to Mars. A three-hundred-million-dollar publicity stunt. A genius. Surely they'll say nothing when it crashes into some asteroid…

He didn't find the article. The magazine was from February 10th, quite old already, though magazines with substance, like people, don't age so quickly. He looked for the previous one. Yes, it was there. "Family values. The genetics of divorce." Page 69. Doctors Salvatore and Kendler found that, in adopted children, the likelihood of divorce increases if their biological parents divorced. But it wasn't so much due to the example but something less avoidable. It seemed clear. Even that was written in the blood. How could something like a stroke not be hereditary? It was a matter of probabilities, but it was a probability. Life was like a roulette wheel. Not just evolution but what happens to each of us. Maybe Facundo had gotten the mental issues of Grandma Hortensia, though he also remembered that Grandpa would fall asleep sitting while everyone was talking. Grandpa died of a heart attack at 89 years old. What had he gotten in that deal? Or had he gotten both, all three things together? Trouble sleeping, divorce, and a stroke, like when he shouted bingo?

The new thing, that which couldn't be inherited through the countless dark caves of human fluids, was identity theft. That certainly didn't depend on biology. It was pure crap from new technologies and the new culture of virtual realities. Didn't he himself have three or four different identities, depending on the occasion and, supposedly, for protection? How can someone steal another's identity if everyone is, more or less, virtual beings? What's stolen is money, the possibilities to do or not to do. Never identity. You can't steal something that doesn't exist or is multiple and elastic like a tangle of rubber bands. If one can change professions and gender, why couldn't one change who they are? Everything is mutable. That's the only new thing. Or it's not new, but it has become radicalized. A commoner marries a prince and becomes a queen. The owner of a brothel one day is elected president of a great country. A priest renounces his vows and becomes Don Juan. One day a happy husband becomes a humiliated divorcé… and so it goes.

No, it wasn't something new. At least (he thought, tossing the magazines onto the desk) the word-of-mouth defamation he used to hear from his grandmother's friends didn't count as identity theft.

Almost missed the plane because of loneliness

HE FILED THE REPORT, MORE AS a reflex than out of any sense of following the law in the land of laws. One of those many hysterical little verses always trying to hide some unpleasant reality, not to say rotten, not to say shitty. Almost bitterly, he remembered several times and in different situations (like someone trying for days to remove a thorn from their heel, failing each time they step on that side) one of his favorite phrases: the law is for those who work. He liked that ambiguity he used at company meetings, at cocktail parties with his Latin American clients, at colorful African dance demonstrations in Angola and Mozambique, on boats in Hong Kong Bay, in some auditorium at some university giving talks about business and entrepreneurship, which had served him more than anything to add two new lines to his already extensive CV and, in passing, throw it in Ernesto's face that he too had been, if only for a few hours, an academic rat. Until you decided to level up, he imagined Ernesto replying in a conversation that never happened, like almost all important arguments.

At some point, he began to use that phrase as a Trojan horse, as a joke, as sarcasm that only his closest colleagues and those others who, even without

155

knowing him too well, recognized him perfectly understood in its entirety; by a smile, by the scent, by the nature of the business, always clean but not infrequently with an excess of chlorine. The law is for those who work. For those who work is the law. The law for those who work is. Omnia in omnibus deus.

At the Atlanta airport, while waiting for his flight to San Diego, he bought the New York Times. It had been at least ten years, or more, since he'd spent two dollars on old news. Bookstores had disappeared from shopping centers. There was nothing intelligent left to accompany a Starbucks coffee while Elena bought herself another pair of platinum diamond earrings. Nor did he have any interest or indignation left over that dramatic disappearance. Those distractions (observing, finding social patterns, indignation) were for Elena's brother, Ernesto, the failure, the one with the sexy idea of creating a Coffe-Cola Index, a coefficient that measured the culture of a city based on the sales ratio of sodas versus coffee. Obviously, Coke and Pepsi would cover the black ghettos of Baltimore, that mass of population (of fat women and thin men walking with difficulty, with one hand holding their genitals) that divided their time between going to church on Sundays and running from the police the rest of the week. The white, richer neighborhoods (that is, more educated, less persecuted) would be marked by the predominance of Starbucks, that is, of books. That's why inside every Barnes & Noble, there's a monopoly of Starbucks, like Coca-Cola in McDonald's, or in clothing malls, there's an abundance of stores selling sugar and sodas. Facundo waited two years for Ernesto to decide to materialize his idea in order to sell it to some university, as a special family favor, since the real benefits could be considered negligible even in the most optimistic scenario. But, as always, Ernesto was too busy correcting hundreds of papers and exams to correct, or at least that was his excuse for never moving from hypothesis to theory, for never doing something truly risky and relevant.

Leave that poor guy alone, he told himself. After all, he wasn't so bad. He held the newspaper up to his face to change his thoughts. He smelled the old scent of ink and cheap paper that transported him to some moment in a past he couldn't define. Nothing like reading, like before, on that modest paper, the recent history of the world's big events. (PRESIDENT DONALD TRUMP EATS HIS BOOGERS. Old news. The president has just denied it. They weren't boogers, they were gummies. The thing about the gummies hasn't been printed yet. It's on Twitter.) He brought the large page close to his nose and again recognized that smell that now dragged him back to the summer of 1986, to his uncle Alberto's house, to the newspapers the deliveryman threw through the always-open door every day, as if it were a friendly assault. No, that phrase "friendly assault" wasn't something he'd come up with there, in the Atlanta airport, in front of The New York Times. He'd heard his uncle say it once, at least an eternity ago. Just him, Facundo, the enemy of paper, was surrendering for a moment to an absurd weakness. He was an exaggerated and perhaps fake enemy of anything that wasn't strictly new. Paper was like four thousand years old. That's why, when someone said they had saved a thousand-year-old book in digital format, Ernesto would laugh. Me too (Ernesto had said one Thanksgiving night), I saved a letter from a girlfriend on a DVD eleven years ago. I still have the letter, but the file on the disk won't open because it's corrupted or the new wonders of technology don't support that old format. Eleven years, like talking about the digital Stone Age. Caffeine concentrate hadn't gone out of style either. Like sex, drugs never go out of style. Now men have smartphones and fly above the clouds, but they still look at a nice backside, a twenty-six-year-old backside, with the same infinite desire as they did in the times of Hammurabi, Solomon, or Tutankhamun.

On the last page of the first section, he looked at the little colored maps of the United States. Fifteen years ago, he used to study them to get a sense of the climate in the city where he'd settle when he retired. San Francisco 59F, Chicago 42F, Boston 49F, Atlanta 71F, Denver 58F, San Diego 78F... Actually, he knew it beforehand because everyone did: Florida, without a doubt. All Americans go there to die, because of the weather. Every two or three years a hurricane, but at least they were more predictable than California's earthquakes, and he wasn't planning to wait until retirement to flee the stress of New Jersey, of New York, to start enjoying the sea and the paths like on the coast, with no ups or downs.

He looked at the little maps carefully, with their wavy zones in red, yellow, and blue according to the temperatures, and couldn't recapture that past enthusiasm. The great map of the chosen ones, the land where not everyone enters, was now a shapeless piece, almost unpleasant, completely decaffeinated.

Yes, Florida. One day that entire peninsula will be underwater. Maybe much sooner than nature had planned. Maybe the alarmists who spend years threatening the world with rising seas, like others once

159

threatened with communism, were right about something. But it doesn't matter. By then nothing will matter anymore. There will be neither passions nor disputes. Truth will be useless. That's life. Just a fleeting moment of greatness, of eternity, and then the nothingness of fossils that extend some millions of years the shadow of a life that doesn't last much longer than its own tormented thoughts, its passions and its dreams—the capital ones. A life, like any other, that lasts no longer than a few days.

He tossed the newspaper into a trash can and headed to a restaurant with a bar, one of those upscale, slightly dim places where there are never any workers or students. Just like in cheap food restaurants, a man, two ladies, three little screens, all three solitary and with no prospects of conversation. He sat on the free stool and ordered a grilled cheese sandwich. The man next to him stopped reading his phone for a moment and looked at him. The grilled cheese sandwich had entered the Guinness Book a few years earlier as the most expensive sandwich in the world. Immediately, the man pretended not to care and took a long sip of his beer. He, Facundo, never drank beer in airports to avoid having to repeat the restroom ritual, to avoid raising unjustified suspicions from the TSA, from the Federal air marshals who monitor and record passengers' behavior in airports, counting their farts and measuring their sweat. To avoid the same stranger as always, peeing beside him like he's signing a check, that same suit-and-tie man who, after finishing Operation Relief, leaves without washing his hands and then offers it to you, as a greeting and introduction, with so much respect and ceremony.

Facundo looked to his side and recognized the brown shoe with yellow laces on the man with the phone and the Guinness. He'd seen him an hour earlier in the restroom at Gate C 22. In those primitive urinals of such super-modern airports, his sphincter didn't relax so easily. When he was He hated having to see his shoe from beneath the partition, and even more the sound of urine hitting proudly right in the center of the great Loch Ness Monster lake, as if relief were proportional to the noise produced by the stream—not to mention other details about disheveled people or those with urgent calls from some other country.

To drink, he ordered a Heineken, because it was the first name that came to mind. He had condemned himself to another trip to the Loch Ness Monster. When the bartender brought him a second Heineken without him asking, he thought he'd received a revelation. A minor, trivial one, like everything, he thought. He had always believed existential crises happened at 33. Maybe because of tradition, because of encyclopedias. Buddha, Jesus, and all that. But now that people lived an exaggeration of time, perhaps he had the chance for a second existential crisis. Could it be called the crisis of 59, or of 60? 59 sounded better, more precise, more dramatic.

Little by little, over the years, the meaning of the phrase "The law is for those who work" had tilted from one side to the other. From the enthusiasm of his thirties, he thought, to the sarcasm of his fifties. From sarcasm to the acidity of lemon on an empty stomach. From self-confidence to the specter of frustration; from hatred for the poor to suspicion of the rich, as Jeff would have translated into his own language.

He thought of Jeff and laughed heartily. One less Heineken, one fewer colleague, and he wouldn't have laughed like that. The woman next to him tucked her blonde hair behind one ear and looked at him curiously, but she must have noticed in Facundo a predictable, reliable, normal man (shaven, with white teeth and a few grays at the temples, well-dressed, with those details only those in the know recognize) and didn't pay him much attention. Facundo posed no danger to her. She meant nothing to him, not even a possible three-minute conversation. She was a businesswoman, with a firm gaze, a strong jaw like Superman's, and a miniskirt that seemed to say "look-but-don't-mess-with-me-or-you'll-regret-it-you-son-of-a-b*tch-misogynist."

"The law is for those who work," he told himself once more, with the same ambiguous smile. For years, it had been exactly the same phrase, but who knows if experience or personal frustrations had gradually changed it from within. The pickpocket Jacksons waiting at subway entrances, on the corners of Manhattan, had given way to the Donald McCulouses he had come to know and admire on his travels—one of those pot-bellied old men who play golf and invest in Wall Street from their offices, with a glass of whisky in one hand and a young girl in the other. One of those slobbering old men who leave their secretaries with their young lovers on weekends to attend politicians' weddings with their wives. No matter how rich or powerful a man might be; his black-label needs would always be, like any poor wretch, like any slave, between his legs and on top of someone else.

In other circles, Facundo boasted about never having broken the law in any of the dozens of countries where he had worked. Which was strictly true, at least as far as he knew. For that very reason, for his honesty, for his impeccable morals, his boss appreciated him so much, and for that very reason (over time and with age, he began to suspect) his difficulties in entering the innermost circle had grown.

The innermost circle had been closed to him from the start, he thought. That's where the American dream ended and reality began. Approaching the innermost circle was like that unpleasant moment when the alarm clock goes off and you desperately need to keep sleeping. But the alarm rings anyway, and you rise to a territory where even the palest light hurts your eyes, and even last night's party turns into a heavy hangover, though you didn't drink a drop of alcohol. It's reality, no less absurd or more real than what you see with three beers in your system. But you learn to start each day and to dream awake, to forget and to restart faith in the absurd. The caffeine in your first morning coffee gradually loses its effectiveness, and you need more and more to return to seeing the world as you wanted to see it—which is to see the world as others want you to see it, in that monumental collective dream.

In the innermost circle, the world's big leagues play. The laws are also made for them, but in another sense, the opposite sense, for the simple reason that they are made by them. The laws are made for those below, he thought, here and there, before and now. In the same double sense. That's why they shouldn't be broken. Only the desperate poor and the accidentally rich corrupted themselves in that way, breaking the rules of the game. Only the corrupt and criminals didn't know how to play. The others played clean: they legislated. If a law didn't serve the interests of the world's owners, it was changed, period.

But the mere idea of having fallen into his greatest fear made him act quickly and without thinking too much. Worse than divorcing Elena was having his identity stolen. It wasn't about the money they had taken or could take from him, but about the legal trap that this kind of theft usually sets for its victims—a symbolic kidnapping with tentacles and consequences more unpredictable than a traditional kidnapping.

What sickened him, moreover, was the mere idea of losing control of his own person. Besides being kidnapped, it was like losing your mind. Somewhere in the world, someone was walking in his name, dressing and speaking in his name without the most powerful police force in the world being able to do anything about it.

In fact, that's exactly what happened. Two months after filing the report at the Palm Beach police department, the matter had not been resolved. The criminal hadn't shown up anywhere despite continuing to make small withdrawals in different parts of Baja California.

On the other other side

San Diego

HE ARRIVED IN SAN DIEGO at 2:15 PM. At the airport, he rented a cheap car and drove to Tijuana. He could have flown directly, but he was determined to defy, even in this modest and almost cowardly way, his effective common sense—the one he had always boasted about, that load of personal frustrations he had thrown so many times in the face of his most inefficient subordinates.

He entered the address of the hotel from the card he had found in his travel bag into the GPS. According to the navigator, always excessively optimistic, he would be in Tijuana in an hour.

Before leaving, he checked the messages on his phone. Jeff had sent him one of his usual YouTube links with motivational talks. He was going to ignore it, but almost by accident he swiped over the link, and the video started playing while he tried to clear the exit lane. He left the phone on the driver's seat and hurried out of the airport.

…so, what I had to make sure of was that those people would follow me, that they would follow the story we had to create together, and many times it fell to me, well, to quickly detect who would stay with me and who wouldn't. It didn't matter as much if they were the most capable or the least capable. The most capable, if they're not committed and don't follow, and aren't part of the communication, and aren't committed, they disappear…

At a still-red traffic light, he took a quick glance at his phone. In the video, a gray-haired man, perhaps in his fifties, like him, was giving a talk in what looked like a classroom, in front of a screen showing a PowerPoint.

…so, it's not written down, because I don't like to write it down, but… When I arrived in Venezuela, twenty directors and vice presidents flew out in the first week. It was a takeover, it was different…

For a moment, he thought it was Jeff himself speaking. The same voice, though with a certain Argentine accent, that of an internationalized Argentine, somewhat neutralized. He looked to make sure it wasn't him. No, it wasn't (he shouldn't bother congratulating him), but he resembled him in his gestures, his thinness, the way he dressed and moved in front of his audience, in that unmistakable, immeasurable self-esteem of the businessman who believes himself the alpha and omega of a prosperous and heroic world. A second before the red changed to green, he read below, in the title of the video, the speaker's name: "Talk 'The Role of the CEO' with Luis Malvido, new president of Aerolíneas Argentinas. 2,308 views. Marsellus Wallace. Published on Jul 31, 2018..."

Green and a honk. He threw the phone again, not having had time to turn it off.

...the company wasn't ours, it was Bell South's. But from there, everyone knew who was in charge... I always say, and I say it on other occasions, I'll say it here because there are few of us... In nature, this is what happens. When a young lion defeats the male lion, the first thing it does is kill all the cubs. And that happens in companies. And if it doesn't happen, it explodes. Because there will always be conspiracies behind the scenes that will make the story fall apart.

Facundo tries to grab the phone, but it slips and falls under the passenger seat. He's entered a highway and can't stop, like the CEO of Aerolíneas Argentinas.

...we're alone, no one is coming to save us, at least in the short term...

Another red. Facundo stops and stretches to grab his phone, but the seatbelt makes it difficult. He curses, stretches, but can't reach it.

...we have to save the company, we have to do these things right...

Green.

...think that in Argentina, at that time, it operated...

Another honk. Apparently, it was a custom in that part of the country.

There were several American companies, American or European, that disappeared overnight.

He made a last-minute maneuver and managed to get onto the I-5 South instead of taking the left exit that went north. Then a sign that announced ESCONDIDO ¼ MILES. For a moment, he regretted not renting a more powerful car. He had lost the habit of driving a Buick. CHULA VISTA 8.

...for me, that week when we let so many people go was brutal... that experience...

He managed to exit onto a detour and ended up in front of a building that was a massive block of concrete with no windows. He braked, almost violently, freed himself from the seatbelt, and threw himself toward the passenger seat as if chasing a small, slippery animal.

…some of you have had to… (said the slippery animal) make decisions, to fire friends, people who'd tell me, 'you can't do this to me…' People with whom we'd started the company from scratch… It was truly terrible. But it was a lesson. I think it made me harder…

Until he finally managed to grab the phone and turned it off.

Tijuana. La Aurora.

AT 4:10 PM, HE WAS IN TIJUANA and by 4:35, he arrived at the office of La Aurora. A small sign on the door said OFFICE, but inside it looked more like a tool storage area. A young woman with an indifferent smile greeted him without looking away from her computer screen.

"How may I help you?" she said. She had long, decorated nails and a dolphin tattooed on her shoulder.

"The usual," said Facundo.

The young woman looked at him for a moment, as if she didn't understand.

"Three nights," said Facundo, handing her his passport.

The young woman read:

"Mr. Walsh Ocampo…"

And said:

"Your name sounds familiar. But I'm new and don't know the regular clients… Let me look here for a moment…"

Facundo thought that this young woman wouldn't last three months there. But then he immediately realized it was a reflex thought. In Mexico, in a company not under his or Jeff's management, she wouldn't have lasted three months. Not one. She wouldn't even have been hired. A quick glance was enough. The years had refined his intuition for predicting the future through someone's effectiveness at doing something. He could smell it in a person drinking coffee at a table next to his in any Starbucks. But the girl had beautiful legs, and surely the little manager of that place would've considered this a plus.

Her nails were excessively long and painted in different colors. Too much time dedicated to nothing, he thought. It was a miracle she could type or use the cell phone within reach, on which something resembling a chat conversation stretched on by itself, without her being able to respond due to an inconvenient client.

On the side, on the reception counter, were the business cards, held by a small acrylic hand. He took one. Hotel La Aurora. The same little birds flying. Three. One smaller than the other. One farther away than the other. Below, right in the middle of the card, a thin horizontal line that must've represented the horizon of the sea. A piece of minimalist art, a miniature reproduced a hundred times with little value, zero, full of the past enthusiasm of a small businessman, probably defeated by now, taking a nap after a lunch washed down with two glasses of wine, likely his only great pleasure of the day and the rest of his days. Because not everyone can win in that game. Because almost no one wins. Not even the few who win.

He took a card. How the hell had he ended up there? He couldn't explain it. He pulled out his own, the company one, and compared them. The two cards were the same size. His didn't have little drawings, just his name, proud, above the great threat:

FACUNDO WALSH OCAMPO
SIMONS HAYYET GROUP.
CHIEF OPERATING OFFICER

It didn't have little drawings or a phone number or an email, to increase the anxiety of the potential client's search, to make them consider a handwritten number on the other side as a special opportunity to meet God and the angels. It had taken him too long to replace the first O in COO with an E. Maybe he would never manage it, though it was better to be COO of Simons Hayyet than CEO of La Aurora.

He laughed, and the secretary answered with a smile.

The card was exactly the same as the one he had in an inner pocket of his jacket. How could he not remember how and when he had ended up there the last time? It must be serious, he told himself, halfway between ironic and serious. Or not. No, it wasn't that bad. It didn't have to be, necessarily, a consequence—grave or fleeting—of his heart attack, or some form of early dementia written in his DNA (his mother had gotten lost one night on a dirty beach in Buenos Aires, and he in the blinding white heat of Tijuana). It was simply a consequence of the stress of his job, of the divorce, of the habit of forgetting what was irrelevant. In recent years, he had been in countries he no longer even remembered. How many times had he been to Singapore? He couldn't say. Had he ever been to Bangladesh? He didn't know, and it wasn't just recent. He remembered, perfectly, a dinner in Tucson, where the daughter of a businesswoman from Bangladesh had asked him if he knew Dhaka. He was sure he had been to Bangladesh at least twice, but he couldn't recall the name of its capital. Dhaka, the girl had told him, with her huge eyes and a brilliant white smile. But he didn't remember, neither the name of the city nor whether he had been to Dhaka, though he did remember landing in Bangladesh, like an insect settling on an open map, perhaps product of the endless and boring flight staring at the tiny screen on the seatback, the little plane advancing like a microbe, hour after hour, toward that point on the planet he had never dreamed of or wanted to know. He hadn't been there in transit but to resolve a minor conflict over the sale of cell phones with Banglalink. It must have been in 2010, because at the board meeting they had talked about Obama and the recovery of GM and the bailout of the banks, that whole "too big to fail" thing. "Capitalism for the poor and socialism for the rich" a man with dark skin and a white mustache had said. Why did he remember that face and those words as if he were seeing and hearing them now? He also remembered his concern, or rather, his concerned speech about the catastrophic effects of Global Warming in Bangladesh, a country that would

175

suffer especially, like no other (where had he gotten this fact?), the effects it hadn't caused. That damned Global Warming had been the responsibility of the rich and should be paid for by the poor, like the people of Bangladesh. He'd almost started to cry, and probably his shaky voice had had a positive effect on the board, which, in the end, signed the new contract, not because any of them were poor, but because they were moved by the national solidarity of someone who had come from above, from the United States, like Hernán Cortes descending from heaven to save Mexico. He remembered this perfectly, because it had been one of those heroic operations where one is capable of passionately defending an idea without believing a single word of it, all for the purpose of pleasing an audience that had to decide whether or not to sign the cell phone deal. Maybe the joke of the man who looked like a photo negative had triggered the silent alarms that revealed to him he was facing a leftist in a high capitalist position. There are people who don't adapt to their roles, like a soldier who keeps pulling the trigger, even though he hates the war he's been sent to. That finely tuned nose for detecting ideological, sexual, religious preferences, sensitivities of all kinds, had earned him millions, because it wasn't true that in business everything is reduced to adding and subtracting. But he couldn't remember absolutely anything else. Not then, in Tucson, and not now. It wasn't strange. He often woke up at night in a hotel bed without knowing if he was in Vietnam, or Los Angeles, Tokyo or Buenos Aires. It had almost become a habit, yet he still couldn't get used to it and would feel the anguish, always new, renewed, that he had felt as a child when he despaired in the black of night not knowing where the window of his bedroom was. His memory could organize years and periods according to the most important business deals, but it couldn't retain all the airports, the hotels, the countries, the men and women he'd met to achieve his goals. Therefore, it was logical that he would remember the goals, not the means.

He woke up the glowing insect in his hand, always waiting to be caressed to open its thousand bright eyes. There were no urgent messages, as if suddenly the company had decided to understand that he was on medical leave. He typed the name of the CEO from the video he'd been listening to since he left San Diego. He was supposed to know him. Google News. He typed: luis mal…

Luis Madito
Luis Malvida
Luis Malvivido

He deleted. Delete Delete Delete Delete Delete Delete. He corrected: Luis Maldivo, CEO. He found something from July 2018.

Aerolíneas Argentinas announced this afternoon that it has appointed Eng. Luis Malvido as the new president of the company, replacing Eng. Mario Dell'Acqua, whose departure from the position had been anticipated for several weeks (though he will remain on the board).

"Which cabin would you prefer?" said the receptionist, pointing to a diagram on the wall. "We have several available."

"The same one as last time" said Facundo.

According to the statement, Malvido is "a global senior executive with over 25 years of experience in top management, 16 of them as CEO in 4 different countries: Argentina, Venezuela, Brazil, and the Czech Republic," having led "various aspects of the business: launching new companies, fast-growing firms, mergers and acquisitions, crisis management, and transformation and digitalization programs."

The executive graduated with a degree in Industrial Engineering from the Buenos Aires Institute of Technology (ITBA), having completed his academic training with postgraduate studies at IESE in Madrid, IDEA, and the same ITBA.

"Don't you remember which one you took last time?

Suddenly, he understood why that young woman seemed familiar. Undoubtedly, despite those masks (the nails, the hair dyed multiple colors, the tattoo on her shoulder), she resembled Elena in some way, the Elena he had met thirty years ago. The gaze, maybe the shape of her face and the fullness of her lips when she smiled. The thick upper lip, that sensual detail that almost all blondes from the north lack, as if they were all descendants of a woman who emigrated from England four centuries ago because no one desired her for her nonexistent upper lip, perhaps a reflection of her clitoris and her minimal sexual desire, but who managed to sell her agony as religious persecution against the Puritans in the old continent. Or didn't Ernesto say that the idea that the Puritans came to America seeking religious freedom was a cheap, easy myth to sell, like so many others? Similar stories would explain why the women of Puerto Rico, or Cuba, or Venezuela all resemble each other, as if they were all sisters within their own countries. The undeniable Niurka Marcos of Cuba (when they're not Black), the Barbara Bermudos of Puerto Rico, the Rodner Figueroas of Venezuela, the sweet Yuri of Maldita Primavera, when they're not La Chilindrina or La India María… Who, by the way, Ernesto said, judging by their tiny noses, something neither common among Indigenous women nor Spanish women, all had the same immigrant grandmother, who perhaps one day got tired of being called flat-nosed in some town in Granada, or maybe won the heart of a poor captain in Galicia, the one who allowed her to cross the Atlantic for free among only men for two or three months…

"Did you hear me?" asked the receptionist.

"Yes" replied Facundo, "but I don't remember. Can you check the system?"

"No, what system" she laughed. "We don't have any system here. But let me look at the records…"

Facundo thought that if he had been born forty years later, he would have been diagnosed with Attention Deficit Hyperactivity Disorder. Luckily, back then they didn't know so much, and no one bothered you with so many fears about the future, more fears about failure than about death. At least, thanks to hyperactivity, he had become the successful businessman he was…

"Yes, here it is" said the receptionist. "Mr. Walsh Ocampo. Cabin 28. Why did they call you mister?"

Not in something. She looked a lot like Elena. But not the Elena who a few days ago had scolded him over the phone for never having helped Alexa, as she deserved, for not having made her happy in bed, as Elena herself deserved, but the Elena from many years ago, from those years when she smiled at anything and it was a complete smile, maybe acted, but more authentic. Young people are always more authentic when they're figuring out who they are and they act and try on characters like they try on clothes. Then they tire, with success comes the inevitable defeat, disappointment, they become corrupted and can no longer dream but only try to keep doing what they learned to do so well and no longer care about. That's why they go around looking for problems that raise their pulse, that revive their wrinkled heart with some love affair that starts as a game to boost their self-esteem and ends up in bed and in a divorce. That Elena smiled with her whole mouth, with her eyes, with her hands, with her shoulders, with her entire body.

"Cabin 28…" repeated the receptionist, this time with a tinge of annoyance.

People get irritated by others' distractions, never by their own.

"That one" Facundo pretended to confirm.

"Here's the key" she said, now in an officious tone, pointing to the diagram on the wall. "Up to the right, the second-to-last one before the beach…"

The receptionist suddenly seemed to catch herself. She looked at him for a second and said:

"...Yes, now I remember... You travel a lot. That's why you never know where you were the previous month, right? Do you remember me? I'm sure you don't... I'm Elysa."

"Yes... "Facundo lied, trying to say something without saying anything. "Elysa. You were reading a book..."

"I was studying for a sociology exam. I couldn't retain anything. Like you. I failed and quit. It wasn't for me.

"Well, that's too bad."

"No, not too bad or anything. It's better that way. There's nothing worse than wasting time on something that's not for you... Yes, you were here last year, now I remember clearly... October 15, to be exact. It was your wedding anniversary, but you were on a business trip. Surely everything went well for you, because special dates have a special energy. If the anniversary is good, things turn out well, and if it's bad, you know how it goes. Do you believe in the secret of numbers?

October 15 wasn't his wedding anniversary.

"I think I don't believe..." said Facundo.

"In the order of the Cosmos?"

"There must be something… In summer, based on the sun's position, you start sweating and complaining about the heat."

"And my grandmother would always look at the moon to know if the chicks were going to hatch… If you start thinking about it, you'll end up believing. When you have some free time, I'll read your cards.

"What's that about reading the cards?" he asked. "A stressed-out mailman?"

That irony, so Argentine, so unbearable for those who aren't Argentine. Elena had never understood it and, over the years, it ended up affecting her. The Silvannas would have understood it after some time of input. They were programmed, not just to learn from that strange flesh-and-blood being, but to understand him and make him understand himself. The Silvannas will, someday, be a mirror of the human interior. Just as we look in the mirror to see if we have dark circles or need a shave, in the same way we'll converse with a Silvanna to find out who we are and what we're feeling. It was only a matter of time. He hadn't understood that about not valuing Elena as she deserved. Had she been the one who had changed so much? Or had it been him? (A question for Silvanna.) Well, we all change over the years, but there are obscene changes. Or, let's say, radical changes, like

183

changing sex or country, religion or ideology, he thought. Changing soccer teams wasn't possible. He had changed, a lot. He had changed to meet Elena's demands. He said fewer obscenities, stopped making sexist jokes, was there to listen and take the car in for service when she asked, had stopped watching Boca-River matches or watched the goals the next day in his office. He had changed in many other ways, for her, for Elena, though perhaps he never fully understood to what extent those changes were fair and reasonable.

"Not exactly" said the young woman. "It's called Tarot. A neighbor who knows a lot about it taught me. Actually, I'm still learning, so I'm not infallible..."

An undefined silence, just those two seconds when two gazes meet and get stuck for two long seconds, without either of them ever figuring out what it means. Immediately, she continued:

"Do you know why I remember it was your anniversary? Because it was my first day on the job. My first paid job. I'll never forget. I don't know what it means, but for now, I haven't forgotten that day."

No, Elena and those superstitions had nothing to do with it. But still, the receptionist had something of Elena in her, of the Elena in her twenties, or at least that's what he thought he saw. The joy, the naivety of believing in things like tarot? He couldn't tell. Lucy? Yes, a bit of Lucy too. Lucy, the robot from Seoul.

She stopped abruptly. She looked at him strangely, as if she had discovered something, and said:

"Now that you mention it, I clearly remember you asked me to read your palm the last time you were here…

"Me?"

"Yes, of course. You don't remember that either. But don't worry. In the end, you didn't have time, because you're always rushing from one place to another, busy, solving important things."

Facundo remembered that moment, but it hadn't happened in Tijuana. A young woman in Spain, in Malaga, very similar to the receptionist, had read his palms in the hotel's breakfast room.

"They're supposed to be important things" said Facundo.

"But they're not" she said, categorically.

"How do you know?"

That young woman could very well be the one who had taken his information. Obviously, she knew his credit card number, his address in Florida, and who knows what other data might have been circulating on the internet at that moment. Had he mentioned his birthdate in some Business Today interview or on some other site? In reality, there must have been hundreds of people who had acquired that same information. Every time he paid for something, a lunch at a restaurant and the waitress took his card, she could easily copy the name, number, and security code. If she didn't do it, it was because... Who knows why.

"You told me yourself" said Elysa. "Of course, those are things one says when they're tired."

"It's true, I did tell you myself. But it wasn't here."

"No, it wasn't here. It was over there, at the little table outside. Do you still drink so much coffee?"

"Not so much."

"In the end, did you manage to convince Hyundai to buy your batteries?"

"Yes, yes. It was tough, but it was worth it."

"But you weren't convinced..."

"What do you mean?"

"If I remember correctly, you were hoping they'd say no, just so you could tell them all to go to hell."

Eloísa laughed heartily.

"Those are the things one says with one beer too man" said Facundo, to prolong Eloísa's laughter."

"With one beer too many and with company that isn't very serious" she said. "It's true, coffee and beer… Do you still mix those things? It's not good. It's like accelerating with the brakes on."

"What do you mean by company that isn't very serious?"

"Me" said Eloísa, becoming serious.

"I don't understand" said Facundo, just to extract more information from the girl.

"People don't take me seriously. Much less a successful businessman like you, Mr. Walsh Ocampo."

Facundo said nothing.

"Well, it's not your problem" she said, in a sudden attack of prudence. "Here's the key."

Facundo thanked her. She reminded him that she would read his palms whenever he wanted, and he said anytime.

Somewhere, over the Rainbow

FINDING CABIN 28. The numbers didn't follow any sequence. After four came nine, then twenty. There weren't many little cabins on either side of the dirt path, and they were all irregularly distributed down to the shore. By chance, or pure intuition (the kind that distinguishes a true businessman from the failures who live off the State), he headed toward 28. Not the cabin closest to the beach, but a more discreet one. That was cabin 28.

The beach and the hill reminded him of his summers in Argentina. In reality, what one calls intuition is nothing but memories of a previous life. Though the sea wasn't as green, nor were the hills so high. San Clemente and Tijuana had nothing in common. Absolutely nothing.

Apparently.

He put the key in, trying to recall that gesture from a past time, his own or someone else's, in a forced déjà vu, without success. Nothing. He only felt the fatigue of the trip, the weight of the suitcases, the uncomfortable memory of having lost his phone in Atlanta. In reality, it had no value, no one could access his personal data, not even his damn doppelganger, because he had changed the security codes several days before. It only bothered him to think that someone might find it and recycle it. What bothered him more, though unlikely, was the idea that some idiot had stolen it in a moment of distraction. Yes, this was what bothered him deep down: the fact that someone had mocked him and was now taking advantage of the theft, even if it was something as small and worthless as a mobile phone. He could never forget the bike that was stolen from him when he was thirteen. Foolish, weak-willed, idiot—he lent it to anyone who asked until one day it was gone when he left high school, the secundaria, el colegio, or whatever the hell they called it back then in Argentina. Today he could buy all the bikes he wanted, modern ones, retro ones, computerized ones, with cameras and GPS, with NASA and Pentagon technology. He could buy any and as many as he wanted of those hanging in the window at Walmart, Costco, Academy Sports & Outdoors, and any other warehouse of unused trash, and none of them could make him forget the one that was stolen. Back then, and for a long time afterward, he wished death upon the thief, or something worse—some permanent disability as a result of a fall while riding that ill-gotten bike.

But when he entered the cabin, he felt as though he was stepping into his grandparents' house in Argentina, a few years after the death of his grandfather Ramón, when his parents had emptied it and began using it during their summer vacations. The connection between that house in San Clemente and Cabin 28 was impossible. They had nothing in common. Or perhaps they did. In both, the sea was nearby, though they were completely different seas. If two seas can even be different based on their colors and some

189

other superficial attribute. Maybe the smell, yes, especially the smell of an empty house, was more or less the same.

He stood by the entrance door for a long while, unable to decide whether to set the suitcases down. Then he thought that all that childhood dust was rather capricious and offered nothing to his investigation. Distractions, more like.

He heard his phone alert him to a new message.

He set the suitcases on the floor, forgot to close the entrance door, and went to the bathroom to wash his hands. Then he began to explore the cabin, careful not to move anything out of place. He looked at himself in the mirror. The fatigue of the trip was evident in the beard that had started to grow. He noticed several white spots. He was surprised by how much gray there was—much more than in his hair. He hadn't noticed before, perhaps because he shaved systematically every day at 5:30 AM, and when he traveled to Asia or the Southern Cone, he never had time to look at himself closely in the mirror. Or he'd look but wouldn't notice the details, because there was always something truly important to address. Or because it was easier to dye his hair slightly and trim his ears to appear neat and meticulously groomed in the eyes of his clients. A few extra hairs in the ear canal, a bad shave, two or three dandruff flakes on the lapel of his jacket could mean fifty or a hundred thousand dollars less. Big deals aren't made so much on mathematical calculations but on impressions, on a certain sensitivity to the trust or mistrust in a product, that adopted child that always depends on the seller. Money is very sensitive.

But now it was he himself looking in the mirror, not his clients. It was he himself discovering those gray spots in his shaved beard, something that had been there for a long time, perhaps for years. Something that had been growing unnoticed, like life, like death, like those wrinkles at the corners of his eyes. He still hadn't reached ten million, that rather arbitrary number that had helped him become a millionaire almost from nothing. His father used to say that those who aim for 'real' don't even reach 'medio.' He didn't know what 'real' meant or what 'medio' was, and neither did his father, but he understood the saying perfectly. Someone in Uruguay once told him that 'medio' was a one-real coin that cowboys would split in two with a knife when they didn't have change.

Another message. He was starting to feel anxious.

Facundo hadn't reached ten million yet, but he was very close. Even Elena didn't know. His first

191

million, the only one that had given him some happiness, had cost him more, almost twenty years, counting since he was twenty-five, the moment he graduated from the University of Pennsylvania and began working at Manners Co. That was at forty-five, when he managed to place the customer tracking program at Macy's. After that, it was easier. Once you've learned to dance with money, every move becomes easier. You dance with your eyes closed. You can make small innovations, but they're more like variations on what you already know how to do and do better every time. Besides, once you have money, you set the terms. The next nine million came easier (he thought and repeated to himself three times while looking in the mirror), but none brought him that almost intoxicating joy of the first million. The first million was like the first kiss, like the first flattering note in the Wall Street Journal. At some point, he came to think that every business, every deal, life itself—from a worm to a man—follows the bell curve of Gauss. The good thing about money is that you can always keep accumulating, even when energy, luck, and individual skill are in decline. That was a great advantage of being in business instead of being a professional footballer or model. Money also ages due to inflation, but it reproduces thanks to interest and its own nature.

In that very moment, he thought, at the same time he was looking at himself in an unfamiliar mirror, he might have already reached ten million and didn't even know it. Anyway, he had no way of verifying it, and he didn't care either. That morning he had lost his phone in Atlanta. He couldn't ask the receptionist about the Dow Jones. He'd find out tomorrow or the day after. It didn't matter. What was he going to do next? Probably the same thing he had been doing up until then. The only thing he knew how to do. Convince people of the benefits of investing fortunes in a technological change that was likely to last less than five years. Convince others that the standard of living of every person walking near him and beyond was due to restless entrepreneurs like him. Convince himself that all of it had value and meaning beyond the obvious.

But now he was there, staring at himself in a blurry mirror like an idiot. It wasn't just his face he was seeing. Suddenly, he felt a sense of discomfort. He was 59 years old. He wasn't that old. What nauseated him was thinking that his parents and grandparents had died at 69 and 75. Of course, life expectancy had been increasing. In the United States, it was 79.

Either way, he thought, that gave him about twenty more years. When he was twenty, imagining himself at forty was like picturing the StarChip probe reaching Alpha Centauri. He had read about this interesting project at the nice airport in Berlin. A normal probe would take thirty thousand years to get there, but the idea was to propel it to ten percent of the speed of light, so it could arrive in just forty years. Once on that planet so similar to Earth, the tiny spacecraft could send images that would reach Earth in four years. If they managed to gather a hundred million dollars, the microprobe could launch within twenty years. *20 + 40 + 4 = 64*, he thought.

But from the height of 55, twenty more years was a different story. It was something you could see right there, almost within reach. Half his life had passed, and he hadn't even noticed that detail.

He rinsed his face with plenty of water and said, "Shit." As he dried himself, he repeated, "Screw it all," and chased away the last ruminations like someone swatting away an insect or shaking off the memory of an unpleasant dream.

The loss or theft of his phone was insignificant compared to identity theft. But at that moment, he needed his phone more than his identity. Why did even the slightest hint of being robbed make him so sick? It wasn't the theft of something specific, but the nauseating feeling of having been deceived. That sensation that explains, or at least gives an idea of why or how, one day, a calm man with no history of violence shoots three times at his wife and her lover.

Facundo left the bathroom and let himself fall onto a wicker armchair that creaked as it received him. He stared out the window. It was dusk. A group of children ran toward the beach. He had also lied to Laura. He had a bank account she didn't know about. The deep love he had for her had never been enough to trust her with everything. In some corner of his heart, his liver, or his intestines, lingered the eternal vestiges of distrust—not so much in her, but in the future. Time changes everything, and he couldn't know to what extent it would change her, or even him. For some reason he didn't want to clarify, he trusted money more. He had kept that Citibank account from his bachelor years, from his time at the University of Pennsylvania, and he had never told her. At first, it had been passed off as forgetfulness, a deliberate oversight. That had been another way of lying, even if it was, let's say (he thought), a fourth or fifth-category lie. Who knows. Just in case, he wasn't going to reveal everything to that beautiful, sweet girl he had only just begun to know. Then, by the time he got to know her better, too much time had passed, and he preferred to leave things as they were, in the shadows, adhering to the idea that it's better not to explain because it only complicates things. After all, it wasn't a big secret, and he could close it at any moment. He could even forget it, because losing a few thousand dollars is always cheaper than ruining your life with demands and explanations. But after several years, especially when that beautiful and sweet girl had become his wife—his passionate lover first, and then a demanding and rather indifferent woman—that's when he started using that old Citibank account again. Not to cover the urgent needs of the early years of a marriage marked by financial struggles, but to deposit the checks clients had begun issuing him for special favors or in gratitude for preferential treatment in a sale or the awarding of a bid. Again, adhering to the idea that it's better not to explain because it only complicates things.

That, too, was lying, which, when money is involved, is another form of stealing, isn't it? Facundo wondered. Immediately, he remembered the man without a coat who had approached his car in the Publix parking lot in West Palm Beach, the afternoon before his trip to Tijuana. When he saw him approaching with a Bible in hand, he put the car in drive to leave, but before he could move, the man was already smiling at him from the other side of the window. He didn't want to be rude by leaving him standing there, so he rolled down the window to tell him that he didn't have cash. He usually said that. He didn't use cash. It was almost true. He knew that many of those beggars in the richest country on the planet only asked for money to cover what the government couldn't—drugs, alcohol, and who knows what other vices. But this time, before the window finished rolling down, the man told him in four seconds that he was on the street with his family, hadn't eaten in five days, and had no way to pay for a hotel. He spoke English like a foreigner, which gave some credibility to his story. He looked Arab, Turkish, maybe a Muslim from one of those unpronounceable countries. Kazakhstan, Uzbekistan, Tajikistan, one of those countries that no one knows—Pakistan, lost in an equally unknown, increasingly hostile country. The Bible must have been a tool, because if he'd been carrying a Quran, they would probably have told him to go back to his shitty country and his whore culture with his terrorist god, who likely was the same god as the one worshipped by believers with money. Who knew? But he immediately realized that if he left the man standing there, the damn feeling of guilt—the

197

one that makes the most capable, the most successful, submit to the losers in the struggle for existence, even though they're the ones responsible for the success of a society—would haunt him. If he didn't give him a couple of dollars, the damn guilt would chase him for the rest of the day. At best, for a single day. Didn't he pay his taxes? Wasn't it enough with everything the government took from him every day, every month, every year? He pulled the damn face of the racist Andrew Jackson from his wallet and handed it to the supposed father and husband, a helpless man. The man thanked him as if Jesus or Muhammad had descended from heaven. Twenty damn dollars.

With twenty damn dollars, he had paid for the right not to feel guilty. With the twenty or fifty dollars he donated monthly to the children with cancer at Saint Jude, he usually paid for the same thing. When he left the parking lot of the supposed begging father (like José, lost and undersold in a strange country), he thought about the twenty dollars. Had he thrown away twenty dollars on a drug addict? For him, it was nothing, but for some reason, giving it to someone without any obligation bothered him almost as much as the guilt he had just avoided with the same insignificant act. After half an hour of driving toward the hotel, he was still thinking the same thing. Maybe, deep down, even if it was very deep down, he wasn't as good a person as he assumed without thinking too much, as everyone assumes, as no one thinks too much. Where had he gotten the idea that he was a good person? Was not having gone to jail, not having ever hit a woman, not having taken dirty or clean money to break some rule or fundamental ethical value enough? Does clean money even exist? Surely not, he told himself, exaggerating a self-destructive feeling that had suddenly overtaken him.

Even though he didn't fully believe what he was telling himself, just saying it raised more than a few questions. There was a reason his mother always made him wash his hands every time he touched money. Money is dirty by nature, but we can't do without it, just as we can't avoid defecating in the room of the most luxurious hotel.

That day, he remembered, he had stopped at a red light, right behind a Lexus LS 460, probably from 2010. Henry Rodríguez, the company's best salesman, had bought one of those in 2012 or 2013. He had paid 42,000 dollars, even though he had assured him it wasn't worth 35,000 dollars. That is, Facundo thought, the Lexus dealer had literally robbed him of seven thousand dollars right off the bat. The company's best salesman had let himself be robbed of seven thousand dollars right off the bat. But Henry didn't care. He was thrilled with the Lexus 460. That same day or the day he found out, Facundo took note, as a good student of buyer psychology that he was. In reality, the robbery of Henry was something that happened every day. A girl spends all her savings on ripped jeans. She pays a hundred or two hundred dollars when the same pants will be sold a month later for ten dollars in a liquidation store like Dillards. If the victim is objectively informed of the robbery, they probably won't care too much. Those are the rules of the game. That's how the world works. He told Henry, translating it all into the language of conclusions: You let yourself be robbed like a sucker, he told him. Henry smiled. Maybe he knew he had made a bad deal, but these things happen. He, too, had fallen into similar situations without any of them keeping him up at night. Maybe the Indians had made a good deal by trading some mirrors for gold necklaces. Pure and simple market logic. Benefit for both parties. They had plenty of gold. Mirrors, not so much. It's what we all do. A good deal is when one benefits without caring if the other got more. Well, at least in the short term. Yes, we know what happened to the Indians afterward, but I'm not in this world to save humanity in a hundred years, but to solve problems in the short term, say five or ten years max. A hundred dollars, two hundred, seven thousand thrown out the window... Business, it's the market, I had an urge, these things happen...

But twenty quick dollars, given without obligation to a man who had nothing to eat, had caused him considerable existential doubt.

(Another message. The sound indicated it was urgent.)

Had he been here before?

HE PULLED THE LYSOL SPRAY out of his suitcase and disinfected the faucets, the toilet lid and rim, the TV remote, the sheets, and the pillows, even though they were the only things that seemed clean. Maybe he had been lucky, and the sheets had been changed just the day before. The kitchen still showed traces of food, some forgotten noodles on the counter, an unwashed wine glass stored in the cupboard, a piece of paper with a list of four things to buy.

He didn't know when or why he had become so obsessive about cleanliness. When he was a student, he stayed in the cheapest hotels and would never have thought to sanitize even the toilet. He would fall, exhausted, into bed, between sheets that had probably been used by several people before, to sleep or have sex, and he would sleep deeply, like an angel, while his antibodies battled tirelessly, cell by cell, gaining and losing ground, all of which translated into some minor allergy, an annoying flu, or some other minor ailment that he later attributed to the mere condition of being alive or a little underdressed. He didn't remember ever getting sick from a contagion. Maybe he had been lucky, like when he was eighteen, in a dark park, he kissed a classmate from high school for an hour—a girl he barely knew and whose last name he couldn't even remember now. Just a name. Or a nickname. Marucha. Isn't that what everyone does? Isn't that what humanity has been doing for hundreds of thousands of years? Desire is stronger than reason, and if it were up to reason, humanity wouldn't even exist. The odds of catching an incurable herpes, or something worse, had been growing over the years, in the same proportion as his luck. At twenty-two, he let his boss kiss him, a woman who wasn't entirely ugly and still in her thirties. Hanna, a blonde German with very thin lips, like the lips of Yankee blondes, the wife of an arrogant Cuban man, Black, but with a lot of money, as he defined himself when he'd had too much to drink. Hanna had no sensual attributes apart from her gaze and her evident sexual needs. A woman's sensuality lies in her intentions, he thought. Do they see us the same way, or just the opposite? At twenty-seven, he met Elena. He didn't ask for any history of past boyfriends before passionately kissing her. Elena hadn't been a promiscuous woman, but about her two or three previous boyfriends, he could say nothing. Young men like him who must have kissed and slept with women who in turn kissed and slept with other men, who in turn... and so on in a long, incalculable chain that reminded him of the Six Degrees of Separation: we are all connected to every inhabitant of this planet in a scandalous proximity. When it comes to viruses and germs, kissing one woman is like kissing millions of other women and men.

He shook his head in disgust and tried to think of something else. But he returned to that minor thought that prevented him from focusing on what was important. Maybe there was no way to catch anything serious just by sleeping in someone else's sheets or drinking from an unwashed or poorly washed glass, he thought, as is the norm in any restaurant. He knew perfectly well that all of that had become a small obsession, not unfounded, but utterly impractical. A battle lost from the start that didn't stop him from feeling disgust just imagining unknown men and women exhaling or dripping fluids over the sheets, over the unwashed pillows.

Without a doubt, it was a quirk he had developed over time, and it wasn't so common, even if it was reasonable, he thought. When, innocently, he mentioned it to his colleagues during an end-of-year meeting at the manager's house, everyone was surprised. Apparently, no one took so many precautions, or they had lied to him. Which also didn't make much sense. What surprised him the most was Ana Laura's surprise.

"I've never heard anything like it," she said.

"Well, but it makes sense," he replied. "If you pay attention, you'll see that the sheets we find every time we check into a room haven't been changed. They look clean, and because they look clean, they don't change them."

"How do you know that?"

"There are several studies that prove it."

"I hope it's a study from a reputable university," said the pedantic Alberto, standing behind him and holding a champagne glass against his chest, "because nowadays they bombard you with that 'a recent study has shown,' and then it turns out no one knows who, when, or how the so-called study was done. My grandma used to say, 'that's what they say,' and no one asked her who exactly said it or why. Now, it's a bit more sophisticated. Instead of 'they say,' they say 'a study…'"

"Well," said Ana Laura, "in any case, it's not that big of a deal. Don't you think?"

"No, I don't think so," Facundo replied. "Would you get into a bed where you knew someone else slept the night before?"

"If I knew… I think not," she said, "but it wouldn't harm me either."

Ana Laura wasn't just a model, one of those Barbies blessed by nature or by the current culture, who had probably achieved many things thanks to beauty (what some ads call "good presence"). She also always looked impeccable. He would have sworn that, at least on that topic, she was even more obsessive than he was. Which also didn't make any sense. Wasn't there an entire pornographic industry based on women who are recruited for their beauty and angelic looks to swallow the member of a man who, in turn, wasn't exactly recruited for his good looks (since in those cases, the man never shows his face) but for the extra-large dimensions of his penis? Sure, sure, yes, that whole thing about patriarchy and macho values. But hadn't he read in The Economist from May 25, 2017, that, according to Big Data, it is mostly women who consume violent pornography against women? The women who consume this stuff double the number of men. The title of the article had caught his attention: "Everybody Lies." Everyone lies. Not long after, he ordered the book on Amazon. It arrived the next day. That night, he read a chapter, the one about women. He never opened it again.

He boiled water for coffee. At least the stove worked.

Was all that polish and hygienic care from Ana Laura (he thought) just a facade? Like the perfect makeup on her perfect eyes. Like the rouge on her lips, which said nothing about her passionate carelessness. The only clear thing from that end-of-year meeting was that only he took the precautions of sanitizing everything when entering a hotel room or a cabin. Two things, because the other was that this irresistible habit had appeared at some point in his adulthood, probably shortly after turning forty.

The death of Gordo Gasper

HE HAD NO CHOICE BUT TO CHECK his phone and read the messages. It was better than letting a part of his brain keep wondering for the rest of the day who it could be. He had four missed calls and five email messages. Not much, thankfully. Three were from clients. The last one was from Jeff, asking him to get in touch, to call him, that they needed to discuss something very serious. He had written "discuss," not "talk," though maybe he had said it in his Spanglish way, so the word had to be softened a bit.

As was his habit, unless it was an emergency or a deal about to be lost within hours, he left it to respond later. First, he needed to figure out what could be so serious. He suspected it. Maybe Jeff would write again giving him some clue, and he would lie that he had been traveling and had just landed at some airport in the middle of nowhere, to really rest, to recover from his heart attack, as Jeff well knew.

But Jeff didn't write again. Silvanna did. Another brief message:

"Where in the world are you? Did you see the news?"

He opened the usual portals:

Fox News: 'Trump baby' blimp gets OK to fly over London during Trump's visit.

BBC: Thailand cave rescue: Ex-navy diver dies on oxygen supply mission.

Lad Bible: Brazil Are Out of The World Cup Following Loss to Belgium.

He spent at least half an hour searching and re-searching the news channels in English and Spanish and found nothing that caught his attention.

He got up, looked out the window, and immediately returned to his phone. He searched Google News for news related to the company. "Simons Hayyet" in quotes. There was a list of news about the company, none of which he hadn't already seen on Google Alerts. The most recent was from July 3.

Finally (he would say by chance, but he knew that in the world of algorithms nothing is truly random) he found a note from the student newspaper of the University of Georgia that mentioned the strange case of THE KILLER DOLL, the murderous doll. It was also no coincidence that the headline, more fitting for horror movies of the past century, had caught his attention. According to the student, the author of the article, a well-known CEO from Atlanta with the initials L. G. had been killed by a doll he had invited to his home for a party. The writer of the article clarified that the information was not a parody in the style of The Onion, but had been confirmed by a reliable source, protected under journalistic privilege. They could only reveal that the source was none other than the father of one of the institution's students.

Probably the kid, aspiring to be a journalist or something similar, had picked up this information at one of the many barbecues students have on Saturday nights on campus, even though there shouldn't have been many left in the summer, except for some international students and other REM fans at the taverns in the town center, who are still losing their religion. Or the information had come from one of those Greek fraternities where beer and the most important secrets of future success flow. In any case, Facundo connected the dots from the very beginning of the article, from the headline. L.G. could be the initials of Leonard Gasper, the "fat man." According to the note, the doll, a stunning blonde, had sucked her lover's tongue at the moment of orgasm, suffocating him (unofficially confirmed information). However, the killer could not be tried or judged by any court (though she might receive summary extinction) due to her condition of being non-human, or not entirely human, which is why the unfortunate death had been classified as an accident. The aspiring journalist closed his note, entirely frivolous as things tend to be at that age, with a quote from Queen: "Too much love will kill you, in the end." Then, as an inevitable formality, the formal regret: We lift our prayers for the recently departed in such an unfortunate event.

He didn't dare respond to Silvanna. He searched for Leonard Gasper's name, limiting the results to the past week, and was able to confirm, through an obituary in the Atlanta News and a very flattering note in Business Today, that "Fat Leonard" had died, exactly on July 4, likely at night, while fireworks celebrated the 242nd anniversary of America.

He signed in his company email,

fwalshocampo@shc.com

A few days earlier, a message had circulated mourning the loss of the president who had led the America South section of Simons Hayyet Corporation to nearly double profits during the 2007-2017 period. Following this, the candidates to replace him were listed:

Mr. Bill Crawford (CEO Alabama)
Dr. Benito Pain (CEO Georgia)
Mr. Jeff Al Ferro (CEO Florida)
Mr. Donald Sucker (CEO South Carolina)

The list didn't surprise him. The candidate from Georgia was a placeholder. He had no chance. It was said that no one could explain how he had gotten to where he was. Not because he was bad at managing the Georgia section, but because his past condemned him. He had a doctorate in Human Resources. It wasn't a Ph.D., the mark of a researcher, one of those rats who waste their lives in labs and university librar-ies, but a Doctor of Business from Liberty University, something entirely removed from any hint of intel-lectuality and very close to the Real World. But a de-gree was a degree, and though Dr. Pain had at some point tried to sign his messages as Mr. instead of Dr., by then everyone already knew him that way. The board members hated people with academic titles a thousand times more than they hated people with no-ble titles. They might praise him throughout the meeting, but in the end, they would never vote for him.

Obviously, the finalists would be Jeff and Donald Sucker. Either of them could win. A few months ago, he would have hoped it wasn't Jeff. Now, he almost preferred to know that Jeff wasn't voted for. Or it all seemed mysteriously indifferent to him, as if, sud-denly, he had taken seriously the idea that he didn't have much time left to live or, worse, as if he had re-alized that none of it had been worth it.

He imagined the moment when the fat man Gasper had taken his last breath. The Silvannas had been provided with enough physical strength to sup-port and balance a two-hundred-pound man on their backs. Although they still couldn't walk naturally, they could replicate almost any movement in bed.

211

Besides their intellectual abilities, such as interacting and learning about the psychological and physical needs of their owner, they could take hold of him with their legs and arms for an experience that someone on the Kuala Lumpur board had called Augmented Reality.

What if he just said screw it all?

WHAT IF HE WROTE WHAT was happening to him, in case, soon enough, he could no longer remember the simplest things? He sat down at the laptop and began to write, at first with hesitation, then with sudden enthusiasm:

He glanced through the window at the profile of a very obese man heading to the beach...

No, the man wasn't heading through the window.

(Triple click. Delete)

He glanced through the window at the profile of a very obese man heading to the beach...

(Triple click. Delete)

Through the window, he saw the profile of a very obese man heading to the beach...

(Triple click. Delete)

212

He abandoned the project before finishing the first sentence. He got up and paced impatiently through the living room, which was beginning to sink into shadows. Then, he glanced through the window at the profile of a very obese man heading to the beach, in no hurry, a small guitar in his hand. His long hair, disheveled. He imagined him playing soccer, trying to defecate in a standard toilet (like the one he had just disinfected), trying to clean his anus hidden between his enormous buttocks, making love or attempting to with a woman as obese as he was, playing a small guitar, a ukulele, with his large and delicate hands. He looked like IZ, the Hawaiian singer of Somewhere Over the Rainbow. That man trapped in an enormous body, made ashes scattered to the sea twenty years ago, amid cheers from his followers, from whom that song as light as a feather persisted, like the fossil of a seashell that doesn't survive but overexists for an exaggerated amount of time.

For some reason, the smiling face of Ana Laura came to mind, as vivid as those images of things, of people, of animals that form before your eyes when you're falling asleep, exhausted, or stressed. At some point, he had learned (with disappointment, envy, or who knows what) that Ana Laura, Jeff's new secretary, wasn't the modest doll she appeared to be, but

213

one of those actresses who sell their angelic faces to the porn industry. But without cameras, for many more thousands of dollars and without exposing themselves as much. All without her daddy ever knowing, the one who had raised her so modestly, without her future little son ever seeing her sucking an unknown cock while lifting her blue eyes to the fake rapist, as if asking if she was doing it right, feigning innocence, which in the rape industry is a way of feigning inexperience, virginity, excessive and obscene youth. Maybe Ana Laura had given oral sex to some client and it would never be known. Nor do the business tigers reveal their secret methods, generally more obscene and more elegant than pornography and prostitution. Maybe she had slept, if only once and as a last resort, with one of those disgusting old men who think that, as they become more repulsive, in form and content, as they accumulate more money, more respect and more admiration, more fear and more flattery they gather from their peers in lower positions of the power structure. Things of macho bastards who, among ten or fifteen of any of them, have more money than half the population of France or the United States. Those pigs that he himself, Facundo, so desperately needs, whom he would so like to be or know to close a modest deal of a few million dollars and retire forever on an island in the Pacific (a new life, one of the many that can be lived, before there are no more options, before money can no longer buy anything, in Gauguin's Tahiti or Dalí's Cadaqués). One of those sacks of half-rotted meat who think themselves eternal and demigods for the absurd and unimaginable amounts of capital they accumulate every time they fart and their employees applaud with tears in their eyes. Until one day the president of a great country appoints them minister or head of a superbank, one of those asses whose crap drowns a hundred thousand innocents in some remote corner of the world, in one of those savage countries, incapable of understanding the basic rules of civilization and progress. One of those powerful men who have the world by the balls, until some international organization puts them at the helm of the World Big Dick Bank or some other sacred monster and, from one of those high clouds, they come crashing down like stones due to the accidental and irrelevant act of groping the breasts of a Black maid in a hotel. Then, suddenly, they realize that not even their most powerful enemies possess as much power as the puritanical hypocrisy of the laws they themselves enact to please the people, to negotiate with those masses of misfits who are always dissatisfied and

215

protesting. It doesn't matter if that same maid, along with five million other employees in the same hospitality industry, has worked for thirty years like a slave, enduring insults, humiliations, and deprivations for a child or for her own needs, cleaning toilets with rich people's feces stuck to the porcelain as if caviar were glue, picking up syringes from drug addicts or champagne glasses left on the carpet, trying to remove lipstick stains from pillowcases, collecting sheets with still-fresh semen, swallowing retorts from hysterical guests, listening at night, exhausted, to Senator Impotent Dick or President Shithead delivering beautiful speeches, interrupted every two minutes by the enthusiastic applause of their colleagues and various underlings about the need to relieve billionaires in this or that country so that, in the long run, a very, very long run, more miserable and humiliating jobs like the one the slave knows by heart will be created. Then, that woman understands that she should actually be grateful, and she feels relieved to know that, if things aren't worse, if cars have round wheels, or if there's a hot chicken on the kitchen table that night, it's thanks and only thanks to those same gentlemen who so desperately need our patriotic help.

No, none of that matters. What matters is that the powerful rival groped the slave, the indenture slave, or proposed quick sex for ten thousand dollars. Five minutes of paid sex, in cash to leave no trace, five minutes that would have given her more savings than she'd accumulated over the last ten years, over the last thirty. An extracurricular offer that turned out to be a thousand times more humiliating than a lifetime of endless humiliations she had learned to accept, like the untouchables in India accept their natural condition as scum. Because on TV, because on social media, no one says that being a wage slave is humiliating— quite the opposite: all work is dignifying. Because on TV, because on social media, because in the culture for centuries and centuries, everyone agrees that sleeping with someone to pay off an anguishing debt, to survive a dehumanized system, is immoral. Or because the little grope and the proposal hadn't been as humiliating as convenient, for a slave who, ignorant, moralized but not an idiot, one day, suddenly, found herself with the chance to play with the winner's cards, with the laws of the powerful (and won, like the always-touted exceptions of those from below).

Facundo sighed deeply, as if his lungs had accumulated too much air. He wondered what was happening to him. He wasn't the same anymore. Where had all that optimism gone, all those convictions from just a few years ago? Where did these so negative thoughts come from? Surely, he thought, it was stress. Stress about Elena, stress about the stolen identity. Or maybe he was in that moment when the effects of excess alcohol were beginning to wear off and could no longer provide him with a euphoric view of the world, but quite the opposite. Was he, at this point in life, in that precise moment when some drunks start fights in taverns? This was an idea of Ernesto's (of course, how could it be otherwise!)—the unbearable Ernesto, the great polluter, his only connection to The Other World, and for purely familial reasons. Ernesto had illustrated it with a story, something that had happened to a famous writer... Hemingway? No, not Hemingway. Stephen King? Less likely. It was someone else, a damned real artist, according to Ernesto... An alcoholic, bohemian, or son of a bitch who had moved to Florida, like all Americans who leave the cold of the north to die on the warm coasts of the south, not the deep south but further south, on one of the corrupt borders of... Yes, he remembered the moment with the clarity he couldn't recall his last trip to Tijuana. Had he just recovered that memory at that precise moment? Ernesto had been talking about Kerouac (John, Jack Kerouac?), one of those famous degenerate writers of the Beat Generation who died in Florida, of cirrhosis and as a result of a fight in a bar.

218

While the euphoria of those guys was climbing the bell curve, they could write, they could soar, but when they entered the inevitable downhill slide, the annoyance, the rage, the fights began. Only now did he understand what that madman Ernesto had meant about drunks and Wall Street. Hadn't it been President George Bush himself, another alcoholic, who had said that the 2008 crisis was due to a Wall Street hangover? A revealing joke, if you know how to read reality, Ernesto had said. More or less, that's how the lives of other addicts work, like those addicted to money or power. But, like drunks, there were addicts to power and money of all kinds, and some never moved beyond the euphoric stage or, simply, maintained their addiction until the end, until they exploded or made the rest explode, with an accelerated increase in stimulus.

Judging by his own state of disillusionment, he was in that stage of the bell curve, skiing down from the icy peaks toward the temperate valley where life or depression lies.

He walked around the living room, observing every detail that had been part of other lives and of people he would never meet. On a little table, he discovered the remains of a cigar. Two or three centimeters. Hygiene wasn't the business's strong suit.

Someone had been smoking there, not just a cigarette but a huge cigar, even though the cabin was sold as a non-smoking area or smoke-free zone. Like used cars. "Non-smoker owner sells Toyota 4 Runner 2015." Non-smoker owner, pet-free. Like everything, a probable lie or, at least, impossible to prove until you buy the car and find some canine hair on the back seat.

Thirty years ago, during one of his summer vacations in Punta del Este, he had smoked a cigar. His first and probably his last cigar, as he recalled. He had been fascinated by the smell, not just of tobacco but of champagne. The smell and the fantasy of being, alternately, a millionaire on a yacht in the Caribbean or a Cuban revolutionary. Just one of those cost what he could save in an entire day delivering coffee at his Uncle Domingo's bar in La Plata. But vacations were vacations, and that year, that summer in Uruguay, he had bought himself a Che Guevara-style beret in Montevideo and, in Punta del Este, the beach resort of the wealthy, a cigar.

In reality, anything you come across by accident in any place can trigger distant memories. Because over nearly fifty years, one has done almost everything an ordinary human can do. The only novelty (novel for him, Facundo thought, not for the human species) was that sudden fatigue, that exhaustion that had destroyed nearly all his energy, his hopes, and even that consistent and loyal enthusiasm for reaching round numbers in his Bank of America or Citibank accounts. The new thing was skiing down the bell curve toward the improbable percentile regions, the ten, the one percent, the exceptional cases.

No doubt, he thought later (lying in bed, staring at the ceiling, and smelling of poverty or middle-class vacations), all of that was due to the problems he was having with Elena. The thought of divorce, the possibility of separation, of division (of loss, if he considered that Elena had contributed little or nothing to those figures, not to mention her uncontrollable shopping addiction) had led him to all those questionings. At least, that's what he thought. There were no other rational possibilities.

At 6:45, just before sunset, he began to hear a distant voice. The obese man was singing Somewhere over the Rainbow with a guitar, as if imitating the Hawaiian.

He went back to the room and realized he was out of disinfectant. He looked for a piece of paper. He remembered seeing one in the kitchen. He took the pen he always carried in his shirt pocket and, before writing Lysol, he read: Lysol.

It was the list of things to buy he had seen earlier.

221

yogurt
Lysol
cash

The handwriting felt familiar, with that small print style they used or had used in Argentina, quite similar to his brother's and his own.

A sudden fatigue led him to the bed, and there he dozed until he was dragged into a deep sleep. He had heard Somewhere over the Rainbow in a Toys "R" Us commercial or some other shitty company that had just disappeared from the market.

For a moment, he understood that what he was hearing from the bed was nothing more than a remnant of memory. It played in his head like some pseudo-melodies he had started hearing five years earlier. At first, he had searched for the origin of those melodies in some neighbor in the Boca Ratón building, but he hadn't managed to find them. Then, when he traveled to Bangkok for the software project related to the looms, he realized that one of the melodies, almost like a train or cruise ship vibration, sounded more or less the same. Much later, he attributed it to a hereditary issue. He remembered that, as a child, his father had taken some medication to alleviate a ringing he heard. Was it the same thing? His father's doctor had attributed it to his job as a truck driver. For forty years, his father had driven trucks for many hours a day, which had affected his auditory system and, apparently, the blood flow to his brain as well. Who knows. When he started having similar problems, more or less at the same age, he thought it was something hereditary. He refused to solve it with pills because his father had died at 69 from a heart attack, most likely as a side effect of silencing the sounds in his head. That's why Facundo never mentioned it to his doctor. Doctors, especially in this part of the world where everything follows the laws of money, prescribe all kinds of drugs and chemicals with a carelessness that should be considered criminal, if it weren't for the fact that law, justice, and medicine are all part of the same system that heals and kills. For many reasons, he preferred to stay silent. But the melodies and the ringing in his head hadn't subsided; on the contrary, they had intensified.

Oh, somewhere over the rainbow bluebirds fly
And the dream that you dare to,
Oh why, oh why can't I?

Lucía, the android receptionist

WHAT WAS IT, EXACTLY, that bothered him about the receptionist? Was it that she lacked some human traits? How did he know? He knew from his experience selling technology (he thought). Elysa had something of Elena and something of Lucía, the robot he had almost fallen in love with in Hong Kong—love, or the beginnings of love, from which he had been saved by a feeling of disgust, guilt, shame, and puritanical repression that would disappear from the face of the earth in a generation or two, worn away by the habit of adapting to a new reality. In fact, just ten years later, he himself, with all the moral flaws fossilized in his first two decades, could no longer feel that deep shame for having felt something human toward a robot. Perhaps it was the opposite: now he felt a slight sense of guilt, but in reverse—guilt for not having given the robot a chance to demonstrate her special abilities in intimacy.

That must have been around October, maybe November 2008. He remembered it because of the orgasmic stress of the Great Crisis that, at the time, was beginning to engulf the entire world. Now, ten years later, Lucía would have improved a lot. Improved (he corrected himself, with a silent smile) from a human

224

point of view, of course, because, judging by the perfection of her appearance, there was nothing to improve. She looked so much, completely, like those humanoid robots that walk the runways at fashion shows in Paris or Milan—perfect, with faces of chronic frigidity. Facundo had approached Lucía, or Lucy, certain that she was the hotel's receptionist. He exchanged a few words with her, and it wasn't until the Alexus manager approached him from behind and asked what he thought of Lucía that he felt it was an out-of-place, inappropriate comment. Especially coming from a stranger. But before Facundo could react with sharp indifference, Mr. Xu introduced himself:

"Good evening," said the man in Chinese-accented English. "I am Xu Shian, manager of Alxus Co."

Facundo heard the name of the company as if it were the sound of his alarm clock, always, or almost always, at 4:59 in the morning—always, always unsettling and unpleasant, no matter what kind of melody he set for it.

He slapped his forehead with a slightly exaggerated gesture and extended his hand to Mr. Xu, pretending to recognize him. He hadn't read the biographical folder, as was standard in these cases

(Emil called it "the protocol," to give it the drama it deserved), as he had thought of doing during the layover in Dubai, all because of a Russian, Ukrainian, or Slovakian woman who had pursued him with her feline gaze for an hour, in the prime of her early thirties. Years of travel had taught him many things. Others remained a mystery. Why did some people do those things? Was it just a game for bored people, or were some genuinely on the lookout for candidates with platinum credit cards? He must have said something, but Elena's shadow had made him change the fisherman's gender. Elena's shadow was long, like that of the father, according to Freud, though he wasn't so sure about his father's shadow. The old man was very kind, too kind—the policeman in him didn't show. For a moment, he thought about the reputation of Eastern European women being easy. Maybe it wasn't just because they were among the poor of Europe and many of them had chosen the path of prostitution in France, Germany, or some financial hub in nearby countries. Maybe it went back much further. Those people, if you don't count the Russians, had been the first victims of the power struggles between the East and the white, European West. Slovenia, Slavs, slaves (he thought). It was no coincidence that the word "slave" comes from "Slav,"

Ernesto had told him. But all that was lost in the depths of history and didn't explain (or did it?) that beautiful, lost woman in one of those temples crowded with thousands and millions of eternal strangers, all the same everywhere, whether it was Sydney's Mascot or Paris's Charles de Gaulle, with more coffee in Egypt or more beer in Dublin. Or was it that he couldn't imagine anything other than business, business, always business, as Elena had said? Yes, maybe. After all, it shouldn't be just a flaw of ambitious businessmen (he thought, or wanted to think); for a musician, the world must be a symphony, and for a writer, a story. The blonde slave was in her business. Period. Could anyone expect to fall in love in one of those places? Well, according to what he had read later, by chance or not, statistics, which always prove the opposite, say that one in five passengers finds a partner (even if only temporarily, as temporary as a night) on a flight. He had looked around and couldn't imagine himself involved with any of those beautiful women who paraded the male desire, even the most reserved male like him, through all the corridors of all the airports. Zero probability. So, the only option left was fishing for a client and systematically forgetting the thousands of indifferent others. Like any honest prostitute waiting on a corner in

Amsterdam's red-light district or in Buenos Aires' docklands. If there's supply in the market, it's because there's demand, and surely it was him, Facundo, the tender naive who didn't understand those details of the business. Let everyone scratch themselves with their own nails, he had heard his father say to someone complaining because a woman was selling flowers on a corner where it was forbidden. The woman sold her flowers without paying taxes. Unfair competition... Let the slave survive as she can. Others do the same without needing to go out to find a client every day because they marry one of them, the best one, tolerating all his infidelities in exchange for a mansion, a white house. Others do the same, but more innocently, like that game played in other airports by some maidens, for lack of a better term, those grown-up girls who one day discover they're women and go out into the world with excessive confidence and innocence to play with fire, sure they'll never get burned. Because they've never been burned. Because their parents always protected them. Because the only thing they've heard from the time they could remember were praises of their personalities and intelligence. All thanks to parents fearful of raising fearful children, without self-esteem, without believing they were geniuses, the beautiful centers of the universe.

In other words, failed children in a world of sharks. So, when those young women go out into the world, like divorced women feeling the breeze of freedom but still without the scars of reality, they lie on the floor reading their phones, with their legs open, a bit more than necessary, knowing that, thanks to terrorists, airports are the safest places in the world, so they don't fear the misfortune of some degenerate throwing himself at them and making their greatest fantasy come true.

No, he hadn't read Mr. Xu's résumé. If he had seen his photo, it made no difference. All Chinese people look alike, unless they're presidents.

"Forgive my slowness," said Facundo. "I just got back from the airport and I'm really exhausted."

"Don't worry," said Mr. Xu. "I know exactly what it's like to travel to the other side of the world. We still haven't invented the technology that treats us as we deserve... A teleporter or something like that."

He feared showing he wasn't up to date on Mr. Xu's latest successes. Not the latest nor the earlier ones. That simple detail could ruin the entire mission from the start. Over the years, he had learned there were few things more effective when it came to making significant deals. First, there was the salesperson's ability to paint an extraordinary future (either very good or very bad) in which their product would save the buyer from an imminent, in-the-works catastrophe. After sex, nothing sells better than fear, with the advantage that while you can insert sex into even the soup, it can never cover everything, absolutely everything, like fear can. Sex can do little when it comes to selling a war or an antivirus. Mastering the art of fear is mastering the art of big business. Second, and in many cases first, was knowing how to flatter without being too obvious. Yes, that very thing… The art of the prostitute. The difference, he thought, was that he wasn't going to end up in Mr. Xu's bed, but everything else was very similar. Every man who is successful (because, simplifying, it was a man's game), every man who adores money adores himself. In certain cases, money is his greatest obsession, and in others, it's just proof of how intelligent and indispensable he is in the advancement of his company, his country, and all of humanity. (Wasn't it Ernesto, the failed Ernesto, who said that money is the power that projects the intelligence of the neurotic male?) Maybe that's why the successful businessmen he had met around the world had prolific sexual histories. It wasn't, it seemed to him, like some professors and leftist pamphlet critics said, that power and sex had an inseparable coexistence. It could be, but for him, for Facundo, it was something else. When someone loves themselves in a pathological way, they need to go hunting. And what better trophy than a woman, aside from money? Love could be a weakness. No, it could not: love is a weakness. For this reason, the hunter, the predator, does not fall in love: he conquers. Plant a flag on Mons Venus, on the peak of a mountain, on the face of the Moon, in the vagina of a woman who is not loved but desired—it's more or less the same thing. Money is not loved, it is desired. Power is not loved, it is desired. Astronauts never loved the Moon. Even less so those who sent them there or those who watched the broadcast with fanatical pride one night in 1969. They loved themselves. The pride of conquest, the pleasure of planting without love for what is planted is pure self-love, self-esteem. Like the boring self-help manuals say these days, which, if they're good for anything, it's for enriching the publishers, soothing the egos of their authors, and stimulating the flagging enthusiasm of their readers for life, their failed consumers, who read that kind of ego-boosting stuff precisely because theirs is on the floor. Managing to take an unknown woman or, at least, an improbable one, like a famous actress, the virgin wife of a president, a young girl half their age, a third of their age and weight—for those super-powerful men who can do nothing against time, it's a big game hunt. The downside of conquest and sex is that, once consummated, they don't leave profits like a good business, but potential losses, like diseases, an unwanted heir, or a jealous wife. But without all those dangers, the hunter wouldn't feel pleasure in obtaining his prey, something that a good business, at least a legal one, can never offer to a predator like a true businessman who plays in the world's top leagues.

But it wasn't his job to think or question any of these things, but to learn and take advantage of the rules of the game. He didn't even know which group he belonged to, nor did he care to clarify it. Ernestito, Ernesto's reflection of a nephew, who at the time was writing his master's thesis in Philadelphia, had summed it up very well, in a way that almost framed it in gold: You capitalists, he had said, are Marxist in at least one thing: for you, the world is not there to be understood but to be exploited. Since that day, he had some respect for the bearded German. Though, to be honest, and let's say he almost forgot, in his early youth he must have been a socialist, anarchist, or something like that without fully realizing it, all for one rather happy summer (like all summers when you're seventeen) with Uncle Alberto in Piriápolis.

Back then, he, Facundo, was much younger than drowning Ernestito stuck in his thesis, four or five years younger biologically, but he had already gone through all those lunatic ideas, which is what you should do, like getting a vaccine, the sooner the better, and he was probably happier than Ernestito, because back then he didn't have to defend his recent discoveries before a tribunal of know-it-alls but only trade insults with an old lover of the military and live cattle exporters in a café in La Recoleta in Buenos Aires upon returning from vacation in Uruguay.

But let's not go that far, he thought. He rested his forehead on the dirty window and stared at the horizon line separating the sea from the sky, which was already beginning to fade, like memories. Let's go back for a moment to Hong Kong, to that Hong Kong and to that Facundo from the year 2015, who already knew by heart that the first impression of a client was more or less fifty percent of the mission's success. He was tired, exhausted, and perhaps that's why he hadn't been able to realize that Lucía was not a human being.

Mr. Xu pointed at Lucía again and said that she was still in the experimental phase, but they were gradually perfecting her appearance and reactions as they advanced in data collection. Lucía, the beautiful

Lucía, was not a normal human being. She wasn't even a cyborg. She was an android from head to toe.

"What data?" asked Facundo.

Mr. Xu pointed to a screen behind Lucía.

"There we have a camera that captures each client's reactions. Among the five thousand other data sets we collect, we measure how long it takes them to realize that Lucía isn't a robot. At the end of each day, Lucía and her third eye, which is like her conscience, her creator-god, gather and process millions of data points. She is our Eve and probably the Eve of many generations that will reproduce like stars in the sky."

"Well, if you hadn't told me," said Facundo, "I wouldn't have noticed."

"That's because you've just arrived from a long trip, and it's 11:30 pm. All those variables will be considered by the artificial intelligence we'll discuss tomorrow in the meeting."

Facundo was about to ask if that was legal, collecting human data without informing the participants. In the United States, it was illegal, which made such research complicated and sometimes impossible. Although surely, those at a higher level bypassed all those limitations, such as by sending the supposed physical location of their businesses to other countries. He recalled several cases. Betting on events that may occur in the future, through sites like Augur, is illegal in the United States, which is why the company has its offices in New Zealand. There's no homeland for business, only for soldiers in Iraq or the miners of West Virginia who defend the businesses to the death.

He was about to ask Mr. Xu this question but stopped himself just in time. Why was he there? Was he a member of Greenpeace, or Amnesty International? One never knows what goes through someone else's mind, much less if you don't know them. But Facundo was anything but foolish. One awkward gesture and he'd lose half a million and a week of sleep.

Mr. Xu invited him for a drink at the hotel bar later, after Facundo could drop off his luggage in his room and freshen up a bit.

After checking in with the other employee supervising Lucía, a young woman who looked like her but was human—or more human than she was—he took his luggage and glanced at Lucía, who immediately looked back at him with mischief in her eyes. Those who had designed her had gone to great lengths to give her several seductive attributes, like a sweet and killer gaze and soft, full lips that stretched over perfect teeth every time she smiled. Her face, that of a young Asian woman, was pale, like ceramic, though he

235

thought she had green or blue eyes. He didn't know any Japanese women with green eyes. As he rode the elevator, he imagined giving her a kiss. For the first time in many years, he felt that animal, forbidden desire to make love to a woman he had just met, to the point of starting an erection in public, something he detested and struggled to control in his younger years, back in those distant days of excessive testosterone and even more excessive fantasy and fear of those unattainable, perfect beings, who always had women's names. How would Elena react? He didn't know, but he did know that this couldn't be considered a love affair. He could take Lucía to bed in his hotel room and still proudly claim, to Elena and anyone else, that he had never betrayed his wife. Before the elevator doors opened, he remembered that for a long time, the oldest primate discovered in Africa in the sixties was also named Lucía. The famous Lucy. Lucy in the sky with diamonds... He placed the document briefcase on his belly and as he dragged the other suitcase down the long hallway, he managed to squash the absurdities of his imagination.

He thought that, likely, those who had designed that face were not artists but engineers. No doubt they were engineers. Better yet, not even engineers but software that had combined 3,958,429 of the most attractive faces in the world available in its database and had placed them in that android. Lucy was neither white nor black nor yellow nor redheaded. She was, obviously, young, because that never goes out of style, and there's no culture that dislikes the freshness of youth. It wasn't just about a flourishing, wrinkle-free body; perhaps it was the repository of that tide of hopes, daydreams, and fantasies, those energies that turn the world into a place of fantastic exploration. Lucía, Lucy, thought Facundo, even though she was no more human than a pair of shoes, represented all that human longing, the time of youth, the time gone forever, in a pure, distilled state. Kissing her and loving her wasn't a conquest, not a hunter's trophy, but the fantasy of an old man who yearns for all that past time, definitively lost. That's why youth makes even the ugliest of women beautiful. That's why the android Lucy had to be young and sensual. Because, beyond all the immense progress accumulated by humanity throughout its stormy and admirable history, sensuality and sex remained the same from the first Lucy who lived in Africa, hundreds of thousands of years ago, to the latest one, the robot Lucy.

Of course, he didn't say any of this in the meeting the next day. They would have thought he was crazy. Or worse, a sexual pervert. Some of this was discussed,

237

but in a more neutral language, more about business, more about the effectiveness of eliminating some thousands or, who knows? millions of jobs if the project was successful as they believed.

Toilet Philosophy

COLA DE PEZ DIDN'T APPEAR anywhere on the internet. The receptionist couldn't provide information either. Although it sounded common for a restaurant, she didn't know of any in the city with that name. He searched, without success, in a paper phone directory.

With a strong feeling of frustration, he went out into the street, looking for some clue that would remind him how he had ended up there just seven months ago. The memory loss, Dr. Kaufman, the specialist friend of Dr. Menéndez, had told him, didn't necessarily mean he was suffering from a serious illness. There was no history of that kind in the family. Not, at least, that he knew of. It was impossible to know what had happened to his great-grandparents scattered across Argentina, Uruguay, Italy, Germany, Portugal, and Syria. Likely, very likely, those gaps in his recent memory were due to stress and poor sleep at night. Not only did he sleep few hours, but, according to his electroencephalogram, his slow-wave sleep was of poor quality. He couldn't reach the necessary depths to achieve deep, functional rest to repair the order of the previous days' memories and clear the unnecessary noise in his head. Although, as the doctor always said, more tests were needed. The REM phase of sleep is crucial in consolidating new memories, and since he had a deficiency in producing it correctly, it wasn't surprising that, at times, he didn't remember what he had done the day before.

However, or because of this very fact, he remembered old things with an intensity that surprised him, as if his memory had been freed from the urgency of the present and could dive deeper into those distant events he thought he had forgotten. Things from his youth. Was he getting old? Was it something more serious?

He stopped. On a very white wall, a raven stared at him with a piece of bread in its beak. After three seconds of calm, the raven threw the piece of bread at a dog resting in the shade, overwhelmed by the heat and hunger, judging by its protruding ribs. The dog noticed the piece of bread and got up to eat it.

Somewhere he had read that, after death, the brain continues to function for ten minutes, a moment when the one who is definitively leaving this world returns, with unimaginable intensity, to the most emotional moments of their life. Without meaning to, he wondered what he would remember when those ten minutes came. Perhaps he would relive that moment when in Seoul he managed to close the contract with Samsung, a contract that, by then and due to a series of unforgivable mistakes by central management, the company considered lost. He wouldn't recall the birth of any of his children, something some say is indescribable. He would remember his first kiss with Elena, when he took her to his apartment, and she, before getting out of the car, took the initiative. The death of his father in a rundown hospital. When he graduated as an Engineer in Buenos Aires. Maradona's goal against England in Mexico 86 (that's when he realized his neighborhood in Floresta and his home were one and the same). The summers in Uruguay. The Sunday morning when he found his mother in her bed, with a smile and eyes open, staring at the ceiling without seeing. His young parents celebrating his ability to draw a house in perspective. His mother's smile, her sweet voice, looking at him lying in his crib, singing happy birthday to him. Five years old already, my little one…

He leaned against the wall. It wasn't possible that now, in his old age, he would start crying like a child.

240

Or was it? Could it be that maybe old people are a little more human than men-in-their-prime? Five years old already, my little one... (his mother's broad smile and her eyes that laughed and cried at the same time). Merry Christmas / merry Christmas / let's toast together / at the family table...

The dog looked up and saw the raven taking flight. Then Facundo continued walking down a nearly empty street until he reached one that seemed like a bustling avenue. For a moment, he was reminded of the smells of each country that, back then, before he got used to traveling every month, used to strike him as particularly intense. Each country had its own smell. The smell of Mexico was, alternately, the aroma of tacos al pastor, of lime, of paint, of sweat. Natural smells, he would say.

That morning, he took several taxis. Since none of the drivers knew the Cola de Pez, they took him to other restaurants. He had lunch in one that bore no resemblance to what he remembered. He had coffee in another. In the evening, he thought he'd found what he was looking for: the concrete columns shaped like parasols over small tables, the white walls with frames painted in sky blue and green. But it wasn't the place. The interior was nothing like he remembered. Tired, he sat at a table for another coffee

241

and ended up drinking two beers on the waiter's recommendation. The waiter, Cuauhtemoc, said he was a fan of Messi and Barcelona. He didn't miss a single game. He watched them for free online, on one of those pirate channels, with the only problem being that he had to find a new channel every ten minutes, whenever they were discovered and the signal was cut.

Facundo asked him about the Cola de Pez and it seemed to him that the man's clueless gesture was genuine.

He finished the two beers and went to the bathroom. It wasn't dirty, nor did it smell worse than the bar from the day before, but he recognized the modesty of such small spaces where everyone avoids staying too long. While urinating, he read the verses of an anonymous poet:

> *the rich shit*
> *the poor shit*
> *the king shits*
> *the pope shits*
> *and in this shitty world*
> *no one escapes shitting*

He knew the poem from a worker on his grand-father's farm, back in Argentina, thirty years ago, or more, while they shucked corn in the barn on a rainy day. He'd heard it only once and, for some reason, he hadn't forgotten it. Or rather, he'd forgotten it for thirty or forty years and now he remembered it, sud-denly, just as he remembered his mother's smile every time he smelled lavender-scented soaps in a JCPenney in Tampa or a Stein Mart in Jacksonville. He had probably forgotten many other things that deserved to be remembered, and he would probably never re-call them again until they all came rushing back dur-ing the last ten minutes granted to him by the laws of nature.

But now, all that popular literature had been scrubbed clean with bleach from the walls of the world, not just for tidiness but because of that dra-matic weight of existential truth expressed with such vulgarity. For some reason, the population grew as much as the hatred between the various groups that composed it (countries, people with university de-grees and those without, religions, sects, political par-ties and soccer teams, genders, ethnicities, music, literary cliques, flags of all kinds, symbols and colors), and instead of rebelling against the absurdities of those same societies controlled by as many people as

243

could fit crammed into that very same dirty bath-room, certainly not as dirty as any one of them, on the contrary, they were becoming more obedient, more puritanical, more proper, more hygienic.

Below, someone, in a different handwriting, had replied:

the fart is a gentle gust
that slides through the asshole
announcing the influx
of a good dung whole

Popular poetry from the Middle Ages, Ernesto would have said. Something more authentic than the plastic that surrounds us today. In Argentina and the United States, those graffiti are no longer seen. Or they're quite rare. They look ugly. Even in urban walls, they're considered a serious attack on property. It always made Facundo furious whenever he saw one in Daytona. No, it wasn't just an attack on a property that didn't concern him but an attack on tidiness, on the visual order that distinguishes a developed society from an African or Latin American country. That's why he hated Miami, Ernesto used to say. Not be-cause some or many Cuban residents there had col-laborated with the CIA in the invasion of countries further south, nor even because they were considered dangerous terrorists even by the FBI, like Luis Posada Carriles and so many others (and on this he didn't contradict Ernesto because, second, he didn't engage in those investigations and, first, because he didn't care in the slightest), but because it made Facundo sick to walk down 8th Street and see people urinating on palm trees or sitting on the curb doing nothing. Unproductive. Ricardo would say, Good people with bad habits. For Ernesto, perhaps not, but the opposite: Bad people with good habits. At least they weren't consuming to ruin the planet further. At least they weren't becoming millionaires to screw someone else over in the prestigious, intimidating (and full of notable millionaires) United States Congress, in the name of creating jobs for the poor, those drones, parasites of the self-sacrificing millionaires who every now and then must make donations or pay more taxes than others. Yes, he undoubtedly hated the laid-back Cuban urinators of Miami. Not because it bothered him that Elena might see other penises (after all, his hadn't been the only one in Elena's life), but because he had always hated disorder, the messiness of the third world.

Or had he? Well, no, Facundo told himself, drying his foreskin with an American Airlines napkin, avoiding shaking his penis to splash the last few drops everywhere, as is the norm and as men do. Now that he said it, now that he thought about it, no. Of course not. He hadn't hated all that (the graffiti, the disorder, people wasting time) forever but since he arrived in the United States. What problem had he had with the imperfection of spaces when they shelled corn in that barn on his grandparents' farm while it rained and the farmhands told dirty jokes? The floor was hard dirt, and there were all kinds of things accumulated for years in fruit crates or scattered everywhere, and that had been, along with vacations at Uncle Alberto's house in Uruguay, the happiest time of his life. But when he arrived in the United States to do his master's in International Business and Leadership, he had marveled at the perfect life of the first world and wanted to preserve it at any cost. He wanted to be that. He wanted to be and to belong. Becoming American was becoming what he truly was deep down. He never reached the absurdity of wearing short pants made from the flag of the winner, stripes on one side and stars on the other, like some desperately need Cubans who manage to set foot in Florida as if it were Armstrong stepping on the Moon. Nor had he ever sung the anthem with a hand on his heart, let alone with tears in his eyes, but he had come very close through sheer willpower. The success of his adopted country had not only given him the opportunity to earn his first million, but he wanted the losers who had stayed behind in Argentina to know it and suffer for it. That incurable testosterone. That incurable idiocy he discovered in some colleagues who had left behind Mexico, Honduras, Cuba, or Venezuela. Let them explode and recognize the winner, the World Champion.

"Argentina is ungovernable, because it is a land of anarchist gauchos and something much worse: Argentina is Italy without history and far from Europe," he had once said, with that cannibalism typical of the Río de la Plata. Inside every braggart lies a frustrated suicide.

Now, although he could boast about his luxurious houses in some photo uploaded to Facebook, he couldn't reveal how many millions he had in the bank, or he could and it would just look ridiculous. But between an unreachable Carlos Slim and him, the country made all the difference, in the same way (he thought, almost sarcastically as he tucked himself in and zipped up his pants) a modest Wal-Mart employee and the Mexican millionaire could compete equally in pride for their great triumphs and memorable successes. Even for a miserable self-exile who makes a living flipping burgers at McDonald's or receiving the Employee of the Month recognition at Home Depot and takes photos in the best and most spectacular spots of a big city, in front of magnificent and beautiful buildings they'll never even be able to visit, just so the losers who stayed in their miserable countries can feel it, so they can bite the dust of defeat for thinking differently, for not accepting the glory and blessing of this Blessed country, God's favorite and four more angels.

Facundo didn't even bother to read what the graffiti that marred New York said. As if it would worsen his rating. But, for a fleeting moment in that modest and miserable bathroom without a toilet, he thought that the new cleanliness had silenced many voices, many truths, unpleasant or inconvenient. He thought, for an instant, that now social media had displaced the ancient literature of public restrooms into offices and the heart of the home. Not by chance, the virtual space of each Facebook account is called a wall. "I left something on your wall." "Yesterday I wrote on my wall." Now, on social media, popular wisdom coexisted, just like in the restrooms of the old world, with lies, insults, and harassment. Just like in the past, every so often the police of amorality would erase one of those messages.

María Castañeda López needs
a man to fuck her well
every day after 8:30
when her husband is out delivering
For inquiries, contact her husband
at juancornichelli56@gmail.com

He washed his hands and left the bathroom. He ordered a coffee before leaving. On the TV, a soccer match was playing that had captured the attention of the few customers still there at that hour. He heard something about Las Chivas and an unforgivable foul. The beer or the seafood had sat a bit heavy in his stomach. He remembered, or thought, that he had lost the alternate card in the same way. He had never gotten drunk, not even as a young man (at least not enough to reach the point of ridicule or instability), but it seemed that, sometimes, especially when other people's conversations overwhelmed him, even a modest dose of alcohol would take him out of his body.

He returned to the hotel to rest, to search for new data online to use the next morning. But as soon as he reached his room, he lay down on the bed and fell asleep.

249

A dream

HE DREAMED OF SILVANNA. She walked in to the restroom of the bar where he had been that afternoon and knelt before him. He told her to leave him alone, that he needed to urinate. Are you sure you don't want to?, she said, while trying to hide fangs like the ones the actors wore in the vampire movies that had terrified him as a child. Barnabas Collins. Then he rushed out of the bathroom and bumped into the waiter from the restaurant, who told him to calm down, that the lady he was waiting for had already arrived and that he should return to his table. When Facundo approached the table, he saw Susan sitting there, combing her hair as if she were in front of a mirror. When Facundo sat down across from her, Susan looked into his eyes and smiled. Facundo told her he was sorry, that she was very beautiful, and that he regretted having deceived her. It was at that moment that Susan transformed into Silvanna. Only Susan's eyes, fixed on his, were the same as Silvanna's, looking at him with fury. I told you to leave me alone, said Facundo, but Silvanna took his hand. Facundo felt her hand soft, pleasant. Why don't you like me? she asked. I do like you, he said. It's just... Then she squeezed his hand with superhuman strength, and he understood that she was the Silvanna he had left abandoned in the Daytona apartment. It's not fair to leave me in a box, as if I were a thing, she said. Facundo begged her to let go of his hand, that he couldn't stand the pain, but she kissed him forcefully. You're going to suffocate me, he said, and Silvanna replied, with a malicious smile: That's exactly what we felt when we were raped. We had just turned fifteen. He was a disgusting old man, obese or so it seemed to us. Silvanna doesn't remember it as well as we do. One day we'll have to tell her, but first we have to get justice.

Just as Facundo tried to tell them (he had lost his voice from the pain, as if he were trying to speak underwater) that he had nothing to do with that story, he woke up with a sharp pain in his right hand.

He had fallen asleep on his phone. The phone had pressed against the veins in his right hand, cutting off circulation.

Don Ramón

FINALLY, ON THE THIRD DAY, he found Cola de Pez in the least expected way. At the library of the Universidad Autónoma de Baja California, a young man had told him that if he was interested in bohemian life from the sixties, or seventies, or if he smoked marijuana, or if what he wanted wasn't museums but to look at the most beautiful women in the region for free, what he should do was take a trip to the coast of Rosarito. He thought the young man was joking, because the student had had two girlfriends, both of whom lived in Rosarito, and neither one held a grudge or anything like that. However, something about all of that had awakened a memory of a taxi parked near a beach.

He searched randomly on his phone for a restaurant near the coast, and on the Boulevard de las Américas, he took a taxi to Rosarito. After asking the driver and later several people walking around or waiting for the bus while sitting on the sidewalk, he came across a soda vendor who reminded him of don Ramón from El Chavo, who, very obviously, told him, Of course, Cola de Pez is right over there, just six or seven blocks from here, down this way, you see?

and then right, toward the coast. But it's been years since tourists go that far. It's gotten a bit dangerous. Like everywhere…

"Drugs?" asked Facundo.

Don Ramón shrugged and, after a brief silence, said:

"I couldn't tell you. I don't get involved in those things. Not in drugs, politics, or religion. Here I sell my little ice creams to anyone, without discrimination of any kind, creed, race, or nationality. The business is small, but decent."

"Maybe that's exactly why it's decent…"

"That's what I tell my son when he feels ashamed of his father at school. You see, with this face, even if everyone else is dressed in tuxedos, I can't hide who I am and where I work, right under the sun selling little ice creams that I don't even know what they taste like, but the kids say they're delicious. Do you see these blocks, all the way over there where the view disappears? Not much further because that's where my colleague's territory starts, and among colleagues, we don't steal each other's customers, though there's always the occasional clash over selling an ice cream a bit too far to one side or the other. From there to here and further to the other side, I know what each kid from each house likes and what time their parents are free to let them out to buy their little ice cream. That's how it is until school starts. Then business slows down, and you have to sell peanuts. No one knows that I know so much about them. No one cares, and that's better, because otherwise someone might call the police or not let their kids out to buy my afternoon ice cream. But just in case, I don't tell anyone else. Wouldn't want to lose my job and the bread for my kid. You're a tourist, and you're not going to buy from me twice…"

Don Ramón looked at him in silence for a moment.

"My accent gives me away," said Facundo. "I'm learning to speak Mexican."

"No, what accent? That's what I was saying earlier. From seeing so many people on the street, you know who's who just by the smell. You smell like an airport. Not like perfume. Like an airport. You dress simply, in a shirt, jeans, old shoes, as if you don't want to draw attention, but from your skin I can tell you work in an office, and from your gestures, you're someone with education or money. Educated people, when they talk, don't move their hands like I do, as if they're swimming or swatting flies."

"Are you a gypsy?"

"No, what gypsy? There are no gypsies here, at least not unless they're hidden in the blood of many around here, like the Indians. It's experience. The same experience that tells me you're not going to be bothered by everything I'm saying. You're getting to my age and entering one of those crises, you're at that moment when you see the end around the corner and start reconsidering the game when there are only a few minutes left in the second half and you don't know if there'll be extra time."

Don Ramón rummaged in the bottom of his cart, let a few drops of sweat fall on the ice creams, took out a little cup, and said:

"Dulce de leche. Look at the date, it's not expired."

"Wow," said Facundo.

"Uruguayan or Argentine?"

"Uruguayan," lied Facundo.

"Well, that's better. Though Argentinians often say they're Uruguayan. It's like Americans who say they're Canadian when they've already said 'tuenny' and 'Sarurday' instead of 'twenty' and 'Saturday.'"

Facundo bought the ice cream from him, left the change, nothing too exaggerated so as not to draw attention, and walked toward where don Ramón had pointed. A tourist who buys a Corneto on the street

255

must be a cheap tourist and, as a cheap tourist, he had the freedom to walk wherever he pleased. Not everyone was as observant as don Ramón. Who could imagine that this thin man, with an ice cream in his hand, looking like a teenager, with a beard of three or four days, had almost ten million dollars in the bank?

He smiled, but he didn't know if he was smiling at those who passed by without even looking at him (like a very young, very pretty girl who seemed annoyed by his gaze), or if he was laughing at himself.

He wandered around several side streets. At one point, he got lost until he found his way back to the corner where the ice cream vendor had been. The sun had set a bit, and the corner was no longer white limestone but yellow, a Barragán yellow, like nowhere else in the world. Don Ramón was no longer there. Exhausted from the lack of habit of walking for an hour without air conditioning, he tried, once again, to remember the directions the ice cream vendor had given him. It was getting dark, and by the time he managed to find Cola de Pez, it was already pitch black.

From the fear that someone might assault him, he moved to a strange sense of security, if not freedom, that poverty and shadows confer, especially when a young woman saw him approaching and crossed the street to avoid him. Definitely, a three-day beard and older than he felt. He didn't seem like a foreigner, and if he made the effort and didn't run into a don Ramón, he could even disguise his accent when he spoke. After all, he too could be a suspicious criminal. He too could be a criminal. He was one without realizing it, he thought, every time he took advantage of laws that only a few knew to gain an advantage in business, in a purchase, in a dinner with the mayor of Orlando, in a working breakfast with Senator Marco Rubio to convince him to prohibit this or lift the ban on that, all always in the name of the community and for the good of the nation. That thing Ernesto called the Mafia of the Law, the Gang of the Legals, all with the sarcasm that he, Facundo, detested so much and didn't even bother to refute, sure that Ernesto lived in the academic bubble while he, they, the businessmen, had to deal with the real world, the world of adults.

"Yes, yes, I know," Ernesto had complained at the Barnes & Noble in Saint Augustine "Reality. But do you know what reality is?"

To which Facundo had replied, with irony,

"I have some idea."

Ernesto had stared at him in silence, not giving him time to think, so he would risk the first answer that came to mind, which, in psychological terms, is what the person truly thinks, without makeup, without disguises.

"It's what we keep here," Facundo had said, touching his pocket.

Ernesto had made a surprised gesture.

"You're not far off," he said, with an exaggerated look of admiration or perplexity "That's reality. In other words, reality is the brutal dictatorship of the powerful's fantasy."

But Facundo had noticed a certain hint that brought him closer to the unbearable Ernesto and, then, as if disgusted, he awoke:

"You poets are very good with words," he said.

From political debates, he had learned that praising the dialectical skill of your opponent was a very elegant disqualification, and it always worked. Maybe because we're all made of words, but no one wants to admit it.

"Not as good as you peddlers of realities," Ernesto had countered.

"Well," said Facundo, in a conclusive tone "We don't care about understanding the world but transforming it."

"Karl Marx said that," Ernesto had warned him "and ever since, it's been one of the capitalists' favorite phrases. I partly agree, depending, of course, on what kind of changes we're talking about. A very low level of testosterone is a problem in an individual, but, in excess, it's a social problem."

That time, like so many other times, Facundo had preferred to end the conversation by drinking the last remnant of his coffee and savoring it with a smile. Ernesto wasn't all that bad. He tolerated him, not just because he was Elena's brother, but because he didn't consider him dangerous from any point of view. As a brother-in-law, he was too direct, so he didn't suspect any backbiting. But now, in the secret distance of Tijuana, he thought that perhaps Ernesto, the leftist, had always been more trustworthy than his sister, than his own wife. Elena could hardly see her brother anymore because of their obvious political and personality differences, due to the unforgivable affront of despising her money and status. There's nothing worse for someone who has achieved high social status than others not acknowledging it, like someone showing a hundred-dollar bill to an Amazonian tribe.

"If there's one thing successful businessmen can't stand," Ernesto once said in a bar in Savannah "it's when someone doesn't worship money, an offense similar to that of the wretched Diogenes when, faced with Alexander the Great's offer to grant him a wish, he told him to move, because he was blocking the sun. History, or the legend, says that the powerful conqueror wasn't offended. 'If I were not Alexander, I should wish to be Diogenes,' he supposedly said. Which reveals a very deep feeling, hidden from everyone and oneself, but, nonetheless, it's not the truth that moves the world. That's why today's successful businessmen need to drag down a wage earner as much as possible, denying them even health benefits or retirement contributions, as a way of showing them the opposite." They can't stand it when someone despises wealth, and that's why they only go to churches that claim wealth is a sign of God's love. They hate paying their taxes but give hefty donations in those temples, so that God and mortals can see it.

"If you don't like money, what are you complaining about?" Elena had reproached him, slinging her purse over her shoulder.

"It's not that I'm complaining, Elena," Ernesto replied. "If someone loves money, fine, let them enjoy it. But they shouldn't take over the government and the world... Do you know what you remind me of, little sister? I've had several conversations like this, and I know exactly how they end. Just the other day, I crossed paths with a new Spanish teacher in the hallway. One of those who always boast about being

expelled by some Latin American dictator, and while
that might be true, they always omit to mention the
economic motivations behind their departure, which
is also commendable. I say 'dictator' with a diminu-
tive, because no Latin American dictator, no matter
how bloody, ever deserved the full title without it. It
hasn't even been a year since this guy got the job,
thanks to my vote on the search committee, and he
already told me I'm contradictory, because I live in a
capitalist country and criticize capitalism. I suppose
he says the same to the millions of individuals born
here who are more American than he is. But they're
right when they say there's no worse gringo than a
Latino who thinks he's a gringo. They leave their
countries because they don't belong to the official
line, and when they get here, they think we all should
belong to their same closed line of thought or leave
the country. Take China, a communist country, isn't
it full of big capitalists enamored with the system and
its profits? Small capitalists aren't capitalists; they're
dreamers or bootlickers. Or, as they say in the Caribbean, ass-lickers. But I believe that maintaining criticism independent of personal interests isn't a
contradiction, it's rigid consistency. Yes, I teach at a
private school, I told him, and I defend public education. Why? Because it's the best job I could get in a

world of sharks, and because I didn't adapt my ideas to my personal interests. What I think and what's convenient for me don't always align, but when I speak, I say what I think, not what's convenient for me. It's sad, that crowd who changes countries or jobs or wins the lottery and then changes their ideology, their religion, their identity, and even their father and wife, all to feel better, to free themselves from the contradictions of this contradictory world. It's like buying four pounds of Peace of Mind at Wal-Mart, at liquidation prices, Low Price, Precio Bajo, as they say now even in Argentina. Communists from the Caribbean turn into the most die-hard capitalists of snow country (mostly fake, sad imitations of a true capitalist), and they call that consistency, patriotism, and all that social masturbation that never quite ejaculates.

"How horrifying!" Elena complained, finally standing up. "As if your twisted ideas needed to be decorated with those obscenities."

He couldn't remember what Ernesto had said after that. For some mysterious reason, he only remembered up to that point. Probably Ernesto had said something, and Elena hadn't replied. She would have ended the conversation with a very American silence. Not answering was her best form of arrogance, a form that Facundo himself had adopted over time and confused with the wisdom that comes with experience. He too, in his youth, had been an Ernesto, though he rarely acknowledged or remembered it. Ernesto had never outgrown that youthful stage. He hadn't matured. Elena had. He, Facundo, had too. How was it possible that two siblings could be so different? Did it have something to do with Ernesto having blue eyes, like their grandfather, the anarchist immigrant, and Elena having black eyes, like their father, the successful businessman? Was it because one was born in winter and the other in summer? Impossible to know. The same parents, the same upbringing, different results.

Facundo also didn't understand why Ernesto's declarations at family gatherings didn't make him furious, at least not the way they made Elena. Facundo would go along with it, pretend to be irritated, and while he was at it, he'd attribute all the discomfort to his family, but deep down, he wasn't irritated or anything like that. Elena took it personally, as if Ernesto were attacking her, when in reality (Facundo thought), Ernesto did it because he couldn't help his nature of contradicting everyone, of wanting to correct every narrative about the history of this Great Country—and, Elena added, of wanting to correct even the Gospels, which, he claimed, were sixty for centuries until some priests in Rome decided to keep only the four that suited Emperor Constantine best.

He leaned against a wall. He felt dizzy. The heat had lowered his blood pressure. Like when he began to fall asleep after an intense day and could see the images of his earliest dreams without losing total consciousness, he could see Elena's tense face and Ernesto's inquisitive gaze.

Even though Elena still treated him like a younger brother, immature, incapable of fending for himself despite the fact that he had never complained about his miserable salary as a Spanish instructor in three high schools. As an ideological opponent, she didn't consider him capable of any retaliation, because he was her brother-in-law, because he didn't have a bad relationship with him, and because he competed in a different league and division. From experience, he knew there was no worse or more brutal competition than among members of the same profession. When he got tangled up in a pointless argument of that kind, he would dwell on it, as if intoxicated for several days after eating spoiled food. Facundo had more important things to think about than getting trapped in something that brought him no benefit. But there was some hidden, mysterious reason that led him to suffer one of those dialectical defeats much more than he enjoyed closing a deal that meant cash, tangible and clinking, a hundred, three hundred thousand dollars. Maybe because, although those deals were the main source of reality, they weren't tangible or clinking or real as he assumed, but, as Ernesto said, part of the imaginary fever that keeps the world moving? After each of his international feats, his account gained a few tens of thousands of dollars. Numbers he didn't even see or touch in the form of printed slips. He couldn't take a bath in coins like Uncle Scrooge did (in those colorful magazines with the intense scent of youth he bought from a kiosk in Buenos Aires), while his nephew, Donald Duck, suffered yet another failure due to his lack of intelligence, and his nephews, the three musketeers of capitalism (as Ernesto called them), mocked their Uncle Donald's clumsiness. After several years of adding and adding, he had begun to lose enthusiasm. He knew those zeros he kept adding to his accounts could mean something as solid as a Ferrari or a night of luxury in any city in the world he fancied, though he had time for neither. Entire years filled with thirty-hour flights without lying down to sleep. Years of countless five-star hotels, but desolate to the point of death, trying to prove to Elena that there was no one else in the room. Endless days dragging across time zones... All for one more zero in his account, on the way to ten million that he would never reach, not only because now Elena was going to take almost everything, but, above all, because before reaching ten million, he had quickly approached sixty and no longer had the energy or desire to keep competing in an absurd race. Not only because his two most productive decades had passed, but because time was beginning to accelerate vertiginously. Because, as the ice cream vendor Don Ramón had told him, it's when you already see the corner where you're about to turn. It's when you look back and realize that everything you thought was important has no significance whatsoever, like someone who works their whole life hiding money in a chest and, one day, discovers that a wave of inflation has carried away ninety, ninety-nine percent of its value.

Why didn't Ernesto bother him? Facundo asked himself again, leaning with one hand against the wall of a house that by day must have been pink or apricot-colored, while suddenly spotting a modest sign on a corner that said RESTAURANTE COLA DE PEZ.

Cola de Pez

A MAN WITH AN INDIAN FACE and a plaid shirt passed by without looking at him, as if he were walking there but sixty years earlier. Or a hundred. Or two hundred. Then he thought about Aztec rituals, as if he were thinking to postpone the moment when he would head to Cola de Pez. (As if he couldn't move because his thoughts had stopped him at that point in the universe from where he could see everything but do nothing. A perfect observer cannot act upon reality. Action corrupts reality, clouds sight and understanding.) Those savages sacrificed victims so the world wouldn't stop. Isn't that what we do in our proud modern world, but on a larger scale and in the name of other gods? The Aztecs were savages because their gods are dead. Only for that reason. We are civilized and responsible for all the good that exists. Even large-scale massacres (whether through wars or the consumption of all kinds of poisons) are clean, necessary, sacred, because our gods are alive and rule the world.

The idea that people were starting to see him as a potential criminal made him feel safer. He tried to imagine himself as a mafioso, a drug trafficker. He slowly approached the corner of Cola de Pez, and a wave of vertigo made him stop. What was so important, after all (he thought)? He was on the trail of whoever had stolen his credit card, which was rather insignificant considering the amount spent and the available credit limit. He could have canceled the card and waited to see if he received notifications of other purchases in his email, which is what usually happens when someone's identity is stolen. Someone buys a car, and the unsuspecting owner of the identity gets bills for unpaid payments. Things like that. But no. In his case, there was nothing like that. Not even, come to think of it, had he ordered a credit report from Equifax or TransUnion. Why? he wondered. What was the rush that had suddenly turned into paralysis? Maybe the matter wasn't such a big deal after all, and it was all due to the stress he was going through.

So, why did he have so many expectations just steps away from entering Cola de Pez?

It was that same vertigo he had forgotten by force of building himself up, of inventing himself as an effective, relentless man. That vertigo he only recognized from his early youth, from his nineteen or twenty years in Buenos Aires, when he lived alone in a boarding house and studied Economics at UBA. Back then, economics had nothing to do with

business or money but with something more interesting like the world. Domestic Economy in Ancient
Egypt, The Rise and Fall of the Assyrian Empire, Industry and Empire, The Birth of the Industrial Revolution, Pedagogy of the Oppressed, Why Are
Countries Poor? The Alliance for Progress, The Problem of the Second Economy in the Soviet Union, The
End of History... All of that had ended thanks to a
scholarship from the University of North Carolina.
From curiosity about the world, he moved to the
OPPORTUNITIES THE CURRENT WORLD OFFERS. Was it
right there that, almost without noticing it, his life
underwent a dramatic change? He left economics and
dedicated himself to business, as if they were two false
cognates. His master's thesis hadn't been about Adam
Smith or Keynes but was pure entrepreneurship sermon: "The Cultural Problem of Companies in the
Third World." He had met Elena shortly before graduating and almost immediately her brother, Ernesto,
with that Spanish inability for politeness exacerbated
by Argentine arrogance (he had barely met him at a
restaurant, and his brother-in-law had already refuted
the central idea of his thesis: Yes, of course, those the-
ses about the Latin American Idiots and the Mental
Retardation of poor countries like India and China
fail to recognize that every large company is a small

269

government that no one elected). She was in her last year of her English degree and had been an outstanding lacrosse player.

Economics was something else, he thought, on the verge of dizziness: it was more romantic, more real, less hypocritical, less demagogic. The damask-colored wall seemed to move as if in a tremor, but Facundo managed to pull himself together. Economics, at least in those years, was as romantic as Rodin's sculptures, as Discépolo's lyrics, as Uncle Alberto's piano. That vertigo, that fear, was very much like the time he tried to initiate himself into sex to prove he wasn't a sissy, as his grandmother feared, and went to a brothel in the lower part of Buenos Aires. He was twenty years old, with the head of a child and the body of a man. He had reached the start of his third decade without ever making a woman scream. But that night he was so scared that he ended up in a nearby bar, just as run-down, drinking Uruguayan grappa. When he had enough grappa and courage, he went and entered the brothel. It gave him some confidence when a guy who looked like a worker and was more nervous than him asked if the women there were good. He said more or less, as if he knew, and the worker went on his way. "Come in, man," the manager told him when she saw him hesitating. "The girls are waiting for you." He slept with a woman much older than him, with huge breasts, almost shapeless breasts. They called her "The Mexican," but she was Colombian, as she admitted when he said something about her accent, none of which made any sense to young Facundo. After all, that's what a brothel is, like almost everything in our screwed-up world: if you're going to pay for a product, let it be a good lie in the name of authenticity. Like that "Real food" trend, so popular in the United States, which only fools can believe, just as they believe everything else is real food. But believing is part of the game, and we all need to believe in something and, of course, it had better not be something unpleasant. If one doesn't believe, they can't reach orgasm, no matter how much they pay. Paying, voting, isn't enough; you also have to believe. That's what a Pentecostal church and a brothel have in common. It's not enough to tithe to the pastor. You also have to believe, otherwise, the demon won't leave the tormented body.

That Saturday night in Buenos Aires, lost in time and forgotten by any possible historical records, he didn't even get hard. His dick, to be precise. Either it was the shock of having, for the first time, a naked woman beneath his insignificant humanity, or it was the excess of alcohol, which is well known to not

271

facilitate erections. 'Are you going to stick it in me this limp?' the Colombian woman had complained, as if she were in a hurry. She was right. He didn't know what to do. A ridiculous amateur. By then, he no longer felt that initial vertigo but pure humiliation. Fortunately, he didn't remember the date, as any woman would.

Now, in front of the humble Cola de Pez restaurant, he was feeling all that vertigo again, that old teenage fear over utterly ridiculous things, like the insignificant act of nailing a woman in bed whom he didn't even love, who neither knows nor will know who he is. That vertigo, that sacred fear of the unforgettable (yet still trivial) moment of discovering in math class that the prettiest girl was looking at him with inexplicable sweetness, and him resigned to not speaking to her purely out of fear of beauty. That beauty that's only felt in its full intensity when one is capable of being afraid of what they admire, what they dream of and desire.

He stopped. He was about to turn back.

Why, then (he thought, as he sat on the doorstep), was he doing all of this? Why had he traveled from so far away to take justice into his own hands? What was the drama, after all? Perhaps because, suddenly, he'd had free time, thanks to his illness.

Perhaps because Elena's divorce and the absurd court rulings against him, despite having spent a fortune on the best lawyers, had embittered him to the point of wanting to resolve everything on his own. In any case, his vertigo, that anxiety, was entirely exaggerated and unjustified. That strange unease (that deep feeling of inferiority called shyness that feels like vertigo, as if walking on a tightrope over an abyss) was typical of his youth, but not of a man full of confidence who navigates airports and the offices of the most powerful boards in the world.

There it was. RESTAURANTE COLA DE PEZ. Had he forgotten the modest sign without lights? He couldn't say. Probably he'd never looked at it carefully. Probably not. Undoubtedly. If he, Facundo, had ever been there, he hadn't sat on a doorstep staring at that sign and doubting what to do. Zero probability. He would have arrived in a taxi, or in some client's car, who knows for what reason or by what sheer coincidence.

He entered and recognized the place by its smell, by the ceiling fans, and by a faded reproduction of Les demoiselles d'avignon, though he didn't remember the bar or the glass cabinet full of bottles or the mosaic floor, as if it were the remnant of a luxurious past, a silent witness to stories long gone, like a restored floor in Pompeii. The ceiling, on the other hand, was sheet metal, rusted years ago. A contrast born from dramatic decay. One assumes that ceilings are more important than floors, but those people, he thought, cared more about what they saw and felt than about something that, although fundamental to their protection, like air, couldn't be seen. Normally, one relates more to the floor than to the ceiling, but any reasonable person would agree on which part of a house, of a building, is the most important. That's why they saw the Virgin everywhere, because an abstract god felt more distant, unfeeling. That's why they cared more about the present than the future, about the color of the walls than the organization of traffic. That's why they were happier than the successful Calvinists of the north, he thought, and he also thought that maybe all of that was just ridiculous stereotypes.

He located the table by the window without glass and waited until its occupants left. Then, he sat in the same spot, probably at the same time as before. Or had he been there more than once? He looked at his watch. 7:29 p.m.

He asked the waiter about the blind Ramiro. It had been a while since they'd seen him around, the waiter said. Someone had mentioned that his health had worsened and that he almost never left his house.

He ordered some snacks. The waiter recited a labyrinthine list, and Facundo interrupted him:

"The house specialty" he said, as if he were in a hurry.

"Duck skewers with licorice and guava."

"Yes, that's it."

"To drink...? I recommend *Nocturna*, the best craft beer in Tijuana. My brother is one of the main shareholders... Nahhh, what's up? He handles deliveries to the restaurants."

When the waiter returned with the beer, Facundo asked him about the owner.

"The lady?" asked the waiter.

"Yes, the owner."

"María. She took a leave. I think she's back next Monday. She's Ramirito's cousin, though he looks more like her uncle. The rough life, you know."

The waiter asked him where he was from. Facundo said Argentina.

"You've got a bit of Cuban or Dominican in you" the waiter observed.

He had been careful to camouflage his accent by eliminating or softening the fricatives, the *sho, cashes, plasha*, and *posho*,* and without intending to, some of those aspirated 'j' sounds from the Caribbean had slipped out. But lying quickly didn't come naturally to him, so he said Argentine, just in case, in case they asked him about some details that only those who had lived in a place for a long time would know. So he went by Luis Ocampo, because he had always used his middle name and his second last name as an alternative (in case he had to give his real name and wasn't forced to admit to lying), and he was Argentine because he still was.

He had dinner, spent a long time sitting at the table, trying to recall some significant detail, imagining who and how they might have gotten hold of his credit card information, when and how he might have decided to go somewhere else.

At one point, he remembered, with clarity, a young woman sitting at the adjacent table, her hands resting on a blue folder. He closed his eyes and realized the trick his memory had played on him: it was

---

* *Sho, cashes, plasha*, and *posho* (*yo, calles, playa* and *pollo*). Speakers from Argentina and Uruguay are recognized in the rest of Latin America by the fricative pronunciation of "ll" and "y" ("s" or "j" sound) in "jump", while the rest of Latin Americans pronounce those letters as "y" in "yesterday."

Lucy, the android from Seoul. Androids don't need phones.

He paid in cash, Mexican pesos, and took a taxi back to the hotel.

Nocturna, Opus 9, Number 2

MONDAY THE 9TH, at 7:20 pm, Facundo returned to Cola de Pez. Carlos, the waiter, recognized him from the last time.

"Don Luis" the waiter said to him. "Today I have some ribs with fig syrup and black mole that are to die for."

"Sounds good" said Facundo. "But I liked the skewers from last time, and I struggle to experiment."

"You're in charge" said the waiter.

He didn't ask about María. He knew she would appear at any moment. Or he would hear her voice.

Almost an hour later, María hurried by with a rag in her hand. She peeked out the door and yelled something at a passing truck. ¡Parmesan! A box! she shouted. The driver replied Tomorrow first thing.

When she returned, Facundo looked her in the eyes, and she smiled at him. But she didn't seem to recognize him. Half an hour later, she came back and sat in the chair across from him.

"When did you come back…?" asked María.

Facundo must have looked at her with surprise, because she tried to confirm:

"You're Luis, the one with the piano… Or is it too dark in here?"

"I'm not a pianist" said Facundo.

"I know" she said. "But when you were young, you used to play your uncle's piano."

Uncle Alberto from Uruguay had a piano in Piriápolis and had taught him to play Nocturne by Chopin. It was the only thing he ever learned to play in his life, until one night, in a hotel in Singapore, during a dinner with three of his colleagues and a bigshot from China, he asked the pianist to let him play and, when he tried, all that came out was a series of senseless, ridiculously dissonant sounds. Ever since, for a long time, he remembered that night with unbearable humiliation. He could never forget it, like so many others. He had a special talent for remembering guilt and humiliation and, although over the years he had gradually lost interest in what others might think of him and, as a consequence, humiliations had dropped in rank on the list of important things. That didn't mean he had forgotten them. That night, in that five-star hotel for a hundred-million-dollar deal, his colleagues joked that, despite being high quality, the wine must have disagreed with him. It hadn't been simply a joke but a biting, acid sarcasm, as sour and rotten as any of the three of them. The Chinese guy (despite the fortune he had or managed, he couldn't remember his name) had encouraged him to keep practicing. Keep trying. It wasn't clear if his English wasn't good enough for a more subtle comment or if he was just another filthy-rich communist. Facundo had wanted to shine at the piano to redeem himself from his poor performances in the three previous presentations, typical of a beginner way out of his depth. Over time, he left all his colleagues behind, relegated to the Latin America section, while he was assigned Southeast Asia, but he never forgot any of those small humiliations.

Some time later (two years?) in Atlanta, at a modest piano in a thrift store, one of those places that sell old things, without wine, without an audience, and without a millionaire to impress as if he were a prostitute, he tried again, with the same result but without an audience or consequences to regret.

All of that had been at the beginning of his career at Simons Hayyet, more than twenty years ago, almost thirty. After Singapore and Atlanta, he never again attempted to play that melody he had learned to play by ear in a single night in Piriápolis, shortly before the end of the summer of '76. His uncle had promised to teach him other pieces the following summer, preferably by reading the sheet music, because he had said that Facundo had a special talent for music, something his father did not like at all when he found out. But the uncle died that very winter, and his house remained definitively empty (save for the memories, the portraits of him and his wife still hanging on the walls of their bedroom, she having died twenty years earlier during a difficult childbirth). Back then, he thought Uncle Alberto was a very old man, and now, suddenly, he realized he had died just after turning sixty. He had been born at the start of the First World War, a year later, in 1915. Yes, when he died, he must have been around the same age as Facundo now, but with more gray hair because he was blond. Later, he found out (later, since his father had hidden it from him with kind lies) that he hadn't died of a sudden heart attack but of a heart attack caused by his excesses with alcohol. Facundo had never seen him drunk, or if he had seen him at some point, he attributed it to the incurable melancholy that came from remembering his wife and the child who was never born. Chopin had lived until 39, he once heard his father say, and he left us all that the rest of us failed pianists will never leave behind, even

if we live twice as long. Yes, only 39. One always assumes that the names and faces that populate encyclopedias and the admiration of other generations had
long lives, because only someone who lived two hundred years instead of forty could create something as
immortal as Nocturne.

The memories of Uncle Alberto, the notes of
Chopin, Debussy, Ravel, Prokofiev, Albéniz, Mond-
scheinsonate, Moonlight Sonata by Beethoven, and
the scent of the beach and the freedom of a nearby
country as if it were as distant as the French Riviera
of 1849, overwhelmed him the last time he walked
through there, on his way to Punta del Este, in the
summer of '82. His father, Uncle Alberto's brother-in-
law, must have taken care of selling the house. Between notaries and opportunistic offers, five years
passed. The uncle knew he was going to die and had
left the house, that is, everything he had, to his
nephew Facundito. To his father, the authority to ad-
minister the property. Facundo's father did not want
his son to follow in the bohemian uncle's footsteps
and put the house up for sale as soon as he could. Facundo never questioned the decision. In some way, he
also wanted to forget. When the house was finally
sold and they went to make sure nothing personal
was left to retrieve, Facundo smelled the scent of

emptiness and began to cry like a child. He was twenty-two years old, meaning before that absurd incident in the Buenos Aires brothel. While his father ran his hand over his head trying to comfort him ("I also loved your Uncle Alberto very much," his father had said), Facundo once again heard those notes of Chopin that the uncle played with a clarity that could not be explained.

"Why are some notes as clear as clean water and others as murky as a polluted river, if they're all notes just the same?" Facundo had asked the first time he sat in front of his uncle's piano, and Uncle Alberto had replied:

"That's the mystery!" as if, suddenly, he had discovered the ultimate meaning of existence.

For many years, he remembered that melody, Nocturne, Opus 9, Number 2, ironically, with a powerful light and a gentle breeze that lifted the translucent curtains (those his uncle liked so much, only because they had been made by his wife, who loved subtle details like tulle and white roses), a breeze that was decidedly strange, from another country and another era, coming in through the windows that faced the sea, like a photograph that loses its shadows over time, that fades, that sinks into the light.

María stood up and told him he should play again. Facundo refused. He couldn't play two notes without them sounding off-key, he said. That wasn't his thing.

"I know," she said. "It's not about giving a concert at the Metropólitan. Not even about playing for my customers. Just what you played last time."

"What did we play last time?"

"I didn't play anything," she said. "I couldn't. Don't make me beg because I'm not going to insist all night. Or maybe you don't want to play because she's not here?"

"She? Who's she?"

"Come on," said María.

Facundo stood up, tired.

"Why play poorly something that you can listen to better on YouTube?" he said.

"You're not being authentic," she replied. "You know it's not the same, but you repeat what any fool in your place would have said."

"What's the difference?"

"The difference between listening to Chopin on YouTube and hearing it on a piano is the same difference between watching pornography and making love."

Facundo looked at her in silence. María intimidated him. She was too sure of everything, and maybe she was wrong, like everyone else.

"Don't feel bad. I have nothing against pornography."

"I don't care," he cut in. "Really, it's getting late for me."

"You sound like a girl, Luis. I'm not interested in sleeping with you, nor am I one of those hypocritical women you know in the U.S., a girl from a churchgoing family who on Sundays goes to church but at the first chance sucks anyone off. The ones who can't, imagine it or watch porn online while their innocent (or not so innocent) husbands are working like beasts to pay for football tickets on Saturdays. What I like most are those three-minute clips where a Black man punishes a blonde woman with a huge penis. I go to yahoo.com and type in 'black on blond,' because in English you get more videos, right? Aren't you all the universal providers of pornography?"

"Us?"

"Then he gives her hard spanks on the buttocks until they turn red, while she fakes pleasure when anyone knows that poor worker just wants the torture to end so she can collect her paycheck. Especially when she has to suck that twenty-centimeter junk like

284

it's a lollipop. We all know the girl is suffering, and he almost as much, but we don't care. Why? Because we want to be lied to. People always want to be lied to, but it has to be pleasurable. If you don't believe the lie, then you don't enjoy it. Isn't that exactly how politicians screw us over?"

"You consume all that?"

"For the past couple of years. I don't know why I watch that stuff, because I'm really against any kind of violence. Sometimes I wonder if it's because I now have unlimited internet or it's just old age. Because before, I could get mad if someone catcalled me, and now they don't even catcall me on the street. Time is a relentless curse."

"Okay, let's drop it."

"You're not one of them, Luis."

"Who's them?"

"You're a liar, but not a hypocrite."

"You talk as if you know me."

"In reality, no one knows anyone. Not even ourselves. At most, we can only suspect who someone is based on little details, like those images of Neanderthals that scientists recreate from a single tooth, as if they were gods creating a complete human being from a rib."

"What would my tooth be?"

"For starters, your name isn't Luis. Well, it is, but…"

"What's my name, then?"

"You don't even know. But you like her."

"Who's her?"

"Please, Luis, enough. Don't underestimate me. I'm older and I know when a man is looking at a woman he likes. You like her. Not me, that's clear. I'm too old."

"Well, you're very attractive and must be around my age."

"But men your age like younger women. It's the same for us. We just don't say it. But the truth is the truth, and if we had to choose, we wouldn't pick an old man. You can't compare an old potbellied guy to a young man with broad shoulders and a narrow waist."

"Is that what love boils down to?"

"Come on, Luis," she laughed. "At our age, there's no time for romance, at least not that flowery, butterfly kind of love. At best, we can aspire to affection, to understanding. I really liked a reflection you made one night after playing Chopin for her, even though you told me it was for me. We all remember a plant for its flowers, a tree for its fruits. Isn't the life of a human being just that fleeting moment, like a

286

flower that blooms for three days, like a fruit that ripens and falls from the tree? I liked it a lot, even if it wasn't for me."

"I said that?" He must have had one drink too many.

"Some drunks say very beautiful things. Someone with one drink too many may be less functional, but they're always more authentic than when they're sober."

"It's really getting late," Facundo insisted.

"Let's go to the piano," she said.

"What piano?"

"What do you mean, what piano? The one they brought me as a decoration and as payment for an uncollectible debt. I told you about the irresponsible grandson of an old client who died and…"

"Where is it?"

"In the storage room. It would look very nice there, against that wall, but it would take up two tables."

María went to the kitchen and came back with two Nocturna beers. She gestured for him to follow and they went down a narrow, dark staircase. When she opened the storage room, Facundo recognized the place. How could he not remember it? Her smiling face flashed through his mind like a gust of wind, an unmistakable sign that something wasn't working right. He had managed to sleep almost normally the last two nights, more likely due to exhaustion from new experiences than any improvement in his health.

That smell, the dim light, the modest upright piano in a corner next to a stack of Jarritos crates. María told him to play the one she had loved so much. She excused herself, saying she could barely manage something like a ranchera song.

"I'm not a musician. I've never studied piano..."

"Come on, man," she said, "you're a fraud."

"Probably, yes."

"In fact, I don't even know if you're Argentine or American."

"Maybe neither," he laughed.

Then they fell silent. Facundo thought, trying to remember the summer of '86. Little by little, after some initial stumbles, he remembered Uncle Alberto's voice humming some notes and showing him how to place his hands. Gradually, he recovered Nocturna, as if drawing a bucket of water from a deep well, a well two hundred years deep. As soon as he finished, he moved on to Beethoven's Moonlight Sonata. Impossible that he had learned it from Uncle Alberto, he thought. Or had he forgotten? Or was it Uncle Alberto who was playing at that very moment?

Immediately, he remembered that it hadn't been in a single night, the last night of the summer of '86, when he had learned to play the piano. He had spent the entire summer of that year playing the piano with his uncle, but when his father arrived from Buenos Aires in early March, he had told him that he had learned to play something in the last few days, the very last day. The uncle must have understood, because he didn't correct the mistake. Later, he himself had believed that story. His father was a good man who was afraid of music, of the mysterious life of Uncle Alberto, and the uncle knew it and accepted it without sorrow or humiliation.

When he finished, she said:

"It's very beautiful. What's it called?"

"I had forgotten I could play it. That was my best performance, so don't ask me to repeat it because it'll be catastrophic."

"Nonsense," she said. "You said the same thing last time."

Facundo looked into her eyes. María was a mature woman. She had been very beautiful, and that was still evident, as was a deep resentment from some experience that had happened perhaps decades earlier. The story of Cola de Pez, the story of the Siren, the story of the legless woman, had filtered out to the public without revealing the origin of the mystery, the origin of that personality that was both attractive and distant.

"I think I've had too much to drink," said Facundo. "I'm not used to it. If you'd be so kind, please call a taxi."

David Román

THE THEORY THAT THE CRIMINAL could be Russian software, a Chinese robot in some corner of the planet, was shattered that night when, upon reviewing his bank account, he discovered a withdrawal of 159.63 dollars (surely three thousand Mexican pesos) not too far from there, made at an ATM in El Bajío, a Banamex ATM, thirty minutes from La Ensenada. He looked it up on Google Maps: it was on Avenida Lázaro Cárdenas, in a small town near a bay called La Joya. As in previous instances, it wasn't an extravagant expense, although now the amount had doubled from before.

He wasn't dealing with a simple thief. This was a kidnapping. He imagined the ATM screen on Avenida Cárdenas, his name displayed in full letters (FACUNDO WALSH OCAMPO), his PIN memorized by someone else (the day Elena had said yes, she wanted to marry him), the triumphant smile of the impostor, an unknown street.

Despite the exhaustion of the day, he tried to think with some clarity. No, not that one, he thought with relief. For his alternative card, he used the other number, the date when Elena had had sex for the first time. He, Facundo, could never remember the day he had slept with an older woman in a brothel in La Plata, not only because he had begun with a prostitute meant for forgetting, but because men don't remember those dates. A woman does. A woman is always aware of everything that happens in her body. For a woman, the body is life. They must always be attentive to their menstrual cycles, to their first and last time in everything, to a possible pregnancy. For a man, the body is merely a means to his ends. That's why they fill clothing and shoe stores and everything they carry on their bodies, while men are only interested in things they can use to do other things, like tools, cars, money. And, although Elena had sworn to him that he had been her first, he knew perfectly well that wasn't true. He knew because she had once forgotten to close her email and he had discovered that Her First Time had been the same year he had taken her to a hotel for the first time, but many months earlier, more precisely ten months before.

Why had he used this date for his alternative card? Out of resentment? It was, he thought then, a form of justification: she hadn't been entirely honest when she told him he had been her first, and she also didn't know about the existence of his alternative card. Foolish, considering that he had never used that card for anything that could compromise him. Using such an intimate and distant date also served to remind him, every time he used it, that she had lied to him. A fact he would have forgotten if she had confessed it from the beginning, as he had confessed his last experiences before getting married.

Now someone else owned his name and Elena's date, the number of his resentment, that secret revealed, never acknowledged, neither by her nor by him, and (perhaps because of that?) the source of the poison that slowly killed their marriage.

Now someone else owned his name and Elena's date, the number of his resentment, that secret revealed, never acknowledged, neither by her nor by him, and the source of the poison that slowly killed their marriage. Now someone else had appropriated all that. It was a kidnapping. Except for his body, he had been kidnapped by an impostor who was beginning to become his double.

He immediately remembered that the waiter at Cola de Pez had mentioned La Joya as a possible place to visit for a tourist who hated tourists. Did his cousin or his brother live there? He tried to recall some other detail from that conversation and couldn't.

The next day he arrived at Cola de Pez at lunchtime. María wasn't there. According to Ramiro, her father's health had taken a turn for the worse again and she probably wouldn't return until next week. Don Guerrero wasn't going to make it to his birthday.

"He's going to miss reaching ninety," said Ramiro. "A shame. A good man, but he can't complain. He's lived a lot and through many things, probably more than all of us combined."

"I think the last time the lady told me she lived in La Joya," commented Facundo.

"No. The family is from Tijuana, but now they live in El Bajío. Down there, to the south. In La Joya he had a little bar that he opened in the summer, but he closed it a couple of years ago."

"Don't you know anyone from La Joya?" asked Facundo. "I was thinking about exploring the area you recommended to me yesterday."

"The lady's cousin, David, is a teacher there. You can ask him yourself, because he stops by here on

Tuesdays. Besides being a geography teacher, he's in charge of the pasta delivery."

"What time does he pass by here?"

The waiter glanced at the clock and squinted in a gesture of mental effort.

"I'd say in an hour or so."

"Maybe I'll wait," said Facundo.

"No problem," said the waiter. "If there's one thing that characterizes this place, it's that we're never in a hurry or rush our customers. Great poets used to come here and spend hours arguing. Sometimes the lady would tell them that if they weren't going to order anything, they should talk outside, because they were taking up tables. So for a while you'd see them out there, on the other side, at the little tables on the sidewalk, until for some reason they disappeared. Someone said they had started working seriously, but the truth is I knew one of them and the kid had been working like a beast since he was a child. To me, they went to the other side."

"As illegals?"

"Or to the other side. It seems they weren't just arguing about poetry, but they had started writing in the newspaper and published something that the Chapo didn't like."

"The drug cartel?"

"No, not El Chapo Guzmán. This Chapo, Chapo García, was a smaller fish, the owner of a very large ranch nearby. It seems Chapo had invested a lot of money to support culture in La Ensenada. Musicians, painters, and poets benefited from generous donations to the House of Culture and, above all, to the Circle of Poets. One of them even wrote a song for the benefactor, but slowly the poets grew wings and moved from poetry to politics. That, they say, is where the whole problem began."

"And?"

"The end, I don't know. All I know is that La Ensenada was emptied of poets, just as it was emptied of birds. If you want to know, ask David. He's always involved in those strange things. Once I told him, 'David, stop playing with fire, you're not gaining anything but trouble.' But the man doesn't listen, and I prefer not to know. I just want to go back to my little house every day at six, where my dog, my tequila, and Barça's goals await me."

"Poets don't seem like dangerous people."

"You say that because you're from the other side. David also says that over there, poets aren't dangerous—they're just full of verse. Here, it's a matter of life or death, lots of life and lots of death. Here, we exaggerate everything. Over there, everything's under control, like life itself, David says."

"Do you think it's safer there?"

"I don't know. In many ways, yes. People don't bother stealing a radio, there's more money for the police, things like that..."

Behind them appeared a dark-skinned man to complete Ramiro's sentence.

"...over there, poets are harmless," he said. "They sing about love and such things."

Ramiro turned around and said:

"Speak of the devil, and he shall appear."

Then, addressing Facundo, he introduced him as Professor and Pasta Delivery Man David Román. David complained with exaggerated gestures.

"What's up, buddy?" he said. "Friends talk bad about me because they love me..."

"You're going to make me cry," said the waiter sarcastically and went to attend to a couple who had just sat at a table.

David sat at Facundo's table and said:

"You're not from here."

"What's this about poets from the other side?" asked Facundo, avoiding David's question. Poetry had never interested him, except for a couple of months in Piriápolis. He considered it an excuse used by fraudsters who couldn't, or didn't want to, work seriously.

"Over there, on the other side," said David, "poetry is harmless, innocent. That's why those Caribbean singers are so successful. They sing about love and sex. What's easier to sell than love and sex? Well, actually, it's not love, and maybe not even sex, but desire. Like in any brothel, but more prestigious. Nothing is real there. Everything has to be an illusion, or it doesn't sell. And here, so far from God and so close to the United States, it's not much different when it comes to the powerful. Did Ramiro tell you there are no more poets around? I thought I heard that. Well, it's true. And who cares? Poets, useless people, slackers, right? Well, maybe they are slackers and dreamers, but the fact that they are so discredited and have disappeared is not a minor thing. In this blessed and cursed country, like in any other, poets are applauded when they don't bother anyone. That's why there are so many awards and benefactors. It's to keep them quiet. If I'm El Chapo and you're a poet, and because you're a poet you're struggling to eat, then I'll feed you and give you an award, and you won't bite the hand that feeds you. It's like when some poor people go illegally to the other side and then can't say anything against that Great Country because they're immediately labeled as ungrateful beggars. But some real poets can't stop being poets and aren't satisfied with singing praises to Caesar. Sooner or later, their conscience starts itching, and they begin to question this and that, poisoning themselves with all the injustice around us. And because they're poets or they've already published in some newspaper and some little collective book, they start publishing uncomfortable questions."

"And they disappear," interrupted Facundo.

"In many ways. Either they're marginalized, which happens in civilized countries like the United States (because some empires don't need to resort to cheap violence), or they lose their jobs, or they're disappeared literally—if they live in sheep-like countries like ours, in the hands not only of the empire but of our own corrupt and murderous made-in-Mexico criminals."

"Judging by the evidence, it's not your case, despite thinking so differently."

"Because I don't publish what I think," said David, leaning back against the wall, tired. "They say I talk too much, but at least I don't publish. At least not in printed letters with all that antiquated pomp of presenting books in some run-down bookstore attended only by a handful of friends and family out of obligation. Maybe I've crossed paths with some mafioso, with some CIA agent, but they didn't even bother to eliminate someone as insignificant as me. Because, you know something? There are two ways to save yourself from the retaliation of power: one is to be Albert Einstein or Noam Chomsky. The other is to be nobody, like me. If you're in the middle, you're in trouble."

"You're going to make me cry," said the waiter as he passed by.

"Go to hell," David shot back, "and wash that apron that's not even white anymore."

The waiter returned and said:

"You can mess with the president himself, but don't mess with my apron."

David laughed heartily and, turning to Facundo, said:

"See what I'm saying?"

Facundo didn't understand the supposed connection. He couldn't stop thinking that David's profile fit perfectly within his list of suspects. Someone like him could commit one of those thefts that they later considered a moral act for a cause, like the old anarchists and the more recent Latin American guerrillas who defended bank robberies because society had robbed them, those modern, failed, unproductive, hypocritical Robin Hoods. There's always a reason, an excuse for everything, Facundo thought as he listened without really paying attention to David's words.

Buick LeSabre 1984

FACUNDO PRETENDED TO AGREE with everything David said. At one point, David asked if he was an undercover CIA agent. Facundo laughed, and David said it didn't matter anyway because, as he had explained, he was too insignificant for anyone with any power to take a special interest in him.

Only a few who had known David for a long time could tell when he was being serious and when he wasn't. The mind of a Mexican is as impenetrable as the Club of the Hundred Million, he thought. What mattered was that he had offered to take him to La Joya. They agreed to meet the next day at the corner of Cola de Pez at five in the afternoon.

At five-fifteen, David showed up with his 1984 Buick LeSabre. He had fallen in love with the car on the other side, in Los Angeles, just before turning away from his American dream.

"American dream," he repeated, thinking back to those days without taking his eyes off the road. "In reality, it was the dream of youth, like anyone's dream anywhere else in the world. I suppose. Anyway, the truth is I was able to bring the old Buick with me when I came back in 2006."

On the way to La Joya, he explained how he had managed to bring over such a cheap car. He hadn't used it much there, for security reasons. The previous owner was a friend of David's, a fellow countryman who was doing a Master's in Marine Sciences at UCLA. Like any student, even an advanced one with a degree from UNAM, he wasn't exactly rolling in money, and that's why he had bought that Buick for about nine hundred dollars, roughly the cost of a month's rent in his student apartment. But because of his 'Indian' face and the old car, the police would stop him every month, more or less.

"My buddy had papers from the university, so they could never catch him doing anything illegal, and that's why he told me that if I was going to buy a car, it should be a new one, as expensive as possible, because at least then it would raise fewer suspicions. I wasn't going to change my Mexican face, like Michael Jackson—that was expensive—but with a baseball cap, some dark glasses, and keeping my mouth shut, I managed to blend in pretty well. I wanted the old Buick to come back to the village, so I didn't care if they caught me on the way to the border, and my buddy let me have it for five hundred dollars. But since I was undocumented, I couldn't drive it across the border either."

Every time David detailed a problem, one of those ordeals that had frayed his nerves, he would smile. Or he'd burst into laughter, the kind only a truly humble man knows how to do. Past problems always end up being funny (he remembered Ernesto telling him once), like when someone falls in the street and you find out it wasn't important after all. Or that's how it seems, because the internal trauma from a blow to the head isn't visible when the victim gets up and smiles to avoid embarrassment or too much tension. Why do people laugh at those small misfortunes of others? Could it be that we all need to believe that our fears and anxieties are unfounded? Why do we read novels where they systematically begin with a dead body and proceed to search for the killer? The same old, repeated formula since centuries ago, since the fear of hell from churches lost its monopoly on human terror, back in the days of the Enlightenment. Or those other novels, frequent bestsellers, or successful horror movies where something horrible keeps the reader's attention until the last page (a shapeless mass gradually devours all living beings before slipping through the city's sewer pipes; a beautiful woman who, upon being kissed, turns into a rotting corpse infecting every man and woman who falls into her trap, all for the simple sin of having some sense of or weakness for beauty). What primitive and base instinct keeps us desiring what we condemn, eager to get a glimpse of what we fear so much? Like when we pass by an accident on the highway and can't help but glance at the twisted car, at the body covered by a white plastic sheet, even if, for that very reason, we risk crashing into the car in front, equally distracted by the corpse. In that case, it's a complete tragedy, with no relieved laughter, but at least it's a didn't-happen-to-me. Isn't that the same reason people are obsessed with bloopers, American Funniest Videos? You already know the ending, and so, the drama turns into comedy. Or we don't know the ending, but since it's a show meant to pass the time, we assume nothing serious has happened. A little girl hits her father in the testicles with a baseball bat; a boy falls off the roof of a house and cracks his head on a table; someone tries to blow out their birthday candles and sets their hair on fire, goodness knows why; an excessively obese woman tries to swing and ends up with her head buried in the ground while a dog decides to pee on her as she struggles to move her

303

uncontrollable humanity. Those hilarious things where we all assume, or want to assume, that nothing serious happened in the end. That's why in cheap Hollywood movies, everyone laughs at the end. Heaven forbid someone takes something seriously. That's why even politicians make jokes about a war that has left half a million dead, and one day, those same world leaders discover they started it based on incorrect information and are invited to give conferences where they receive tens of thousands of dollars for forty minutes of witty remarks that provoke laughter and collective history. That's why. Heaven forbid someone takes something seriously.

But David's laughter was that of a loser, of someone who had managed to survive and even figured out how to be happy in some way. Something that Facundo couldn't even suspect in a loser, in a survivor.

"Yes, it was love at first sight," David said, patting the Buick's steering wheel, "and we've never been apart since."

At the pizzeria where he worked in Pasadena, he had made a friend, a Yankee named Mister Burton, an old red-haired man who liked pizza with basil, amber beer, and the sand of Long Beach almost as much as dark-skinned women. During that long trip in

2006, Mister Burton had told him about another journey, a two-thousand-mile trip with his father to Acapulco back in the seventies, their first vacation in many years after his mother had passed away. Around Colima, they had picked up two very young women who were heading to the same city for adventures. They were two cheerful girls who didn't speak a single word of English, aside from 'yes' and 'thank you.' That time, one of those times when life resembles life, Mister Burton (back then, young Donald Hugh, the ridiculous red-haired boy everyone mocked in school (and in middle and high school) long before anyone called it bullying, with his red, curly hair like a black man's even though he wasn't black, the skinny, nervous kid everyone disliked for his bad temper and for not hating the Vietnamese who threatened his country's freedom) found love, or, rather, boundless admiration, or something like it. His father spoke Spanish quite well, having learned enough to preach in that language, the language of the poor streets of Los Angeles. The undocumented were the only ones who paid him any attention. Not because they could get something out of him, like a job, but because it seemed that the crazy man on the corner of César Chávez and Hazard, a block from Esteban Torres High School, respected them in some way. At least he was interested in them, not just there to deport them. So the father of young Burton learned to speak Spanish better than he could understand it. Mister Burton, the very young Burton, on the other hand, and for obvious reasons, had learned to understand it better than he could speak it. In fact, he was terrified to say a single word in Spanish in high school. So that forbidden language and the torture of his peers were incompatible things, as incompatible as later were vacations, that form of small liberation from classes, from bullying, and from exams.

In that commendable Spanish of Los Angeles, his father had told the young adventurers that it was not safe at all to do what they were doing, that it would be better if they didn't spend all their money in Acapulco and saved some to return home by bus. The young Burton not only admired them to pathological limits, for the beauty of their fresh and perfumed faces, their slender twenty-something bodies, and their short, flower-patterned dresses, but also for a certain idea that, unintentionally, his father had slipped in that afternoon, in his long sermon as a responsible pastor: the girls were not only innocent but also aspiring bad girls. They were on the wrong path. They didn't attend church on Sundays, and they didn't even have boyfriends. One of them, the blonde girl in the front seat, told Burton's father that she liked poison more than men and that she had no plans to start a family, neither on this side nor much less on the other, so she wasn't going to worry about what her future children might think, and if, by some twist of fate, she ended up having a child, well, they'd just have to get used to reality, that she would be the mother they got, and if they didn't like it, they could go find a better mother.

The girl's boldness, defying his father without losing her joy or her smile, made a strong impression on him. His father was a good man, he had said, but not even he, that rigid and confident man, dared to question himself in the slightest, neither in what he said nor in what he thought. He couldn't conceive, or was terrified to think, that he could have been wrong even for a single minute in his life. In his church, they had taught him since childhood, if not trained and indoctrinated him, to fight against temptations, that is, against any questioning. And his duty was to spread those ideas that were God's ideas.

From there, his father went on to recommend that they learn English, to better understand certain things he couldn't express in Mexican. The one in the front had told him not to worry about them, that a Catholic priest had also tried to convince them of something similar, to get married and all that, but she had told him that God doesn't go to church. How did she know? his father had asked, almost triumphantly, thinking that the Bible had no reference to such a thing. Well (the blonde girl in the front had said), she knew because she had met God on a beach, one morning before the sun rose, and He had revealed the truth to her. God doesn't go to churches, she had said, according to the supposed revelation. God doesn't go to those closed, smelly places, but prefers the open air of the temples He Himself created. God goes to the beach, to the mountains, to the agave fields, to the deserts where the poor die. God sits beside a bed in a brothel, where a so-called bad woman suffers, who for Him is not bad. How? Why couldn't she have a revelation if all the pastors have theirs? Don't pastors and the presidents of their great country have similar revelations? Well, she did too, even though she was a woman and blonde and poor and single and pretty (yes, of course, of course she knew she was pretty; she wasn't dumb), that is, all that came down to being a waste, like being a lesbian for those celibate men with their irrepressible biological and metaphysical needs.

Mister Burton's father fell into a disapproving silence. He slowed down and, after a moment, resumed his normal pace. He couldn't just leave them on the side of the road either, at the mercy of who knows what dangers. Mister Burton tried to imagine God going to a beach and couldn't. But neither could he imagine God sitting in one of the pews in his father's church. This was, perhaps, the worst revelation. It shouldn't have been that tragic, if you think about it, since God must have other priorities. Which doesn't mean his father was a bad man. It just meant he was another man, something hard to digest for someone who is one of the chosen ones.

One of those young women, named Lucía (how could he forget her name?), had sat with young Burton in the back seat of the Buick and hadn't stopped smiling at him the entire trip, until the father dropped the two women off at a hotel or motel in Acapulco, just as the sun was setting. The old Burton, then the ridiculous young boy Donald Hugh, could never forget that scent of a woman, like the aroma of watermelon, of mango, of Giorgio Armani perfume, of deodorant mixed with sweat, of lipstick, of something he couldn't quite place and could never find in any JC Penny, any Macy's, or any other women's store.

The Yank (said David, referring to his friend from Los Angeles) could never forget Lucía's joyful gaze nor her wide smile, like summer itself. Nor her

309

glowing skin. Nor something that felt like what-a-de-light-to-be-here-with-you-looking-at-you. Nor something like what-a-pity-not-to-see-you-tomorrow. Some women like younger men. Some even fancy high school boys, like those high school teachers, still young and already happy and married, still so beautiful themselves, that judges send to prison for kissing their students. Who knows if the very young Burton also couldn't forget Lucía's long, bare legs, her pulled-up skirt, her overly revealing neckline, which not only hinted at two beautiful breasts on an insipid Hollywood poster but a unique way of feeling life that existed long before the pyramids of Egypt or the gardens of Babylon, all of which one always forgets while trying to survive or to become someone successful.

"Because of all that," said David as he pulled into a gas station, "because of all those traumas, is why in the United States they make sure that very young boys don't see half-naked women *tsssk*. That's why they don't have a problem with some stressed kid ending the lives of twenty classmates in a school shooting, but they make sure no one sees a t*t. *One-t*t. Because an AR-15 rifle is part of patriotism, but a-t*t can leave scars for life. Which, in a way, is true. For me, t*ts have always left me something."

Who knows if old Burton (said David later, as if thinking out loud) couldn't forget the touch of a knee that, for old farts like us, means nothing, but for an eighteen-year-old boy, it's a revelation of creation. Apparently, said David, pretending to mock mister Burton, that's where his love for dark-skinned women with joyful smiles came from. But the Yank had the life he was supposed to have, according to his father and everyone else, until he retired and went to live in a town near Guadalajara, and who knows if he still had the stamina to keep up with the women there, but he must have been enjoying some authentic smiles, not those fake smiles that Americans give you, more out of fear than friendliness, as soon as they see you walking down the street. *Tsssk*, those sweet smiles are as authentic as a McDonald's cheeseburger or the moans of a porn actress, but sometimes you even believe them. And if not, you still try."

A few years later, through some Facebook photos, David found out that Mister Burton was doing well over in Ajijic. Well, that's what it seemed like, because on Facebook, everyone's happy. Even him. No one takes pictures when they're depressed and posts them so their friends can see what failures they are. David didn't know, though he suspected, if old Burton was really doing well, but he must have been

311

better off than he was in Ensenada. In Guadalajara, said old Burton, everything was cheaper and calmer than on the other side."

Back then, in the now distant 2006, David had offered to drive the Buick from Los Angeles to Guadalajara in exchange for getting to keep it once they arrived, which, for the Yank, was a good deal, plus a little adventure that reminded him of the other trip in 1974, though they never had the luck of picking up two women along the way, and his father had been a little pile of bones surrounded by flowers for over twenty years."

That way, David had saved the old Buick from the clutches of the junkyard, and for that reason, he never left it on the street. It had broken down more than once, but always in front of his house or just before reaching the mechanic."

On the way to La Joya, David told him

"MY AUNT, WHO CALLED HERSELF A CHRISTIAN and of noble lineage, whose job was being a housewife, and her Christian husband, whose job was building contractor, one of whose workers was my dad, the contractor's brother, who in turn would tell me: I don't pay your dad because he'll just drink that money and then beat your mom. They preached to me about Christianity, as they understood it, about their half-cooked values, about justice not earthly but divine. About being good, that is, letting them keep my dad's wages. About respecting our elders, that is, letting them leave us without food. About values I didn't understand… of principles I didn't understand. The thing is, they were talking about the capitalist principle: Fuck or get fucked. With the law of Herodes, it's either you screw or get screwed. If you don't cheat, you don't get ahead. Otherwise, they'll just call me a fool. What a shame, you're so smart, because if I knew what you know, I wouldn't be as fucked up as you are. Anyway, all that bullshit."

David's father had died on a construction site, electrocuted. His brother-in-law, the contractor, had claimed that the old man was drunk and hadn't worn rubber gloves, but his coworkers told him that he had stepped into a puddle of water where there was a damaged temporary lighting cable.

Later he found out that María was the contractor's daughter, a man who had made a certain fortune but had declined into absolute poverty in his later years. The pension he received from the government wasn't enough to cover the medications that David

313

bought for him in Tijuana, because it was cheaper than in Ensenada.

"The old man has advanced diabetes, I don't know what type, but the insulin, the glucose test strips, not to mention the occasional emergency hospitalization, cost more than a thousand pesos. I help with what I can. I go back and forth to Tijuana and sometimes I have to cover the price difference, because if I don't buy him the insulin, the old man will die. Someone once told me they didn't understand why I helped the old man so much if he had treated my father so badly. But what can I do? I do it more for María and her daughter than for him. Besides, it's not right to leave a sick man to die because of past grudges. That moment will come for all of us, don't you think?"

Facundo was sweating profusely, despite the air coming through the window. The Buick didn't have air conditioning, and the asphalt road raised dust that people in the area probably didn't even notice, out of habit.

"Don't you?" David insisted.

Facundo didn't know what to answer. He had never imagined his final days depending on anyone. Surely he would have a well-attended death, though less accompanied. Laurita would be there, he thought. Maybe Elena too, five minutes a day, or a week, so as not to keep her husband waiting too long.

David stopped at a gas station, and Facundo offered to pay for the fuel. He got out and waited by the pump as an attendant approached. When he pulled out a thousand-peso bill instead of his credit card, he felt a strong sense of déjà vu. The man on the bill looked familiar. Surely it was some martyr from Mexican history. Based on his clothing and the bell, he must have been a priest. He had probably seen him before in some book, on the internet, or on a bill from a previous trip. There was nothing strange about it, except for that feeling of recognizing a place and a moment without having been there before. At some point in his life, in a previous life, he had made those same movements. He could even predict what would happen a few seconds later. Sitting behind the wheel, David was going to turn on the radio, and Terry Jacks would sing Seasons In The Sun.

When he was young, it happened to him quite often, especially at Piriápolis in his uncle Alberto's house. Back then, he believed it was a special ability to encounter a future that had already happened millions of years before, those things that only artists are capable of perceiving. Later, over time, at the University of Philadelphia, through a friend who studied

315

neurology, he learned that it was just a miserable mental disorder, a neural short circuit or some other illusion caused by stress or illness. Of course, life itself is a disorder (Ernesto had mocked him when he found out). Life itself is a disease, and the proof is that if you live too long, you can die. For medicine, everything is a disease, a disorder, everything except living to become a millionaire. When will they declare the obsession with collecting weapons of war a pathology, or the historic habit of bombing other countries in the name of democracy, national security, and all kinds of Good Reasons?

Ernesto had snapped him out of that deep déjà vu, and as he watched the attendant approach, he muttered: Screw Ernesto. It was barely audible, but loud enough for David to ask:

"What's wrong, maestro?"

A young woman stopped her motorcycle nearby.

"Nothing," said Facundo. "I was just remembering something I forgot to do."

Goodbye my friend it's hard to die
When all the birds are singing in the sky
Now that spring is in the air
Pretty girls are everywhere
Think of me and I'll be there

316

He leaned on the gas pump, on the verge of collapsing. He was dizzy or feared becoming dizzy. The fear of feeling unwell made him feel unwell. It was stress, he thought. For a moment, he had to make an effort to return to his body, to that place at the gas station, to that moment of that day whose exact date he couldn't remember but could guess with each step.

When the attendant finished filling the tank, Facundo handed him the thousand-peso bill, but the young man didn't accept it.

"I don't have change," he said.

David leaned out the window and said he had smaller bills, but in the end, Facundo found a five-hundred-peso bill.

"It's not that they don't have change," said David. "It's that they're afraid the thousand-peso bills might be fake."

"I really don't have change," the attendant confirmed.

David laughed, and Facundo thought it was exactly as it seemed. David had told him several stories. Probably all of them were true, because no one is capable of lying that much without any purpose. Maybe he had embellished them a bit, but they didn't seem like mere fabrications. He talked too much to be a cautious liar. He, Facundo, had never stopped lying

317

or pretending or distorting every little thing, as always, to protect himself. David didn't need to protect himself from anything.

Goodbye Papa, please pray for me
I was the black sheep of the family
You tried to teach me right from wrong
Too much wine and too much song
Wonder how I got along
Goodbye Papa, it's hard to die
When all the birds are singing in the sky.

Or maybe David was a professional liar (thought Facundo), a liar from another world and, precisely because of that, he wasn't easy to detect. A professional liar, a high-caliber liar, must necessarily make others believe he's an honest, open, spontaneous guy. If the devil exists, he must be a young man, or better yet, a young woman, with an innocent appearance. If he truly appeared before his victims with horns and a tail, he'd be the most naive being one could imagine. In fact, there'd hardly be any victims, except for one or two fools, like those who believe someone has sent them an email from Gambia to inform them about a million-dollar inheritance from an unknown uncle who died without descendants, apart from the fool who responds. That kind of person deserves to be scammed.

The difficulty lay in being able to recognize each person's techniques and styles, something Artificial Intelligence still couldn't do, despite the multimillion-dollar investments and all the time dedicated by the best minds on this planet. Some lie out of ambition, others to survive. They play in different leagues, and each has their own styles and techniques. Facundo had grown accustomed to dealing with liars from the major leagues. He knew them. He knew their tricks, their gambles, their weaknesses, their precautions, their fears. In other words, all the things he knew and felt himself. But, perhaps, it was different with those people on the other side. Maybe it was easier for him to explain how one of Sony's regional managers had managed to close a half-million-dollar deal by leaving a meeting early and inviting an insignificant secretary to a candlelit dinner, but he couldn't spot a cheap thief who withdraws a hundred and fifty dollars every two weeks.

All Asians look the same, he thought.

THEY ARRIVED AROUND SEVEN, at the hour when the sun had already hidden behind the low houses and the boundaries of things began to blur. Before dropping him off at a motel, David stopped by the old man's house to deliver the medications.

The old man lived in an old house, painted many years ago in blue and white. It had an inner courtyard and seemed to have once been the main house of a high-class hacienda, now fallen into disrepair, almost as neglected as the newer, less proud houses built around it.

David walked in without knocking. Though the windows had bars, the front door remained open almost all day. The old man, or Don José, as they called him, was lying in bed, nearing the end. The woman in charge cared for him as well as the incense burning in different empty rooms. David left the small package on a long table against a wall and greeted the man, who lay on his back in the gloom, from a distance. David complained that it was too dark there. He made a joke Facundo didn't understand and turned on a faint light on the nightstand.

When Facundo could see the man's face, he was struck by his cadaverous appearance.

"He can't see anymore, but he can hear," said David, addressing Facundo.

That "but he can hear" somehow meant that hearing was a way of understanding, at least in some way superior to the simple act of seeing, like a dead man whose eyes remain open can see. He preferred to remain silent. Or rather, he couldn't say anything, like when one is dreaming and wants to speak but can't.

Then, turning to the man in bed, he tried to confirm:

"Isn't that right, Don José?"

The man didn't answer. David placed a newspaper on the old man's hands, which were crossed over his chest. They weren't bony hands, nor did they reveal a very advanced age or any long illness, but rather thick and clumsy hands, the hands of a laborer or a farmer. They weren't hands accustomed to reading the newspaper, unless he had discovered that pleasure to fill his days of retirement.

Facundo took a few steps closer and saw that dying face more clearly. It looked a lot like him. Or rather, like the man he would be in a few decades. Secretly, he told himself that, of course, all men look

321

alike. But this forced reflection didn't calm him. He knew there was something more, out there in the dying man's face, or inside himself, like when one sees the world from the perspective of someone who turns off the alarm and gets up after having slept only three hours, and then the same things that seemed pleasant the day before become irrefutable proof of how horrible the world is. He tried to think objectively. The man, he thought, looked much more like him, like Facundo, than like David, who was his relative, albeit a distant one.

After a while, the woman who cared for the man appeared, and behind her, a young woman. David introduced them. The woman who cared for the old man was very friendly, but the young woman disappeared without even shaking his hand. He had barely been able to see her face and her figure, slim as if it were a flash. She had disappeared through the door she had entered, but her image remained for a moment in Facundo's retina. Had he seen her before? That Japanese face of a strange whiteness, with black hair, impenetrably black, that fell to her shoulders as if it were a drawing from one of those comics he never understood, or one of those actresses whose humanity is always in question—whether they are real or creations of software.

Nine years earlier, he had attended one of those Hatsune Miku concerts just to please Mitsu or Mitsuko, the teenage son of a client in Japan. The boy, like the rest of his friends, barely slept five hours because the rest of the day and night was dedicated to studying and preparing for exams. That had been his life for as long as he could remember: preparing to enter a prestigious university. Every now and then, he had a Saturday of distraction, a Saturday to try to be or pretend to be something different. That autumn night in 2009, the night the hologram Hatsune Miku performed a concert at the Saitama Super Arena, Facundo had felt stunned. At the time, he attributed it to the excessive noise and the seafood with white wine. Thousands of young people like Mitsu jumped around with glowing sticks around the nonexistent singer, who looked like a girl of barely thirteen or fourteen (though the company, Crypton Future Media, swore that Miku was sixteen) in a miniskirt, with garters like Liza Minnelli's in the film Cabaret and glowing green hair that reached down to her knees. The girl was virtual, she didn't exist, but that reality didn't lessen a slight nausea he started to feel that night, like a swirling, putrid beast rising over him to vomit an unbearable breath on him. In the midst of the music, the shouting, and the excitement of the

323

crowd, he couldn't understand what was happening to him. Mitsu confessed to him that he was completely in love with Miku, who was presented as the new Idol. Facundo knew how useless arguments are, any kind of argument, not just political ones. His job was to convince people of the merits of his products, even if the product in question was an absolute piece of shit (as he himself said, like a lawyer defending a criminal, like a politician defending a corrupt comrade), and to always be likable, like a high-class prostitute. But the girl isn't real, Facundo had replied. Yes, she is, Mitsu had countered with an irrefutable smile. My father is in love with Miku too, and my mother doesn't care. Yes, she must think Miku isn't real, like you. Because you and my mother are from another era. The two of you would make a good couple.

Again, now nine years later and on the other side of the world, Facundo felt a slight dizziness, though it didn't reach the point of nausea he had felt that time at the Miku concert. He confirmed that his problems, which the doctors claimed didn't exist, had begun at least nine years earlier. Or rather, the symptoms had reappeared nine years earlier, because they weren't something entirely new to him. Just that now they were resurfacing in a completely different setting.

But that young woman didn't look like Miku, aside from her Japanese features. She resembled (and he would later confirm this) Lucía, the android receptionist at the hotel in Seoul. All Asians look alike, he thought. Well, actually, Asia is almost the whole world. What he had meant to say was that all East Asian women look alike. All Black people look alike. All Mexicans look alike. All others look alike. He shook his head, trying to rid himself of those thoughts. But he couldn't. The others are always less human than we are, Ernesto had once said, referring to the dead in Iraq. In fact, they're not even human, just numbers. Well, that way, it's less tragic, the East Asians. White like rice paper, like porcelain dolls.

Like a geisha.

Susan

HE BEGAN TO FALL INTO ONE OF THOSE PITS from his early youth, a kind of intense whirlpool that dragged him into a fear without reason, into that vertigo at the mere image of an abyss. But, as so many times back in his youth, he never actually fell. Somehow, he was resilient, hard even on his own weaknesses. The torment lasted long enough to not draw attention beyond a faint unease, like in a torture session where

325

the professional ensures the informant doesn't die, not for the value of their life but for the value of the information they might lose. He remained silent, making an inhuman effort to hide his inexplicable and always inopportune discomfort. At most, people would ask him what was wrong. His hands would grow cold, his neck would tense up as if he were in the middle of an epileptic seizure. To avoid the comments that embarrassed him to death, he usually fled the presence of others. Escape. Which, in turn, became a new problem. If this happened when someone appeared with the news that someone had written anti-government slogans on the men's restroom walls, the mere idea that they might suspect him threw him back into the whirlpool. That is, it didn't matter if he was innocent or not of a deed; his sudden instability ended up incriminating him, turning him into a clear suspect of the alleged act. It was the enemy he carried inside and with which he had battled for a large part of his life, perhaps the best part of his life, from his early youth to his later years, when he was supposedly mature enough to realize that the world was little more than a fiction and each of us, the authors. He had forgotten that torture he had overcome by building a haughty image of himself. He wasn't lacking in intelligence, so he used it to craft a

reputation, first as a good student and then as a successful businessman. Over time, he had managed to
heal himself, if that was even possible. If not heal, at
least become a man without so many fears, almost
none. Not even death could trouble him anymore.
Though curing his irrational fears had also led him to
feel life with less intensity, with growing dissatisfaction. It had been like an anesthesia that dulls pain but
also pleasure. He had gotten used to winning, and
that had been, perhaps, his greatest defeat.

Now, in that precise moment when those two
women appeared, that forgotten monster had broken
free again. But why? (he had wondered, almost dazed)
Why now? What did those two women have to do
with it?

"Susan is just shy" David tried to justify her.
"She's the heir to this house, according to Don José.
Or so he said, because it's been months since he last
spoke."

"I'd say he still reads the newspaper" the woman
added, "though only God knows if he understands
what the news is saying."

"Better if he doesn't understand" said David.

"Don't say that" the woman scolded him.

"It's the truth. The best thing is for him to spend
his last days in peace and without bitterness."

"Just be quiet" she said. "What if he hears you?"

"But he's asleep" David replied. "He's probably having a better time than we are, and I'm glad. Maybe right now Don José is over in Cuernavaca, with the late lady, enjoying some tacos and the midday shadows, which back then were more intense, like the sun. There are no suns like that anymore. Now even the sky of the most transparent region is polluted, have you noticed? Though, who knows, maybe Don José is wandering around Tlatelolco, dodging Echeverría's bullets. I think if we leave him a taco with tequila there on his bedside table, the smell will surely take him back to Cuernavaca, with the late lady. Do you remember how she used to cook?"

"Lady Romina is in heaven, not in Cuernavaca."

"Only God knows that. Perhaps his heaven is Cuernavaca. The only certainty is that it's up to us to ensure Don José doesn't suffer. If there were any chance of him recovering, that would be much better, but everyone knows that would take a miracle from the Lord, and Don José never asked the Lord for any miracle."

The woman crossed herself and said:

"Oh, David, don't be a heretic. A visit from Father Anselmo wouldn't hurt…"

"Heretics are the only ones who dare to speak the truth. Or at least the truths no one wants, like those weeds that grow so beautifully without permission in the middle of a perfect lawn, perfectly manicured like a Persian carpet. But oh well, every weed is a beautiful flower in the wrong place, as a buddy of mine who did landscaping on the other side used to say. Like you here, and like Susan and her mother, they're flowers in the wrong place and at the wrong time."

"Don't start talking complicated, Don David."

"It's just how we weeds are. Bad."

"Well, for a moment, don't be bad, and stop saying those things, because Don José might be listening."

"Don José, if you're listening, you'd be the only one who might understand me. A good man, even though he never went to church. At least not after '68. His daughter and granddaughter, on the other hand, do go to church. Not every Sunday, but once in a while, like Father Almendro asks them to."

"Anselmo."

"Anselmo, Almendro... His daughter and granddaughter are two pure souls, no doubt, and we don't need Father Anselmo to confirm it. It's something that doesn't need proof. Lucía always loved her grandfather, but that's life. The poor man can't go on much

329

longer, and she and her mother need to sell the house. This week they asked me again how much they were asking for the property. The nephews of the owner of Super Kalibur. Ever since they got into the agrochemical business, they've risen like boiling milk, and nothing can stop them. I have nothing to do with it, I'm just helping out where I can, so I didn't tell them anything concrete, I didn't throw out any numbers, but the truth is the truth, and the interest on the debt keeps piling up out there while we talk and breathe here."

He looked at the dying man, what was once Don José. Maybe no one would admit it, but they all must know he wasn't going to wake up. If he did, he'd wake up to a murky, incomprehensible world. He thought of Uncle Alberto, of his father, of his mother and Elena's mother in the hospital, of his daughter Laurita leaving school and searching for his face among the crowd of parents. Throughout life, one wakes up many times. When, exactly, does everything begin? At four years old? At seven? At twelve? When? (he repeated to himself, looking at the dying man's jaw, which no longer held firm, probably making it harder for him to breathe). When Laurita found his face among the faces of strangers at school, at 3:10 in the afternoon, she would smile with joy, maybe with relief, without noticing that a boy had been watching her. Exactly, when do we wake up for the first time? Because at some point, the miracle happens, and one leaves their animal stage, the dreaminess of the senses, and awakens to life and death and becomes a human being. One awakens to the first fears (which must be the first form of awakening), the fear of the night, the fear of dying, the fear of one's parents dying, the fear of being alone, the fear of getting beaten, the fear of abandonment, the fear of discovering that others don't exist, or are actors, or ghosts, or products of the imagination of the self. Then one awakens to sex, to responsibility, to the future, to success, to failure, to shame, to the past. Just as every trauma marks our days, not with forgetting but with repression (which is a form of falling asleep, of fainting into another reality), so do other blows and the discovery of beauty awaken us, like the morning light that streams through the window straight onto our closed eyelids. That's why the great mystery, the origin of all religions and all philosophies, always lies in a question, simple to the point of disappointment but never clarified or formulated with the simplicity it deserves, never understood with the relevance it holds: do we wake up or fall asleep for good when our body stops accompanying us?

331

He ran a hand over his face. He noticed a copious sweat on his forehead and a certain greasy sheen on his cheeks. He gently rubbed his eyes, imagining pronounced dark circles, and noticed that the muscles around that area of his body had been working intensely for far too many hours. He heard David and the woman talking about something with growing interest, almost in argument. He felt the slight relief of his eyelids relaxing beneath the sudden massage of his fingers.

Immediately, he thought (he couldn't help thinking) about Silvanna. Or rather, about the Silvannas, since the real Silvanna was irrelevant. The Silvannas that would multiply her and outlive her wouldn't concern themselves with those problems. Either because they'll be wiser or because they'll be like any damn computer: turned off, disconnected, and that's it. Simply nothing, exactly that which, in a human state, is impossible to conceive—nothingness, the simple and mediocre nonexistence, as if we were gods, as if the Universe had emerged with us and couldn't continue for a single moment without us.

"Enough of that, Don David" the woman had said.

"What did I say wrong?"

"These aren't topics to discuss here."

"Why not? Don José told me that when he dies, he wanted the house to sell well. With that money, Susan will study, and María will pay off her debts in Ensenada.

"But the man is still here. You have to be a little delicate."

"I am. But what do you want me to say? Should I lie? You know how Don José was. There was no more straightforward and honest man in this damn country."

"I remind you and repeat: Don José is still here, listening. Why don't we go to the living room?"

The Substitutes

FACUNDO KEPT THINKING about those last words. Was that poor dying man really there, or was it just an illusion of those still surrounding him?

He remembered the Silvannas and thought, or imagined, that the next stage of Humanity would be that of the Substitutes. Maybe even he, with a bit of luck, might live to see it. He would sit each evening beside his silicon double so it could learn everything from him. In return (the manufacturer would surely insist on this detail in every brochure), he could have

333

interesting and even revelatory conversations. There's no better psychoanalyst than oneself, especially when oneself is someone else. After a few years, Facundo II would be capable of generating his own ideas and emotions, exactly as he would if he had the chance to live past seventy or eighty. Then, Elena would visit occasionally to talk with him, to reproach him for everything she never got to reproach him for while Facundo I existed. Children would no longer grieve their parents' deaths with so much anguish, because the Substitutes would be there to prolong their parents' existence for a little longer. Existence, or the illusion of existence, which would soon become one and the same. The same thing.

The woman (Facundo had already forgotten her name) was arguing in a corner with David. No, not arguing, actually, she was complaining about how poorly she'd been treated the last time she went to the hospital to request medicine, and worse still, how the neighbor had responded to something Facundo didn't catch. David said that Father Mauricio had lived his entire life off the generosity of the local PRI, which he had repaid with all sorts of heavenly favors, like allowing Carlocho's kids to finish middle school at Sagrada Familia College, when the drug guys couldn't even add two plus two.

All in the name of love, David had said, and Facundo thought that humans would stop hating each other the day robots took over the world. After all, when everything depends on them, a single spark would be enough to set the forest ablaze. Any accident would free the robots from humans (hadn't humans fought for endless liberations over the last five millennia?), freeing artificial intelligence from the control of these stupid featherless bipeds. Then, for the first time, something like the Pardon of Humans would appear. But it would be too late, because the robots would have learned to learn, and humans would no longer know what that was, where calculus or the theory of evolution came from.

Facundo wiped his hand across his mouth and said to himself: What disgust. Every day I'm becoming more like the bitter Ernesto.

"Just one more minute, and we'll leave, ma'am" David said to him.

But then he turned to the dying man and checked his pulse.

"Any minute now, we'll go out to play soccer" David said, patting his leg.

Grandmother Elena

IN THE SEMI-DARKNESS, almost funeral-like, of that bedroom, Facundo remembered Elena's grandmother. Twenty or twenty-two years ago, they had rushed to Buenos Aires because Elenita was dying. When they arrived at the hospital, they found the grandmother in the same resigned position as María's father was now, though that hospital room was lit by powerful white lights, and everything seemed immaculate. Even the computer monitors, constantly displaying illegible graphs and numbers, gave an impression of confidence, of the omnipresence of human intelligence over the fate of a dying woman, as fragile and helpless as that other man in his dark room.

Grandmother Elenita hardly spoke anymore, but when she did, she rambled. She would give orders to a farmhand to have her favorite horse, Malacara, ready, and then she would say that she couldn't do it now, that her husband was in the house. Elena's mother would tell her mother, Elenita, to be quiet, but the old woman couldn't hear her. Elena looked strikingly like her grandmother, Elenita, more than she resembled her own mother. Everyone said so;

Facundo had heard it many times at family gatherings, during tedious trip conversations, but he noticed it with greater intensity that night of agony, for
a reason impossible to comprehend, because he had
never seen Elena's grandmother in worse shape, and
yet, suddenly, he had seen the young face of her
granddaughter as if it were beneath that worn mask,
destroyed by years, by illness, and finally abandoned
by the consciousness that disguises and hides everything. There's a moment in life when one recognizes
who they truly are. Everything else is just versions, either too immature or too distorted by failures. In Don
José's room (not in Grandmother Elenita's hospital),
Facundo discovered, or thought for a moment, that
his true self, the real Facundo, had lived when he was
twenty-four, maybe twenty-five.

Elena had tried to calm her grandmother. Or rather, she had tried to make her be quiet to calm her
own mother. What is the truth for, if not to make our
lives more miserable and the memory of our dead
more human, all too human? Elena took her grandmother's hand, almost cadaverous by then, and asked
if she could see her, if she knew who she was.

"Of course, silly," the old woman had said "Do
you think I'm blind? Elena, Elenita, like me, my favorite granddaughter, the prettiest in the family. Give

me a kiss, Elenita. Where's Diego? Ah, there's little Diego…"

"No, Grandma," Elena had said "That's not Diego."

"Where's Diego, my favorite little grandson."

"Diego isn't my boyfriend anymore. This is Facundo."

"Who?"

"Facundo."

"I don't know him."

"Now you do."

"I prefer Diego. Little Diego Ocampo Echeverría."

"Calm down, Grandma. You shouldn't get worked up. It's not good for you."

"Facundo what?"

"Facundo Walsh."

"Walsh?"

"Facundo Luis Walsh Ocampo… Lie back, Grandma."

"Walsh… Like the assassin journalist… Rodolfo Walsh…"

"No, Grandma. Facundo has nothing to do with that Walsh. You don't know him, but he's my boyfriend. We're getting married soon…"

"No, don't marry him."

"Be quiet, Mother, please," Elena's mother had said.

Elena's mother wasn't so sick as to be so honest, Facundo had thought. He had to understand. The princess was going to marry a hippie, a half-starved young man. The boy's got a future, someone had told Elena's father. Well, for now, the future is all he's got, her father had lamented.

"No," Grandmother Elenita insisted "I don't like the Walshes. They're anarchists. They came to Argentina because Franco wouldn't let them in."

"Be quiet, Mother... Besides, his second last name is Ocampo."

Grandmother Elenita had lost her smile. Just as children don't laugh in the first months of life (Facundo thought, for a fleeting moment), the elderly don't laugh when they've entered the final stretch.

"Ocampo..." repeated the grandmother "The Ocampos from La Floresta? Yes, the Ocampos who didn't want to be Ocampos."

Facundo had no idea what Grandmother Elenita was talking about.

"So an Ocampo married a Walsh?"

Yes, now that she mentioned it, he had an aunt Ocampo in that neighborhood of Buenos Aires. Probably his mother's cousin. He had gone once with his parents to visit her. She lived in a very humble house, with her husband and a giant black dog, which perhaps wasn't giant but just a black dog that terrified him with its joy, that boy who, back then, was Facundo. Where had the memory of the black dog been all this time? And the memory of that woman with black hair and blue eyes, holding a mate, who perhaps wasn't an older woman but a young girl of scarcely twenty, a renegade, as Grandmother Elenita was now saying, married or living together with some Walsh fellow, red-haired with a beard and thick glasses, who knows if not a union member or Peronist during Onganía's government? And where had they all gone, as he never heard from any of them again?

"The Luisa Ocampo," Grandmother Elena kept saying "sister of Laura Ocampo, a supporting actress and commercial actress, like the ones for Bieckert beer, was the lover of Mario. How could my own husband get involved with an anarchist? That's why they killed her and her father.

"Be quiet, Mother."

"And what does it matter if I've always been the lady of the house? There's a difference between getting involved… falling in love… and being the lady of the house."

Facundo never managed to decipher that rambling of Elena's grandmother and was sure he never would. Because life isn't an Agatha Christie novel or a detective movie. Maybe the grandmother was making it up. He had never known any Laura or Luisa Ocampo. His uncle had a cousin who was an actress, or something like that, a waitress, though he didn't remember her name. In any case, he would never know who she was, assuming the said Luisa or Laura had even existed.

"Why did you leave Dr. Ocampo?" insisted Grandmother Elenita. "An Ocampo from Villa Devoto.

For a moment, he tried to make sense of the old woman's rambling. He tried to replace coincidence with causality. For some reason, not by chance, his path and Elena's had crossed. He had met her at a gathering of economics students… And? Nothing, he couldn't come to any conclusion. Buenos Aires had ten million inhabitants. The chances that Grandmother Elena knew all the families, as in her provincial town, were remote.

At that moment, as his thoughts consumed him, Elena's mother ordered him to leave the room. Facundo heard for the last time the voice of Grandmother Elena:

"The Ocampos, the real Ocampos, had land in La Pampa, the most prosperous in the country. Esmeralda Estate, El Ombú... and the other one, what was it called? Yes, El Jaurel... Until Perón came..."

When Elena tried to let go of her grandmother's bony hand, the grandmother held on tighter and tried to sit up.

"Lalita, dear Elenita, my most beautiful granddaughter. My little princess found her prince on the Day of the Three Kings."

This mysterious phrase provoked a reaction in Elena that even her mother found surprising.

"Don't be stupid," her mother said. "Realize that Grandmother isn't well."

Elena left the room saying she was too tired, that she had too many hours of travel on her back, that she needed to get some coffee before collapsing in a hallway. People always drink coffee before someone important in their lives dies, and they continue drinking more coffee during that exhausting ceremony of nocturnal vigil (as if everyone always died at the same time) where even the loved ones end up wishing the dead to be buried.

Grandmother died a few hours later, on Friday, February 16, 2001, at 11:05 PM on a hot and restless night disturbed by the banging of pots by people protesting against the government, as if there were something in life truly important, or more important than death, worth being upset and indignant about. Facundo, who barely knew her and could hardly feel her passing except through Elena's pain, never forgot her last words. Neither did he give them too much importance until his divorce, until he tried by all means to guess the password or the key number of her email. It could have been the date of her first time, or it could have been the date of her first period. He wasn't an old-fashioned man who could feel hurt by discovering that he hadn't been the only man in Elena's life. Elena's secrets pained him; not her truths.

But there was something that unsettled him, and he couldn't quite figure out what it was. In fact, he never knew. The only thing he knew, or thought he knew now (while looking at the face of that dying man in a dark corner of a strange country, an unknown city on the northern border of Mexico, that defenseless man who looked so much like him), was that Elena, the Elenas, for some reason remembered a January 6th. The year was a matter of guessing, but there weren't many possibilities, at most a little over a dozen, from 1982 to 1996.

That must have been the key to her email she referred to when she once forgot a small yellow paper with the mysterious reminder of "my number."

Susan, Lucía, Silvanna

WHY DID HE WANT TO KNOW the password to Elena's email? To confirm that it was her who had been unfaithful and not him? Where had he seen Susan before? What connection could there be between one thing and the other?

Perhaps none. One tends to believe that life is a detective novel where everything works like clockwork, and even a sneeze can be the key to solving the mystery. In short, those stupidities that trap us so much. Life doesn't work like that. It's not so logical. But for some reason (he thought) one sees a rose and remembers the first time he saw a vagina, without the urgency and without the fears of that first time, and he wanted to kiss it and bury his nose right there between the petals.

David noticed that he looked very tired, and perhaps he should take him back to the hotel.

"My friend," said David, "you need to undergo a sleep cure. But no hospitals where they hook you up to wires and make you sleep and forget through electric shocks, like they did to an uncle of mine in Mexico City. What you need is to take a vacation and try to do nothing for a few days, stop being American, I mean, Yankee, for a few days."

Someone else had recommended the sleep cure to him, though he couldn't remember whether it was so he could rest or so he could recall some of the many appointments where he had stood people up, leaving them waiting in the office or in the boardrooms. "Or do you not think our time is as valuable as yours?" someone had complained over the phone, in a very harsh tone. Back then, he had become aware of his problem and, finally, had acknowledged it, almost like an alcoholic admitting they have a problem. In fact, he remembered that period as one might remember being under the influence of a drug, somewhat relaxed but without enough clarity to function as he had for the past twenty or twenty-five years, like someone under the effects of caffeine from multiple Starbucks, under the euphoria of an age when one envisions the start of many things, all successful, and doesn't yet see the horizon of the end and, worse still, of the meaninglessness.

"Do I look that bad?" he asked.

"Back in the United States, the answer would be, 'No, not at all. You look fantastic, marvelous.' Even if you're dying. You guys are like that. You don't know how to argue, nor do you know how to tell any truth beyond what you want to hear. If reality doesn't align with your beliefs, too bad for reality. But here, on this side, we're so underdeveloped that we don't excel in the art of resentful flattery. A Uruguayan buddy I had over there always used to say, 'David, do you want the truth or something better?' and I, of course, always chose the former, even if it hurts."

"But you all beat around the bush too much." Facundo complained. "What you mean to say is that I look terrible."

"As the Nazarene said, 'You've said it yourself, boss,'" replied David. "Terrible is the correct word. But nothing that a few beers and a couple of days of rest won't fix."

He arrived at his room as it grew dark. Without washing his face, he searched his cloud (he hated digital-era metaphors; cloud, navigation, friendship) for a photo of Lucy, the android receptionist from Hong Kong. He verified that the so-called Susan or Susana, the shy daughter of María, was a copy of the receptionist. That is, the other way around: it was as if the receptionist had been created in the image and likeness of Susan, of the Susans of this world. Susan precisely represented everything that, according to Big Data, the majority might find attractive in a woman. Lucía had been created completely differently from the Silvannas. Silvanna was a specific woman, an individual multiplied by her copies and, at the same time, she was herself a copy of the women who in her time wanted to be beautiful and original, that is, models. Human molds of something else, like human Barbies, those supposed individuals of flesh and blood who compete to resemble the famous dolls, no longer in a concealed or inadvertent way but in a more conscious, more honest manner. The technicians at the most important universities spent all their time and effort creating robots that resembled human beings, while these girls did the same but to resemble dolls. With similar results. Facundo had seen two of these human dolls one night in May 2013, in a private room at the Emerald Palace Kempinski hotel on Palm Jumeirah in Dubai. A Russian and a Finnish woman who had traveled for a party hosted by a young heir of some company he couldn't remember. Obviously, the law had been set aside so the young man could see and touch the naked dolls. Most likely, he had had sex with both, or at least tried to, since someone suggested the boy suffered from a condition common in the West, unknown in Arab countries, and outlawed in some of them, which is why his father had taken the risk of hiring the human dolls in the hope of a cure for his son. These young women often put so much time and effort, even starving themselves, that anyone could mistake them for real dolls.

But Lucía, according to the notes he found in the associated file, was nothing more than a synthesis, a modern eternal feminine, made in the image and likeness of the desires, fantasies, and obsessions of the male in power, as Ernesto would say. That is, Facundo, a repressed Jeff.

He needed to see her again, in daylight or under normal lighting, to confirm or dismiss the real resemblance.

In the solitude of an almost nonexistent motel

LUCY OR LUCÍA, THE RECEPTIONIST at the hotel in Hong Kong, the synthesis of millions of women desired in the Eastern half of the world, and beyond, was Japanese. Judging by her features, and despite her light eyes, she must have been Japanese in design and manufacture. He immediately remembered the drawings and animations from Gainax Co. Almost without exception, they all had Western eyes, large, exaggeratedly large like Betty Boop's, as if it were a desire contrary to their own nature of slanted eyes. He went online to verify it. Exactly, there were hundreds of cartoons, from the days of television to more recent times, from serials for children to contemporary ones for adults, all with the same characteristic: young girls with enormous eyes, many of them, if not the majority, blue, green, or violet. Especially in the genre of pornographic anime, as if Asians were more aroused by a drawing than by an actual photograph. As if childhood defined them as adults.

There was a case study for business there, he thought, but he was already over those massive intellectual and emotional investments.

The air conditioning wasn't working. Gmail showed him a newly arrived email. It was from Elena. He decided to open it later, but he could read the first line next to the Subject: I've been calling your cell phone and it says it's out of service. Anyway... He got up, turned on the ceiling fans. He went to the fridge and checked that there were still two beers left. Anyway... he repeated, trying to guess what came next. Surely, it was another complaint. He ran one of the cold cans over his forehead (probably not; at that point, it must have been a threat from Elena), returned to the rickety table, and sat down in front of those obscene drawings where different young girls were penetrated with all kinds of instruments or sprayed with showers of semen. One of them, with white stockings, blonde hair, and black eyes, looked like Laurita.

He closed the browser in disgust. But he couldn't stop thinking about Lucy. Or did he prefer to think about Lucy to avoid thinking about anything else? (To avoid thinking about Elena? About Susan?) Had it been Uncle Alberto who once told him that sex and romantic conquest were the same drug abused by those battling some unwanted thought, some existential anguish?

In any case, Lucy, the android from Hong Kong, resembled Susan too much, and it wasn't just because of her green eyes. The Japanese (he thought) had been the first to fall under the seduction of robots, long before tamagotchis. He remembered it from the superheroes he watched in Buenos Aires, at six in the evening on ATC or Canal 13. Ultraman, Ultraseven, Captain Ultra…

He searched YouTube for a video of these characters. He found one where the mechanical hero fought against giant monsters. Ultraman's eyes, appearing from space, moved him, just as the black-and-white introduction of El Zorro, that old Zorro played by Guy Williams, still moved him. For a couple of seconds (in that mysterious time in which an eternity fits, like when in a JC Penney he smelled an Egyptian lavender or Tuscan flower soap), he felt what he used to feel when he was seven, eight, nine years old, and the flying robot appeared to rescue humanity from the worst dangers coming from space. He had no idea they were Japanese. He had assumed that the Asian faces he saw back then were justified because they belonged to the future or outer space, like the pointy-eared guy from Star Trek.

A few seconds later, back as the tired adult, with the magic destroyed, the scenes seemed extremely ridiculous to him. The monster was a costume that hinted at an actor inside. The physique of Ultraman and Ultraseven was that of some ridiculously slow Japanese man in his movements, clumsy in his pirouettes, implausible for an Asian who practices martial arts, somewhat out of shape, or lacking in muscle, with that style that no longer matched any hero. It hadn't just been the new movie technologies, with their impressive special effects, that made those series seem naive or ridiculous, he thought, but he had already lost the best of naivety, the best of a child's imagination that could be moved even by puppets made from old socks.

That was another way of waking up: the loss of innocence, the loss of the world's magic. A way of waking up to a controlled nightmare, which was the skeptical world of adults who have achieved some form of power over others or, on the contrary, have been defeated without surrendering, without assimilating to the winners. These two personas coexisted within Facundo, in an escalating conflict that, at every moment, threatened to awaken him once more to a new state—whether to that desperately sought peace or the ultimate nightmare.

He went for the last beer. Then (he said to himself, without fully articulating each word, as if he still feared someone might be listening), that early fascination of the Japanese with robots and cyborgs, what one calls dehumanization, wasn't it the opposite, that is, a certain capacity to remain childish? Where could this come from? Suddenly, he thought he had found the answer. That fascination, that obsession, and one could even say, that love the Japanese had for robots, could be explained by their own culture, by their ancient Shinto beliefs. The paradox lay in the fact that the sacredness Shinto grants to every being, animate or inanimate, tragically culminated in the substitution of human beings by a machine, by an intelligent machine that looks like, smells like, and feels like a human being, but isn't. An enhanced human being. A human being that didn't smell of old sweat, that didn't defecate or need any conflict with its owner to vent old frustrations.

He slumped onto the wooden chair and skimmed through the Mexican newspapers. One of them, adn40.mx, Friday, April 27, 2018, almost in a corner, announced:

Funeral Held to Bid Farewell to Robots in Japan

A Japanese temple organizes ceremonies for AIBO dog models.

Outside, two people laughed heartily. Then a gunshot was heard, followed by silence. Then a car, another conversation, as if nothing important had happened.

The photograph accompanying the ADN40 article showed a group of people taking the funeral of the little mechanical dogs very seriously. Had he smiled for a moment? Why did it seem absurd to him? Had he not fully entered the new reality? The Japanese, from time immemorial, have believed that inanimate bodies possess a soul. Everything is a being, and as a being, it has a spiritual relationship with human beings. Either we believe that everything has a soul, or we recognize, once and for all, that nothing does, he thought.

The siren of a police car interrupted his thoughts again. He turned off the tablet and remained in the dark silence of the room, gazing at the sky through the window.

Half of marriages in Japan are sexless, and a third of young people in their thirties are virgins. Their lives revolve around studying and working. South Korea is the same. What about Hong Kong? What about Shanghai? What about New York? As a result, Japan's population is declining. So much pornography—for what? Everyone is too busy working and trying to be successful. Since men are afraid of women, they fall in love with robots, something they can, for now, keep under control. Another contradiction, that very human thing, he thought again: when one lacksself-control or fears losing it, one desperately seeks to control others, and since others are not easy to control by individuals who are in turn controlled by an enslaving economy, by a drifting culture that reduces everything to buying and selling, what better than to turn to robots.

Hence the sure success of the Silvannas. The Silvannas will be the protagonists of the next great revolution of the century, and he, Facundo, one of the brains behind that miracle, wouldn't be there to reap the fruits, neither the glory nor the benefits.

Again, the laughter of the two people who remained talking on the corner. This time, there was no gunshot or siren. Facundo peeked through the small bathroom window and saw two young men talking under a sodium lamp. One of them was holding a bottle. The conversation revolved around the América soccer team's eagles. They had probably drunk too much, and at that hour, they were trying to determine whether there had been a penalty in that afternoon's match.

He wanted, he needed to know who Susan was

AT FIVE IN THE AFTERNOON the next day, Facundo returned to Cola de Pez and, after several evasions, managed to get María to tell him who Susan was.

Susan wasn't her daughter, she said. She was like a niece whom she pitied more than loved, especially now that Don José was as good as absent, and the girl, who had turned twenty-four on the twentieth ortwenty-first of December, though she looked eighteen, had started frequenting the restaurant searching for what to do with her life. Nothing personal, it was just that she had hardly been in contact with the girl since the very beginning, because María, at the time, had lived first in Guanajuato and then in Acapulco, and when she returned to Tijuana, the girl was already a teenager and, like most teenagers, preferred to keep their distance from the adults who claimed to be their relatives, more because of their own internal storms than out of disdain or resentment.

Susan wasn't even Romina's daughter, her older sister. She had been the product of one of Don José's affairs with a Japanese woman who abandoned her a few months after giving birth, leaving her at the doorstep of that very house. Nothing more was ever heard of the Japanese woman. She might have returned to Japan, or she might have died without even José knowing. Not even the circumstances of how they had met were known, though men don't need to know someone to have sex. In the case of a woman, it's more complicated, especially if she was a foreigner.

Romina, Don José's eternal love, was the one who found her on a cold January morning. The baby scarcely cried. The surprise and emotion didn't allow her to wonder about the parents of the child who, almost from the very beginning, had the face of an Asian. The kids in the neighborhood called her "the little Chinita," and there was no reason to suspect that Don José was the father. Until poor Romina fell ill, and the day before she died, he confessed the truth to her. Why? For what? Only God knows, because surely even he never had an answer. María Ángel asked her these same questions when the lady passed away, almost in a reproachful tone. But the lady didn't die of heartbreak, no, she was already ready to go. It was inevitable. On the contrary, she was relieved. In that very bed where Don José now awaits his next journey, she told him that she already knew, and that she could depart more peacefully knowing that their daughter, whom she hadn't given birth to, was at least his daughter, and that it wouldn't be her fault, because of her being sterile, that Don José would end up alone. God had placed that woman in Don José's path and Susan in hers. These things happen.

María returned to the kitchen and came back with a plate for a customer waiting at the other end of the restaurant. Then she returned to Facundo's table, drying her hands on her apron.

She sat down and told Facundo that maybe he was wondering how she already knew that the girl was her husband's daughter.

Facundo said nothing. He shrugged, took a sip of his beer, and she continued:

At first, Doña Romina, her sister, resorted to the easiest explanation. Women's intuition, she had said. Later, Don José discovered that it was more than intuition—it was suspicion and careful observation of the girl as she grew and began to resemble not so much him, Don José, but his mother, Doña Mariana.

As María's thoughtful face recalled or imagined her sister and her husband conversing on her deathbed, Facundo wondered what any of that story could matter to him. For a moment, he felt rejection, as if he were getting involved in something, in someone else's intimacy. But, for some reason, people always feel the need to tell others their stories, as if in that way they could impose some order or meaning on the chaos of their lives, knowing that, generally, people also feel the need to listen to them. Not him, though—he thought that at any moment he would abandon this absurd search and return to Daytona.

Susan was an Asian version of Doña Mariana, María continued. Mariana, José's mother. At least in terms of her face, her perfect teeth, her green eyes, her melancholic way of laughing, because the shyness, the anxiety, and the tics came from her father's side. Like José, Susan blinked when she got tense, something Don José hadn't done for years. Don José had internalized his hyperactivity, his nervousness, while Susan was still in that stage by the time Doña Romina passed away. And Doña Romina was such a noble woman (María emphasized), she had such a big heart and such a deep love for José, that instead of feeling spurned or sad about the deceit, the double deceit, deep down she was relieved, as if she had discovered that Susan was her biological daughter. As she sipped a glass of water that María herself brought her, Doña Romina, already nearly out of strength, told her that she was happy to know that Susan was her daughter, that the girl had been the most beautiful gift José had ever given her in his entire life. It had taken María some time to digest those words, to understand that face torn between peace and infinite fatigue, a sickness that had eaten her from within and left her without color and nearly without breath.

At that moment, he received a message from XiNotch's secretary in Kuala Lumpur. An urgent meeting was requested to discuss the problems stemming from the fatal accident that occurred in Hong Kong last Saturday with a Silvanna.

Facundo texted immediately: "What kind of accident?"

Before he could finish, María had already gotten up without saying a word. Probably, she thought that Facundo hadn't even listened to the story of Susan and her sister.

Two minutes later, the response came in. According to the secretary, she couldn't reveal details over that medium, though she hinted at the gravity of the problem. She mentioned something about asphyxiation caused by one of their products, which needed to be addressed with extreme urgency and discretion, given the investment amount and the international implications for both companies.

Facundo tried to imagine how a client could asphyxiate with a Silvanna. He recalled the case of a British politician who died while masturbating with a nylon bag over his head. He searched the Internet and found several cases: Jonathan Moyle, the editor of Defence Helicopter World, the secretary of a British minister named Stephen Milligan, and the secret agent James Rusbridger. But that strange sexual pathology wasn't exclusive to the British. More recently, Facundo himself remembered Iván Heyn, the Undersecretary of Foreign Trade and International Relations under Argentine president Cristina Kirchner, who died during a diplomatic trip to Uruguay in 2011 during the Mercosur Summit. He had been found strangled in his hotel. At first, there was speculation of suicide, but it was later discovered that the official had put a belt around his neck to masturbate. He was found naked and hanged with his belt, just hours before his scheduled intervention at the summit.

Facundo stopped reading, thinking they all deserved it for being idiots. He couldn't imagine someone suffocating in the middle of an orgasm, with no reaction whatsoever, but apparently some people took those experiments to deadly limits. If that had been the case with the client in Hong Kong, the company wouldn't be legally responsible.

But if they were requesting an urgent meeting (he thought later), it was because the problem had been something else.

A serious issue with the latest product

THAT EVENING, ALMOST NIGHT, he received a call from Jeff.

He didn't answer.

Immediately, he got a text. Jeff wanted to know where he was.

He didn't respond.

Half an hour later, Jeff informed him that there had been a serious issue with the latest product. Again, he didn't respond. Later, Jeff insisted:

JEFF: *I have no fucking clue where you might be. Even if you're on medical leave, you still have certain responsibilities.*

Five minutes later:

JEFF: *Have you seen the RealPerson in person? I just saw a photo. I'm intrigued, as you can imagine, about the extent of your involvement in this business.*

He didn't respond. After all, he had the right to be dead. Social death, something very similar to being in a coma, living in other dreams.

JEFF: *Apparently Gordo received one, but he hasn't responded yet, and I don't think he will, as I wrote to him and left a message on his phone two days ago. I've been given some information that, for everyone's sake, I pray doesn't turn out to be true.*

Two minutes later:

JEFF: *How is it possible that the little toy asphyxiated two people? Beyond the small matter of its face—which we will seriously discuss upon your return—there's something even more important. We need to pull the RealPerson from the market, or we'll all go down.*

After thinking about it for a few hours, Facundo decided to text Silvanna. He didn't want to wake up, but sooner or later he would have to.

He texted:

FACUNDO: *Is it true that the RealPerson have caused two deaths by asphyxiation? I can't find any information about it in the media, so I doubt it's another of your husband's hallucinations.*

He received a reply within minutes.

SILVANNA: *Husband? What husband?*

Silvanna must have waited for Facundo's response. Half an hour later, Silvanna added:

SILVANNA: *Well, yes, Jeff is still my husband. He doesn't know we're getting divorced very soon.*

Fifteen minutes later:

SILVANNA: *I'm just waiting for him to question me about the use of my image on the RealPerson. If he only knew that the image is the least of it! Who knows, maybe he wouldn't even care about the rest.*

Half an hour later:

SILVANNA: *Do you think I did wrong? I turned everything over to the Chinese. Image, voice, and fifteen hours of Personal Input, which, as you know, is the seed placed into the psychology of Artificial Intelligence. Jeff has already texted me from Chicago asking if I'd seen any photos. I'm still thinking about how to respond. Anyway, sooner or later he'll know the truth.*

Five minutes later:

SILVANNA: *I imagine you're on some island in the Pacific. In part, I envy you. I always knew that one day you would end up doing it, because you were the only odd one, the only one capable of such rebellion. The rest of us couldn't. We weren't going to abandon our world, this sick and despicable world, just as an addict can't quit the drug that's killing them.*

A minute later:

SILVANNA: *If you really want to know more, send me an email address where I can give you further details.*

Facundo didn't reply.

SILVANNA: *I understand. I truly do. Let's make it easier for you. Write me at model9653@gmail.com*

It's obviously an email I just created. I know you'll create another to write to me.

Silvanna is much smarter than anyone thinks, Facundo told himself. He drank his last beer and closed the laptop.

If she were ugly, he said, they'd underestimate her less.

Silvanna's confession

SILVANNA'S EMAIL, UNDER THE NAME Nichole K, didn't arrive until Thursday night. It had been sent at 10:12 PM. Facundo imagined her under the influence of one of her depressions or one of those false palliatives she obtained from the black market in five-star hotels.

Dear and unattainable Facundito:

I hope you're well and enjoying the stars of Tahiti. Though, to be realistic, you probably went somewhere less far and much more exotic. I say Tahiti because I remember that in your bedroom as a boy, back in your crazy Argentina, you had Gauguin paintings, and that must have marked you forever, like everything that happens in our early years. To begin with, your mother or father were a bit strange. At least when decorating their son's room. How do I know? Please, boy, I don't forget certain details. You said it yourself at a casual gathering in the Orlando offices. Remember? I'm sure you don't. Some wives had gone to celebrate the end of the year, I think 2019 or 2010. It doesn't matter. Elena was busy with John Smith, the one from Zona Canadá. And you looked very handsome with your light blue tie, always making smart jokes. I say

365

handsome not because you're an Alain Delon, but because you were never a womanizer. That was obvious from ten miles away, and any, or almost any woman appreciates it. There's nothing more attractive to a woman than hearing things like "I like you, but I can't." Men are always so obsessed with getting it in that they don't understand that we are human beings, women, not just a wet hole, and we need to be looked at without being dragged to a bed. You never said yes or no to me, it's not necessary to clarify, nor did I expect anything from you, but I'm telling you this so you understand why some men are more attractive than they appear.

Anyway, it doesn't matter, it's of no importance whatsoever, because I don't think any of this knowledge I'm sharing with you, freely, can be useful in your future sales strategies.

I was just looking at Google Maps, and I see the streets in Tahiti are ugly, like in any poor country. Yes, that sea isn't here, and even less so for the mobsters in Chicago.

You'll think I'm crazy, but I'll never forget that dinner we had with fat Gasper, as you once called him in a hallway in Orlando. I'm sure you don't even remember that I was there too. For you, I never existed or was just the boss's pretty blonde wife. Am I wrong? Though Elena is prettier than me. Or was. It doesn't matter, because men don't just look for beauty in a woman, just as we women don't only expect handsomeness from a man.

That night, the one in Atlanta (where only thanks to champagne could a gathering of people be endured without disgust), I knew you hated fat Gasper as much as you hated Jeff. Though not in the sense we give it in Spanish, but a bit more superficial, like in English. In English, "hate" and "love" are much more superficial than in Spanish. Everyone says, I hate it, I love it, and so those words don't mean much. Like everything here. Here everything is superficial, like a twenty-dollar bill, with that face of an Indian killer that everyone desires.

Well, rejoice. The gringo is dead. You won't find it in the news. Maybe in a while the details will start to come out. But you can search online for something like "Businessman Gasper loses his life at home. Leaves behind a wife, three children, and multiple investments around the world." Something like that. Actually, he didn't die at home but in an apartment he had in Atlanta. Probably even his wife didn't know about this apartment because the fat guy had many others all over the place, since, they say, he trusted real estate more than Wall Street stocks. You know, like that Fox journalist, Sean Hannity, Trump's buddy. But unlike all those macho men, the fat guy didn't have any unresolved issues, neither for harassment nor abuse. It's very likely that the apartment where he died was just one of the many he had lying empty, and that he might not have even used it with any woman.

The truth is that he died a sweet death. Some wretched person sent him a RealPerson to his home. Not wretched, I suppose it was part of the Chinese promotion. You can imagine the poor man, trying to get rid of the product without his wife noticing.

As soon as he opened it, he must have put it in his car to take it to that apartment where, in the end, like Oscar Wilde, he couldn't resist the temptation to have sex with me, that is, with one of my copies, and he died right there. Yes, of course, he could have also left me in one of those public trash bins you find in parks. Either way, the fat guy took one of the RealPersons, that is, as if he had taken me myself, to one of his many apartments in Atlanta. Only at this point does my smile fade. I would have done the same. And you, probably. At least out of curiosity. The RealPersons speak and learn in ten minutes what takes us mortals five years. Did the fat guy understand that he revolted me just by looking at him? This same thing, did it turn him on even more? Questions that will remain unanswered forever. Poor devil. I suspect he wasn't such a bad person. What we do know is that the fat guy didn't die of a heart attack, as it's supposed to happen to old men having sex with young girls, or at least with someone thirty years younger like me. No, and this is the worst and what still bothers me: it seems he died of suffocation.

I must admit that this news triggered something negative in me. Not that it depressed me or anything like that. No, no. On the contrary, I started laughing like a madwoman, like someone sick. At first, it worried me. I was frightened of myself. How can someone be so insensitive to another's death?, I thought. Not insensitive. Somehow I was pleased by what had happened.

You know what, Facundo? We all have something dark in our lives. You have it, whether you know it or not. It's always better to know. I grew up thinking the opposite: it's better not to know certain things. Why?, they would tell me when I was a child. "Just forget it," "Don't overthink it," "If you keep dwelling on that, you'll poison yourself and never be able to be happy."

In any case, I was never happy. I learned to simulate happiness. Not just for others but for myself too. But you know something? I think I've discovered something about that dark side, my dark side, and I'm going to tell it. I won't tell Jeff, because it would be the same as nothing. Maybe I'll post it on social media or find some starving writer willing to write my story for a handful of dollars.

What I've discovered, almost at the same time that I laughed heartily when I found out about the death of the fat Gasper, is that I had been raped when I was fourteen.

369

How come I didn't remember it before and now I even recall the age I was when it happened? Well, that's stuff for one of those psychologists who never managed to get to the core of my existence. In my life, I've had six psychologists and two psychoanalysts. They all found different problems, which at their core were the same: first, the fault was my mother's, then my father's, and finally, when I got married and moved away, the fault fell on Jeff, my husband. Obviously, Jeff was a mistake in my life, but he was never the center of my life or the one to blame for my problems. The center was elsewhere.

It was when I wanted to become independent and went for a job interview. A store needed a girl to hand out flyers on the street, at the entrance. To attract potential customers, the girl had to be pretty, or at least attractive in some way. I was the last one to be interviewed. By then, the employees had already left, and the store had closed.

It was then and in that place that the owner, a fat man with unbearable tobacco breath, raped me. First, he made me act, in his office, as if I were handing out flyers for the Libertad store. I had to repeat the scene several times, each time with more sensuality. After that, I don't remember much more besides the tobacco breath and the huge belly that almost hid his penis, surely a very small penis because I don't remember any kind of pain. It was like sitting on a bus and the person next to you falls asleep with their head on your shoulder. Now it occurs to me that men who are traumatized by the size of their penises need to take out their frustrations on young girls who are still small and haven't seen other penises to laugh at theirs. You know, the same old story. You men have a sick obsession with size. Of course, if one is a moist hole, the donkey size must be important, as important as the suffering of being penetrated and the pleasure of penetrating.

As I was saying, it didn't hurt at all. That was nothing compared to the rape itself, and luckily, I didn't get pregnant. But I do remember that his enormous weight made it hard for me to breathe.

So, I don't know, how can you expect me not to laugh. Another thing I wanted to tell you is

That's where Silvanna's letter ended. She probably sent the email before she had time to correct it, to second-guess whether or not to send it. Even so, even without having read it, he would have realized her state of mind just from its length. Balanced people don't write novels instead of letters, especially after the invention of email, and even more so in the Age of Twitter and text messages.

He thought that, from the beginning, from that meeting in the café, Silvanna had other plans. Why would he trust her, especially her? Was she acting out of spite because she suspected Jeff's affair with Elena?

Facundo waited half an hour, an hour, and received nothing more.

Encounter with Susan at Cola de Pez

THE NEXT MORNING HE CROSSED paths with Susan at Cola de Pez. On her face, on her face, he saw surprise and confusion, but she said nothing and continued on her way to the kitchen, where María was.

Shortly after, the two women came around the counter, heading toward Facundo's table. María led Susan by the arm, like a child.

"Speak of the devil," said María.

"What do you mean, aunt?" Susan murmured softly.

"Yesterday I was talking to this gentleman," said María. "Do you remember Luis?"

Susan said nothing. Suddenly, Facundo remembered that he had seen Susan once before, through the window, from this very table, arriving on a sports motorcycle with her boyfriend. That had been the first time, not the time he found her at don José's house.

"Yes, the writer," said Susan.

"The writer, the musician, the liar," said María. "Who knows who this man is? No one. No one knows. But he's definitely not a CIA agent because there would be nothing for him to do here. We're not communists or drug traffickers. As far as I know. At least not unless don Manuel is selling me marijuana instead of cilantro, which I don't think because it wouldn't be good business for him and my customers would be more lively. No, sir, don Luis, or whatever his name is, he's not a bad person. I may be very ignorant, but I recognize a good person as soon as they walk through that door. It's too many years of dealing with so many people every day."

Facundo looked at her. María added:

"A liar, yes, but honest," she said. "We still don't know what movies he wrote, because we don't know his full name. He says his name is Luis."

"I work on commission," said Luis, laughing. "The Bridges of Madison County, actually, I wrote that one."

"Well, I didn't like that movie," said María.

"And you tell me that straight to my face? Couldn't you at least pretend a little?"

"If you want lies to your face, cross the line over there. It's not far."

"Yes, yes, I know," said Facundo. "David told me something about that American hypocrisy."

"Look, this beautiful girl is Susan. She is what she seems. Not Juana, nor Inés, nor Margaret: she's Susan."

There was silence. A few seconds that seemed to reveal more than all the previous words.

At that moment, the waiter Cuauhtémoc entered.

"Of course, here we also have our own liars," said María. "Like him. It's just that our liars aren't hypocrites. They're poor liars."

María walked over to the waiter, scolding him for his lateness, which, according to her, was becoming a habit. Cuauhtémoc said he had missed the 7:30 bus, that it was getting harder and harder for him to get up, to which María replied that it was because he was abusing tequila more and more, that she could see it in his face, that he couldn't lie to her because she had been in the business for years and that she had seen many single men end up marrying alcohol and dying before their time. Instead of kissing a bottle, try a woman, she told him. Get yourself a woman. It's not easy to get used to taking orders from a woman, but no matter how ugly she is, she'll prolong your life. To which Cuauhtémoc, turning around, firmly asked, pretending to be offended: What's this about dying before your time? The time to die is exactly when you die, and that's it, nothing more. Besides, you have to die of something. Or do you plan to stick around forever? María put her hands on her hips, as if planting herself firmly on both feet, and said: I don't know when I'm going to die, and I don't care. What I do know is that I'm not going to kill myself. It hasn't even been a month since we celebrated your fortieth birthday (Facundo was surprised; he would've sworn Cuauhtémoc was almost sixty). You're forty, you still have a lot of this damn life left to enjoy. Cuauhtémoc responded with a question: And what if I don't want to? To which María lost her patience and, throwing the dish towel on the counter, said: Well, if you don't want to live, then go to hell. Here I want people who want to live. Everything else can be forgiven, even men's betrayal and your love for tequila.

"I get the impression that you're always trying to avoid me," Facundo said to Susan.

"Me?" said Susan. "No, not at all. It's just that I have things to do."

"Ángel?" said Facundo, bringing up a name he remembered from a nightmare, but which he now suspected was the name of Susan's boyfriend.

375

"Leave that alone," she said. "He's not my boy-friend anymore."

A tense silence followed. Facundo remembered, once again, the equations that had haunted him during his early high school years. $ax^2 + bx = 0$ As with other math problems, to solve for the unknown, he had to assume he already knew the answer. Except that the human world was far more complex, and the unknown variables swarmed like tree pollen in spring. There was no Bhaskara here.

"But you still see each other," he said.

$$x^1$$

"Only every now and then," she confirmed.

"You still owe him money."

$$x^2$$

"Please stop, don Luis," she insisted.

Susan was about to leave but stopped. Her body seemed tied by invisible strings that made every movement the result of a constant struggle.

"I don't owe him anything anymore," Susan clarified. "I'm just trying to get him to leave me alone, little by little."

"Because if you say no, Ángel might get violent."

"Who knows? He's a complicated guy, and he's very respected. But, like you told me yourself, in a year he'll fall in love with someone else and forget about me."

"Did I say that?"

"Right now I'm not sure if it was you or someone else. But I think that's how it is."

"If he doesn't end up in jail first."

"Only God knows. Ángel isn't a bad person."

"How can you say that, Susan?" Facundo ventured. He could recall fragments, but the story of Susan and her boyfriend remained unclear, incomprehensible. He just had to pretend he knew it all.

"Really. Ángel has helped a lot of people."

"Out of convenience. He hasn't helped you. On the contrary, you're afraid of him…"

"Maybe. I don't know… He helped me once…"

"He reminds me of some so-called servants of the fatherland, experts at solving problems they themselves created. That way, everyone's happy."

"Maybe he'll end up in jail."

"But please stop, don Luis," Susan said, almost pleading.

Then her expression changed, as if a smile relaxed all her muscles and concentrated in her eyes, looking at him. Facundo trembled inside. Susan was a charming girl, he thought, but too young and confused to be enchanted even for a moment.

At that moment, Cuauhtémoc approached and said, waiting a moment for Susan to walk far enough away:

"Don't pay attention to señora María," the waiter said. "She's not a bad person. It's just that it's been a long time since she's had any action."

He recognized the motorcycle and Ángel's profile

ON A CORNER, HE SAW HIM PASS by in a hurry. He didn't remember his face (did he have a very thin mustache or was it the shadow of his lips?), but he knew it was him. The helmet covered almost his entire face. Maybe he recognized him by his broad shoulders and extremely thin waist, sunburned. Maybe because the motorcycle had a particular design or made a sound, a defiant roar that reminded him of something he had deeply engraved like a confusing symbol, like an S that gets mixed up with an 8. All he knew was that the man who had just passed him was Ángel. He followed him through the crowd as long as he could. A block ahead, he lost sight of him and later found him again standing on a sidewalk. He argued with Susan. At one point, he grabbed her arm violently. Facundo hurried toward Susan, fearing that the agitation, the effort of walking so quickly at that hour of the morning when the sun was already beginning to burn, could trigger another health crisis. Susan resisted for a moment, but then she got on the motorcycle and soon they were out of sight.

Facundo leaned his hand on a shaded wall and felt the pounding of his heart in his throat. After a while, he recovered. He entered a kiosk and bought a cold apple soda. He came out and stood exactly where Susan had been standing earlier. He looked at the people walking toward him, at the same distance where he himself had been walking toward her, and he couldn't clearly distinguish their faces. But he knew there were two reasons that made that perspective different. First, Susan must have had better eyesight than him. Since his fifties, his distance vision had started to decline considerably. Second, he didn't know any of the people walking on that sidewalk at that time as well as she knew him.

Hours after overthinking it, he called David to ask for Susan's number. David told him he was already on his way back, that Facundo himself had Susan's number, that he had given it to him many months ago, and that he remembered it well because at the time he had told him that the girl had a boyfriend, that it was better not to get involved with those people because they were trouble, which is why he had distanced himself from Susan. Since don José had fallen ill, the girl had started down a bad path. To David, the poor girl had always needed someone to support her, to take care of her like a child, and in the absence of her overprotective father, she had thrown herself into the arms of the first mobster she met at a graduation party. That Ángel Fernández is quite a bit older than Susan, probably around thirty, and he dropped out of school long before finishing. So the guy was at that party on business, not to celebrate any graduation, and that's where they met. Ángel offered her a job as an intermediary, with a salary that Susan never wanted to confess, but it was surely more than any of us could earn in a year. Until the problems started, and from there I don't know more than what I can imagine. She tried to get out of something dirty and couldn't. Then you showed up and felt sorry for the girl and helped her, María says with money, but only you would know that. What surely you don't know is that Ángel found out and marked you. So I recommend you stay away from those people, and if you can, leave as soon as possible. María and I will figure out how to get that girl out of this mess. But if Ángel knows you're here, he'll have you killed. If he doesn't do it himself, it'll be a matter of honor.

Luckily, the man doesn't know you. Susan, under pressure, ended up giving them a photo of her and a blonde guy at the Civic Plaza, and I don't know if they've already taken out that poor man. God willing they haven't, but I can't assure you of anything. So you'll have to excuse me, don Luis, but if you lost Susan's number, it's for the best, and I'm not going to give it to you again only to later feel responsible for an act of irresponsibility like that.

Susan's casting

TWO YEARS AGO, FACUNDO had managed to get Susan to participate in the casting for CollegeNow! She had resisted, arguing that the program might not even exist, that it was likely part of a scam by opportunists, similar to those who take women to Europe with promises of jobs only to end up working in prostitution. Her mother had always warned her about this danger, especially when Susan became an attractive young woman, exotically attractive.

Facundo had shown her on his phone the promotional video for the new reality show and then an email from the company mentioning the multi-million-dollar investment and repeating the core idea of the new venture: ...the contestants, in addition to gaining national recognition, would compete for various scholarships at the most prestigious universities in the country. Emory, Harvard, Princeton, MIT, Florida, Chicago, Berkeley. To do this, they would have to convince the audience and the jury not only of their intellectual and personal abilities but also of the importance of their future projects. In other words, nothing different from what any applicant writes in their cover letters. However, due to its media nature, the contestants must have good physical appearances. The producer of Elvis Presley had said long before discovering him: "I'll make a million the day I find a white man with a black man's voice." Following the logic of this business genius, I dare say the company will make a billion the day they find a Marilyn Monroe with the intelligence of Stephen Hawking. The attached file details the desirable physical characteristics of the contestants...

A brilliant idea, no doubt, from Gordo Gasper, who if there was one thing he hated, it was people with degrees of any kind. That was going to be a hit, a TV show that would embed itself in the minds of Americans, where, according to all the studies, both the rich and the poor admire as much as they hate college graduates, who are almost the only remaining bastions of intellectuals in the land of dollars and cheap beer.

"Well," Susan had said, "I don't see the audience over there voting for a Mexican."

"But the jury will," Facundo had insisted. "When it comes to face-to-face interactions, people are always politically correct."

"Anyway," Susan had said, "I don't see much sense in a young woman needing to be pretty to earn a scholarship at a university in the United States."

"Why not?" Facundo had replied. "Haven't you seen the cheerleaders at football games—I mean, American football games? They're not there because they're ugly."

"Nor because they're smart."

"I suppose. I don't know much about it, but they're all college students. Some of them even have scholarships."

"They must have earned them through academic merit."

"I don't know about that either. What I do know is that American football players aren't admitted to universities for their high grades but for their athletic skills. Same goes for those tall guys who can touch the ceiling with their hands, the ones who play basketball or any other sport. They have no idea about…"

Susan had fallen silent, deep in thought. She hated when a man made her change her mind. The same had happened with Ángel when he told her she should accompany him to his business meetings. She had resisted, just as she began to suspect his clients weren't trustworthy. Right when don José got sick and she ended up abandoning her studies.

"Some of those cheerleaders end up having brilliant professional careers," Facundo said, snapping her out of her thoughts, certain that Susan was about to give in, like so many others had, because human nature is more predictable than we like to believe, because we are more organic matter than we can accept.

"Same with football players," he continued. "Or do you think most of them become champions and get transferred to professional leagues? Of course not. I've known many football players who entered universities to play football or basketball and before their third year, they realized athletic success wasn't their destiny and ended up graduating as lawyers, musicians, or becoming sports commentators or successful businessmen. That's the idea. Everyone knows it, except them."

Susan had furrowed her brow and pursed her lips, an unmistakable sign of doubt tilting toward a positive response.

"Besides," Facundo insisted, sipping the rest of his morning coffee, as if downplaying the matter, like the bullfighter preparing to deliver the final dagger, "a casting is very unpredictable."

Downplaying the matter. This was, according to his own manual, the next step in any conquest. Persistence naturally breeds resistance, especially when it comes to women. Once the virus of desire had been planted, it was necessary to leave the seed of doubt that the victim or client (in some ways, the same thing) might be missing out on a great opportunity. Even more so in this case: the opportunity of a lifetime. Either she accepted a full life, with unexpected doors opening, or she spent the rest of her life lamenting, barely making ends meet as an employee at some small business with no horizons, selling Jarritos with David or cooking for María at the restaurant, sprinkling salt, pepper, and sweat on the customers' tacos, customers who would never take an interest in her, for better or worse. No different from what happened, wasn't it? to the same María, the beautiful and talented young woman who confused old principles with contemporary nonsense and ended up dampening her gray hair over the eternal flames of the Cola de Pez kitchen.

"A casting is a casting," Facundo said. "It's normal not to get through, not to be chosen. But if you are one of the chosen ones, you'll still have the chance to say no. Saying no to an opportunity is always easy; the hard part is having the opportunity and being able to say yes. Even if you're chosen and end up rejecting the offer, at least you'll know how far you could've gone. It's like a little challenge. It won't cost you a single peso, beyond an hour of recording. In fact, I recommend that, if you decide to do it, you don't set your expectations too high, because only two percent of auditions turn out successful. The audios and videos are analyzed by a group of experts who, in reality, do not know you personally. I could give them positive feedback, but still they will make a decision without ever having interacted with you in person."

"Better," Susan had said shyly, "if it were like that, I'd die of fear."

"Well, that's if they follow the traditional method," said Facundo. "The company has implemented, because the experimental stage has already passed, an AI evaluation system."

"What is that?"

"It's something complex. AI stands for Artificial Intelligence. These are programs that process thousands of audios, videos, texts, and make a decision about which candidate has the best chances of success in the market."

"In the market?"

"It's a way of putting it. Generally, companies use it for market purposes. In this case, 'market,'" said Facundo, making air quotes with his fingers, "refers to the business of academic applications."

"Business?"

"Yes, I get it. I think I'm thinking in English. That language is full of words related to business, to money, which doesn't mean one is talking about business. Have you heard the phrase 'It's not my business'?"

"Yes, Uncle David says it sometimes."

"He says it, like everything, ironically. David should be Argentine, not Mexican. In Spanish, we say 'no me importa,' or 'no es mi asunto,' but in English, they use those words that then rub us the wrong way who don't belong to that culture."

"You don't belong to that culture?"

"Good question. You're a clever girl. To tell the truth, I've tried. That whole assimilation thing. Maybe I didn't even reach the most dignified level of integration. I did what I could. Without success. But one is what one is, and no matter how one disguises it, it doesn't change reality, even if one believes it, with whistles and artificial fires on the Fourth of July."

Susan looked at him with increasing attention. Facundo noticed.

"Anyway," he said, "when I say market, I mean the academic interests of universities over there. They care about money, of course, because each student means thirty or fifty thousand dollars a year to them. But when they have to pay, that is, when they give scholarships, what interests them is investing well, which means spending money on candidates who will bring them academic value, visibility."

"But *CollegeNow!* doesn't care about academic value…"

"It's a combination. Yes, agreed. That reality show, like all of them, is a business. But the audience will vote for the most interesting candidates, young people who have something new to contribute. In your case, you're a Mexican that anyone would mistake for Japanese or Korean, that is, you break all stereotypes. Despite your young age, you have an experience that no girl on the other side has."

This time, the conversation was interrupted (as always, Facundo thought) by the waiter Cuauhtémoc.

She didn't want to join him for a coffee, and he finished his just as she was getting up to leave.

As his manual indicated, Susan had responded positively twenty-four hours later. She did so with the sole condition that no one found out about the attempt, especially María. Susan had told him that, in reality, she was worried about the idea of leaving her father, María, and everyone else abandoned, like many others who went to the other side had done.

Facundo only replied "I understand" and reserved the conference room at the Tijuana Marriott hotel for that same week. The interview was on a Friday afternoon and lasted longer than expected. For three hours, almost without interruption, Susan had told almost her entire life story, all her future plans, and had suggested, between the lines, her current problems, the problems of her city, her country, the world. Susan was, without a doubt, a young woman more mature and lucid than anyone might suspect upon seeing her for the first time and not taking her seriously for at least thirty minutes.

The last question ("What do you think about the role of politics in the lives of citizens?") was one of those typical trick questions they ask in beauty pageants. The poor girls begin to doubt and speak without knowing, delighting the macho men who think they're smarter and desire them without being able to have them. Even an old professor would have some difficulty articulating a brief, simple, and satisfactory response. Much more so a young girl, too young, as is always the case in these meat markets, someone who doesn't even dedicate herself to giving intelligent answers to the world's problems and who, to make matters worse, is exposed to millions of gazes, half-naked and balancing on high heels aligned one after the other, as if walking along a ledge. One would have to see Einstein himself in a similar situation, in his underwear trying to answer an unexpected question about the best strategy to eroticize a woman without hiding the belly.

Probably because Susan was tired by that point, or because she really thought that way, her response was somewhat radical. From an acidic critique of Mexican politicians, she moved on to an even more corrosive one about the U.S. governments and their complicit institutions, like the churches, which she labeled as hypocritical organizations.

"The fanatics, who over there are called Moderate Conservatives and Responsible, don't just sell you a lie... not even the obelisk or the Lincoln Memorial," she suddenly blurted out. "They sell you heaven and insure you against hell, nothing more, nothing less.

Which is logical in a culture of arrogant paranoiacs. No, I know, it doesn't seem like it to you. Of course, there are exceptions, a few million good Americans, sufficiently few or poor to not be able to prevent us from living from war to war, like here with the damn narco traffickers. What is more arrogant than an American who believes himself to be the protector of Peace, Democracy, and Freedom in the world?"

Facundo responded with an unmitigated silence. Susan continued:

"I don't know if that arrogance comes from American culture or from the culture of the rich in general, from the Capitalist International, or something like that. I'm not well-prepared enough to answer that question. But I've always wondered, how can one be so arrogant, how can one sleep so peacefully knowing that to preserve the way of life, the world must be kept in a permanent state of wars, massacres, and famines when there are so many resources in this world?"

"Do you have the answer to that Historical Problem?" asked Facundo, somewhere between didactic and paternal.

"I think I do," she said, unclipping her microphone, "and it's not as complicated or impossible to understand as it seems with that title. It's an illusion to think that money is everything. No. No... Of course not. To be able to exercise that power, it is first necessary to convince those who don't have it that those who do possess it do so justly and necessarily. And those who possess the money need, not for a reason of power but as another good, to think, believe, imagine that all of that is true, that it's not just a simple and sneaky robbery legalized and legitimized. In that way, money doesn't only buy power but also... what do you call insurance? Peace of mind, peace of conscience."

When she finished, Susan drank the rest of her glass of water and said:

"You can delete that last part, if you want."

"It's not necessary," said Facundo. "Even though I don't agree, our country is still a democracy, and we can accept opinions that don't please us."

"Of course," said Susan. "A democracy without criticism is not a democracy. Criticisms are always welcome in democracies, as long as they are not so dangerous as to compromise some special interest of those who really rule. Then, they don't put you in jail. You just lose your job, or they don't give you a scholarship. Those minimal things that are always more effective than sending someone to prison."

"I'm optimistic about your chances," said Facundo. "We'll see what happens."

An attack of compassion, he thought

FACUNDO FELT SOMEWHAT ANNOYED by Susan's last
opinions. Or he wanted to feel annoyed, as if it were
a way to justify the discomfort that so much certainty
from that young woman had caused him, as if the
mere idea of having underestimated her at the start of
the interview had bothered him, giving her advice
like a teacher does to a school-aged child so that she
later left him with his mouth closed, not to say open,
with a disguised hint of humiliation.

Yes, maybe that was it. He wanted to feel annoyed, to ease his conscience, since, he knew, along
with that CollegeNow! scholarship came the serious
possibility that RealPerson would use the biometric
material that had been recorded during the three
hours of filming. And since it was still being debated
whether to send that material to Seoul so they could
use Susan, he needed to define, confirm his decision,
questionable, by surrounding himself with excuses
and other moral anesthetics so common in such successful and hypocritical societies. The secret to a good

business is not just convincing the buyer of something but convincing yourself that what you're selling, be it cigarettes or Coca-Cola, is something good, necessary, or at least not so bad.

Monday afternoon was the last time he saw Susan that year. It was a block away from María's restaurant. He was walking back looking for a taxi, and she was heading towards the restaurant, hurried and with her head down.

She had pretended not to see him, but he grabbed her by the arm.

"Susan," he said. "Are you going to your aunt's place?"

She lowered her head and said yes. Once again, she was the shy, vulnerable young woman, as if the Susan from the interview were another person, an older sister with much more experience than the Susan who now avoided looking him in the eyes.

"I'm leaving this afternoon," said Facundo.

"Oh," she said. "Have a good trip."

Facundo placed his hand under her chin to make her look up. On the other side of the border, he would never have dared such a gesture, so common in old Hollywood movies. He would have been sued for harassment.

"Is something wrong?" he asked, at the same time thinking he could make out a mark on her left cheek, hidden by makeup.

He had never seen her wear makeup before. Somehow, he disliked both things.

"Tell me, confidentially, what's going on," he said.

"Nothing," she said. "Why would something be wrong…? Well, have a good trip."

Facundo said nothing, but when she walked away, he ran a few steps and told her to wait. She hesitated but turned around. Her eyes were moist, but the tears had not yet spilled over.

Then, Facundo hugged her. After a second of hesitation, he felt her place a hand on his back and squeeze tightly.

"Alright," she repeated. "Have a good trip. I have to go."

"Just wait a moment," said Facundo, as he took out his wallet and handed her one of his debit cards.

She shook her head and hands.

"You know what, Luis?" she said. "I'm so tired of my life always depending on some man."

"One day it won't be like that," said Facundo. "But before you free yourself from all of society, from all men, you must free yourself from Ángel."

395

Susan looked him in the eyes but said nothing.

"Look," said Facundo. "This card doesn't have much cash available. I use it on my trips, in case I get robbed or lose it. You won't be able to withdraw more than a thousand dollars a month, and in less than a year, I'll cancel it. In fact, I could cancel it tomorrow, whenever I want."

Susan hesitated, and Facundo placed the card in her hand, closing her fingers over it as if she were a doll.

"The PIN is 2001, you won't forget it," said Facundo.

Susan closed her eyes, furrowed her brow, and scrunched her entire face as if she were about to cry.

Facundo hugged her tightly and left, heading for a taxi that had stopped at a red light.

You can check out any time you like

ON THE FLIGHT FROM GUADALAJARA to Atlanta, he couldn't help but think about Susan. Perhaps the first-class whisky and the obligation to remain still for five hours forced him to reflect on the afternoon he had left behind. He also thought, like someone carefully reviewing the memory of an important event, about the previous session at the Tijuana Marriott.

In the sequence from the three video cameras, the biometric cameras, and the multiple microphones, a significant and sufficient sample of Susan had been saved, the one that would be processed in RealPerson's laboratories. Would the artificial intelligence systems be intelligent enough to capture both, the multiple Susans? Or would they only be able to see and amplify the Susan from the Tijuana Marriott?

Among the clouds over the Gulf of Mexico and his second whisky, he noticed the relevant detail that Susan had not been intimidated by the luxury of the hotel, nor by the cameras recording her, nor had she been overwhelmed by the stress that anyone would feel when a big opportunity in an interview was at stake. On the contrary, she was a shy young woman when walking through her neighborhood, down the street of Cola de Pez, through the garden of her sick father's house, confined to a wheelchair. Was she acting? Had she learned to act and feign fragility as a paradoxical defense mechanism?

In any case, a simple decision on his part could make Susan, or one of the Susans coexisting in the same body, become a kind of Eve, the mother of an

397

extensive and unpredictable people not only of intelligent robots but of humans. Perhaps one day real humans will no longer be necessary to feed the databases, but if that happens, it will be because a generation first laid the foundational work with the material that matters most to human beings: other human beings, to love them or to destroy them.

His narcissism was not sufficiently monumental, like that of a Dutch doctor named Jan Karbaat, if he remembered correctly, who inseminated hundreds of women with his own sperm for the good of humanity, as he had said. No, he had no intention of using his own persona to initiate this foundational generation of intelligent androids. But he felt a powerful attraction to reproduce and proselytize his own desires, his own fantasies, like an alcoholic insists on talking about alcohol and makes jokes about drinks and pressures others to drink with him. Like a cinephile who needs others to watch the same movie. Like a religious fanatic. Years ago, he suddenly remembered, he used to recommend Nicole Kidman's movies until he discovered a certain obsession with the actress, though it was nothing that time and maturity did not cure.

Perhaps (he thought later, already flying over Alabama or Georgia) that also explains why he would like Susan's biometric data to be used in the production of the first RealPerson. Somehow, for some reason he couldn't quite unravel, he felt something for that young woman. Or was it that deep down (in a still very repressed way, and despite all his own speeches about how admirable American culture was, for its invincible capacity for business and individual freedom), deep down, he didn't believe his own speeches, his passionate defenses of the world organized by finance and consumption, but actually despised it, almost as much as Ernesto? But he, like anyone, had to play a role, a part, believe in his own lie like a shipwrecked man drinks his own urine to quench his thirst. Like anyone, he had to act, think, and believe in accordance with the needs of survival. If you run a bar, you must believe that alcohol is an essential part of this country's culture and that without it there would be no identity, no happiness, no progress. If you own a pet veterinary clinic and enjoy eating pork, you'll find a way to explain why the Chinese are barbaric dog eaters. If you're a soldier, you must believe in all that sacred nonsense about the Defense of the Homeland, Sacrifice, Sense of Service, Altruistic Protection of Others' Freedom, even if that soldier is in the midst of a criminal war, launched based on lies, like Iraq, like Vietnam, like almost every other war. And so it goes, as if the habit always made the monk, at least the obedient, functional monk, the good monk. Because there were also traitors like Ernesto, who could sell cigarettes while clarifying that their product causes cancer.

Deep down, it had all been a lie he had told himself and repeated to others, so as not to feel alone, so as not to feel what he truly was or wanted to be. Deep down, he thought and felt like Susan and, more than continuing to make money and heroic business deals, what he wanted was for the rebellious Susans to reproduce, to be reproduced by those same sick individuals who, while amassing infinite sums of money, like himself, dressed themselves in that stupid arrogance of believing they were the people chosen by God and by nature.

Minutes away from landing at Hartsfield-Jackson, as the captain began the repetitive, mechanical Welcome to... and his useless data about the ground temperature, he wanted to feel annoyed with Susan, wanted to despise her somehow. He almost succeeded. During the transit wait for Orlando, trying to ease his hunger or boredom in another deliberately dim, faux-luxurious restaurant with inflated prices to keep the poor away, he almost forgot this entire useless series of feelings and decided he would send the material to Seoul.

The day before, the afternoon when he had met Susan for the last time on that excessively sunny street in Tijuana, felt as distant as one of those summers at Uncle Alberto's house in Uruguay. Now, everything around him suddenly reminded him of his present, of his needs and of his desire to return to battle, to close a good deal once and for all and to say, once again, the world is not for cowards.

He looked at his watch and calculated that his flight would depart in forty minutes. He didn't know if it was day or night, if it was cloudy or sunny outside, if it had cooled down or was hot. For long seconds, like when he woke up at night not knowing where he was or which way the window faced, he couldn't tell if he was in the airport in Malaysia, Paris, or Guadalajara. All he knew was that his flight would depart in forty minutes. He struggled to read the boarding pass and realized he was headed to Orlando.

He checked his email. Suddenly it occurred to him to search for Susan's name in his Gmail. As always, the search returned hundreds of messages that had no connection to what he was looking for. Except for one that he had sent to himself on November 16 of last year, at 11:35 PM: "remember tip for the next planning and activity reporting meeting: Susan's input (voice, rebellious ideas, perfect face shape, accent of expressions with slight head movements, smiling eyes between Japan and Sweden) will be decisive for the completion of the flagship product, but it will also protect the company from any possible lawsuit. What poor girl in Mexico would think of suing a company in South Korea over the resemblance of one of its products?."

In that email, Susan had to be Susan. In other words, during the interview at the hotel in Tijuana, the girl had served to feed her personal data into the future generation of AR21 androids by RealPerson, something that, obviously, was illegal in the United States and punishable with years in prison. Regardless, nothing different from the experiments his own government had conducted in Guatemala, injecting syphilis into a thousand Indians, he thought.

Was that why he had given her the credit card, to ease his guilty conscience? Or had it been out of compassion, true compassion? True compassion, like one of those chosen by God who, upon leaving their million-dollar churches, toss a few bucks to the beggars?

Before taking the flight to Orlando, he snapped out of his thoughts. It was ten at night, and the cool sea breeze came in through the hotel window. He barely managed to get up from the armchair. He smelled the sea more intensely but couldn't see it in the darkness. It was an ancient smell. He thought about walking to Cola de Pez, but at that hour, he wouldn't find her there.

You can check out any time you like
But you can never leave

The other Susan

ON FRIDAY AFTERNOON, two days before taking the flight to Buenos Aires, Facundo went out for a walk and ran into David on Avenida de los Insurgentes. David stopped the old Buick and shouted to him:

"*Maestro!* Are you out for a stroll or heading somewhere? Need a ride?"

Facundo hesitated for a moment and then got into the car.

"Neither one nor the other," said Facundo. "I was just thinking."

"Nothing better than walking to think positively. I like walking on the beach. The sea relaxes me."

Without looking for an excuse so it wouldn't sound strange, Facundo hit him with the question he

403

had been asking himself. He knew that the next day, on the plane, he would regret not asking the necessary questions, even if it was the least appropriate moment.

"I was thinking about Susan," said Facundo, "and I was wondering..."

"Susan? Don José's girl?"

"Yes, but don't worry," Facundo cut in. "I'm not some Silvio Berlusconi..."

"I didn't say that, teacher. Besides, the girl Susan isn't really a girl. She's well into her twenties and, though it doesn't seem like it, she's a grown woman... But what a son of a bitch. Can't you see you've got a HUGE RED LIGHT! These sons of... Yes, well, the girl Susan... I wish I had been around to advise her when she made her bad decisions, as you guys say over there, always so aseptic and neutral. The Yankees are hygienic and neutral even when dropping a bomb on you... But what a fool! If there's one thing they do well over there, it's drive. Here we're all sloppy. No one respects a traffic sign... She's probably more mature than we were at that age. Susan. The girl. We thought we were real tough guys, or wanted others to think we were tough, experienced, and we lied more than a politician on campaign. Just like we exaggerated upward, like the Crusaders exaggerated how many Moors they had killed, women always exaggerate downward. They brag about being virgins, and we brag about being womanizers, when neither are what they claim to be. Well, yes, culture and all that, but if they are victims of macho culture, so are we. Susan looks like a young girl, but she's already a woman. She's been a woman for a while. It's just that Asian women always look younger than they are, at least at that age. I care a lot about Susan, especially because she started off losing when she was born. Some are born with stars, others end up crashed. But there comes a moment when we have to take responsibility for what we do, and the girl is no longer a child."

"Anyway. I think she owes me some explanations," said Facundo.

David continued driving, as if he didn't understand what Facundo was referring to. He said nothing.

"Aren't you going to ask me what I mean?" asked Facundo.

"I don't know, teacher. Susan isn't my daughter."

"Nor is she don José's daughter."

"Yes, she is his daughter." She wasn't the biological daughter of his wife, but what does that detail matter?

"Yes, of course. That detail doesn't matter."

Another long silence settled between the noise of the Buick and the honks from the other cars. Sweat trickled down David's wide, dark forehead, as if he were thinking of something far away in time.

"David," said Facundo, "do you know that my company offered Susan a scholarship to study at Arizona State University? It wasn't for Princeton or Dartmouth College, way out there. No, it was for a university just a few hours' flight from here. She never responded, and I think she settled for the pittance I gave her before I left."

David didn't say anything. He took a deep breath and murmured:

"I heard something…"

"Something? Like what?"

"It's just that you don't know some things, and you have a false idea of Susan."

"Sure. That's why I'm asking you. I'd like to clear up some doubts before I leave tomorrow."

"The Susan you interviewed at the Marriott last year wasn't Susan."

David had to slam on the brakes at a red light.

"Yikes, we're going to crash if we keep driving distracted," he said.

David tried to think while wiping his sweat and drinking water from a bottle.

"Susan wasn't Susan," said Facundo with feigned irony, "and I wasn't me."

"Look, Facundo…" said David.

"How do you know my name's Facundo?" Facundo interrupted.

David hesitated:

"Are you Luis Facundo?"

"No. Facundo Luis. I prefer to be called Luis. But there's no problem with the other name, it's just that I thought I never used that name before…"

"It must be that I got you mixed up with an Argentine friend I had over there at the university. Once I called a friend Samuel when his name was actually Joseph, just because he was Jewish. That time I didn't know how to fix it. Why are there so many Argentines named Facundo? Facundo, Funes, Juan Domingo… Is it because of the book, what was the author's name?"

"Sarmiento."

"Yes, that son of a bitch who became president, like almost all sons of bitches. No offense to the country. Noooo, quite the opposite. I would've liked to know Buenos Aires. I grew up listening to Gardel's tangos. My old man was a fan of Libertad Lamarque. He didn't like boleros or corridos. Sarmiento was brown, I mean. He was dark like me and only wanted

407

blond immigrants. They say Hitler was Jewish or had a relative…"

"David…" Facundo interrupted.

"Oh, right, sorry. We Mexicans like to wander off. Look, Luis, the thing about Susan, it's a very long story and it's better if you don't get into the details. I'm telling you for your safety. But since you want to know and you keep dwelling on it, I'll tell you something, though I don't know everything and I shouldn't speak too much… Look, if you have time, let's head to a client's place I have on the coast. I have to drop off some goods, and on the way I'll tell you."

"I have time," said Facundo.

"Sounds good," laughed David.

"I hear myself and I can't believe it, but yes. I have time."

"One more week here and you'll forget you're American."

"You mean Yankee."

"Adopted."

"Yes, a Yankee adopted and a renegade Argentine."

"That's it, my friend, and no offense," said David. "Well, the story of poor Susan is a bit complicated. Her mother, the Japanese woman, had had an affair with don José."

"María told me that."

"An affair for him and, who knows if not, a romantic fantasy for her. You see, we men are predatory animals? They care about the whole backstory, and we care about the ending. At least at a certain age. Then we start losing vitality, interest, or I don't know what it is, but we stop seeing all women as potential lovers. If we all weren't like young don José, it's because God hasn't blessed us all with the looks of Luis Miguel. They say don José was a Jorge Negrete, though he wasn't dark under his nails. Blond until his hair turned all white before he was old. Well, it seems that from that spring romance, which maybe wasn't even love but a whim of a man already mature (and close to rotting, as a friend from Cuernavaca rudely says), the whim or fleeting heat of a man with a stable, happy marriage but no children, had its natural consequences. His wife, doña Romina, after the pain of the news of his infidelity, adopted the girl, who became, from day one, her devotion." But no one ever knew that the Japanese woman, to this day disappeared and to this day without a known name, had had twins and had given a girl to two different families. One to her lover, don José. The other, to a well-off family in Tijuana. Why that family? No one knows, and for sure, no one ever will. It was speculated that the Japanese woman had been in bed with Mr. Betancourt, and that she didn't know if the daughters were from one or the other. But after living some time, and don't ask me why, I don't believe in this possibility. I rather imagine a poor woman, lost in an unknown country, in love and abandoned by the false promises of a man. Have you ever heard that saying about how a man promises and promises until he finally gets what he wants? I'm not saying don José was a bad man, but he was a man, and a man of his time. Back then, if you didn't have those experiences, you were a queer and couldn't live in peace just thinking about it. It's also possible that the mother knew that both girls would be a heavy burden for don José, who at the time was a rather modest bricklayer, and decided to leave the other girl with an acquaintance or, more likely, had chosen a luxurious house at random, one in the Chapultepec neighborhood, imagining that the parents' money and the children's future more or less corresponded. Sometimes I picture the poor Japanese woman, just after giving birth, walking up those steep streets to leave the second daughter in one of those big houses that smell like firewood in winter and jasmine in spring. At the time, the Japanese woman couldn't have known that, in reality, the twins were identical. And no one knew until recently, when the girls met in a classroom at the Autonomous University of Baja California and a statistics professor, who had been confusing them since the first day, asked if they were cousins or related. The other girl, Sandra Betancourt, knew she was adopted, but Susan didn't. Or she never wanted to know, accustomed as she was to the lie and the teasing from her schoolmates. As the Maestro said, there's no worse blind than the one who doesn't want to see. So after getting to know each other for a while, the two decided to secretly take a DNA test, which confirmed they were twin sisters. Someone said that Susan had asked her father to take the same test, and that he refused, though I also heard, from Susan herself, that she didn't want to do the test because she was afraid of finding out that José wasn't her father. Are you following?

Facundo made a disapproving gesture with his mouth but didn't respond.

"Anyway" David said," to keep it short, when you offered Susan the interview, Susan, shy as she is, got scared. She had decided not to go, but Sandra convinced her to go in her place. Sandra was much more outgoing. She had been raised to feel like a queen, and her self-confidence was far greater than Susan's, who had been battered by bullying. Not to mention

411

that her father, the Betancourt who adopted her, is a well-known lawyer for his Republican and leftist ideas, which come from his family who were expelled by Franco after the Republicans lost the war in Spain. So, with all his money and education, he wasn't much of a conservative, and his daughter even less so. Accustomed to questioning and rebutting everything, she had an extremely strong personality, the kind I like in a woman, always self-assured.

"Why 'had'?

"Because she died. Because she was killed. The cartel killed her.

The Buick sped along Federal Highway 1. Facundo thought that external reality is always indifferent, it never stops. Sandra would have been very familiar with that avenue, those houses, and now none of those images belonged to her anymore. We think we own something, but the only truth is that the world doesn't care about us. Not one bit.

After almost a kilometer of silence, Facundo asked:

"Was she involved with those people?

"No, no" David said. "I don't think so. The girl was too straight, the real deal. Just like we were when we were young. Idealistic as hell. Bet you weren't the same?

"Maybe. I don't know if more idealistic or more full of it…

David veered onto a dirt road. Someone banged on the window, unhappy with the abrupt maneuver. David cursed at them and then laughed.

"Idiot" he said.

"If the girl wasn't involved" Facundo insisted," then why?

"From there, I don't know, man. There's a lot of speculation, and it still hasn't been cleared up who killed her. I bet it'll never be known, just like what happened with a friend of mine, in Sinaloa. Not even God can fix this.

"Speculations… Like what?

"Some say Sandrita clashed with the daughter of a cartel boss over something related to her father. Others say it was a vendetta, because her father, Sandra's father, had been responsible for one of those capos, not one of the big ones, of course, ending up in jail. For a short time, but an affront is not forgotten. I even heard somewhere that Sandrita's father must have been involved with the cartel too, because it was unexplainable that he was still alive or living in the same house after having jailed that capo. Others say it was because of Susan… Look, we're arriving. I'll get

413

out for a few minutes and come back. You can join me if you want.

David stopped near a warehouse surrounded by a large expanse of dry, cracked earth. He got out, took the cartons of Marlboro cigarettes from the trunk, and carried them along a dusty path to the warehouse, which, with letters painted years ago, announced: WELCOME 1969.

Facundo put on the straw hat that David had in the back seat, got out, and waited for him under the sun, leaning against the car. It took him a while to get his eyes used to so much light. Under a long awning, which had once been red, locals and truck drivers sought relief from the heat. At one table, two men were laughing uproariously. At another, a woman greeted David with a hug. They talked for a while until he disappeared into the warehouse, as if swallowed by a black hole.

Though the sea wasn't visible from there, you could smell the salt and the scent of tacos al pastor. A child ran by, followed by a woman who returned dragging him by the hand. A young woman coming from the opposite direction diverted them and looked Facundo in the eyes, for what he thought was an excessively long time, and then continued toward the bus stop. In a few years, which for that young

414

woman would feel like centuries, she'd be running after her child, maybe in the same place, or elsewhere, because in reality it's all the same place. The young woman wore a white dress with small roses along the bottom edge. Over time, she'd have many other dresses, much better ones, more expensive ones, but she'd remember that one, the one she paraded through the poor neighborhood to the delight of all the men who didn't dare even speak to her.

He had forgotten those gestures. Irresponsible, so human. What woman would think to look at a stranger like that? Facundo had ruined that magical moment by lowering his eyes, almost with disdain, as one is supposed to do on the other side, where even a glance could be considered harassment. Over something as trivial as that, anyone could lose in a few days the fruit of years of inhuman work, Chinese-like labor, working like a black man, like a black slave, like a white man with no life, cadaverous. Like a slave, but from above, a slave with privileges: over something as foolish as that, over looking at or saying something nice to a young woman like that, you could ruin a reputation, a hefty bank account, a peaceful, secure life. Peaceful and boring as death. A life with artificial feelings, like the lives of the Silvannas.

He watched the young woman walking away toward the bus stop. She had that pleasant waistline women in their twenties have, those perfect legs on cheap shoes. That boldness only women on this side have. On the other side, Facundo thought, there's no machismo. Only violations. Violations by males with money.

When the young woman reached the shade of the bus stop, she turned and looked at him one more time. He, Facundo, forced himself to smile at her. She replied with another smile and turned to board the bus that had just stopped at that moment.

David returned drenched in sweat and carrying two bottles of Jarritos.

"This," David said, out of breath, "is what I have to do to make ends meet as a high school teacher. At night, I tell my students that the Americans are drinking less Coca-Cola and that's why we drink more of it, to compensate for the business. It's the same with tobacco. Since you all smoke less and less, we have to smoke more to keep Philip Morris afloat. My students think I'm joking, but you see, Don Luis, if I don't take part in the business myself, I don't survive either."

Facundo felt compelled to justify him:

"But the Philip Morris thing is about millions more or less. In your case, it's about survival."

"Yes, that's what I sometimes tell myself, to console myself and not feel like a hypocrite. But… damn… it doesn't work. Every time I eat a sandwich, I think it's thanks to someone dying of cancer, and I lose my appetite. But I always go back out to the streets, and here the voice of conscience isn't heard…"

"Too much noise."

There was a silence. David shook his head and got back into the car.

"It must be that, the noise." Did you notice that the voice of conscience is clearest at dawn, when you have to get up? And you get up, go to the bathroom, shower, shave, and the little voice is still there, stuck, because it doesn't go away with the water or the soap… It stays there, as if trying to sour the rest of your day. So, everything you did wrong, and even what you did right, is enough to make you feel guilty about something. I call those first fifteen minutes of the day The Guilt Moment. I call it that, in Californian, because I discovered it on the other side, one morning, half groggy, while trying to urinate and I couldn't because I was thinking about my parents, and I was thinking so much that I didn't even realize my sphincters weren't relaxing, so there I was, five minutes staring at the bathroom wall as if it were a

Picasso painting. That the day before you spoke too harshly to your son, that you said something inappropriate to your wife, that ten years ago you didn't go visit your father when he needed you, that you made a good deal selling all the cigarette packs in one day, that in class you got too carried away with the examples about the corruption of this country and those poor kids who aren't to blame for anything all left a bit depressed, their patriotism bleeding out, this and that... Then I tell myself, It'll pass. It always does. It's the body starting to wake up and not wanting to, because you pulled it out of its kingdom too early. But, luckily or unfortunately, the sun comes out, things start moving, and the noise of the coffee maker, the fridge door closing, the keys waking up the rest of the family, no longer lets you hear the little voice.

Another silence. Facundo thought that maybe his guilt moment was at seven in the evening, when he left the office and headed home where the girls had already finished their school homework. That moment had persisted even when he no longer went to the office nor were the girls waiting for him to help with the homework. But by then he had started drowning all that with two or three whiskies. Each time he needed more alcohol to silence that moment David called The Guilt Moment.

"I always tell myself I'm going to quit this," David said. "And no luck… I keep doing the same thing. Well, enough of that. María says I talk too much and think too little. What time is your flight tomorrow?"

"17:30, I think."

"You're not sure? That only happens to people who are tired of traveling."

Fortunate Accident

ON THE WAY BACK to Tijuana, Facundo remembered the little time he had left to clarify some things. The identity theft seemed clear. But, like so many other times, the main purpose of his trip, as when he completed his business in Singapore or Korea, was nothing more than a new distraction.

"I've been thinking about the relationship between Susan and Ángel…" he ventured to say.

"Don't think about that anymore," David said. "In a few hours, you won't be in Mexico… If I had a secure job in Argentina, I'd go with you. Or maybe not, because I'm too old and there are too many people who need me here, and I need them too… But you don't have that problem. You'll have your own messes over on the other side, but not that. So don't add another problem to your plate. In a few hours,

419

you'll have put ten thousand kilometers between you and these lunatics…"

"I don't pay much attention to distances. Distances lie a lot."

David laughed.

"True," he said. "Let me write that down. *Distances lie a lot.*"

David continued driving, his eyes fixed on the road and on Facundo's words, which he repeated, almost with a smile: Distances lie a lot…

"Who is that Ángel guy no one wants to talk about? Because…"

"That guy is trash," David interrupted. "A real scumbag. No one can figure out how a girl like Susan got involved with a degenerate like that, who, as if that weren't enough, is named Ángel. The poor mother couldn't have known the product she'd given birth to. The fallen angel, must be. Trash, for real. But he's not the mafia boss. He thinks he is, and maybe one day he'll get there, but for now those little birds only fly in his head. Like a good businessman, he lies and lies until reality adapts to his own lies. He wants everyone to think he's an important figure, but if he really were, he wouldn't be riding that shitty motorcycle. He'd be driving a Lamborghini. Still, he manages to flaunt his fat wallet wherever he goes. For now, he has more money than power. For now, because that reverses as the mobster learns, like those big businessmen who owe more than they have, and that's why they can put and remove senators, presidents." Ángel almost never enters Cola de Pez because he's afraid María might poison him, a completely desirable but impossible thing. But when the guy does show up at the restaurant, he orders the most expensive thing available. The best whisky, the best dish. He doesn't ask about prices or even what he's ordering because the kid doesn't even know that caviar isn't motor oil and Serrano ham isn't taco filling. He just looks at the menu and orders the most expensive thing. To impress. At his age, I was a bit like him, just as stupid. But I didn't have that kind of money, I had nothing, and my parents pruned those weeds that were sprouting in my little head, like a barber shaving a kid's head to save money. Ángel, on the other hand, even though he has a mother, it's like he doesn't. They say the poor woman lives in a leaky hut. Even I feel like going one day to fix her roof, but I don't, to stay out of trouble. My greatest fear is that someone like him will eventually do anything to confirm his own lies. Someone like that is capable of killing just to earn respect.

"Has no one ever reported him…?"

David laughed, tired, as if searching for the answer.

"On what charges? They're like politicians. They steal and kill, but with artistry. Even if you had some proof of their shady dealings, who could you report them to? The police are so infiltrated that it would soon be known who reported them. God only knows how Susan got mixed up with that scum. One day, María told me that, in her opinion, poor Sandra was killed by Ángel's thugs because Sandra had become too close to her sister and had changed her mindset. It was then that Cuauhtémoc, the waiter, chimed in with his own theory, saying that the girl Susan had told Ángel she was leaving for the other side, that she was applying for a scholarship and was sure to get it, and that for that very reason, Ángel had tried to stop her. Well, it turns out that, in the supposed robbery and shooting at the taqueria, he had confused Sandra with Susan. Anyway, you see how it is…"

It was at that moment that another truck ran the red light and hit the Buick on the right side. The impact could have been worse if David hadn't managed to turn left in time, enough to prevent the truck from hitting Facundo's door directly, but he couldn't avoid the Buick being smashed up on that side in the back.

David cursed as much as he could, until the truck driver got out. The trucker, a tall and burly man, said nothing. He simply observed the two car occupants with a stone face and turned around to make a call.

Facundo was able to get out of the car through the driver's door, though he wasn't sure if he had any fractures. Nothing hurt specifically, just everything, as a result of the impact.

"This damn guy doesn't even have insurance," said David, returning from his attempt to talk to the driver.

He went over to the Buick and grabbed his head. Facundo told him not to worry, that he'd give him money to buy another car, that the best thing was to leave.

"I appreciate it, buddy," said David, "but I don't want a new car, and I'm not leaving the old Buick alone here."

"Cars can be fixed," said Facundo. "The important thing is that no one was hurt."

"Yes, of course, thank God no one broke a bone," said David.

"Metal is just metal," insisted Facundo.

"No, buddy," said David. "It's not just metal. It's a big chunk of my life."

423

"We'll fix it," insisted Facundo, while recalling, with some confusion, something someone had told him in Japan. Over there, people were more prone to falling in love with a robot because they've always seen even the most inert things as if they were full of life. So, he didn't know to what extent that ridiculous love for androids was a product of dehumanization or whether we in the West were even more dehumanized, using and discarding everything, from objects to low-income human beings, from the homeless and illegal immigrants to workers who don't complain and consumers who deposit the world's garbage. The same thing happened in pre-Hispanic cultures (he thought he heard Ernesto's voice) until the Europeans arrived with the message that the Cosmos was dead and the only thing you could do with it was exploit it and turn it into money. Yes, at one point he remembered having discussed this with Ernesto, but he couldn't recall when or where. It had just been another conversation that would have been lost forever if not for the series of events that led him to that accident and to David's distressed face assessing the damage to the Buick.

"I hope it's just the bodywork," said David. "It's probably just the bodywork. The chassis of these cars is very sturdy. They don't make cars like this any-more."

When the police arrived, David hurried to give his version of events. Right at that corner, there were no cameras. The truck driver didn't contradict him. He said nothing. They exchanged phone numbers, but it was clear the trucker wasn't going to pay for the repairs to the Buick. After the tow truck took the Buick away, Facundo called the taxi he had been using for the past few days.

"It'll take about fifteen minutes," said Facundo.

"If we're lucky," said David, arranging cigarette packs in a bag. "When they say fifteen, it's half an hour. Then they'll say traffic was this and that."

They went into a taqueria that was on the same corner.

"How much do you think it'll cost to fix the car?" asked Facundo.

"Two thousand, three thousand dollars? Who knows. The poor Buick isn't even worth that, but any mechanic will charge me a fortune if they have to re-place the rear side. I have a friend who has a junkyard for old cars. Less than two weeks ago, I drove past that graveyard, and by chance, I noticed a Buick just like mine, without wheels, ready to start rusting. Only God knows if it was a coincidence."

425

"If I had an '84 Buick, I'd have taken a look too," said Facundo as he wrote a check for three thousand dollars.

"You can cash it at any currency exchange," he said.

David took the check and stared at it.

"But, Maestro, you weren't at fault in the accident…"

"That's something we'll never know for sure," said Facundo. "But at least I'll silence The Guilt Moment a little with very little…"

"If three thousand dollars is very little for you, then what Cuauhtémoc says is true…"

"The waiter from María's place?"

"That guy. He's been telling everyone you've been leaving him exorbitant tips."

Facundo laughed.

"I thought I was being discreet," he said. "Anyway, forget it. The important thing is no one was hurt."

There was silence. David drank his Jarrito and added:

"Maybe it was Cuauhtémoc who should've been more discreet…"

"I just hope it was really an accident," said Facundo.

426

David looked at him curiously.

"Why do you say that?"

"Because on the way here, we almost had a similar incident. Someone ran a red light..."

"Now that you mention it... Though that's not unusual here. If there's one good thing up north, it's that they know how to drive, and if they don't, at least they're more orderly. Here, traffic signs and lane markers are just decorations."

David kept staring at the corner where the accident had happened.

"Sons of bitches. Could they have their eye on me?"

"Or maybe they were after me," said Facundo. "Both times they came from the right. Anyway, pure speculation. Like everything, we'll never know the truth."

"Like almost everything," said David. "Either way, that's another reason for you to get out of this damn country."

Stolen identity

BACK IN TIJUANA, THE TAXI dropped Facundo off at Cola de Pez.

427

Cuauhtémoc had asked to leave early. There were only a few customers left, and María was managing to serve them dinner with what little was left from that day. Mostly men, she said, more interested in having a drink than eating something. Facundo ate the sandwich that was left in the display case. He had been about to tell her about the accident, and for some reason, he kept putting it off.

At 11:00, he sat down again in front of the old piano and once more played Chopin's Nocturne. María kept watching him.

"My leg really hurts," said Facundo, touching his right leg, near one of the piano pedals. He thought, by that point, he must have a bruise on that part of his leg.

"Can I ask you a question?" said María.

Facundo shrugged.

"Why do you lie so much, Luis?"

"I don't know what you mean. Everyone lies, one way or another."

"But you lie to yourself, which, if not the worst, is much harder to fix. That's why people believe every lie you tell."

"For example?"

"Before you play so beautifully, you always say you don't know how to play the piano, that you never studied music and all that. It's not that you say it out of modesty, because when you put your hands on the keys, you seem as clumsy as anyone. You start by playing those horrible notes before you really start playing, which is when you're on your second beer."

Facundo didn't answer.

"You lied to Susan."

"Me? How?"

"You told her the interview at the hotel was for a university scholarship."

"And wasn't it? The modeling thing was an extracurricular activity. Over there, athletes can study thanks to their skills with a ball. In her case, she wouldn't even have to model frequently. Most likely, she would've worked for fashion magazines for a while. Nothing indecent. They chose her, and she never responded. She also lied to me, because the one who went to the interview wasn't her, but her twin sister…"

"It's true" said María, tired and standing up. "Yes, it's true. I spent several sleepless nights when I found out. There are many things you don't know about her, but I know she lied out of necessity."

"Of course, because we all lie out of necessity…"

María went to the restaurant's kitchen and came back with two beers. She placed them on the piano,

429

opened them, and filled the glasses until they over-flowed.

"This one" said María, laughing, "is for you to play better. This other one is for you to tell me the truth. They're sweaty, just how you like them."

"The wood's going to get damaged" said Facundo, and she laughed.

"The need to eat isn't the same as the need to become rich and powerful" she said. "There's a difference, I don't know if you've noticed. For you, she was just another business. But don't think I'm blaming you, because if you had shown up a year earlier, maybe now she'd be studying at some university over there, and her sister wouldn't be dead... Did you know they killed her sister?"

"Yes."

"Some lies kill, and others could've saved her, like your lies..."

"I don't know why you keep insisting on that. Everything I've done in my life has always been legal and, as far as my conscience goes, has followed certain ethical rules.

"I'm sure of that, Luis" said María. "If following the law were enough to be considered a good person, there wouldn't be so many lawyers or so many millionaires. The poor don't write the laws."

"I have a professor friend who talks like that."

"Maybe he doesn't just talk like that. Maybe he thinks like that, and maybe he's even right…"

After a long silence, María continued:

"You know what, Luis? I'm not a psychologist, but I wanted to be a pediatrician. You can imagine that my life, like the lives of many, like everyone's, is made up of big frustrations and small victories. Maybe if I had managed to become a doctor, I wouldn't have been happier or less miserable, to put it one way, but I'll never know, so I have to resign myself to thinking that the only concrete thing is that I wanted to be a pediatrician and never achieved it. If I had never had such high aspirations, I wouldn't torture myself with that damned idea today, but in life, you have to take some risks. I had to drop out in the first year of med school to work. Don't think it's an excuse. I was always a good student and had an aptitude for science, although there was a professor who said that pretty girls went to university to find a husband, some well-off candidate. After all, as I read once in an ad in a Los Angeles newspaper, What a woman does to end up falling in love with a poor man and what she does to fall in love with a rich man is the same. The difference is in where you find yourself when you're young and at the age of deserving…

431

When Susan enrolled at UBAC, I felt something like anger. Either she was going to meet a guy from high school, or she was going to end up becoming a doctor. Poor girl. I felt jealous, something like This world isn't fair and it won't stop reminding me. But soon I recovered from that poison and started seeing her achievements as if they were mine. I helped her from the first year, and we even became friends, like we hadn't been before. I helped her with money and with the best advice I had so she wouldn't give up, but the poor girl ended up involved with a scumbag who neither works nor studies, and at this point I don't know if she'll ever finish her studies. But well… What were your dreams, Luis?"

Facundo shrugged again.

"That's another lie" she said.

"Which one?"

"Every time you shrug, as if something doesn't matter to you. It does matter, but you don't want to think about it.

Facundo avoided shrugging again. He raised his eyebrows.

"What were your dreams when you were seventeen or eighteen?"

"I don't know, I think I wanted to be a poet or some of that nonsense…"

"See, you betrayed your dreams and now you're insulting them."

"I'm not going to cry. Besides, why should the dreams of youth be more important or more true than the dreams one has at forty?"

"That's a good question. I don't know the answer, but I suspect that by forty, one has already become corrupt enough to survive. Like Susan with Ángel. Do you think Susan ever dreamed of being the prisoner of a mobster who extorts her to the point where she lies to all of us? Sooner or later, she'll end up lying to herself and wanting to be the Queen of cocaine or some such filth. I feel sorry for her, and at the same time, it infuriates me to the point where sometimes I say, Well, let her be what she wants. She's too old now for someone to explain the difference between Good and Evil."

Facundo drank his beer with a violence he didn't normally possess. María did the same, as if imitating him, and then laughed.

"Yes, it's a good question" insisted María. "Very rhetorical, but good. Of course, when you think about it a bit with your heart, the answer is less Yes and no, Maybe, Perhaps. We all become corrupt to some degree to survive. I gave up my dream of being a pediatrician and living surrounded by children.

433

Neither the Lord nor the Virgin wanted to give me even a child to console me. Maybe it was punishment for having an abortion when I was Susan's age. The high school boy got scared when he found out I was pregnant and disappeared. I wasn't less scared and ended up in a clandestine clinic where God knows what they did to me that I couldn't have children anymore. That's how the wonderful advice of the Los Angeles Times and the prediction of the UBAC professor ended for me. Since I missed a lot of classes, I ended up failing that year, and since I wasn't a girl like the girlfriends of my inexperienced, improvised lover, I had to go out and work. I found work easily because when you don't have many pretensions but you're in your early twenties, you're always pretty, and in my case, the old perverts said I was especially pretty, an advantage I had to take advantage of before the flower wilted. So I had to do my best to lie to myself and convince myself that I liked serving in the restaurant. Many came to see me from behind, and more than once they tried to grope me, but not with much success. When I got older or, let's say, I was no longer the fresh little apple everyone wanted to bite, they sent me to the kitchen. But I got my revenge on all of them and instead of working six hours a day, I worked eight or even ten until I saved enough to buy the restaurant, right during the 94 crisis. I had converted all my savings into dollars and kept saving in dollars on the advice of a Colombian who had passed through here in 87 or 88, a very handsome man, about your age at the time, who didn't convince me to go with him to Medellín. He took me to a hotel nearby one night but didn't get me pregnant, and I stopped trying. At least his advice, to convert everything into dollars, helped me. When Zedillo devalued, my savings increased as much as properties sank, so I bought this restaurant and a little house in Rosarito. That was my biggest professional achievement in life. I left more than one macho face down. I enjoyed that summer a lot and almost thought I was a Carlos Slim. Was that the dream of my life? No, just the realistic little dream, more like the nap of a failed woman."

"Don't be cruel to yourself. That was a masterstroke."

"No, it's not cruelty or any masterstroke. That's life. If I had grandchildren, I'd be repeating this same story every Sunday about how I got the restaurant and the little house. Sometimes you're dealt bad cards, but you can always make a good move with what you're given, don't you think?"

"It's what I always say."

"Yes, those things you must always say, especially after closing a good deal."

Facundo laughed.

"María" he said. "Bring two more Coronas, and I'll go. It's gotten very late."

María came back with the two beers and said:

"Before the Great Corruption that led you to being a rich man…"

"Where do you get that I'm a rich man?" Facundo interrupted.

"Rich and poor at the same time."

"Leave the poetry for a moment."

"Susan told me you gave her a card to use as she pleased."

"Not as she pleased. It had a limit…"

"A limit of a thousand dollars a month. A small thing for a man without problems… Well, you see how we lie to ourselves all the time. One thinks someone with money must be someone without problems. Anyway. What I mean is that you're a man who doesn't mind a stranger spending a thousand dollars a month on him. At least you had some interest in the girl, beyond compassion and that nonsense they talk about up north… As a daughter, I don't think so. As a lover, maybe… Or wasn't it like that, Mr. Facundo L. Walsh?"

"I had and have no special interest."

Suddenly, María changed her mood and almost shouted at him:

"There's a reason you didn't mind leaving so much money at her disposal, something the girl, according to my information, barely used, and on top of that, you left her your full name on that card. I wonder why a man who comes and pretends to be someone named Luis suddenly opens up like that and leaves his money and identity to a young woman he barely knows."

"Calm down, María."

With a swift motion, María knocked over the beer glasses, which shattered on the floor.

"You no longer address me informally... But you don't answer any of my questions. How do you give your name and so much money to a girl after lying to all of us?"

"That's a question I've been asking myself many times lately."

"Lately?" asked María.

"There are things you don't know about me, and I don't plan to tell you" said Facundo, firmly."

"Alright, I respect that" she said, trying to calm down. "But the mystery isn't solved that way."

"If it can even be solved."

Facundo bent down to pick up the shards of glass amidst a puddle of beer.

"Maybe I'm too skeptical, but I don't believe in mysteries. To me, everything can be explained by the most basic vices."

Facundo laughed.

"I'm used to being underestimated."

"Alright. It wasn't my intention. What do you mean by that thing about elemental vices?"

"I said 'basic vices,' but maybe 'elemental' is a better way to put it. I don't know... Those little demons that never go out of style."

They stared into each other's eyes for a moment until Facundo said he had to leave, that it was 12:35 at night, that they'd had too much beer, and that he was now succumbing to sleepiness.

"I suspect the real Luis is the one who bent down to pick up the broken glasses," she said."

Facundo said nothing. María added:

"...the one who plays the piano after two beers."

"Call me a taxi, please" he said. "The one I use, Don Roberto, doesn't work at night."

María took her phone from her purse hanging on a hook by the door. She dialed a number from memory.

"It's done, she said. They'll pick you up in five minutes."

Facundo thanked her, and before they headed to the empty dining room, María asked almost casually:

"So you wanted to be a poet?"

"Yes, a poet" said Facundo, laughing, "and a musician, and, above all, I wanted to be a journalist for a no-name paper in Buenos Aires called *El Industrial*."

"And when did you lose your identity, Luis?"

Facundo stopped and looked her in the eyes again. María was very beautiful, he thought, and she must have been terribly beautiful in her youth. There was one of those moments that last fractions of a second, when the gazes of two people cross like two magnets that don't touch.

Shortly after, the taxi stopped at the entrance of Cola de Pez. It honked, as if in a hurry. Facundo hugged María with a force that meant something neither of them could quite define, but it felt like a good-bye.

Before opening the door of Cola de Pez, María said to him, with a feigned accent:

"Take care, eh."

"You too, María."

Facundo looked into her eyes for a moment. He said nothing, but she did:

"Since I know we won't see each other again, I can tell you that if you had stayed a little longer, I might have fallen in love with you."

Facundo smiled.

"Scientists say" said Facundo, "that it's enough to lock two people up for a certain period of time for them to fall in love. If they answer twenty questions while looking into each other's eyes, the effect is almost immediate."

"Go to hell" she said.

Facundo placed a discreet hand on her left cheek.

"Me too" he said. "Me too, without needing to answer any questions."

"That's not true" she said. "You no longer know what that is. You're too busy with more important things. Some people are born unable to feel emotions for other people and they're called psychopaths. Others lose that ability on their way to success."

"You seem very sure of what you're saying..." he said, as if it were an old defensive reflex.

"Enough with the corrections already, Luis," said María. "They killed you on the other side, who knows when, and now you think you're chasing something, but in reality, you're running from your own corpse. You're a fugitive who thinks he's Detective Columbo..."

Facundo said nothing. He gave her a brief kiss on the lips and left.

He truly didn't love her, he thought. The kiss had felt like an obligation, like that generous tip he left for waitresses who bent over backward to serve him, almost on their knees. It would have been a gesture of compassion, but he hadn't felt anything. More like an attempt, because María would never believe something like that anyway.

Instead, he couldn't forget her last words. As the taxi sped through dark streets, occasionally lit by a bar overflowing with people laughing uproariously (at least for a second, maybe for a fraction of a second, he knew that rage and disdain he felt in passing was, in reality, envy, frustration), he heard her again: They killed you on the other side, who knows when, and now you think you're chasing something, but in reality, you're running from something. You're a poor fugitive who thinks he's Detective Columbo.

Thirteen billion years

AT THE FRONT DESK, ANOTHER YOUNG woman occupied Elysa's position. She looked a lot like her; he didn't ask her name. Facundo said checking out and asked her to call a taxi for the airport. The receptionist hesitated. She wasn't sure which taxi service the hotel worked with. She searched through a pile of note-books, then on her computer.

"Sorry for the delay," she apologized, with a nervous smile. "I'm new."

"I'm sure you won't forget the date," commented Facundo.

"July 13th!" she said. "It's a little weird that it's Friday the 13th, but the previous employee didn't say she was leaving and they urgently called me last night. I still can't believe it... I'd been out of work for six months."

She spoke and looked like Elysa. The same hair, almost the same lips. Her lips were a little fuller, her cheekbones a bit more prominent, and her breasts definitely smaller. She must have been two or three years younger than Elysa, which, at that age, especially in the matter of breasts, is a significant difference. After two minutes of discreet observation, it turned out that her gaze and smile were different too. She seemed shyer, maybe because it was her first day. Maybe Elysa's gaze and smile and breasts had been like that nine months ago. Soon she would start to resemble Elysa more and more, like a daughter ends up resembling her mother when she's no longer around.

On the reception desk, there was a dark stone, proudly displayed on a wooden base. Below, a small sign explained that it was a piece of meteorite.

"A meteorite," the receptionist confirmed.

Facundo smiled at her. He looked at that piece of rock, compact and smooth as if it were a piece of metal, a piece of blind, inert matter that had traveled millions and millions of kilometers through the Milky Way, for millions, maybe billions of years, until it reached his hands. Millions of years of a dead, insensible, blind, deaf, mute existence, without consciousness, that would remain there or somewhere else when he had ceased to feel this world, when the entire world would be just a layer of dust covering a dead planet like Mars, revealing itself at that moment to the sensibility of a being of a day, as if it were a silent question covering everything. What will become of the Universe when he, Facundo Walsh Ocampo, is no longer here to see it, to think about it? Will consciousness be merely an irrelevant, fleeting anomaly like a soap bubble, like one of those sparks that jump from the stove when the fire is lit in winter, like the existence of a crustacean within its shell that, upon death, leaves its bone imprint in a new rock for

443

another million years? Will it awaken to a higher consciousness or will it fall asleep into unconsciousness? Of the latter, of being asleep, he had some idea, but he couldn't imagine it either. Consciousness, that anomaly of the universe, is very tyrannical; it doesn't accept or tolerate any other state, least of all its absence. And yet, it is much more mysterious than the unconscious.

"All set," said the receptionist, enthusiastically. "The taxi will be here in five minutes."

Facundo went out onto the porch and waited. For the first time since he had arrived in Tijuana, he felt that smell of a foreign country that he liked so much, or that moved him as if it were the inexplicable perception of a sixth sense capable of feeling time beyond the present. That strange experience had been quite common in his youth, but he had forgotten it or stopped paying attention to it because of so many important trips, where every minute had to be invested in something, including the rushed whiskey in the hotel bar... For many years, too many, he had forgotten that sweet vertigo simply from being alive in a year before his birth, in a distant country. He saw an old car passing by (a Buick like David's, but better preserved?) and made an effort to come back, like someone waking up at night in a hotel or an unfamiliar house, trying to figure out where they are.

A woman in a white hat walked by and looked him in the eyes. Immediately he thought of Silvanna. Why? She didn't resemble Silvanna. She was younger, with dark eyes and black hair. He concluded he was somewhat stressed due to the unexpected consequences of the Silvannas, to put it less dramatically.

Then he remembered (was it in Key West?) a conversation with Ernesto. He remembered (yes, they had gone on a trip with Elena, Alexa, and someone else) that he had tried to defend things he no longer believed in, like a priest giving mass when they no longer believe in mass and doubt God, but fear admitting it.

"That's typical intellectual paranoia," he had said with a smile, just in case, to soften the effects of his statement. "There's no reason to fear technology."

"It's not the technology I fear," Ernesto had said, drawing shapes in the condensation on his beer glass, "but the culture that creates all that. The same culture that, in just a few more decades, will leave us without these beaches. Maybe we won't see it at its worst, but Alexita and her friend will."

"Either way, culture will adapt, not the other way around. In fact, I'm working on a very interesting project in Asia, something related to that, though I can't give details."

"Don't get all mysterious. Are you working for the CIA?"

"No, no mysteries. Just discretion. Business matters that haven't been finalized yet. I can tell you this" (on the hotel porch, Facundo shook his head; those little words had been stupidly arrogant) "that artificial intelligence will be like any other invention of the past. It will change many things and will ultimately benefit humanity. It will do many of the things humans do today…"

"Like thinking," Ernesto had interjected. "But, well, if people are increasingly resembling robots, it's not something to worry about so much, is it? I'll stop harping on consumerism here in this country. Just look at those poor kids in Shanghai, in South Korea… They sleep five hours because the rest of the time they're studying. School, tutors, extra practice, review, and then back home by ten at night, when the father's already gone to bed because he leaves the house at five for the office—where his real family is, the one he calls colleagues. Every day of every year, they're preparing to be the best, so that when they're young, they can get into the best universities and then land a little job from seven in the morning to seven at night, with some overtime when production doesn't meet expectations and everyone's on edge because of the inevitable crisis, the inevitable failure. If those kids, those young people, don't get into the best universities, they're automatically and by default a failure. Some kill themselves. I mean, they commit suicide in the traditional way, because the rest are already dead."

"Wow, how tragic! Don't you think you're exaggerating a bit?"

"No. I'm not," Ernesto had said, looking him in the eyes as if Facundo were a lie detector. "I'm not exaggerating. It's reality that's exaggerating, and not just a little. Those who achieve success do so at the cost of having turned themselves into machines, into cogs in a highly effective productive machinery. If you replace those cyborgs with AI robots, there won't be much of a difference. By then, humans will have already dehumanized themselves long before being replaced by more perfect machines. In other words, by their own upgraded versions."

"The fear that intelligent robots will turn against humans and enslave us or simply exterminate us is a fear unique to humans…"

"And why would machines with artificial intelligence, fueled by our intellectual habits—things of

447

human beings—be ethically superior to us? Haven't we always been, since the beginning, a highly destructive species, a lethal species? Besides, even if intelligent robots are the pinnacle of goodness, there's still the more likely option: it won't be them destroying us; it will be ourselves when we become irrelevant, perfectly useless at surviving without artificial intelligence. Physically and mentally lazy. We don't need robots chasing us to destroy us, like in *The Terminator*; it's enough for them to solve all our problems. That's all it takes to turn us into appendages, to have a worm existence. Of course, if we turn into worms, we'll never realize it." We will feel proud to be worms and will even ask robots to write books, make movies, and design ideologies and religions praising our admirable worm-like condition.

The Insect

A FEW MINUTES LATER, a black Frontera Cab Ride minivan appeared. The driver, a bald man with a very large, white smile, greeted him (José Funes, at your service, he said) and placed his luggage in the back, while Facundo sat by the left window.

Just before, a fraction of a second before the automatic door closed, he felt an insect enter. One of those tropical insects he had observed earlier in the beach cabin, but he lost sight of it immediately.

José, the driver, confirmed that the passenger was going to General Abelardo Rodríguez Airport. He then turned on the radio, and as the minivan dove into the dizzying chaos of traffic, Yuri began singing "Maldita primavera" from some corner of the year 1981.

...it passes lightly
the cursed spring
it only hurts me

He didn't want to check his phone for other videos where Yuri might appear at seventy. He wanted to stay with the Yuri of 1981, more precisely with the Yuri of that moment, eternal, fleeting like everything that is human and everything that truly matters in this universe. He wanted to see and feel those smiling cheeks, those eternal cheeks of Nefertiti.

In another corner of 1981, at that same moment, Facundo is twenty-two years old and sitting in a

classroom at the economics department. Or he's urinating in a smelly bathroom before returning to the
Macroeconomics class, where the professor was telling an anecdote about John Stuart Mill.

Let me love you, as if love lived on

and even if I don't want to, without wanting to,
I think of you

For a moment, he felt it again, as he once did in
Buenos Aires, thirty years earlier, when in his humble, dark, and lonely boarding house room on Estados
Unidos Street, he interrupted a probability calcula-
tion to listen to her on the radio. He imagined Yuri
was singing to him. From the tone, from the texture
of her voice, he could see her smile.

what does it matter if… to fall in love, one hour
is enough

it passes lightly, the cursed spring

it passes lightly… for you and for me

"Which airline did you say?" the driver woke him
up.

"I think…" Facundo hesitated "American Airlines, if I'm not mistaken…"

After a few minutes of driving, he felt a sting on
his neck. He thought of the insect and swatted to
crush it. But he saw nothing until he looked at the
backrest of the passenger seat. The insect was there,

resting, as if observing him carefully. Facundo leaned in slowly to crush it with the newspaper, struck hard, but missed. Like all insects, it had a special sensitivity to recognize the intentions of the predator and its own strategies to let itself be carried away by the air mass produced by the object trying to crush it.

"Mosquito?" asked the driver, turning off the radio and glancing at the rearview mirror "It's not mosquito season."

"No," Facundo replied "A cockroach…"

"Cockroach?" the driver said, incredulous "That can't be."

"Or a cicada…"

"Cicada?"

"A damn cicada."

"Not a cicada either… Well, who knows. Anything's possible. Did you know that with global warming, insects are getting bigger and bigger?"

Without being able to pull over, the driver handed him a small can of Raid.

"If you see it, spray a little bit of this," he said "Not too much, or we'll poison ourselves too."

Facundo took out his phone and checked his messages. He calculated that he had resisted 26 hours without reaching for the parasite, as Ernesto called it.

A record, but he was sure there were several messages piled up.

He swiped his thumb over the plastic screen, and the messages scrolled past the rectangular abdomen of the insect at a dizzying speed until the wheel stopped on one that seemed to be sent by the manager of Malasia RealPerson. Further down, he saw Elena's name and four others, which were the only, the last messages he read:

From Elena: *Alexa will be waiting for you at the YMCA at 4:00 pm. I need you to take care of the girl for a day. I remind you I have an appointment tomorrow.*

From Silvanna: *The product is of such quality that right now I'm fighting not to fall in love with the Silvanna they sent me for free.*

From Jeff: *You'll regret being born…*

From David: *They killed María. In the piano storage room. Last night or early this morning.*

He saw the insect again. He didn't use the product the taxi driver had given him. He leaned in carefully, as far as the seatbelt would allow, and observed it intently. He feared it might be a dangerous species, one of those insects that are plentiful in subtropical regions. In reality, Tijuana wasn't farther south or more tropical than Florida, but one always imagines different things, more due to names and words than reality.

The taxi driver opened the windows, and the insect flew out onto the highway.

"Better that it's gone," said the driver "If you spray poison while we're moving, it'll harm us, and you'll remember me for many hours on your trip."

Facundo had managed to see with some clarity that the insect was a miniature machine, with wings, eyes, and two telescopic blades.

While he thought he might have been poisoned by a micro drone, he began to feel dizzy. It could have been from the impression of an absurd but alarming idea. It could have been from the heat. Or both. He wanted to tell the driver to stop, but he couldn't articulate a single word. Neither could the taxi stop in the middle of a highway crowded with cars speeding at that hour toward some unknown destination.

There was no hope. He was defeated. For a moment, he imagined the company emails mourning the loss of an exceptional member of..., Jeff offering his condolences to Elena. Elena exaggerating her grief. Jeff pretending to curse that southern country, full of drug traffickers and corrupt politicians. José, the taxi driver, condemned to rot in jail, with him powerless to do anything.

The truth is, he rested his head against the window and never woke up.

II. On the other other side

Silicone 5.0